Dear Reader:

The book you ~~~~~~~~~~~~~~~~~~~~ stseller from St. Martin's True Crime Library, ~~~~~~~~~~~~ *he New York Times* calls "the leader in true crime!" Each month, we offer you a fascinating account of the latest, most sensational crime that has captured the national attention. *The Milwaukee Murders* delves into the twisted world of Jeffrey Dahmer, one of the most savage serial killers of our time; *Lethal Lolita* gives you the *real* scoop on the deadly love affair between Amy Fisher and Joey Buttafuoco; *Whoever Fights Monsters* takes you inside the special FBI team that tracks serial killers; *Garden of Graves* reveals how police uncovered the bloody human harvest of mass murderer Joel Rifkin; *Unanswered Cries* is the story of a detective who tracked a killer for a year, only to discover it was someone he knew and trusted; *Bad Blood* is the story of the notorious Menendez brothers and their sensational trials; *Fallen Hero* details the story of O. J. Simpson which stunned the nation.

St. Martin's True Crime Library gives you the stories *behind* the headlines. Our authors take you right to the scene of the crime and into the minds of the most notorious murderers to show you what really makes them tick. St. Martin's True Crime Library paperbacks are better than the most terrifying thriller, because it's all true! The next time you want a crackling good read, make sure it's got the St. Martin's True Crime Library logo on the spine—you'll be up all night!

Charles E. Spicer, Jr.
Senior Editor, St. Martin's True Crime Library

ABOVE SUSPICION

JOE SHARKEY

ST. MARTIN'S PAPERBACKS

Published by arrangement with Simon & Schuster

ABOVE SUSPICION

ISBN: 0-312-95394-1

Printed in the United States of America

Simon & Schuster hardcover edition published 1993
St. Martin's Paperbacks edition/November 1994

St. Martin's Paperbacks are published by St. Martin's Press, 175 Fifth Avenue, New York, N.Y. 10010.

10 9 8 7 6 5 4 3 2 1

For Christopher

ACKNOWLEDGMENTS

The material in this book comes from my own conversations with the people involved, as well as from police and FBI files, court records, and historical research.

There are numerous passages of reconstructed dialogue. These are based on the recollections of at least one person who was directly involved in the conversation. In dialogue involving Susan Smith, I satisfied myself that what someone recalled her saying in a specific instance was consistent with what other people who knew her recalled about her attitudes and state of mind at the time. I have depended on Mark Putnam's recollections to reconstruct the final conversation between him and Susan.

In over a year of research, I found no significant disagreement among the principals in this case over what they said or heard, and very little disagreement on what they meant. In the few minor instances where I had to act as a referee between opposing viewpoints, I called them the way I saw them.

Many people showed me extraordinary hospitality in Eastern Kentucky, and their names will be found throughout the book. I am especially indebted to John Paul Runyon, the commonwealth attorney for Pike County, and Richard Ray, formerly of the Kentucky State Police, for sharing their insights with me and for opening doors that would have otherwise remained shut. I am also grateful to Mable Dotson, of the Phelps Public Library, for many kindnesses.

I spoke at length with Mark Putnam at the Federal Medical Center in Rochester, Minnesota. He was always frank and forthcoming, both during our meetings and later, in lengthy correspondence. Kathy Putnam, likewise, answered my questions in detail, even the ones that no outsider had the right to ask. Her honesty, grace, and intelligence—not to mention her courage—were crucial. I should add that when inner thoughts are attributed to Mark, Kathy, or others in these pages, they are given in the words they used in describing them to me.

My editor, Rebecca Saletan, contributed mightily to this book. Any writer is fortunate to find an editor who is either a skilled craftsman or a perceptive conceptualist. Few find both of those qualities together in the same editor, as I did. I greatly appreciate her assistance, her patience, and her unfailing good humor.

Finally, and most importantly, to my wife, Nancy—thanks for everything.

1

The baby threw up just as the eighteen-wheel coal truck with the word *Jesus* across its front plate barreled out of a blind switchback and bore down on them in the rainy February afternoon like a forty-ton avalanche of soot.

Skidding on the slick mountain road, Mark Putnam managed to pull the 1980 Oldsmobile far enough off to the side, where he slowed to a crawl, the passenger door nearly scraping the granite wall that went a hundred feet up. The coal truck rumbled by with its horn shrieking.

"Oh, my God," Kathy Putnam said in a low voice from the backseat, where two-year-old Danielle lay across her lap, miserable with car sickness and fatigue.

When they caught their breath, Kathy cleaned up with a diaper. Her gaze met her husband's dark eyes in the rearview mirror. "Listen, Kat, we don't have to do this," he said with a grimace, and added, only partly in jest, "Do you want to turn around and go back to Connecticut?"

Kathy was nothing if not a good sport. Three years before, when she and Mark had dashed off to get married in New York City, she had known what she was getting into. Mark was a young man with one overriding goal: he intended to be an FBI man. Theirs was a marriage remarkable for its synergy—her hard-nosed realism applied to his unchecked zeal, his fortitude to her diffidence, creating a force that augmented their individual strengths. Together, they'd gotten him into the FBI. If Mark's first assignment out of the academy was a forlorn outpost in the isolated mountainous coalfields of eastern Kentucky—in Pikeville, a town neither of them had heard of until two weeks earlier—they would make a go of it and wait for a better assignment in years to come. Kathy smiled and tickled the baby's chin. "It's going to be okay. You'll see." Mark guided the old car, its engine straining, up the steep mountain road.

"The road has to end somewhere," he said disconsolately from the front seat, where he was wedged uncomfortably between the door and a stack of pillows on top of a picnic cooler and some cardboard boxes that took up the passenger seat.

In a while, they were relieved to see a road sign, CON-GESTED AREA, but it only marked the truck pull-off for a coal-mine operation below the blasted rocks and stepped contours of a strip-mined mountain. Heaps of coal chunks clattered noisily on conveyor tracks that crisscrossed down from outcrops high up the ridge. Broken trees and shattered boulders lay scattered on the site in huge heaps. Staring in wonder, they drove past and started another steep climb.

Kathy frowned at a Triple-A road map, but it was clear there was no real choice except to go straight ahead on the winding two-lane. There simply weren't any intersections. After a while, they saw evidence of a settlement: unpainted little frame houses set onto shelves of land hacked into the hills; tumbledown bungalows and rust-streaked trailers pushed up close against the highway, as if waiting to pull out into traffic. On a sagging front porch, a woman in a faded print housedress and muddy field boots studied them from a rocker.

A mile farther, the highway bored down abruptly and swept open into four lanes at the base of a deep gorge blasted through the rock, with walls one hundred feet high, the surfaces of which were veined with glistening narrow seams of coal that might have been drawn in by a thick black marker. They sped past another road sign, PIKEVILLE—POP. 4,500, and past an exit that wound around into a small community shadowed by mountains all around and skirted by a meandering river. A jumble of neat buildings dominated by a brick courthouse with a weather vane on top, Pikeville looked like a village in a model railroad display.

A mile beyond the exit, the road narrowed and began to climb once more. Mark made a U-turn and drove back into town.

Kathy Putnam was twenty-seven years old in 1987, six months younger than her husband. She and Mark had both grown up in Connecticut, where they had met five years earlier. With their daughter, they made a handsome and cozy family—Mark, dark and sensitive, a muscular young man who had been a star athlete in college and stayed in shape by running and lifting weights; Kathy, with her delicate features and untamed light brown hair, hopelessly unathletic; and amiable Danielle, already chatty, with her mother's quick smile and her father's flashing eyes. If the FBI had commissioned a recruitment commercial to get young families to consider a career in the bureau, the Putnams would have been in it.

But the commercial would probably have shown the family arriving somewhere other than isolated Pikeville, the seat of Pike County, Kentucky, a corrugated chunk of land shaped, in fact, like a lump of coal. It sprawls over 785 square miles, most of them situated between two rivers, the Levisa Fork and the Tug Fork, which tumble out of the high watershed of the western Appalachian range down to the Cumberland Plateau. They flow north for about a hundred miles and join at the old railroad town of Louisa to form a river known as the Big Sandy, which plunges northward under rocky escarpments on the border between Kentucky and West Virginia and finally empties into the Ohio River.

It is a land extravagantly endowed with mineral and other natural resources and thus cursed with plunder. Timber barons cleared the mountains of their magnificent hardwood forests after the Civil War, and when they were gone, coal barons slashed their way in for the wealth underneath. Under a thin veneer of modest prosperity in small towns such as Pikeville, the toll of over a century of feverish exploitation is evident both physically and socially—as Appalachian historian Harry M. Caudill put it, "exhaustion of soil, exhaustion of men, exhaustion of hopes."

"Dogpatch" is what some new arrivals call the place, a term that conveys not only the disdain outsiders often bring to their first encounters with "hillbillies," but also the condescension that has always seeped down the map to Appalachia from the urban media centers. Dogpatch is, after all, the fictional world of "Li'l Abner," the comic strip whose characters embodied popular conceptions of hillbillies as perpetually befuddled lummoxes, sexually amenable Daisy Maes, bumptious elders, and assorted shotgun-toting wild men, all coexisting in dim-witted timeless bliss in a junkyard Eden where tranquillity is occasionally shattered by a thumping mountain feud. As with most enduring stereotypes, there is always authentication available to those who look for it. Pikeville and the neighboring Tug Valley along the border with West Virginia were in fact the locale for the Hatfield and McCoy feud of the late nineteenth century. In the hilly rural areas out of town, grown men still go barefoot in the summer; the dole is a way of life; the teenage pregnancy rate is among the highest in the country; feuds simmer over generations like stew pots.

It is here in southern Appalachia that the liberal imagination stumbles into the back alley of the industrial revolution, on a vast, fan-shaped plateau of deep, sinuous valleys and hulking mountains where wealth has been found, and carted off, since the days when the first agents of capitalism descended with pockets full of coins to claim the land.

The settlers of this place were pioneers who came through the Cumberland Gap seeking not the rich farmland of the Ohio Valley, but the nearly impenetrable hills to the east, hacking their way along animal trails into the Tug Valley, a rugged terrain that offered no guarantees except solitude. This is the hillbilly stock, described by Caudill as "a population born of embittered rejects and outcasts from the shores of Europe, as cynical, hardened, and bitter a lot as can be imagined outside prison walls."

It is a place whose young people have long plotted to leave

if they had the capability. By the end of the 1950s, three-quarters of the annual crop of high school graduates were migrating out of the plateau, according to Caudill. What they left behind was a society as stratified as its landscape, one still nearly feudal in its relationships between rich and poor—the rich clustered in small towns like Pikeville, among the banks and courthouses, the poor clinging stubbornly to life in smoky hollows and along the ridges, with walls of granite at their backs and thick veins of the richest bituminous coal in North America underfoot. Long accustomed to the appraisal of outsiders, inured to flash floods, mudslides, mine explosions, and rockfalls, alert as guerrillas, this remarkably homogeneous population includes some of the most cantankerous and individualistic humans alive on the continent. These are the people Mark Putnam, special agent of the Federal Bureau of Investigation, twenty-seven years old and all of one week out of the academy, was sent to serve.

The job had a long legacy of futility, left by the land-deed agents, railroad cops, coal-company detectives, government revenuers, federal officials, and social reformers who had trampled the hills for a century, outsiders attempting to exploit—or in some cases, to save—indigenous interests. Mark brought with him an analytical wariness unusual for a young cop off on what others might have looked forward to as a great adventure. Just before graduation from the sixteen-week training course at the academy, when he got his orders to Pikeville, he had approached an agent who had lived in Louisville, in the bluegrass flatlands of Kentucky two hundred miles across the hills. The agent had whistled softly as he looked over the rookie's papers. "Pikeville? I can't *believe* they're sending you there—a pretty Yankee boy in his first office! It's the mountains, Mark. You don't know what you're in for. Just watch your young ass down there, buddy."

Mark was worried not by the potential danger of the post, but by the lack of supervision. Pikeville was a two-agent office, far from Lexington or Louisville. Shortly after the Putnams arrived, the senior agent from the Louisville office, a man seldom seen from year to year in Pikeville, drove down to offer a welcome. He told Mark frankly that he would have been better off in a central office like Lexington, where there were dozens of more experienced agents to teach him the ropes. But the supervisor pointed out the bright side to Mark's situation. A small, isolated office such as Pikeville offered certain career opportunities for a rookie looking to make a name for himself. It was the political and adminis-trative center of a region that always ranked at the top for the sorts of crime and mayhem that can keep a cop's life inter-esting. And besides, he would not be following a tough act.

"I'll be right up-front with you, Mark. You're right out of the academy. This is an office that needs new blood. It has a lot of potential that hasn't been worked at for years. We thought that you would benefit from this. You could do a lot of screwing around down there, but you're obviously gung ho, and there's a lot to keep you busy if you want to work it. Anything that comes out of there is a bonus for us because we don't expect much from Pikeville. Look at it as a potential career-maker."

"I'm going to bust my ass for you," Mark told him.

"Just do your caseload. You don't have to bust your ass."

It puzzled Mark not to have heard at least a pep talk. The senior agent left him instead with this concession: "I won't kid you—nobody else wants to come here, which is why you got it—luck of the draw, I guess."

There was another unspoken reason for the assignment. The FBI, with its deeply entrenched regard for record-keeping, likes to insist that its files be as neat as its agents' attire, but over years of indifference, the Pikeville bureau had become an administrative disaster. The office needed more than new blood—it needed a clerk to straighten out the mess. Whatever his nascent abilities as a crime-fighter—and Mark Putnam had been considered one of the most promising rook-ies in his graduating class—he had another skill that put him at the top of the list for Pikeville. For four years after college, while he and Kathy worked toward getting him accepted as a special agent, Mark had served as a clerk in the busy FBI office in New Haven, Connecticut, where he had soaked up everything he could learn from the fifty agents assigned there, while shrugging off a depressing bureaucratic refrain: "Clerks don't make good agents." Now, having overcome that prejudice to finally gain admission to the ranks, he realized that he also had to demonstrate the obverse—that in his case, at least, an agent must also make a good clerk.

It was characteristic of the Putnams' marriage that Kathy had been the one to shore him up and motivate him for the assignment—after initially intervening and trying to have it changed. Before they packed up the car in Connecticut, Mark had told her about his anxiety, saying, "I'm afraid I'm going to screw this up and ruin my career before it gets going. I'm a rookie and a Yankee, with no law-enforcement experience." His wife had called the special agent in charge in Louisville to point that out, but she was told that the assignment was firm. "Tell him the Pikeville office can be a career-maker if he handles himself well," she was told.

Apprehensively determined to labor day and night to do just that, Mark reported to work on a Monday morning in late February 1987. The Pikeville FBI office was a tiny room on the ground-floor front of the federal building, with a window that looked out on sleepy Main Street. It was still staffed by Mark's two predecessors, Dan Brennan and Sam Smith, who were awaiting transfer to more appealing locales. The new man had to squeeze past their desks to get to his makeshift work area, which consisted of a chair, a telephone, and a cleared space on the table that held the paper-shredder, mail bin, and answering machine. There was no secretary; after they settled in, Kathy would begin to fill that role for him, fielding calls and passing on messages from home. When she came in to visit during Mark's first week on the job, she was surprised by the humble surroundings, which she thought looked like the cubbyhole in an automobile showroom where the customers sign the loan papers.

The office fleet consisted of a beat-up Dodge Diplomat with nearly a hundred thousand hard miles on it and a four-wheel-drive Bronco, both of them already claimed by the two veteran agents. Kathy needed the Olds to get them settled in their new home. With a territory of several thousand square miles to cover in Pike and the adjoining counties in eastern Kentucky and West Virginia, Mark resented having to arrange for a bureau car like a teenager asking his father for the keys.

"Where are you going? I need to know where you're going," he would be told.

"I need to go out and interview this guy. You're not using the car, dammit."

"Why don't you wait till tomorrow? We'll go out and do it together."

"Come on, man. Days are passing! I want to get rolling."

Again and again, he heard the same frustrating message: "Relax. You've got a big career ahead of you. You're not supposed to go overboard down here—this is a sleeper office that nobody cares about."

He wasn't prepared to accept that. He finally talked Dan Brennan into a compromise arrangement to fit the twelve-hour days he'd already begun to work, every day but Sunday. Late in the afternoon, he would drive his colleague home. Then he'd use the Dodge well into the evenings to get into the hill towns to do investigative work on the cases that piled up. Because Mark reported to work at seven in the morning, two hours earlier than his colleagues, he would leave the car in Brennan's driveway that night and jog home, then jog the mile back to work the next day.

On Saturdays, he often brought Danielle into the office, installing her at a desk to draw with crayons while he went through the mail and official dispatches, lining up the coming workweek. Sundays were family time.

"Mark went to church and usually took Danielle with him," Kathy recalled. "We actually acclimated pretty quickly to the new environment. He had the job he'd dreamed about, that we both had worked so hard for. Danielle was the center of our lives. It didn't matter if we were in Pikeville, Louisville, or Florida at that point because we had each other. When he came through the front door, she'd be right on top of him, he'd scoop her up. We read to her together every night, without fail. When he wasn't working, there was no time for anyone else but the three of us.''

But Mark's long workdays left Kathy largely on her own to establish their home in a place where many things about her, not least her New England accent, marked her as a stranger. She worked gamely at it. Thanks largely to her skill at managing money, they had enough saved up to make the down payment on an $89,000 two-story colonial on a well-tended street in Cedar Creek, a small subdivision that had been built on a tract of level land at the northern edge of town, accessible across a sway bridge over the Levisa Fork. The house, on the market for over a year, was of ''modular'' construction; that is, large sections had been trucked in and assembled on the site. Kathy's father, a building contractor in Connecticut, had inspected it with a cold eye and pronounced the house solid and well built when her parents came to visit for a week not long after they arrived, but a neighbor soon set her straight. ''The reason the house was a bargain is, if a house isn't 'stick-built,' people think it's like a glorified trailer.'' Their new neighbors—dentists, small-business people, accountants, faculty members at the tiny Christian college in town—had, in fact, filed an unsuccessful lawsuit to block construction of the house.

Kathy, however, loved it. ''We could never have afforded a place like that in Connecticut,'' she said. ''It had seven rooms, with hand-embroidered curtains, a nice kitchen, two full baths, nice appliances, lots of room, nice landscaping. It seemed perfect for a small family like ours.''

Mark's only objection was the mountain that pushed into the backyard. Kathy remembered him the day they moved in, standing at the sliding glass door and staring at the muddy hulk that left the house in a cold, damp shadow for much of the day.

In any case, he had little time to brood about it. Mark started in on his first case a few days after he reported to work. Several months earlier, a roadside bank had been robbed in a tiny town on Johns Creek called Meta. The robber got away with $18,000 in cash.

"We got a call from this lady who believes the guy she lives with did the robbery," Brennan told him. It looked like a break in the case. The two agents took the car and bumped along mountain roads to the trailer where the woman lived. She invited them inside. Brennan took out his notebook.

"Why do you think it was him?"

"Well, he come home that day with a potful of money."

"How much money?"

"It must of been over ten thousand dollars."

"Why are you telling on him?"

"The dirty son of a bitch won't share none of it. He's been going out, drinking it away. I need a new dress and he won't get me one. I'm mad at him, is why."

"Where is he now?"

"I ain't seen him in three days. He done took off, and he took all the money I had saved up, too."

Mark listened, thinking back to his training: the strategy of interviewing, the criminal mind, the psychology of informants. He plunged in:

"Ma'am, I'm kind of confused about something. What exactly is your relationship with this guy?"

For the first time the woman regarded him.

"I think I'm married to him, is what," she said, somewhat affronted.

"What do you mean, you think you are?"

"Well, we was talking about getting married, and he wrote out a piece of paper that he was going to be bringing down to the courthouse in Pikeville, with twenty-five dollars that he borrowed from me. And he went down there and come back later that day and said we was married. I still have the note here with the writing on it."

She went to a drawer, withdrew a wrinkled sheet of paper, and showed it to Mark. "I don't read," she said casually, as if she were declining milk and sugar with her coffee.

The scrawled note said: "By this hereby, advices that these two are legally married," and below that both names were printed.

Mark surmised that they had their robber, but Brennan warned him not to jump to conclusions.

In a few days, they discovered that the man's story was somewhat different. He had gone into town to file for divorce against his actual wife, and he needed the $25 as a filing fee. He volunteered to take a lie detector test and passed it without any problem. The woman had apparently named him as a bank robber only in retaliation for his reneging on a promise of marriage. To a young agent who still studied his notebooks from the academy at night, it was a small but important lesson in gratuitous deceit, banal revenge, hidden agendas, and the perils of easy assumptions.

Without supervision, desperate to assimilate and learn, Mark soon found a way to get into the hills during the day without a car. He surprised some local law enforcement officers, who tended to resent the FBI for its haughtiness and its preoccupation with its image, by asking to tag along on their patrols. At the academy, the value of good relationships with the local cops had been stressed. Mark's purpose was to see and to be seen—he wanted to cover eastern Kentucky like a Bible salesman. It amused him that the cops who befriended him from the beginning were named Hatfield and McCoy. Paul Hatfield, Fred McCoy, and Bertie Hatfield, all of the Pike County sheriff's office, let him ride with them and introduced him to the old coal towns and hill settlements. Bertie, a laconic sheriff's deputy who also sold used cars from a small lot in Freeburn, an old coal company town on the banks of the Tug, "three mountains away from Pikeville," became a particularly good ally.

Bertie was endlessly amused by the young FBI man's driving skills. "That the way they teach you to drive up in Connecticut?" he snorted one afternoon as Mark cautiously maneuvered the sheriff's car around a blind curve on a narrow asphalt road cut into a sharp ridge high above the treetops. On the way back, Bertie took the wheel and showed him how it was done, racing around the switchbacks with tires squealing. "This is the way us hillbillies drive," he said. Bertie was pleased to see that Mark Putnam learned fast.

Yet as he got to know the local cops, Mark found that the lines of his dealings with them could get just as tangled as they had been in the trailer of the woman who reported the bank robber. Once, deep in the coalfields to serve a federal fugitive warrant, he was approached by a local police officer.

"I hear you're looking for this boy."

"Yeah, I am."

"Well, can you kind of leave him alone?"

"What do you mean, leave him alone?"

"Well, he's my second cousin. He's a real good boy."

"Hey, man, I got a warrant for him. I can't do that!"

"Hell, sure you can."

When he didn't, word got around.

Money talks, as cops know, but its voice carried particular resonance in eastern Kentucky, where information has long been a commodity. All law enforcement agencies paid for information, but the FBI had especially deep pockets—money was readily available for most criminal investigations. All an agent had to do was fill out a voucher with the amount and a few sentences describing the information likely to be yielded. Within a week, a check for $500 or $1,000 would come from Louisville.

Later, Mark would recall his amazement at discovering how the system worked. "I'd go to an informant, 'I've got something for you.' And then the guy would be just awestruck that I was actually giving him the whole five hundred or thousand dollars and not holding out like two hundred dollars of it for myself. It was incredible how fast the word got around that I was good for the money. People would actually call the office offering information for sale. After a while, I didn't have to go out anymore and drum up business—it just came to me.''

By summer, Mark felt a long way from the academy. While his rookie classmates were still processing paperwork or working routine details under the supervision of senior agents in Chicago, Miami, or Denver, Mark had already set up a network of informants and, he thought, established himself as a streetwise crime-fighter who was living the life that he had always dreamed about.

One sultry morning while he was on the phone, gazing out at Main Street, he heard the crackle of gunfire, and a federal probation officer burst in from the hall shouting, ''Boys, there's bodies on the ground!''

Gun drawn, heart pounding, Mark tumbled outside with Brennan, who ordered, ''Watch the buildings, Putnam—snipers! I'm going up to the bank.'' The bank was a block away.

Mark scampered across the street where two women lay on the sidewalk. Outside the bank, Brennan crouched over the body of a man.

The older woman was dead, but the younger one was still alive, bleeding heavily with gunshot wounds to the neck and shoulder. ''Don't let me die . . . help me,'' she gasped as Mark crawled to her side. He reached her and said, ''It'll be okay. *Look at my face*. Hold on to my hand.''

She grabbed his hand tightly. She was still alive when the paramedics came.

When they took her away, the agents pieced together the story with help from state police officers who arrived on the scene. The gunman was the young woman's husband. He had shot her and her mother as they were on their way to the county courthouse to file for a restraining order against him. Then he had turned the gun on himself.

''Family feud,'' one of the state cops said with a shrug. ''We see a lot of it.''

2

To a bank robber, eastern Kentucky offers unusual challenges and unusual opportunities. In some ways, it is not an ideal place to rob a bank. For one thing, the region has an FBI office, and bank robbery has been a federal crime since Dillinger's days. For another, robbing a bank is usually a daylight pursuit requiring the capacity to get away in a car—not an easy task in a place where the roads run up one side of a mountain and wind down the other, and the nearest interstate is two hours of bad road away.

But on the other hand, banks in isolated mountain settlements tend to be guarded with about as much fortification as a hot dog stand, in towns without full-time police protection. So they draw freelance opportunists who haven't always clearly thought through their plans, such as the robber who hid on a bank roof to pounce on the driver for the Piggly-Wiggly store making his night deposit—and missed, knocking himself out cold in the parking lot. Or the hapless gang who held up a bank on Peter Creek, found themselves stranded when the getaway driver got lost en route, politely borrowed a teller's car keys, and ran out of gas a half mile down the road.

This atmosphere of benign ineptitude underwent a change during the late spring and summer of 1987 in the hill towns of the Tug Valley. Small banks were being knocked off, not only efficiently, but in a similar manner. Bertie Hatfield soon had the answer: apparently Carl Edward "Cat Eyes" Lockhart, recently released from prison on probation, had gone back to work.

As bank robbers go, Cat Eyes had much of the audacity

of John Dillinger, only a little of the skill, and none of the discretion. A proud man, he had announced his return to virtually everyone he knew in the valley.

Cat Eyes was a soft-spoken, dark-haired local boy with luminous green eyes that provided him with his nickname and helped establish his amiable reputation. From childhood on, his stated goal in life had been to be a bank robber. Having achieved that, he had just been released from a Virginia penitentiary after serving seven years of an eighteen-year sentence for a brazen robbery in 1980. He had gotten away with $300,000 from a bank in Grundy, Virginia, a small town at a crossroads near the corner of the Appalachians where the borders of Virginia, Kentucky, and West Virginia touch.

Cat Eyes was a legend in the Tug Valley, mostly for having spent the $300,000—all of it—in a wild three-month spree driving through several Southern states in a white Cadillac El Dorado with a friend. The desperadoes' odyssey had culminated in a truly spectacular week of debauchery and gambling in Nashville, where the boys dropped their last $50,000 before turning up frazzled and broke back home. There they were promptly arrested.

After he got out of prison, one of Cat's favorite haunts was the small wood-frame house in West Virginia, where Kenneth and Susan Smith lived. The house sat next to a little bridge that crossed the Tug Fork. Beside that bridge, on the Kentucky side of the river, was Bertie Hatfield's car lot. Cat Eyes even had the courtesy to wave.

In June, Bertie called up his new friend Mark Putnam and told him he thought he knew who was behind the latest spurt of bank robberies.

"Who's that?" Mark said.

"A fella named Lockhart. Cat Eyes Lockhart." Bertie described the man.

"How do you know it's him?"

"Well, all of a sudden, he's rich. One thing about the guy, he spends it." Bertie also explained that all the reports mentioned the robber's bulky coveralls and ski mask, Cat Eyes' favorite disguise.

"Any ideas on how we catch him?"

Bertie had a good one. He offered to introduce Mark to Kenneth Smith, Cat Eyes' boyhood friend, unabashed admirer, and, it appeared, host.

Cat Eyes' chief virtues were gregariousness, loquaciousness, and generosity—qualities admirable in law-abiding citizens, but problematic in bank robbers. Cat was so likable that many people would hide him, but so gracious that he made it a point to publicly acknowledge the hospitality. He liked to think of himself as Robin Hood, without considering the fact that the ancient English outlaw stayed out of custody by hiding in the forest. Cat preferred a more public role. When Cat had money, his friends prospered. He would not only share booze, cocaine, and cash, but also make other gestures certain to gain attention, such as buying sneakers and clothing for their wives and children.

After Cat was paroled, Kenneth Smith—himself on probation for drug possession—invited him and his girlfriend, Sherri Justice, to move out of the tent where they had been living in Cat's mother's backyard and come to stay awhile. Kenneth had been married to a Freeburn girl, Susie Daniels, for five years, and though they'd divorced a few years earlier, they still lived together, off and on. Susie claimed that it was for the sake of the two children, although people close to her knew that the drugs that Kenneth usually managed to get were part of the allure. Kenneth liked cocaine and booze. Susan preferred pills. Their four-room bungalow had long been a social center for the disaffiliated, a place to drop by, borrow clothes, drink beer, smoke cigarettes, or snort cocaine at the kitchen table, and, to those so inclined, crash for the night on the couch.

Oblivious to Susie's haphazard efforts to maintain a household like the suburban ones she saw on television sitcoms, Kenneth invited Cat and Sherri to "stay on the place, do odd jobs for your keep," for as long as it took them to find their own place and settle down—a goal that Cat set out to finance the way he knew best.

Cat liked to embellish his legend by discussing bank-robbing strategy to the shifting population around the Smiths' kitchen table: when banks opened and closed, whether they were constructed of brick or clapboard, where the alarms were located, how many employees they had, when they got the cash deliveries for "check day," when welfare checks arrived at the start of the month. A thorough appreciation of such minutiae, Cat maintained with elaborate gravity, was what separated the amateur from the professional. All summer long, Kenneth and Susie Smith listened with fascination. Susie, who thought of herself as a practical woman, was especially taken with Cat's investment advice: "Trailers. You buy a bunch of them and sit back and collect the rent."

As both a car salesman and a part-time cop, Bertie Hatfield made it a point to keep posted on who had spending money in the small universe of the upper Tug Valley. He suggested to Mark that Kenneth Smith, chronically broke but with expensive tastes, might be open to the kind of persuasion that the FBI's deep pockets could provide. In August, there was another small bank robbery. Mark and Dan Brennan spent several days visiting dozens of bank branch offices to warn them of the robbery spree and discuss security. Meanwhile, Bertie had Kenneth come to Pikeville to see Mark.

The meeting wasn't promising. Kenneth had a list of demands. He would cooperate—without specifying as to exactly what that would entail—only in exchange for being removed from probation and given protective custody. He also wanted a weekly salary, with bonuses for specific information, such as the activities of Cat Eyes. Afterward, Mark contacted Kenneth's parole officer, who said, "Forget it. The guy is totally unreliable." Besides, for a small-time drug dealer, Kenneth had a notoriously bad memory. His ex-wife was the one who kept track of the details.

Bertie, who had known twenty-five-year-old Susie Smith all her life, suggested to Mark that they approach her instead. He warned Mark that Susie "ran her mouth" frequently and did not have a good reputation for telling the truth. Still, with the suspected bank robber living in her house, she had the right connections, and she had secretly provided Bertie with useful information in the past. He thought she would be worth pursuing.

By this time, Susie had begun to weary of her house guests anyway. She liked having people around, but Cat, who ate like a wolf, ran up the phone bill calling his former prison buddies long-distance. Having his girlfriend in the house created extra tension because Susie was pretty, and Cat flirted with her incessantly. Besides, Cat was broke again. Even though Susie was working a common Tug Valley welfare scam and collecting monthly checks from both West Virginia and Kentucky, money didn't go far with six people in the house—more, if you counted Susie's troublesome younger brother, Tennis, and the others who drifted in and out. She also worried about the effect on her two young children, Miranda Lynn, five years old, and Brady, who had just turned two. By the summer, she and Kenneth were fighting openly over the situation.

To get to Susie, Bertie decided to introduce Mark to Tennis, whom Bertie had also used as an occasional informant, with the pittances of $50 or $100 that the sheriff's department parted with from time to time. On the night before they were to get together, however, Bertie called Mark at home.

"We got big problems. Tennis shot somebody."

They went directly to Susan's house. It had been a family dispute. Tennis had fled after the shooting, but while they were there, he walked in. Mark persuaded him to give himself up. "They'll be a hell of a lot easier on you. We'll try our damnedest." They called the West Virginia state police barracks just up the river past Matewan. As they waited for the troopers to arrive, Susie Smith, her eyes blazing resentment, took the occasion to unload on Mark. A relative of hers had once helped the FBI in a case, she said angrily, and never got the money that was promised. Fair, she insisted, was fair.

As they drove back to Kentucky, Mark said, "Bertie, that girl is trouble."

"You're right about that," his companion replied.

Mark said, "Keep working on her, will you?"

A few days later, Mark found Cat Eyes himself fishing in a dirty pond near a strip-mine site halfway up a mountain. He said hello, and the two young men chatted for a while. Cat, ever cordial, denied robbing banks, but added that he appreciated the courtesy of an introduction.

Not long afterward, when another bank was robbed in a mountain town just across the river in Virginia, Bertie called Mark and said, "Okay, she wants to meet."

They drove to Williamson, a gritty river town in the rocky coalfields on the West Virginia side of the Tug. Susie arrived accompanied by Kenneth and Tennis, now out on bail on a manslaughter charge. They sat at a table in a small restaurant, Kenneth dominating the conversation while Mark made eye contact with Susie, who at least gave him a smile. After a while, he asked her, "Listen, could I talk to you alone for a minute?"

Kenneth stopped talking long enough to glower when his ex-wife, tossing back her brown hair, followed the FBI man outside. Through the window, he watched them get into Bertie's car and sit there talking.

Mark tried to size her up. She was street-smart, that much was obvious. There was an edge to her, which was something he liked in women. She wasn't about to be pushed around. He didn't think she was particularly attractive, although she was generally considered to be fairly pretty, with small features and a smile that was definitely engaging when she turned it on. Like most young women in the valley, she put on makeup every morning, whether she was going somewhere or not.

"So what do you want to talk about?" she asked with amused anticipation.

"Listen, I want to know if you're interested in helping me."

"Now, why would I want to do something like that?"

He explained that money was available. She shook her head disdainfully. He kept at her, thinking, *I am going to break this girl.*

She changed the subject.

"I see you're married. Tell me what your wife looks like."

"What does that have to do with anything? We're talking about—"

"Pretty?"

"Yes, she's pretty."

"She have a good body?"

"She keeps herself in very good shape, Susie," he said, glancing at her legs, exposed in high-cut shorts. Momentarily flustered, she placed her palms unconsciously across her thighs. At five feet five and 125 pounds, she was self-conscious about the ten pounds she had put on during the summer.

"Don't call me Susie. I hate it. It's Susan."

"Okay, Susan." He smiled at her. "Will you help?"

She said she'd think about it, and they went back to the restaurant, where Kenneth and Tennis sat glumly waiting.

Over the next week, Mark and Susan met twice more, privately, and as an understanding evolved, he explained the payment process: "First, you have to give me something to take back." Taking out a notebook that she eyed nervously, Mark got her talking about Cat Eyes.

"Him? Oh, he might be involved in them bank robberies, I surely don't know." She crossed her arms. "He is a robber, after all."

She doled out information in expert increments, and he let her talk. Mark, like many naturally quiet men, was an exceptionally good listener, and it was apparent to him that this was a woman more accustomed to giving attention than to getting it. From time to time, he would ask a pertinent question, and she would add a pertinent piece of information. It was a complicated negotiation of egos. Before long, they had arrived at an accommodation. Yes, she finally said, she thought that Cat Eyes was planning on robbing another bank.

"How do you know?"

"He's living with me and Kenneth. Him and his girl-friend."

She knew that Mark was well aware of that, but he played the game. "How come?"

"He's broke. Kenneth likes him."

"Do you?"

"I suppose. I just don't want to adopt him. I already got two kids."

"Doesn't he pay you?"

"No."

"I thought he was so generous."

She shrugged. "He is when he has it."

"Sounds to me like he's taking advantage of you. Exploiting you, like he doesn't give a shit about you."

That got her attention. She agreed to meet Mark in Pikeville. Before long, they were meeting two and three times a week in a pattern that would continue for the rest of her life.

In sixteen weeks of training, new agents received a few lectures on what motivates informants: greed, money, revenge, or occasionally a sense of duty. The delicate business of actually developing and maintaining relationships with informants, which is the backbone of the FBI's investigative process, is passed over with a few rhetorical nostrums, the most important of which is "Don't get personally involved with your informants." Even the dullest rookie recognized this as pure bullshit, since the only way to develop a worthwhile informant was through personal trust and loyalty.

Money paved the way, however. To "open" a new informant, an agent was allotted $5,000, to be distributed at the agent's discretion, and more down the road, with virtually no limit on the amount, depending on the usefulness of the information. From the beginning, Susan understood that she stood to earn thousands of dollars for cooperating, if she could deliver. But Mark was nervous about spending the government's money. He had determined that Susan was willing to talk, that she could provide specific information in a criminal case, and furthermore, could probably open doors to him in future investigations. He wrote out a requisition and sent it to his supervisor, Terry Hulse, who ran the Covington branch office near Cincinnati, more than two hundred miles away. When Hulse phoned to talk about it, Mark wondered uneasily if he had done something naïve. Hulse did not sound encouraging when he asked, "Mark are you sure about this money for this informant?"

"What do you mean?"

"You're only going to give this girl five hundred dollars?"

"Talk to me some more."

"Well, I mean, she's giving you information on this guy—you know this guy's doing this robbery, don't you?"

"Yeah, I'm about ninety-five percent sure he's doing it."

"So keep her on board. Give her more money."

Mark thought about that for a moment, then said, "This girl's holding back—we're playing a kind of cat-and-mouse game right now. I just want to get her in the habit."

"Okay, I'll buy it. I like it. But let me tell you something: The money is there. Use it. Especially in your area. Don't feel like you're prostituting yourself by giving these people money. They want it. You've got it to give."

"Thanks."

At their next meeting, when he gave Susan the $500, she seemed a little upset.

"Hey, there's more, but the information has got to back it up," Mark said. "My boss is a real prick when it comes to this money."

Mark didn't realize that to Susan, taking the money was a major step, a break with her past. He wouldn't understand until it was too late that once she made that break, for her there would be no going back.

*   *   *

Susan Smith was born in 1961 in Matewan, West Virginia, an heir to two famous legends of the Tug Valley. Her mother, Tracy, was directly descended from the McCoys of the Hatfield-McCoy feud. And her birthplace, which had the nearest hospital to Freeburn, a few miles south on the Kentucky side of the Tug Fork, was the scene of one of the great dramas of the bitter coal mine union organizing wars, the 1920 Matewan Massacre in which nine men died in a shoot-out after a force of private detectives working for Tug Valley coal companies evicted miners and their families from company houses. The hero of that insurrection was the police chief, Sid Hatfield, who stood with the miners.

The Matewan Massacre was historical fact. The Hatfield-McCoy feud is one of those curious specimens of American folklore that, like much of the popular mythology of the Wild West, owes a certain amount of its historical longevity to the invention of the high-speed rotary printing press and the coinciding imperatives of market capitalist expansionism. Which is to say that while the Hatfields and McCoys did indeed shoot and kill each other over a period of many years from their respective turf on either side of the Tug Fork, the commotion would have gone largely unnoticed if it hadn't been exploited by outsiders looking for profit.

The two legends are nevertheless closely related. "In American history and folklore the Hatfields and the McCoys symbolize the backwardness and family violence most Americans associate with Appalachian mountain culture," the historian Altina L. Waller wrote. The Hatfield-McCoy saga, the most famous of many long-running mountain feuds, is actually "a story involving competition over rich timber resources and the desire of Eastern corporations and the state government to foster economic development in the region. The feud was more a foreshadowing of the era of the bloody coal mine wars than it was the final gasp of traditional mountain culture."

The Hatfields lived, by and large, on the West Virginia

side of the Tug Fork and the McCoys kept to the Kentucky
side, although the boundary has never been regarded seriously by the people who live there, isolated together by the
mountains at their backs. (The boundary was in fact drawn
somewhat arbitrarily during an all-night drinking session in
1799 by members of a joint commission.)

There were long-standing animosities between the Hatfields and McCoys, as is inevitable in isolated areas where
generation after generation face each other, keeping track of
grudges over the decades. Like many neighbors, the clans
sometimes fought over property. In a time just before outside industrialists would begin plundering the Appalachians
for hardwood, both families made money from cutting and
selling timber on their lands, and deeds were not always
firmly fixed in mountain areas. But the trouble really came
to a head with the theft of a pig.

In 1878, a Hatfield boy was accused of stealing a hog
from the patriarch of the less-prosperous McCoy clan, a
cantankerous man known as Old Ranel McCoy. The dispute
went to trial in Kentucky, but the Hatfield boy was acquitted
thanks to a not-guilty vote by one of six McCoys on the
jury, introducing an element of betrayal into the rancor. A
few years later, acrimony escalated when Old Ranel's
daughter, Roseanna, ran off with Johnse Hatfield, a son of
Devil Anse Hatfield, the ferocious but generally law-abiding
patriarch of the Hatfield clan. Over Johnse's protests, Devil
Anse adamantly refused to allow his son to marry her; the
girl was sent back home across the Tug, literally barefoot
and pregnant.

Roseanna's brothers set out to avenge the family honor
by kidnaping the Hatfield boy, whom they intended to transport to Pikeville and charge with the only criminal violation
they could prove, moonshining. But the lovesick Roseanna
thwarted them by stealing off at night on horseback to warn
Johnse. Meanwhile, on election day, when whiskey flowed
freely and voters stumbled across the river to cast ballots on
both sides, tempers flared. During a brawl between the
young men of both families, Devil Anse's brother, Ellison,

was beaten and stabbed by Hatfield boys, one of whom finished him off with a shotgun. A Pike County judge, on the scene to purchase votes, ordered the arrest of the perpetrator and several other McCoy boys. But on the long horseback ride to Pikeville with the boys in custody, a posse of Hatfields, led by Devil Anse himself, overtook the party, kidnaped three of the McCoys, and shot them on the riverbank, near what is now Matewan.

There were sporadic instances of violent retaliation between the two families, but the feud didn't reach its full intensity until five years later. That was when Perry Cline, a Pikeville lawyer who had once fought a legal battle with Devil Anse over five thousand acres of disputed land, decided to reopen his claim, since the property's value was rising sharply as the timber industry expanded and the railroads blasted through the hills into the Tug Valley. Cline prevailed on Kentucky authorities to press the five-year-old murder indictments against the Hatfields, who soon had lucrative bounties on their heads offered by lumber and railroad interests. Devil Anse and his men fled into the hills, pursued by hordes of private detectives and other bounty hunters. Their exploits were celebrated in newly established mass-circulation newspapers like Joseph Pulitzer's *New York World*, where the legend of "white savages" clinging to a primitive region "as remote as Central Africa" caught the fancy of millions of urban readers. By the time the feud died out at the turn of the century, a dozen or so Hatfields and McCoys had been killed, and one of the most enduring caricatures in American culture—the bellicose hillbilly—had been created. Significantly, according to Waller, "many Appalachians themselves had been convinced of the inadequacy of their own culture, and industrialization proceeded with little opposition." Within decades, the largest hardwood forest on the continent—7 million mountainous acres of virgin tulip poplars towering 150 feet over walnuts and white oak, hickories and maple, buckeyes, basswoods, ash, cedar, and pine—had been reduced to less than a thousand acres.

*   *   *

Two hundred million years ago, the Cumberland Plateau of eastern Kentucky was a plain that had risen from the floor of an inland sea. The earth cracked, leaving a jagged fault, pushing up mountains of limestone and slate, seldom more than three thousand feet high, that ripple like a rug bunched against the northern watershed of the Appalachians. As the ancient sea receded, it left a vast trough of peat that would ultimately curse the land and its people when the overlying mountains compressed it into what regional historian Harry M. Caudill called "a mineral the steel age would esteem more highly than rubies"—coal.

Timber had been hauled out chiefly by push boats and steamboats along the swift currents of Tug and Levisa forks to the Big Sandy, and thence to the thousand-mile sweep of the Ohio River. The railroad arrived in 1881 in Louisa, where the two forks meet, ushering in a new era of exploitation. This time the prize was the region's vast resources of high-quality, low-ash bituminous coal that lay in fat four- and six-foot seams. Gangs of immigrant construction workers, whose prowess would become embodied by mythical steel-driving men such as John Henry, slashed rights-of-way through ridges and laid bridges between cliffs as the railroad pushed inexorably up the valley, crisscrossing the hills with an intricate web of spurs and short lines. With the railroad came the speculators, agents of Wall Street and the mineral companies. These "foreign lawyers," as they were called, were expert at providing slick legal documentation, often certified at the courthouse in Pikeville, to lay claim to tenuously deeded property.

The greatest entrepreneur of them all was one John Caldwell Calhoun Mayo, a Pikeville prospector. After studying the newly completed federal geological surveys and obtaining financial backing from banks, he tramped the hills securing claims from gullible—and naturally hospitable—hillbillies with an innovative contract that acquired mineral rights independently of surface land rights. Such deeds, thousands of which remained in existence well into the

1980s, gave to the developers broad rights to all minerals in the land—including the perpetual right to make roads, knock down trees, buildings, and even cemeteries, pollute water supplies, or do anything else "necessary or convenient" to exploit the minerals, without liability. A standard rule of thumb among the speculators was that fifteen thousand tons of coal could be gouged out of an acre of such land. On many of his forays shortly after the turn of the century, Mayo was accompanied by his wife, Alice, who had dresses specially made with pockets for $20 gold pieces, which she ceremoniously dropped into the hands of hillbillies, who sold their rights for as little as fifty cents an acre. To attract Eastern capital, Mayo even arranged "safaris" into the hills of the Tug Valley for parties of bankers and developers, who were outfitted in khaki and pith helmets, with meals on the trail whipped up by the world-famous New York chef Oscar of the Waldorf.

From Mayo's expeditions, which within ten years would lay claim to mineral rights on more than 90 percent of the land in Kentucky counties such as Pike, Floyd, Harlan, and Letcher, sprang scores of coal-company camp towns—some well-maintained, many others squalid, all featuring rows of houses arranged in monotonous similarity—with names like Jennings, Neon-Fleming, Happy, Sassafras, McRoberts, and Freeburn. The coal camps sprang up independently of normal migratory patterns, in the isolation of the hills and backwaters. Their economies were based on company-issued "scrip," currency usable only in the company store, with sharp social distinctions between the miners and their families in their squat company houses, and the "big bosses," the executives and foremen, who lived in comfortable and sometimes luxurious residences, typically built on higher ground with a commanding view of the dust-covered shacks, coal tipples, and slag heaps below.

Freeburn, by the time Susan Smith was born, had long since been abandoned by a succession of coal companies that had maintained it until machine-driven strip-mining revolutionized the industry in the 1950s. But there were still a few old-timers in town who could remember the days when patriotism and company loyalty were inseparable, when coal miners, their wives, and children would gather at the company auditorium, known to all as simply "the Building," to recite the Freeburn Creed:

> I believe in Freeburn, its splendid traditions, its present greatness as a mining prospect, its magnificent prospects for the future.
>
> I believe in the Portsmouth By-Product Coke Company, its high ideals in matters of relations between the employer and the employed, its earnest and just consideration for the happiness and welfare of its workmen, the policy of its officials to deal foursquare with everyone.
>
> I believe in the people of Freeburn as among the best created.
>
> I therefore believe it is my duty to my own town to love it, to support it, to respect it, to boost it, and to defend it.

The Building and the company store had burned down before Susan was born. Even the union, which had transformed miners' lives in the Depression, was barely a factor. By the 1980s, the United States was producing more coal than ever—85 percent of it going to produce cheap electricity in the United States, Japan, and Europe. But coal prices dropped by more than a third in the first half of the eighties, and unemployment in the region sometimes exceeded 40 percent. Federal relief funds that had poured in with the Great Society programs of the 1960s—most of the spending actually went to build roads—virtually dried up in the Reagan era. Coal trucks roared down mountain roads, overloaded by as much as fifty thousand pounds, with drivers speeding to make two trips a day, getting $1.30 a ton to haul coal to the Ohio River port at Catlettsburg. Ironically, in the urban areas of America where the cheap electricity provided by low-priced coal was being devoured, it cost as much as $100 a ton to haul garbage.

Today, and throughout Susan's lifetime in the Appalachian Mountains, creeks and streams flow red with toxic runoff from strip mines; mudslides, on hills bereft of topsoil and trees, routinely cut off populated hollows for days at a time. Impoverished mountain hamlets, which themselves have no trash-removal services, are inundated with applications from outside companies who want to use the land for dumps, incinerators, and nuclear waste disposal.

Even the land itself has become unstable. Mountains gutted for coal sometimes settle like sand castles; fissures tear open like earthquake faults; visitors are told about hunters who have lost good dogs into a sudden break in the earth. The noise of settling mountains, frightening even to those who are used to it, is a hellish, primordial cracking of rock.

Resentment of outsiders festers. In 1992, two unrelated columns appeared on the same feature page of the *Floyd County Times*. One defended the area against a central-Kentucky newspaper account "about how we bare-footed, nasal-whining, whiskey-drinking, cock-fighting, illiterate, illegitimate scumbags have become full-fledged dope addicts." Another excoriated a two-year-old network-news report on Appalachia that focused on a local town: "Pretty much everybody else in the country thinks we're nothing more than toothless hicks playing the banjo on the front porch of our shacks while we stare out at our front yards filled with rusted-out car bodies, old washing machines and outhouses with half-moons crudely carved into the doors."

Not long afterward, a Mingo County, West Virginia, newspaper reported on a shootout between two local families that left one dead and nine others wounded. The argument was over a woman who had dated a member of the opposing family.

A woman of Susan's age who grew up on the same hollow as her in Freeburn remembers sharing a room with four sisters in two beds, and fetching water on winter mornings from a well whose chain was caked with ice. Clothes were laundered outside in the butter churn and hung on long lines up the hill like battleship flags in the wind. She recalls school days hiding from the truant officer because she had no shoes; breakfasts of biscuits and gravy for the week after check day; bread and milk the rest of the month. She remembers her father trudging home across the mountain from Majestic at night, his face smeared with soot. Like many of the old miners, he died of black lung disease, an oxygen tank by his bed.

A child who grew up in such circumstances learned early about physical, natural, and economic and social hazards. By the summer of 1987, Susan had already lived a hard fifteen years since she announced at the end of seventh grade that she had "better things to do" and dropped out of school in Freeburn. If she'd gone on to eighth grade, she would have had to ride a school bus each day along Peter Creek and around the mountain to Phelps, a settlement somewhat more cosmopolitan than decrepit old Freeburn. She had already been in a couple of fights with girls in elementary school, and she fought easily and ferociously enough to be ostracized among her better-mannered classmates. In a household where a smack across the face was a routine occurrence, in a social world where a young girl with a fast mouth sometimes had to defend herself with her fists, Susan arrived at adolescence with physical threats already firmly established in her life. She was poor—her family was on welfare nearly all of her life—and she resented it. Susan had grown up the fifth of nine children of a chronically unemployed coal miner, Sid Daniels, and his long-suffering wife, Tracy Eldridge Daniels. The children shared clothes, and even shoes, in a drafty house high up a mountain gulch in Freeburn known as Barrenshea Hollow.

It was a place where trouble never was far away. Susan started school in 1966, at a time when cheap oil was flooding the country and the Appalachian coal industry, already battered by unemployment caused by the growth of efficient strip-mining, sank into one of its cyclical severe depressions. At the time, only one in four students in Pike County finished high school; the majority had already dropped out by ninth grade. In isolated areas like the one in which Susan grew up, the graduation rate was as low as 7 percent. Dropping out of school came naturally to Susan, who saw that people simply fled the hard times all around her. In 1960, the population of Pike County was 81,154; ten years later, it would be 61,059.

Natural peril intensified the fatalism of a child's life in a mountain hollow, where mine disasters were a routine part of life, and spring rains often unleashed great mudbanks of strip-mine debris and boulders from eroded mountaintops onto populated areas below. Catastrophic floods devastated the Tug Valley twice during her youth, in 1963, and again in 1977, when she was fifteen. That year the river, swollen by fifteen inches of rain that fell on still-frozen ground, crested at fifty feet and swept away hundreds of homes in the valley.

Few of the four hundred or so people in Freeburn had telephones in Susan's childhood years, but many acquired television sets. When she was a little girl, Susan decided that she wanted to be a secretary like the ones she saw on television shows. Secretaries had respect from men. Secretaries dressed beautifully and lived in cities. Secretaries were helpers, and Susan, at her best, was a helper.

Like most out-of-work miners, her father drank hard. Like most women in the hollow, her mother remained in the background. Susan had few friends. "She was like a stray kitten with a temper," one woman who grew up with her would later recall sadly. "A girl with fancy ideas and an attitude and a temper to boot don't make a lot of friends."

Instead, she had what were referred to as "notions." The highlight of Susan's grade school years was belonging to the Patriotettes, the all-girl drill team. No one in town knew the history well enough to enlighten her, but the drill team had actually been organized early in the century by the Portsmouth-Solvay Coke Company, the firm that had built the squat rows of miner's houses along the Tug Fork and named the town Freeburn, after the valued properties of the indigenous bituminous coal. The little girl from Barrenshea

Hollow loved her red-and-white Patriotettes uniform and
wore it proudly in ragtag holiday parades. In her seventh-
grade yearbook, Susan's picture stands out among those of
her classmates with pigtails and scrubbed faces. She is the
only one wearing a beret.

In 1977, the year of the big flood, when Susan was fifteen,
she saw her first opportunity to get out. She met twenty-
two-year-old Kenneth Smith, a good-looking local boy who
could be charming when he wanted something—the kind of
young rogue a girl's father warns her about, if the father is
paying attention. When Kenneth spotted her and whistled,
Susan simply got on the back of his motorcycle and rode off
with him to a trailer he rented on the far side of the mountain, in another old coal company town called Majestic.
   Kenneth, who fancied himself a successful gambler, actually earned his money by selling drugs. Like most dealers,
he visited cities from time to time. Susan resolved to go
with him, and he was smart enough to realize that she was
an asset since she had a good memory and an affinity for
numbers. She helped him with small-time deals in cocaine,
marijuana, acid, and bootleg depressants and stimulants,
known locally as "nerve pills." In time, she began refer-
ring to herself as his "executive assistant," a phrase she
had picked up from television. Another favorite term was
"charming," a word that none of Kenneth's friends had
heard anyone actually utter before.
   For the first time in her life, Susan was able to go up to
Matewan, the nearest town with stores, and buy the clothes
she liked—not only for herself, but for friends and relatives.
But the prosperity didn't continue. When Susan was seven-
teen, Kenneth was arrested for drug possession, jumped bail,
and fled, sending her on to Louisiana to stay with one of his
brothers and his wife. While there, broke and miserable without Kenneth, she worked for a time in a fast-food restaurant.
When that didn't pay, she turned to occasional prostitution.
   In time, Kenneth joined her. They later moved to Indi-

ana, where they married and had a daughter, Miranda. Thrilled at being parents, they tried to settle into respectability. Kenneth, promising to straighten himself out, took a job as a carpenter's assistant. They were living in a trailer, but Susan worked hard to decorate it with frilly curtains, throw rugs, and pillows. She liked good restaurants; he hated them, suspecting that the waiters looked down on his uncertain manners. As the novelty of parenthood passed into drudgery, they again turned to drugs for recreation and then, after Kenneth lost his job, for financial support as well. They began fighting. Kenneth would beat her and vow in the morning to reform. It was a pattern that Susan never managed to break out of.

From Indiana, they moved for a while to a cheap apartment in Cicero, Illinois, a run-down suburb just outside of Chicago. There their small-town drug-dealing expertise took on some big-city sophistication as they established contacts that would later keep them supplied in the Tug Valley. Among their friends in Cicero were some men who held up a bank. Susan had listened to them planning the robbery at her kitchen table.

By the time she was twenty-four, Susan and Kenneth had run out their string up north and were back in the Tug, in a life once more squeezed between dark ridges. Facing trial on the old drug charge, Kenneth pleaded guilty and got off with probation. At home, the fighting got so bad that Susan ran away from her husband and child to live with a sister in West Virginia. Leaving there, she wandered for months, staying with friends and relatives, who would sometimes find her curled up on their couch in the morning like a child.

During this time, she began showing up regularly at a country and western bar that attracted a spirited crowd on Route 23, the main highway through Pikeville, across from a road called Harmons Branch. The owner, who was also the featured singer, was a burly man named Marlow Tackett, who had hopes of making it as a star in Nashville. Borrowing clothes from her sister, Susan sat at a table night after night and pined for Marlow. Once he gave her an autographed publicity picture of him in his cowboy costume, and she cherished it. She told people that she was planning to become his manager and help take him to the big time. Years later, when asked about her, Marlow would barely remember the girl from Freeburn.

Miserable and destitute, Susan finally returned to Kenneth. A second child, Brady, was born in 1985. She and Kenneth divorced soon afterward, which enabled her to get better welfare benefits. They were still living unhappily together in the rented house beside the river in 1987 when Mark Putnam came into Susan's life like a knight on horseback. In Susan's world Mark was a novelty, a handsome, motivated, polished, polite man who was *interested* in her as someone who had something to offer. With no special effort, he treated her like a lady, and she responded.

The payoff for Mark came in September. Susan told him that Cat Eyes, still living at her house, had brought home a duffel bag containing two sawed-off shotguns and some ski masks. She found it in the children's room, which Kenneth had given to Cat and Sherri, forcing Miranda and Brady to sleep in the living room. Cat was clearly making big plans, Susan reported to Mark. "Watch the papers," Cat had told her with a sly wink. "Easy street is just up the road."

The FBI quietly alerted local banks to be on the watch.

Cat had chosen a branch of the First National Bank in Ferrells Creek, in the hills fifteen miles from Pikeville and five miles from the Virginia border. The bank, which was near a town called Elkhorn City, population fifteen hundred, usually had plenty of cash on hand. It was housed in a one-story building with a parking lot, beside a used-trailer dealer. In Virginia, the roads were good. Cat had arranged for a getaway van and an accomplice to drive it.

On the morning of September 10, Cat entered the bank and approached the teller's window, waiting patiently for a few seconds while a woman in front finished tucking money into her wallet. The teller looked up with some alarm. Cat was wearing a huge pair of lumberjack's coveralls that swathed him from neck to foot, and a black knit ski mask turned around backward, with two eye holes clumsily cut out in front so he would not expose too much of his face, especially his distinctive green eyes. He was holding but not brandishing a sawed-off shotgun. Cat was having some difficulty seeing because the eye holes in the knit mask shifted whenever his head moved.

The teller, Rosemary Childers, had been an employee of the bank for eleven years, working her way up to branch administrator. She was filling in at the window that day because the regular teller had called in sick. Cat plopped a pillowcase down on the counter and said, "Fill it up with money." She thought to take note of the pillowcase itself, which had a print of pink flowers but was grimy, as if it had been used to haul fishing tackle.

While she took stacks of bills from her cash drawer, Cat Eyes raised the gun and swung around, ordering the six or seven other people in the bank: "Freeze, and put your hands up!" Some were confused at the sequence of the command; tentatively, hands went up.

Childers took this brief opportunity to drop a dye pack into the pillowcase along with the money. A dye pack is a clever security device that looks like a standard stack of bank money, a hundred bills thick, with a real ten-dollar bill on the top. Once it passes through the electronic beam at a bank's door, a timing switch is triggered. The next time it is jostled, the device explodes like a firecracker, splattering red dye on the fleeing culprit and his loot.

"Into the vault," Cat Eyes shouted to the bewildered group of employees and customers. There was some commotion while Rosemary Childers went to look for the key. When she found it and opened the vault, Cat ordered her to take the stacks of bills from a shelf and drop them into his pillowcase, which he held open like a trick-or-treater. She made a show of dropping in a second dye pack. Cat Eyes

spotted this one. "And no dye bombs," he said. Sheep-
ishly, the woman removed it. The pillowcase now contained $12,807 in bills, including the real ten-dollar note
stuck atop the hidden dye pack.

Cat Eyes closed the vault door, thoughtfully not all the
way, and ran to the exit with a shout of glee. Just outside,
he paused to perform a small victory jig like football players
do after grabbing a pass in the end zone. At once the dye
pack exploded, initially causing Cat to think he had been
shot and was watching his own blood spurt. When he realized what had happened, he dashed for the van, screaming
at his accomplice, who had been lying on the front seat, to
get going. As they tore out of the parking lot and turned
south toward the Virginia border on U.S. 460, a bank employee coming to work sized up the situation, chased after
them, got the license number of the van, and stopped at a
gas station to phone the state police.

The number was busy.

The van was found ditched on a side road at Ferrells
Creek, along with a couple of hundred dollars soaked with
red dye.

Cat didn't return to Susan's house, which the authorities
were watching. But a week later, in the Tug Valley branch
of Pikeville National Bank in South Williamson, another
alert bank teller, Debby White, became suspicious when a
very polite but highly nervous dark-haired man with amazing
green eyes came in to exchange a wad of two-dollar bills, 182
of them in all—all stained at the edges with red dye. "Usually two-dollar bills come in only in deposits," she later told
the police. "You never see exchanging of bills like that."

As Cat left the bank, she called the state police, who
promptly notified the FBI. Mark was out of town to serve a
fugitive warrant, and Dan Brennan finally got through to
him on the phone and explained the situation. "Talk to
Susan," Mark said. "She'll fill you in."

Susan refused. "I only talk to Mark," she told Brennan.

When Mark found her the next day, he was baffled by her stubborn loyalty. "It's your case," she said. "I don't want you to give away the credit. You worked on this case very hard."

She told him where Cat was—at his mother's house in West Virginia. When Mark and Dan Brennan arrived with state police to handcuff the suspect, Cat insisted that he walk beside Mark, for the benefit of the newspaper photographer who showed up.

Susan was furious that Mark had to share credit for the arrest. She stopped by the office the next day and found him there alone. He counted out fifteen one-hundred-dollar bills and gave them to her, but she tried to give one back. "I want you to have this."

He shrank from it. "I can't take that, Susan!"

She insisted, "You did all the work and you're getting screwed out of any credit."

"You don't understand how this organization works. You're making me a hero. Maybe I didn't get the big write-up in the paper, but my bosses know who did the work, and I get the credit for you."

"I want you to have this. I won't take it back."

She dropped the money on his desk and walked out.

In a panic, he thought, *Is she trying to set me up?*

He phoned his supervisor at the Covington office, who told him not to worry. He should write a covering memo and put the money in the safe toward the next payment, which would come if and when Susan testified against Cat Eyes.

Later, when Mark broached that subject with her, Susan said she would consider testifying, but that she was afraid for her life. If she testified at the trial, she wanted enough money to move out of the area with her children.

Mark asked, "How much money do you think you'll need?"

"Four thousand dollars."

"No problem," he said.

3

Mark knew enough about what he was up against in eastern Kentucky to regard Susan as more than a source of information. To an outsider anxious to assimilate, she offered the invaluable cachet of acceptance: being seen with a local girl made him look more like one of the boys. It never occurred to him that for her, the opposite was true. To the extent that he found camouflage with her, she was flushed out into the open. Susan had known instinctively that once she made her pact with Mark, there would be no turning back. As if to ensure that, she had made it a point to tell everyone in Freeburn that she was working for the FBI.

Far more than her husband, Kathy implicitly understood Susan's dilemma. From the beginning, she approached Susan with a mixture of empathy and wariness that enabled Susan, a woman acutely alert to opportunity, to find the rapidly blurring zone between Mark's professional and personal life and quickly step onto it.

In fact, Kathy recognized in Susan a kindred soul. No one else ever really understood that—not her husband, and certainly not Susan herself, who seemed to have drifted into the Putnams' life as aimlessly as a cloud trailing under the sun.

The unlikely alliance between the two women developed on the telephone as the Putnams settled more securely into their new home during the summer and fall of 1987. Susan had taken her role as an informant quite seriously, regarding it as a full-time job that required her to be on call and to report in frequently. Since Mark was out on the road so much, and the office had no secretary, Kathy stepped in to help as an unpaid receptionist, fielding many of his phone calls from their home. Susan called the house for the first time about a week after her initial meeting with Mark.

"Kathy? This is Susan Smith," she had begun in a matter-of-fact tone. "I'm working for the government. I don't know if your husband told you about me or not. I'm working as his informer on an important case. Is he there? He was supposed to meet up with me at the office, but I don't know where he is."

Kathy said she'd relay the message when Mark got in. Mark had already told her about his introductory discussions with Susan, including the meeting outside the restaurant in West Virginia. He'd also told her something that they both found amusing and somewhat curious. According to Bertie, right after the meeting, Kenneth had stormed around Freeburn maintaining that the FBI man had actually "screwed" his ex-wife in the backseat of the car, in broad daylight.

This alone was intriguing enough to whet Kathy's curiosity about what sort of person would be living with a wild man like Kenneth Smith. Kathy was pleasantly surprised to find that she liked her. She decided that Susan was friendly, sincere, refreshingly self-deprecating, engagingly ditsy at times, and, she thought, more than a little bit vulnerable when it came to relationships with men. Her first and abiding impulse was to help Susan.

Kenneth's fabrications aside, it was nevertheless apparent to Kathy that Susan was enthralled by Mark, a situation that she accepted with the practiced equanimity of a faculty wife toward an eager female graduate student with a harmless crush on the professor. Besides, in close-knit Pikeville, where Kathy didn't know many people and her neighbors made it clear that they kept to themselves, it was nice to have someone to talk to.

Susan began to ask Kathy's advice on grooming and etiquette, while probing subtly for information about Mark. She found out that he ran every night and told him that she had started running, too. Did he read? Susan began showing up at their meetings with a paperback in hand. As they got to know each other better, Mark began noticing odd little changes in her, as if she were trying to transform herself to become more like the women he knew. Even her manner of speech changed—she would correct herself crossly when she said "heered" instead of "heard," for example.

"The calls got more personal as we got to know each other," Kathy would later recall. "I actually enjoyed her calls at first, but you could sense right off that this was someone with an odd fascination for our personal life. Within a couple of weeks or so, she wanted to know things like, 'What are you making for dinner? What does Mark like to eat? What did Danielle do today?' The more I got to know about the awful life she had, the more I saw this as her attempt to understand our life. And I thought I could maybe show her that she had options, if she would just identify them and work at them.'"

Before long, Susan was calling at all hours, sometimes several times a day. Every time she picked up the phone, Kathy expected to hear Susan's hillbilly twang. In time, Kathy decided that Susan's attitude toward Mark was akin to that of an executive secretary's toward the boss. "She wanted to know where he was and how he could be reached all the time. She expected him to be available. She always claimed that she had important information for him. It was glamorous for her to be working for the FBI. On the one hand, she seemed to have the idea that it was like a regular job and Mark was her boss; then on the other, I think she saw him and her as Bonnie and Clyde." Susan was persistent. Soon after she started working as an informant, she began showing up at the courthouse nearly every day, looking for Mark in the FBI office. Since he was often out, Susan would pass the time bantering with courthouse employees, especially the officers in the probation and marshal's divisions, where she managed to establish the impression that she and Mark had a close working relationship.

Mark's take on Susan was less complicated than his wife's. He had noticed, for example, that Susan tended to boast about sexual relations with men at the courthouse, men who he was quite sure had never been involved with her. "She has a big mouth, Kat," he warned his wife. "Watch out."

But Susan's dependence on Kathy grew as the friendship deepened. They sometimes spoke for hours, Susan's troubles spilling out one after the other to a receptive ear. The dead-end relationships, money problems, despair, abysmal self-esteem, half-baked aspirations, and chronic ineptitude—Kathy readily recognized these afflictions because she had overcome them herself. She believed that in time she might be able to help Susan do the same.

Patiently, she would say, "Listen, Susan. I have been there. Believe me, I know where you are coming from. You can get yourself together."

To look at her then, poised and happy, ensconced in a solid marriage with a spouse who loved her deeply and a bright-eyed young daughter who would be a delight to any parent, it would have been difficult to imagine what similarities in their lives Kathy was alluding to. Kathy Ponticelli and her younger sister, Christine, were daughters of an autocratic but devoted second-generation Italian-American father and a mother who offered quiet, unassuming encouragement to her girls. The household had strict rules: no chatter at the dinner table, help out around the house, be home by curfew and not a minute later, make good grades, go to mass on Sunday, and don't get in trouble with the nuns.

A smart and perceptive girl who felt that there was probably more to life than the tedium of Manchester, Connecticut, a small town aspiring mightily to become a suburb, Kathy managed to break all of the rules except the one about good grades. She coasted through St. James parish school and then East Catholic High School, sullen and bored. Unable, she thought, to do anything right, she compensated for her lack of self-confidence with a brashness that some would misconstrue as brazen effrontery. Her high school misdeeds, still painful to recall even after she'd grown into a well-adjusted young woman, had begun innocently enough, with hemline-length violations and back talk. If social acceptance meant dating the loutish captain of the football team, opening a purse to brandish a stash of joints, talking street-tough, copping cigarettes in the girls' bathroom, flouting the rules—in general, courting the fires of hell in the next life, and detention, threats of expulsion, and inclusion on lists of suspected school troublemakers in this one—then so be it. She was in, and who cared? On the other hand, not many of her female classmates pointedly carried, as she did, a well-worn paperback of *Catcher in the Rye*. At East Catholic High, such an attitude led right down the slippery slope to what her devout parents saw as the worst of all ignominies: public school, to which Kathy was banished in her junior year, and from which she dropped out a few months later, days after she turned eighteen.

She was one of those skinny, fresh-faced girls who would grow up to become a winsome beauty, yet never quite appreciate that it had actually happened. Nearly two decades later, she continued to see herself through a clouded lens as a gawky, self-conscious kid holding back tears of rage. *Ponticelli, your ears are sticking out! Look at her ears! Look at her ears!*

After Kathy dropped out of high school, the similarities to Susan's life became more pronounced. She horrified her parents by moving into an apartment in a run-down, crime-ridden part of East Hartford with a jealous boyfriend who drank heavily and had a propensity to punch any man who glanced more than casually at his girlfriend. The young man's mother tended bar in a club that featured go-go dancers, where Kathy took a job as a waitress and bartender. Keeping her shirt on didn't make her feel any more virtuous than her friends who danced, some of them young mothers trapped in the gritty economy of divorce on the fringe of postindustrial America.

The boyfriend was thrown into jail after a fight with a man who had flirted with Kathy in a bar. Things got worse. A man who followed her home one night forced his way into the apartment and raped her. She reported it to the police, who arrested the man immediately, but at the station house she was unnerved by questioning that implied that she had invited the assault, since she worked in such a disreputable bar. She was afraid to testify, and the assailant went free.

She resumed the relationship with her boyfriend, driving off with him to North Carolina, where they rented a trailer near a military base. When their money ran out, he stranded her there. Ashamed, she phoned her parents for the plane fare home. In the stultifying sanctuary of their house—"If you're going to come home, you're going to live by our rules"—she tried to accommodate herself to their diminished expectations. When a man ten years her senior who had a steady job in a gravel factory entered her life, she married him, virtually on impulse. Her father gave her a job managing an apartment complex that he and his father had built in Manchester, and she got her high school equivalency diploma and enrolled in community college. It looked like things were working out at last.

But there was a dark side to her new husband that Kathy hadn't seen. Her husband deeply resented the "airs" he said she was putting on by insisting on continuing in college. He was also insanely jealous. The marriage, which lasted four months, ended one night when, in a drunken rage, he smacked her around in the car and pushed her out, bruised and mortified, onto her parents' well-tended front lawn.

Not at all sure that she was getting through, Kathy tried to make Susan see the parallels in their lives, by way of showing her that it wasn't too late.

"We both had lifelong feelings of inadequacy," she would say later. "We got involved with the wrong people, looking for love wherever we could get it, always looking for easy answers. We both got involved with impossible men. We both had a history of running away. We never felt we were good enough. We didn't face reality and just assumed it would somehow magically work out.''

Susan confided to Kathy that she was a regular drug user, ''pills, to help me relax.'' Kathy had never abused drugs, but she'd spent enough of her life with people who did to understand the predicament involved in being around them. ''I was scared by cocaine, but I was pulled into that world. It was the same thing as Susan's life, basically—the people around the kitchen table, people coming and going all day, strangers asleep on the couch when you got up in the morning.''

By the age of twenty-one, however, Kathy was on track at last. ''My overriding resolution was not to have to crawl back to my father. I was determined by then. I was no longer married, and I got my associate degree. I had a decent job managing the apartments, I was living in a nice apartment that I'd furnished beautifully from secondhand shops. I even had a new Datsun 280ZX. Then I saw Mark and he changed my entire life.''

They met serendipitously on a Friday night in July of 1982, two days before his twenty-third birthday. In the apartment next door to her lived an avuncular, hard-drinking elderly man, who had asked Kathy to join him for dinner at a local restaurant where a woman he was dating would be singing. At dinner, however, he drank so excessively that he was listing severely by the time the singer came on. At an adjacent table, a sprightly middle-aged widow sitting with a male friend noticed Kathy's plight and caught her attention.

''Men,'' the older woman commiserated, rolling her eyes.

Kathy smiled back. ''What are you going to do with them?''

The woman looked Kathy over appraisingly and asked a few tentative questions about her age and marital status.

"You know," she said, pulling her chair closer, "my son would be perfect for you. He's a good-looking guy. He just graduated from the University of Tampa, and he's going to be an FBI agent. I can call him and ask him to come over."

Sure, Kathy thought. *Some guy sitting at home on a Friday night while his mother hustles dates for him? And what kind of guy wants to be an FBI agent?* But the woman was engagingly persistent. "Come on," she said, getting up. *"Come on!* We're going to call him."

"Listen, we need to leave," Kathy protested, noticing that her companion's elbows were sliding off the table. "I have to get him home." But the man got unsteadily to his feet and wobbled across the dance floor to join his friend the singer between sets, announcing that he was going home with her.

On her way to the ladies' room, Kathy passed the older woman at the pay phone. "You've got to meet this girl," the woman was saying into the phone. "She's beautiful." She grabbed Kathy by the elbow and thrust the receiver into her hand. "Talk!"

Flustered, Kathy mumbled, "Hello?"

There was embarrassed laughter on the other end, and a deep voice said, "I have to apologize to you for my mother putting you on the spot. The woman is incorrigible."

Kathy was intrigued by the sound of his voice. They talked for a while and seemed to have things in common. She liked his sense of humor. She heard herself saying, "Well, why don't you come down here then, if you want to talk?"

"Would it be worth my while?" He didn't sound arrogant, just assertive enough to be worth a look.

"Yeah, it would be worth it."

Twenty minutes later, a dark-haired young man with flashing eyes and a dazzling smile walked in. He shook her hand, held her chair, made her laugh, and treated her like the most important person in his life. By the end of the night, she was hopelessly in love.

"We connected right away," she recalled. "We talked all night long. He told me about his plans to get into the FBI as a special agent by working his way up from clerk. I told him about my own hopes to have a husband and a family, a good, working marriage, security, and simple happiness. It was very clear very fast that this was the man I really wanted in my life, and he felt the same way about me. We talked and laughed, and we made love for the first time in the morning, in my apartment, as the sun came up."

When he met Kathy, Mark was two months out of the University of Tampa, where he had been the captain of the championship soccer team and from which he had graduated with a degree in criminology. In September, he was to start work as a clerk at the FBI office in New Haven.

Mark, his younger brother, Tim, and his sister, Cindy, had spent part of their early childhood in a public housing project in East Hartford. But their father worked hard to provide a better home. A burly, soft-spoken man who always had another job or two to do after his regular workday driving a truck for Sears, Walter Putnam soon put together the down payment on a comfortable house in middle-class Coventry. He had dropped out of high school to enlist in the Navy, and he and his wife, Barbara, placed great value on his children's education—although it was Tim, not Mark, who was considered to be the brains of the family. Tim was "college material." Mark was the jock.

However, in his freshman year of high school, Mark was offered an athletic scholarship to the prestigious Pomfret School in Pomfret, Connecticut, fifty miles away. Going off to prep school posed a tough decision for a boy who stayed close to home and was already a star soccer and baseball player in high school. His mother opposed it, advising him, "Stay at home. You're going to be all-American." Characteristically, his father's response was to throw the question back at him. "Think it out. I know the answer, but think it out."

In time, Mark knew, too. He recognized the opportunity

and welcomed the chance to prove himself to his father. He knew that he wouldn't be able to coast through Pomfret, as he had so far through public high school, on a soccer ball and a smile. His teachers had been padding his grades and told him so. Mark had already decided that he wanted to be an FBI agent, although he hadn't told anybody yet, and he was aware that the FBI was fussy about taking only college graduates with good academic records. His father, delighted that Mark opted for Pomfret, told him, "If you want to go, you go. I'll handle your mother." Despite the scholarship, it would cost Mark's parents about $1,000 a year to send him. They'd make do, his father said.

Later, Mark would recall his apprehension about leaving home for an expensive school like Pomfret. "For the first time, I had to study. I had to prove myself in a group of people who I knew were intellectually superior. I was so intimidated by that. I absolutely hated the place when I got there. It was such a totally alien environment. My initial impression was that I was surrounded by these prissy rich kids who had it made all their lives.

"I was never comfortable having people know much about my private life, so it took me a while to acclimate. But then I began to realize that some of these kids, their parents had just shipped them off to get them out of the house. And others I got to know and found out they were in the same boat as me—working-class kids who were there on grants or scholarships. I began to relax."

The summer before he went to Pomfret, Mark broke his leg in a soccer scrimmage. The cast came off only a week before classes began, but he started anyway on the team, playing through the pain, never mentioning the injury to any of his teammates. He rapidly assimilated. "The soccer team was going great—we were winning games right and left. Friends started coming, girls started coming around. My grades were good, and this time I worked hard for them. And boom, before I knew it, I was back in a fold again, a nest."

Meanwhile, his relationship with his father, who had overcome a drinking problem a few years earlier, underwent a significant change. The man who had been a distant figure through much of his childhood became a confidant. Mark sensed that through him, his father was vicariously living out a part of life that he had never been able to experience.

"We began to have meaningful talks on the phone after I went to prep school, which was odd because the man usually hated the phone. He wanted to know what people were doing, what I was studying, what the rich kids were like, what the girls were like. I was dumbfounded. I had never heard the guy talk that way. He had left school at sixteen, so I guess it was a world he had always wondered about." Mark's father and mother made the trip to watch him on the athletic field on weekends. Mark maintained a B average, played baseball, and captained Pomfret's undefeated soccer team in his senior year. He graduated in 1978 and enrolled at the University of Tampa.

The relationship between father and son grew even closer during the summer between prep school and his freshman year in college, when Mark frequently went out on the road with his father.

"On the road at night, we would come into a truck stop and my father pointed out, many times, where guys would come up and offer him like twenty thousand or thirty thousand dollars for his load. You know, the deal was he could leave the truck, go in for a cup of coffee, and come back and report the cargo was hijacked. He told me, 'It would have been no skin off my teeth, and man, there were times when we really could have used that money. It was easy money. But it would have been wrong. And there's no two ways about it. You be honest in life, Mark. That's it.' "

Mark never forgot. At the start of his sophomore year, he decided to major in criminology; in his earnest way, he told his father that he intended to become an FBI agent because he believed in what he had learned about honesty, as corny

as it might sound. "My old man was the one person I knew
I could talk to about the FBI and not get laughed at," he
remembered.

During Mark's sophomore year, his father died of lung
cancer. The broken relationship would leave him with a
powerful, nearly overwhelming sense of incompleteness.
At the funeral, he told his mother, "If I could be half the
man that he was, I will be happy. I'll have made it."

He returned to school an even more serious young man,
with goals firmly in place. Mark had developed a reputation
as a heartbreaker among campus women, and he was cha-
grined by it now. He began dating a chemistry major, independent, self-sufficient, and assertive. He liked that in a
woman. He liked someone who would stand up to him, who
knew what she wanted, who could goad him and keep him
laughing at himself, and who would share his values without question.

When his mother introduced them in the summer of 1982,
Kathy Ponticelli, it appeared, was just such a woman. He
fell in love with her with the same force that she did with
him. From the first night, they were inseparable.

"We were like teenagers dating," Kathy said. "We
played, we talked—it was just us, there wasn't room for
anyone else in our lives. By the end of the summer, we
moved together to a tiny apartment in Middletown, about
halfway between New Haven, where he was going to start
work in the FBI office in late August, and Hartford, where
I had just got a job as a paralegal at an insurance company."

Many weekends, they drove down to New York City, to
explore, to have dinner and see Broadway shows like "A
Chorus Line" and "Dream Girls." They rode a horse-
drawn carriage in Central Park, had their portrait sketched
in charcoal on Times Square, and went to the top of the
Empire State Building to watch the lights of Manhattan
twinkle on at twilight. On a Rhode Island beach, they made
love in the sand and skinny-dipped. He took her to Fenway

Park in Boston for her first baseball game. Her parents liked him enormously. The summer seemed endless.

"I was already pretty well straightened out, but this was the icing on the cake," said Kathy many years later. "I loved hearing about his life—things like prep school, senior proms, college pranks, graduation day—things that I had missed. Mark had done everything the right way, always.

"God, we were a perfect fit. For everything I learned from him, he learned something from me. He was more or less attracted to the self-assurance I had developed by then. I'd gotten all As in community college, and by now I wasn't ashamed of who I was or what I had done. I taught him how to manage money and balance a checkbook. He was so naïve about some things—like he'd never count his change. He was an impossible sucker for garage mechanics. I showed him life: you shop around for a garage; the bills come due; the rent has to be paid; the oil has to be changed in the car. We seemed to fill in each other's blanks."

They lived together for almost two years, putting away money for marriage and a baby. When they agreed it was time to get married, Kathy decided that it was important to tell him every detail of her past. He listened in stony silence, then walked out without a word. She didn't see him for three days, during which time she thought she would never see him again. When he came back, he said only, "I don't ever want to talk about that again. Any of it." And they never did.

After he was promoted to night clerk at the New Haven FBI bureau, where he fielded agents' after-hours phone tips and edited their investigative reports as part of his duties, Mark took a second job during the daytime as a clerk at a liquor store. On Easter weekend of 1984, without alerting either of their families, they drove to New York City to get married. They'd chosen New York for the wedding because they thought it would look more romantic than Hartford on their marriage certificate. The only objection came not from their families but from the bureau, where Mark's supervisor let him know that the FBI frowned on elopements, even by clerks.

But they had other things on their mind than the FBI. They wanted to have a baby.

Kathy would always remember the night Danielle was conceived. "My doctor had told me I should go off the pill a few months before we planned to conceive. Mark had come home from his night job; we were lying in bed, and he kissed me in that way. I reached for my diaphragm, but he put his hand on mine and said, 'It's time. I want you to have my baby.' We made love. This is difficult to say, but our lovemaking was always intense. This time it was so different—even the way he looked at me was different. He was making love to me as the mother of his baby, and I remember that as the most perfect moment in my life."

She remembered something else. "As soon as I started to show, he would not make love to me. He was petrified that he would hurt the baby. He treated me as though I was a queen."

Danielle was born on New Year's Day of 1985. Eighteen months later, after years of work and a long period of anxiety awaiting the results of his application interviews and tests, Mark was finally accepted into the FBI academy to begin training as a special agent. They both would later recall this period as the happiest time of their lives, happier even than their first summer together. Kathy's most enduring impression of her husband comes from the days right before they left for Pikeville, when Danielle was just two. She simply remembers Mark sitting, at Danielle's insistence, on her Fisher-Price toddler's chair, a friendly giant at a little girl's tea party.

4

$\mathbf{F}$ederal agents have been paying informants to provide information on illegal activities in Appalachia since the days of the bloody "moonshine wars" of the Prohibition era, when the Cumberland Plateau was one of the chief sources of bootleg alcohol for Midwestern cities such as Chicago and Cincinnati. Heavily armed teams of government agents were so diligent in their crusade against the prosperous hill-billy moonshine industry that railroad cars had to be chartered to haul thousands of natives off to overcrowded federal penitentiaries. To the mountaineer, already seething under the tyranny of outside agents hired by coal companies to thwart union activity, the invasion of "foreign" law enforcement officials, operating with the assistance of local authorities, left what Harry M. Caudill called "the deep-seated conviction that he is governed not by just laws but by corrupt and venal men—men who would betray him when it was to their purpose and reward him when it was to their gain."

This unspoken paradigm was still firmly in place two generations later when a wild man barged into the FBI office in Pikeville late in the summer of 1987, filling the doorway with his bulk.

"I'm telling you, gentlemen, it's a million-dollar operation," Charlie Trotter boomed. The two agents' first impulse was to reach for their guns. But Charlie held up his palms and motioned for them to relax, settling himself into an empty chair and saying expansively, "I want to give you guys the biggest case you are ever going to work."

Suspiciously, Dan Brennan said, "Yeah, what's that?"

"Stolen trucks," Charlie replied, folding his arms and

looking from Brennan to Mark to see who was looking back hardest. "A goddamned Sears catalog of them."

Brennan tightened his lips and found something to read.

Charlie leaned forward to scrutinize Mark, a grizzled grin showing under his Fu Manchu mustache. A solid six feet and 190 pounds, wearing a tight muscle shirt over arms festooned with prison tattoos, Charlie adjusted the little leather cap that sat jauntily on his shaved head. Mark had never seen anything quite like him.

For the next four hours, as Mark made notes and encouraged him to go on, Charlie spun out his tale of betrayal and indignation. At the heart of the story was a willingness to sell information, and perhaps to testify if the price was right, about what he described as a huge multistate operation in stolen vehicles, truck parts, and construction and mining equipment, an elaborate "chop shop" located on a secluded mountain somewhere near the town of McRoberts, just over the Letcher County border twenty miles southwest of Pikeville. Since he was a member of the ring that ran the operation, Charlie had details. He identified the "brains" of the operation as one Vernon Mullins, who over the past several years had recruited a gang of thieves who stole the trucks and other equipment throughout several states and towed it back to the Letcher County site, from where it was being sold.

"It's going to cost you, but it'll be worth the price," Charlie promised. Was the FBI interested?

Mark thanked Charlie for his time, took a number where he could be reached, and said he'd be in touch.

When Charlie left, Mark called a local cop he knew in Letcher County and asked him what he'd heard about the operation. "Yeah, we've been after that son of a bitch Vernon Mullins for a long time," the cop replied, "but you can't get near him. He supposedly runs a big chop shop somewheres."

Mark checked Charlie's criminal record. He was a certified desperado, a hardened criminal involved in drugs and robbery, who had also done time for attempted murder. Such a résumé was not necessarily a bad thing in a potential informant, assuming you could keep him on your side.

Brennan, looking forward to his transfer to another office within months, tried to discourage his young partner's obvious enthusiasm. "Mark, you don't want to mess with that," he warned.

"Why not?"

Brennan whistled. "Stolen parts, man oh man. You're overwhelmed with paperwork. It's a real hassle. The reporting requirements are unbelievable." He pulled out the bureau's procedural manual to illustrate the complications: Every part, every vehicle, would need to be thoroughly documented and traced to its source, which could be anywhere in the country. Fingerprints would have to be matched, owners of the stolen equipment notified and assuaged. It would require tracking down original police theft reports from every jurisdiction involved, not to mention insurance reports and claims documents. If the operation was as major as Charlie was maintaining, it would be a full-time job.

As always, Mark considered Brennan's advice. But he knew that, if Charlie's information was good and if the investigation was thoroughly professional, such a case would break new ground in the territory. It wouldn't be just another bank heist, fugitive arrest, or drug bust. This—sophisticated data-based investigative procedure—was what made the FBI, at its best, the finest law enforcement organization in the world, Mark believed. This, he understood, could be a career-maker.

"I'll give it a shot," he told Brennan, who shrugged and said, "Suit yourself."

Obviously, the first question was, what was Charlie's motive? The answer appeared to be fairly simple—money and a desire for revenge. The chop-shop operation employed teams of spotters, hot-wire artists, and mechanics to steal the equipment, transport it, and then disassemble it into parts. The way Charlie described it, his specialty—stealing trucks and delivering them to the site—was worth $300 to $500 a vehicle, with an extra commission on each individual part subsequently sold. Charlie was angry because he hadn't been paid for the last truck he'd brought in, and he figured that if Vernon Mullins and his boys weren't going to pay, the FBI was. It was no secret in the hills that the FBI paid well for the right information. Charlie figured he could become a rich man and settle a score at the same time.

Money talked, but not all at once. Mark realized that Charlie was impetuous; like most outlaws, his plans rarely extended more than a week or so into the future. Charlie was mad, but he was wily, and before he got himself killed by spoon-feeding the FBI, the anger would have passed. Mark knew he would have to work him carefully, step by step, over the weeks and months. Eager to get going, he called him back and set up a meeting.

It helped a lot that Mark came to genuinely like Charlie as their alliance evolved. They met once or twice a week. Usually, Charlie would stop by the office, and they would get in the car and drive off into the hills, where they would be able to talk without being observed. Snapping open a can of beer from the six-pack he invariably brought along, Charlie was curious, laconic, and, Mark thought, hilarious when he went into his hillbilly act: "They done me wrong, Mark boy!" he would wail. "The varmints done me wrong, and they will pay!"

But Mark also realized that Charlie was working both sides of the fence, maintaining his activities with the chop-shop gang in a clearly dangerous balance between conflicting demands. While Charlie claimed that he had returned to the good graces of the gang only to facilitate the gathering of information, Mark knew that he couldn't drop his guard against a double cross. Once, when Mark caught him in a lie, Charlie responded with a look of grave injury.

"You're a ruthless bastard, Mark. A shabby bastard, and I thought you was my friend."

"I am, Charlie. But I have a little bit of smarts and I know when somebody is trying to screw me over. I check things out, Charlie. Always remember that."

"What was them college girls like, Mark?" Charlie said, abruptly resuming their friendly conversation. "I'll bet they wasn't like a good wild mountain woman."

Bit by bit, Mark built his case. Charlie liked not only the money, but, it appeared, the attention. And he delivered.

In the fall, not long after Cat Eyes was arrested, Charlie had gone along for the hijacking of three trucks in Maryland. They were coming across the mountains toward Kentucky when Charlie realized he had forgotten to call Mark, as arranged, to let him know when the convoy was on its way. It wasn't time to make arrests yet, but Mark insisted on knowing what Charlie was up to. At the Putnam house, the phone rang around ten o'clock.

"Charlie, where are you?"

"Pay phone, man. We're coming in around midnight."

"Charlie, aren't they wondering who you're calling? Aren't they suspicious?"

"The other two trucks went on ahead. It's just me and this old boy. I coldcocked him, punched his lights out. He's out."

"Why the hell did you do that?"

"So I could call, man."

"Is he all right?"

"He'll be okay."

"What are you going to tell him when he wakes up?"

"I'll just say I didn't like the way he was a-looking at me."

Kathy, already well accustomed to telephone intrusions, merely added Charlie Trotter to the growing list of people—Susan prominent among them—who called at odd hours, usually with an air of urgency, wanting to talk to Mark. As she had when he was a clerk, Kathy happily pitched in to help with the official work, fielding the calls and even spending hours some nights going over his laboriously hand-written interview reports, known in the bureau as 302s. That sometimes involved interviewing Mark to clarify the account. As she edited and neatly typed the 302s for him to send on to his supervisor in Covington—well aware that an agent was judged by his paperwork—she became vicariously fascinated herself with the quirky outlaw world of eastern Kentucky.

As a chilly autumn arrived, they were looking forward to the birth of their second child. Kathy had become pregnant a month after they moved to Pikeville. They'd planned on having two children, and as in everything else, they were right on schedule. In late October, six weeks before she was due, Kathy intended to take Danielle with her to Connecticut, where they would stay with her parents until Mark joined them for what they hoped would be a three-week Christmas vacation centered around the birth of a son.

Life in Pikeville had settled into a pleasant routine, Mark's long working hours and the incessant phone calls notwithstanding. Sam Smith had been transferred out of the office, allowing Mark to finally have his own desk, and enabling Dan Brennan, now the senior agent, to claim the Bronco. Mark made do with the wheezing old Dodge, consoled by the fact that the car's decrepitude at least provided cover, since no one would have guessed that it belonged to the FBI.

His initial apprehension about being a rookie in an unsupervised environment had abated. Mark's superiors made it clear that his work was appreciated—suddenly, with his presence, the office seemed to be bustling with activity; the paperwork was humming back and forth between Pikeville and the supervising office in Covington. His success in cultivating Susan and Charlie as informants was impressive; so, too, were the reports that he had significantly improved relations between the bureau and the Kentucky State Police, whose Pikeville post was one of the busiest in the department. State cops had long resented the FBI as exceedingly

glory-conscious and aloof, but the word filtering through
the overworked Pikeville post was that Putnam was different. Veteran state police officers there had never before
come in contact with an FBI agent who made it a part of his
routine to stop by the post and shoot the breeze, trading
information, offering to help out on minor criminal investigations of the sort that the FBI often disdained. Mark
Putnam established himself as someone who showed up
even for the scut work, the excruciating night-long surveil-
lances in mountain backwaters, the down-in-the-mud
searching for physical evidence at a crime scene, the inter-
minable routine interviewing, the warrant-serving in places
that required a hike into the woods. Hungry for the camaraderie of police work and anxious to learn what he could
from experienced state cops who understood the region,
Putnam worked, as one of the state cops would later recall,
not entirely complimentarily, "like a damn rented mule."

"I was basically a sponge, soaking up everything I possibly could," Mark would later concede. "Maybe I was
overeager. Work was all I wanted to do."

When he wasn't working, he applied the same fervor to
his family life. For a young couple just starting out in a new
home, on a salary of just over $30,000 a year, money was
adequate but not plentiful. Mark and Kathy seldom went
out, preferring to have intimate late-night dinners at home
on weekends. He always tried to get out of the office at a
reasonable hour on Friday nights, which was designated
"date night" with Danielle, who wore her prettiest dress to
accompany her father to the Dairy Queen or the McDonald's out on Route 23.

Kathy regarded their family routine, happy as it was, as
fairly mundane, and she was baffled by the deep allure that
it seemed to hold for Susan. She knew that Mark was somewhat concerned about the intense nature of Susan's interest,
which he couldn't easily defuse because he needed to maintain his relationship with her at least long enough to ensure

that she testify at the bank robbery trial of Cat Eyes, now scheduled for January. Furthermore, the bureau had encouraged him to keep Susan active as an informant, since she was promising to develop and pass on information about other, as yet unspecified, criminal matters in the Tug Valley. This meant that he met with her regularly, and unbidden, she continued calling the Putnam home almost daily. For Kathy, who sensed that Susan felt neglected, empathy began to overcome prudence. She shrugged off a disquieting sense that Susan's inquisitiveness about both her husband and her family might have started to become obsessive.

The initial evidence of this was innocent enough to be vaguely flattering. By the end of the summer, Kathy, five months pregnant, had decided that she was tired of having shoulder-length hair, which had lost its bouncy curl. She went to a beauty salon in Pikeville and had it styled and layered shorter and told Susan that night how pleased she was with it.

"I guess Mark likes short hair, huh?" Susan asked.

Kathy replied, "Mark likes women who take care of themselves."

A few days later, Mark mentioned that Susan had had her long hair cut short and had asked if it was like his wife's.

Not that Mark had much time to ponder an informant's hairstyling. By late October, after months of painstaking detail work and hand-holding with an increasingly nervous Charlie Trotter, Mark decided that the groundwork was well enough laid to move on the chop-shop case. He had brought Brennan up to date on the investigation and alerted the Covington and Lexington offices, as well as the state police in Pikeville and the sheriff's department in Letcher County. The last step necessary before a full-scale raid was to photograph the operation itself. After Charlie drew him a map, Mark persuaded a pilot from the state Department of Mines and Minerals to fly him over the site in a small plane.

Through wide gaps in the thinning autumn foliage they saw it—an expanse the size of two football fields littered with trucks, bulldozers, radiators, axles, engines, coal scoops, end loaders, and hundreds of other pieces of equipment—a veritable supermarket of stolen parts, displayed for sale on graded-out shelves cut into a mountain.

The raid was scheduled for the last week of October, which would be right after Kathy and Danielle were due to leave for Connecticut. The timing was excellent for Mark, who knew that the real work would come following the raid and the arrests. He would have to spend weeks on the scene, carefully taking inventory of thousands of pieces of evidence to begin assembling a major federal case of interstate theft. With his family out of town, he could work at it around the clock, if necessary, without guilt.

After work on Friday night, the Putnams drove to Lexington, where they spent the night in a motel. When he went to check in, there was a message to call the office.

Kathy could see that something was wrong. "The raid is going down tomorrow," Mark told her disconsolately. "There was some kind of glitch with the search warrants and they had to move fast."

The next day, after seeing Kathy and Danielle off at the airport, Mark drove the three hours directly to the site, but he was too late. Dan Brennan was on hand supervising the dozen or so officers who had conducted the raid and were crawling over the location, marveling at the extent of the operation. His news was not good. There had been no arrests; someone had apparently tipped off Vernon Mullins and his men, who were nowhere to be seen when the police stormed up the hollow. The only living creatures anywhere in the vicinity were a pack of menacing Dobermans, who weren't impressed with badges and guns.

As Brennan briefed him, a heavy downpour erupted from black clouds over the mountains. Most of the officers fled to their cars, and Brennan departed, saying he'd see Mark back at the office. Furious at what he regarded as an oper-

ation that had been botched despite all of his careful prep-
arations, bewildered that someone could have tipped off the
suspects, Mark stood on the hillside, ankle deep in cold
mud, and took out a notebook. He crawled under a bulldozer to look for its vehicle identification number.

For three weeks afterward, he stayed at a tiny motel in
Whitesburg and spent the daylight hours on the muddy
chop-shop site, often accompanied by sheriff's deputies, a
state cop who had helped to prepare the case, and a technician from the National Auto Theft Bureau, representing
the interests of various insurance companies. They photo-
graphed hundreds of vehicles and parts, recording whatever
identification numbers they could find. As Charlie had
promised, it was quite a haul. Mark was conservative about
placing a dollar value on the cache of stolen material, but
after the preliminary inventory, he estimated that they had
recovered $2.2 million in stolen equipment that was trace-
able directly through serial numbers to its owners. Newspaper accounts of the raid, quoting state police estimates,
put the total value of all the equipment at $6 million and
called it the biggest single recovery of stolen vehicles and
parts in recent memory. But, the newspapers also pointed
out, no arrests had been made. Police were still looking for
the thieves.

The trucks and other equipment were moved to a
fenced-in area nearby for safekeeping. It was almost
Thanksgiving when Mark was able to get back to the office
to continue his statistical work, which involved entering the
mass of serial numbers and other data into the National
Crime Information Center computer. When numbers
matched, the next step was to locate and notify the owners,
who were spread out over a five-state area. The owners then
had to be interviewed, one by one.

Brennan was right. The detail work was staggering.

But Mark had been prepared for that. What he didn't
expect, when he returned to the site one Saturday, was to be

confronted by Charlie Tackett, one of the men whom Charlie Trotter had named as a ringleader in the operation. Tackett, aware that no arrest warrants had been prepared and that no evidence yet linked him to the crime, strode right up to Mark with a broad grin and held out his hand. Mark had spoken with him once in the initial phase of the investigation and was left with the strong impression that Tackett felt he had protection.

"Mark, how you doing, son?" he said, clearly amused at his own audacity.

Mark narrowed his eyes. "Hey, Charlie, where have you been?"

"I don't want to be telling you that."

"Where's your boss Vernon these days?"

Tackett laughed. "Let me tell you something: Vernon and I have a lot of friends in this area. We're businessmen, son. A lot of people depend on us for parts. I don't know how many people have come up to me—"

Mark lost his cool. "Charlie, is that some kind of threat? Because if it is, you can just shove it up your ass. If they want to shoot me, go ahead and let them. But I guarantee you, there'll be about eight thousand agents who'll come down and bust every fucking thing that's going on down here, every business you got going, and every business your partners got going. So I don't think that would be a very good move."

"Oh, man, nobody's threatening nobody," Charlie said, kicking at the dirt and chuckling. "I'm just fucking with you, man. No threats. This is a game with us—a *game*. They're not going to get us. You don't even have enough to make an arrest warrant."

So far, that was true. Mark was depending on Charlie Trotter to supply that. "Charlie, this isn't state court where you can buy your way out of it."

"Time will tell. Time will tell. You'll come around. We got a lot of people that we know, a lot of people on the payroll."

"I know you do."

Both men glanced off to where a local detective was standing with a clipboard, looking down at some parts.

"Like I said, there are a lot of people on our payroll."

"Shove it, Charlie. It isn't going to work."

But Mark had reason to wonder as the case wore on.

Twice, the site where the parts were stored was broken into by thieves, who carted things off at night. Angry and frustrated, Mark moved back to the motel after Thanksgiving and even spent several nights on the site in a sleeping bag. When he went back to Pikeville, he had a call.

"Bad news," said a local cop who was also on the case. "We got broken into last night. They got all the CB radios."

In all, there were four burglaries within seven nights.

Mark was in the area one morning when a battered pickup truck pulled up. "You Putnam?" the driver called through the open window.

"Yeah," he said, approaching the pickup. "Who are you?"

"Well, I ain't going to say. But they say you're a good boy, and I hate to see you wasting your time."

"What do you mean?"

"Well, you know that guy you been working with?" He named one of the cops.

"What about him?" Mark said.

"I hear he's been selling CBs," the driver said, and rumbled off.

The next morning, Charlie Trotter came by the office with more unnerving news for Mark. He looked nervous. "I had a problem last night. I was a little drunk, and some of the boys jumped me, took me aside." He lifted his shirt and turned around. From shoulder to belt line, a crude X had been carved in his back.

5

Though she hated being away from Mark, Kathy was glad that she had chosen to go back home to have the baby because she developed some minor complications late in the pregnancy and felt more confident knowing that she would deliver in a hospital in Connecticut. In December, Mark managed to get the time off to fly back east. He was with her on December 9 when Mark Jr. was born, the image of his father.

In the baby book Kathy bought to match the one they'd kept for Danielle, the new father wrote:

> Who would have thought that your mom and I were capable of producing a son? From the moment I saw you, healthy and strong, I realized you were going to be special. Your mom and I have been through so much during the pregnancy, and the fact that you made it through unscathed meant only one thing— your sister and I won't be calling you Looie Loser. Seriously, every man needs a son to do things with. I only hope you know how to fix cars and machinery so you can teach me. I would like to take this opportunity to welcome you to our family and wish you luck—you will need it in dealing with your mom and sister. Right now you appear to be your mama's boy, but that will change in time. Ever hear of the Sox?

> Your old pop

It was invigorating to leave the problems of Pikeville behind for a few weeks, but Kathy could see Mark's distress, barely masked by the glow of the new baby and the holidays. The botched raid at the chop-shop site had bolstered his conviction that he needed to do everything himself. Sidelined in Connecticut, he fretted about the implications of what had happened. Recovering stolen goods was only half of the job, and even with the material in hand, that aspect of the case still needed months of hard work. The other half was bringing criminal charges against thieves brazen enough to laugh in his face and claim that they had protection. His key informant had obviously blown his cover—that X on Charlie's back was a bloody message not only to its victim but to his supposed protector as well. Mark brooded over the possibility that he wouldn't be able to come up with criminal indictments of the Mullins gang as easily as he had come up with the stolen trucks and bulldozers. There was also the problem of Cat Eyes, whose trial was coming up right after New Year's, with no guarantees that a mountain jury was going to return a guilty verdict. Susan's testimony would be crucial—again, with no guarantees that she would go through with it and publicly expose herself as the accuser. He wondered if he was in over his head.

With a sense of foreboding mixed with impatience to get back on the job, he returned to Pikeville with Kathy, Danielle, and the baby a few days after Christmas.

Susan was in the office waiting for him with a big smile. She surprised him with a kiss on the lips and said happily, "I got you a couple of things for Christmas. I'm sorry I didn't wrap it, but you know how it is."

He was bewildered. "Susan, don't buy me anything."

She took out a pair of expensive running shoes and a Nike T-shirt and set them proudly on his desk. "Well, you wear those ratty old sneakers all the time, and I think you could use these."

"I can't take these, Susan!"

Her face clouded like a scolded child's. "I will be very insulted if you don't take these. You've been very good to me this year. This is just between us."

Not wanting to hurt her feelings, he muttered thanks clumsily. But as soon as she was gone, he got on the phone to Terry Hulse in Covington and asked him for advice on what to do with a gift from an informant. Again Hulse told him not to worry, just to write a memo about it and put the stuff in the safe. But he also wondered whether Mark was worried about more than a pair of sneakers and a shirt. "Hey, is there anything going on with this girl?" he asked.

Mark considered his response for a moment before replying, "Well, she has made her intentions known, if that's what you mean."

His supervisor didn't seem concerned. "Just be careful," Hulse told him. "And do good work. See that she testifies."

Seeing that she testified was the main reason he had been going to the trouble of sustaining his relationship with Susan, who required high maintenance, not only from him but from Kathy. Susan, he had come to believe over the fall, was a loose cannon. She continued to shoot her mouth off about working for the FBI. What little information she had managed to pass on since the Cat Eyes arrest—mostly, tips on small-scale criminal activities in the Tug Valley—wasn't worth the effort. Partly thanks to connections he'd developed through her, and partly thanks to his own hard work, he had a growing network of informants. For that, he was grateful to Susan, which complicated things. She had been among the first people to accept him in his new post. But she'd been paid, regularly. It was time to move on. Mark was looking forward to putting an end to his work with Susan as soon as the trial was over. Because she had, indeed, made her intentions known.

It was during their last meeting, in December, before he'd gone to Connecticut. He had been driving Susan home to Freeburn and, as was their routine practice, pulled off on a mountain siding to talk. She seemed unusually pleased with herself. "I lost ten pounds, you know."

He hadn't noticed, but he told her, "Jeez, you look terrific."

"I started running every night, just like you."

"That's great, Susan."

"Just in case you're interested."

"Interested in what?"

"Oh, like a little fling."

"A *what?*"

She gave him a coy look. "A fling, Mark. You know?"

"Jesus, Susan, I'm a married man. I got a new kid on the way. I can't be doing stuff like that."

She persisted, "Come on. I like you, you like me, right? I'll tell you right now—whatever you want, we'll do it."

"What? What about Kathy, Susan? She's your friend, for God's sake."

"Why's she have to know?"

He started the car and tried to make light of the situation, and Susan found other things to talk about as he drove her home. Not that propositions were especially startling—in his first month on the job, for example, a bank teller had passed him a note with her phone number on it and the message, "Call me anytime." But Mark realized that his relationship with Susan, developed partly through a social process that almost necessarily involved elements of flirting, had become confused, in her mind, if not in his. Susan's attentions had been on his list of things to worry about over the holidays, as he came to wonder whether he really knew what he was doing in Pikeville.

In the interim, he had to work closely with Susan as the trial date approached. She was apprehensive about testifying—she said that Kenneth was making her life more miserable than usual, raging about her "ratting on a friend"—but she seemed to take comfort in the implicit protection offered by her alliance with Mark, who felt that he could not risk doing anything to shake her confidence. Sometimes, Susan managed to talk her younger brother, Billy Joe Daniels, known as Bo, into driving her the thirty-five miles from Freeburn, a task that he resented. Bo had already decided that his sister and Mark Putnam were sexually involved.

But she came through valiantly. At the trial of Cat Eyes Lockhart, the fact that a local woman was actually taking the stand to testify was the talk of the courthouse. Informing was one thing. Standing up to admit it in front of everybody was something else entirely. It was an impressive coup for Mark.

At the trial, Cat Eyes maintained his innocence with a sense of injured pride, though he did so with the rococo lexicon that any parent recognizes as a sure sign a child is spinning a whopper. According to him, he had been arrested and unjustly accused by authorities who would never let him live down his past.

"It seemed like, wherever my personal being was, they would always be law enforcement agencies such as FBI, local authorities, whatever, because when the circumstances of a bank robbery would occur, in specifically speaking in the areas, which was a number of bank robberies, I would be the first individual they came to, regardless of my whereabouts," Cat explained.

Susan was more direct when she took the stand, avoiding the glares of Kenneth and her brother, who came to court with her.

"Mrs. Smith, do you know a person who is Cat Eyes Lockhart?" the prosecutor asked.

"Yes, I do."

"Is that person in court today?"

"Yes, he is. He is on the left in a plaid shirt."

"During the summer of 1987, did you have any occasion to see Mr. Lockhart with any firearms?"

"Yes, I did. He stayed in my guest bedroom, with Sherri, and he had this green duffel bag—it looked like an army bag, you know, and a pillowcase that he had a lot of stuff in. And he had two guns. . . ."

"They were both shotguns?"

"Yes."

"Were they both sawed off?"

"Sawed off," Susan said.

"Did there come a time that you were aware that a bank at Belcher in Pike County had been robbed in early September of 1987?"

"Yes."

"Turn your attention to the few days before that, and I want to ask you if you had the occasion to see Mr. Lockhart and Ms. Justice a few days before that robbery."

"Yes, I did," Susan said as Sherri looked daggers at her. "It was at my home on a Friday night a week before the bank was robbed, about eleven o'clock. They came to my house. They were very nervous, upset. . . ."

"Was there any discussion by Mr. Lockhart and/or Ms. Justice in your presence of robbing a bank?"

"Yes, both of them was speaking at the time to me."

"What did they say?"

"About robbing a bank. They didn't say what bank, they just said a bank in Pike County."

Susan's testimony, with her positive identification of the shotgun, clinched the prosecution's case. Cat Eyes was found guilty and sent back to the penitentiary, but even as he was going to prison once again, he refused to believe that Susan Smith, a woman he said he loved, had done it to him of her own free will.

"That Kenneth, he put her up to it," Cat Eyes said sadly.

A few weeks after the trial, Dan Brennan was due to be transferred out, and Mark considered the possibility that his replacement, Ron Poole, an agent coming down from the Chicago office with a reputation as a good undercover investigator who liked to handle drug cases, might be the man to solve his problem with Susan. Most of Susan's tips lately had to do with drug cases, which Mark himself had little interest in, since he thought they were too easy and accomplished little. Still, he reasoned that if his new partner was

interested, he'd be able to pass Susan on to him, neatly
solving one looming problem with a gracious gesture of
welcome besides.

Brennan asked Mark to accompany him to the Landmark
motel to meet Poole, who was staying there while he found
a place to live.

Brennan had already met him, and he had a word of
caution on their short drive across town. "This guy's a
little, uh, different from what you would expect in an
agent," he said tentatively.

Mark soon understood what he meant. At over three hundred pounds, with shaggy hair, perspiring heavily, Ron
Poole looked like a hill-town school-crossing guard on a
patronage job. *Holy shit,* Mark thought when he saw Poole.
*Maybe this guy does such great undercover work because
the last thing you'd take him for is an agent.* Not only
Poole's appearance, but his attitude as well, offended
Mark's idealized sense of what an FBI agent should be. It
was clear from the start that this was going to be an uneasy
relationship.

Poole invited them into his room and looked over his new
partner sharply. "I don't care who I work with," he told
Dan in a cool tone, "as long as it's not a goddamn Yankee."

"Surprise," Mark replied curtly, holding out his hand.

Poole obviously cultivated his unruly image and let Mark
know right away that he had no intention of "carrying" a
rookie. Staking out his position clearly, he said that he
worked alone, without interference, which suited Mark fine.
Poole let it be known immediately that he had been transferred out of the Chicago office after receiving threats on his
life by drug dealers. But he was also known, during eight
years in the bureau, as an agent who delivered the goods—
Poole did, in fact, manage to infiltrate criminal activities
because he looked like anything but a cop. He was in fact an
agent who delivered, but whose superiors apparently pre-

ferred to keep at arm's length, even if it meant teaming him with a rookie in a remote office without on-site supervision. Moreover, Poole had been an accountant before he joined the FBI. Using Poole to fill the vacancy opened by Brennan's departure seemed eminently logical on paper—in Pikeville, the former accountant could be paired, with perfect bureaucratic expedience, with an ex-clerk.

Mark, hoping to have a new partner from whom he could actually learn things about police work, didn't quite see it that way. A few days after Poole arrived, Terry Hulse phoned Mark from the Covington office to sound him out on his new partner, whom he extolled for his investigative expertise and bravery. But Mark's impression was that there might have been a certain laxness in the paperwork.

Does he want me to cover for this character? Mark asked himself. But all he said was, "I'll do anything I can to help."

It didn't improve matters much when, a few weeks after Poole began work, he met a young Pikeville woman named Myra Chico. Myra, who worked as a part-time reporter for the local radio station, made it a point to know all of the local cops, whose cooperation was always useful when a story broke. When she introduced herself to Poole, she tried to break the ice by complimenting him—on his partner. "To me, Mark Putnam is the epitome of what an FBI agent should be," she chirped.

Still, however skeptical he was about being teamed with an agent who he thought looked like a goddamned magazine model, not a cop, Poole had to concede that Mark had obviously managed to put together sources, not the least interesting of whom to him was Susan Smith. And Putnam certainly was amiable enough. Even his wife had made a real effort to make Poole feel welcome in Pikeville.

Kathy asked Mark to invite Poole to the house for dinner. Poole eagerly accepted. Kathy recalled that he spent much of the time regaling them with war stories about his undercover work in Chicago and, before that, in the mountains of North Carolina, from the bureau in Charlotte. He also disarmed her by discussing his weight problem, which he said his previous supervisor had humiliated him over, going so far as to bring a bathroom scale into the office and make him weigh in publicly. Immediately sympathetic, Kathy described to him the diet and exercise regimen she'd used to firm up after having the baby. He remarked that he could see that it had been successful.

A few nights later, when Mark was working late and on the road, Kathy was surprised to get a call from Poole. Danielle and the baby were in bed; she'd been doing aerobic exercises and answered the phone out of breath.

"Breathing heavy?" he had said in a manner that struck her as suggestive. But she brushed it off, and Poole said he was calling to see if he could borrow a diet book she had mentioned at dinner. They talked for about a half hour, mostly about diets, but also about the long hours Mark put in. Innocently, she mentioned that she was looking forward to the day when they would get out of Pikeville.

Poole reiterated his experience in Chicago, when he'd been transferred after receiving threats. "That's all you need," he pointed out in a tone that she thought sounded almost hopeful. "Guaranteed. You'd be out the next day."

It occurred to her that Poole might be jealous of Mark, and she wondered whether she should warn her husband about him. But she decided that Mark would think she was being silly. She could handle Poole herself. When he phoned back a few nights later to thank her for the diet book, she commiserated with him about the difficulties of staying in shape. He told her that he appreciated the help and added that he'd make it a practice to check in on her when Mark was working late "since you're there by yourself with the kids." In very short order, Ron Poole had joined Kathy's motley little group of regular nighttime callers.

In the meantime, Mark was looking forward to the time when he could pass Susan along to Ron Poole, but his supervisor cautioned him to think long and hard about her proven value to his career. Good sources like that didn't grow on trees in eastern Kentucky.

"Listen, you started out with a bang down there," Hulse told him when Mark broached the subject during one of his infrequent trips to Covington to review case files with his boss. "You were there a few months and you got this informant. And she actually *testified*. Keep on this woman. Look at the potential!"

Mark readily agreed about the potential; he just didn't want to be the one to develop it any further. He was worried that he was stretched too thin already. But he felt his resistance weakening in the face of his supervisor's blandishments. "She can mix in with anybody, that's for sure," Mark had to concede. "She can talk to politicians, she can talk to drug dealers—anybody. I know we should keep her on, but I'm not sure I can get much more out of her. Poole thinks he can work with her on his investigations."

"Do you think she's blown her cover for you?"

"Maybe. Maybe not. With her, it's hard to say. She's full of surprises, that one."

On the three-hour drive back to Pikeville, annoyed with himself for not standing his ground, Mark tried to assess his position. As fond as he had become of her, he was uneasy about Susan, professionally and personally. On the other hand, every time he decided she had outlived her usefulness to him, she managed to come up with something to make him reconsider. For example, after his impressive first year in Pikeville, he had decided that once the chop-shop case was finished it would be time to shift gears and move aggressively into what he regarded as the big time: political corruption. Through the bureau grapevine, he had heard that the U.S. Attorney's office in Lexington was starting work on a major, top-secret investigation into interlocking networks of corrupt politicians, judges, and sheriffs in the region. A web of kickbacks, shakedowns, extortion—the essence of official corruption—lay like a drying fishnet over

eastern Kentucky. Once the investigation got going, there
was no telling where the trail would lead.

With uncanny prescience, Susan showed up in the office
at primary election time carrying a bag of red, black, and
white pills that she held up to Mark's face for inspection.

"Where'd you get that stuff?" he asked nervously.

She named a politician who she said had given them to
her in Freeburn "to pass out for votes."

Thinking it incredible that anyone in her hometown would
trust her enough to give her illegal drugs, Mark took the pills
away and flushed them down the toilet. While he couldn't be
sure where she'd got them, the last thing he wanted was to
have a sack of illegal drugs on hand. He knew by now that
Susan's stories only checked out about half the time.

But with her, the problem was he never really knew
which half. One day that spring, she sauntered in with new
information. She named two men who she said were planning to rob a bank in Phelps, on the way to Freeburn.
Overwhelmed with work on the chop-shop case, worried
about Charlie Trotter wavering as an informant, Mark didn't
want to encourage her. He knew that Susan felt neglected
and had been crying on the phone to Kathy about how
miserable her life was, especially with Kenneth on her back
all the time about her work with the FBI. She was broke and
desperate to get back into action. But Charlie Trotter had
also started crying on the phone about feeling abandoned.
By this point, Mark didn't have either the time or the energy
to coddle Susan, a task he more and more often left to the
much more sympathetic Kathy.

"Susan, how do you know they're going to rob the
bank?" he asked her doubtfully.

Petulantly, she insisted that she had heard it directly from
one of the robbers himself. She identified the man as an
uncle of Cat Eyes' who lived near Freeburn.

This sounded even more preposterous to Mark. "Susan,
he knows you testified against Cat Eyes. Why would he tell
you that?"

"Well, he wants to get in my pants."

Everybody wants to get in her drawers, he thought. "Susan, I can't believe this, that he would tell you something like that."

She insisted that it was true. She said she had driven the man to the bank herself to look it over. To prove to him that she was not working for the FBI anymore, she had even given him the gun that he planned to use in the robbery. She had set the whole thing up, she claimed.

"No way," Mark told Poole when she left. He wrote up a standard note to the miscellaneous file summarizing what she had said and forgot about it.

A week later, Mark went to Washington for a few days of work on a case involving a fugitive terrorist. He was in the office of the FBI Technical Services Division when an urgent phone call from Poole interrupted him.

"The bank in Phelps got robbed!" Poole cried. "What the hell do I do? I don't even known where this place is!"

Mark groaned and suggested, "Call Susan."

Poole was happy to do just that. In his conversations with Kathy, he'd made it clear to her that Susan interested him greatly. He'd also said that he believed Susan was in love with her husband—which came as no surprise to Kathy, since Susan herself had confided the same thing. Kathy thought it pathetic rather than threatening. She was worried about Susan's increasing drug use and despaired of ever being able to help her straighten out her chaotic life. Kathy warned Poole, who was separated from his wife, not to get involved. But Poole abruptly snapped that he could take care of himself and startled her by hanging up.

For her part, Susan realized that Mark was shunting her aside, and the knowledge only made her more miserable.

"Poole wants me to work with him on these drug cases, but I need to work with Mark," Susan told Kathy through angry tears.

The bureau money was there, of course—and Susan was

desperate to put enough together to move out of the house she shared with Kenneth into an apartment in Pikeville with her two children. So she began working small drug cases with Poole. She complained, however, that more often than not, they ended up alone at a bar or a restaurant.

By the summer, Kathy decided unilaterally that it was time for a real vacation. Except for the Christmas trip back home when little Mark was born, they hadn't been away together since before Mark went into the academy, which now seemed like ages ago. Kathy had quietly squirreled away enough money to do it right. She announced to Mark that she had already made the arrangements. Like it or not, they were going to a place they had visited once and loved: Myrtle Beach, a resort on the coast of South Carolina. At first, he resisted mightily, insisting that his workload was too staggering even to think about getting away. She was adamant.

"We're going," she said. "You'd better go find your bathing suit."

She prevailed. In August, they packed up the car and the kids and drove across the Appalachians and the coastal plain beyond to the sandy sweep of Myrtle Beach, where they spent ten glorious days. It was a sun-drenched island of peace, serenity, and intense joy in their still-young marriage, but it would be their last.

6

The vacation reverie faded quickly. The night after they returned, Poole was on the phone, telling Kathy the last thing she needed to hear, which was that the bureau was cutting back on spending and that "first-office agents" such as Mark, who could usually expect to be transferred after two years or so in one place, were now likely to spend four or five years before being relocated to one of the offices of their choice.

She was crying when Mark came home. He didn't want to talk about it. Instead, he read Danielle her bedtime story and without a word went out for a longer run than usual. While he was out, the phone rang.

"Is this the FBI's wife?" a gruff voice said.

"Who's calling?"

"Just this: your old man's fooling around with a girl named Susan Smith. That's all." The caller hung up.

When Mark came back, she tried to talk to him about Susan. But all he would say was, "Don't be ridiculous."

Mark in fact was enraged by the rumors about him and Susan, not only because they weren't true, but because they confirmed that he had allowed the situation to get out of control. Out of his depth and stretched to the limit, he felt himself sinking under the weight of his inexperience and hubris. At the same time, at home with two small children, in a place she had come to despise, besieged by an increasingly distraught Susan, annoyed by constant calls from Poole and Trotter, Kathy had fixed her hopes on getting out at some point soon. Not having that to look forward to plunged her into a state of depression that deepened as the sunlight began its steady fade into fall.

Meanwhile, Susan, herself dejected about Mark's indifference, depending on pills to lift her spirits in the morning and to put her to sleep at night, threw off any semblance of discretion. In Freeburn, she told anyone who would listen that Mark Putnam was in love with her and was planning to leave his wife, describing herself as being under FBI "protection." In Pikeville, she did everything she could to encourage the notion, now widespread in the courthouse, that she and Mark were having an affair. It was as if she were on a campaign to make it come true.

When she managed to cajole her brother into driving her to town, she'd drop into the FBI office unannounced, and when she didn't find Mark there, she would poke her head into one of the nearby offices, put on a long face for the marshals and probation officers, and say, "Where's Mark? He promised to meet me."

When Mark got back, they'd say, "You're in trouble, buddy. You stood her up." Mark refused to get drawn into an explanation. He'd just force a grin.

Once he stopped to chat with a small group of courthouse workers.

"That girl is nuts," one said.

"Today she come in looking for you. She had a tank top on, no bra," another put in. "Somebody made a remark about her chest, you know, and she said, 'Well, you want to see?' "

"She pulled up her shirt! She's flat!"

Later, Susan told her own version of the event. It was obvious that she believed she could make Mark jealous.

Mark understood that some of this was his own fault. For a time before the Cat Eyes trial, he had thought it helpful to keep certain people with their eyes on courthouse comings and goings from thinking that Susan was acting strictly as an informant. But he sensed that it was more complicated than that. In ways he did not care to explore, he did presume a degree of possession toward Susan. The more unhappy his wife became, the more pliant Susan seemed. And in painful moments of introspection during his long laps alone in the night around the high school track near his home, he wondered whether he was exploiting Susan's unconditional trust just to prove that he had, in fact, fit in.

Susan, running on her own mental track, gave him no room to maneuver, and none, either, to Kathy, who had begun to take her calls not with the attitude of a concerned friend but more often now with that of worker for a crisis hot line.

Susan's family was furious with her because of her testimony, which had sent a local boy to prison. As she became brazen in her insistence that she would continue her work as an informant for the FBI, the abuse from Kenneth intensified. She made no attempt to put on a brave front with Mark. "My family doesn't like this at all," she told him. "They don't talk to me anymore. Somebody gives me a hard time in a bar, they won't come to my rescue. Shelby doesn't agree with me working with a Yankee cop."

Shelby Jean Ward was Susan's older sister; often, during her battles with Kenneth, Susan stayed at her house in Freeburn. Mark had only spoken to Shelby on the phone a few times, when he needed to reach Susan. He was well aware of her animosity toward him.

Years later, Mark tried to sort out how and why the experience in Pikeville deteriorated so drastically.

"Both Kathy and I would talk about her at home," he remembered. "Kathy would say, 'That girl has it so hard. Kenneth beats her up, the other people are threatening her for testifying for you. Social Services is trying to take her kids away. She's doing a lot of coke and pills.'

"The first thing they teach you at the FBI academy is, don't get involved with your informants. That's rule number one. I knew I was already over the boundary with Susan. I thought, 'This girl had really helped me out. She's put me on the map with the bureau, and because of my association with her, more and more people are helping me out. And she has this incredibly shitty life.'

"Man, I was starting to go over the edge. I was feeling

sorry for Susan, but the truth is, I was feeling sorry for myself, too. I knew the invitation was there with Susan. At home, things between Kathy and me were sporadic. We'd hook up, we wouldn't. I was always working. We weren't communicating at all. Kathy was miserable—I would come home from work, and she'd be crying. And I just didn't want to hear it because I heard so much crying from people all day long. I just wanted to come home and relax without any problems, but there she was, laying problems on me: 'I hate this place and these people; we've got to get out of here; you're working too much; you don't care about me; all you care about is that job.' I'd go out for a run, or I'd drive back to the office and do paperwork until Kathy was asleep. I just abandoned her."

Meanwhile, Susan's calls to Kathy became frantic. Kathy hardly even mentioned them to her husband anymore, although she did pay attention when Susan told her how "close" she had become to her husband. There was no denying now what she meant. Kathy discounted it as drug-induced fantasy, but still warned Mark, "Don't you ever get involved with this woman."

He scoffed, "Kat—"

She was furious at him for a naïveté that she had once found charming. "She will get pregnant and she will ruin you."

"Kathy, I'm not stupid. I love you."

As winter approached, with the sun behind the mountains for much of the day, shacks clustered on the ridges and far up into dark hollows were exposed under bare trees, with wisps of chimney smoke curling into a gray sky. Kathy resented even the season. Susan's calls persisted like a cold drizzle. Fielding them at night, Kathy would tell Susan that Mark was out when he wasn't, using hand signals to convey to him how drugged and agitated Susan sounded. Yet she maintained her sympathy, even when the drugs and despair turned a conversation with Susan into an emotional ordeal.

"What's the matter, Susan?" Kathy said, hearing her familiar sniffles one night.

"Oh, Kathy, I don't know what I'm going to do. Kenneth, he just makes everything so hard. I know I got to get out of here, but he'll come after me, Kathy. He won't never let me go."

"Susan—"

"It's always about the money, and Mark. He knows about my working with Mark, and he won't let me just do what I need to do and get paid for it. He wants it all. He's saying I should give him the money."

"Listen, Susan, calm down. We can work this out."

The sniffles became sobs. "I keep telling him, I'm the one that's in danger, Kenneth! I can't even think straight no more!"

"Susan, you have to calm down and tell me what happened. Are you listening to me?"

"Kathy, is Mark there? Is Mark listening?"

"No." She caught Mark's eye sternly as he lay on the living room rug playing with the kids. "Why?"

"I don't want him thinking I'm crazy or nothing, Kathy. If he thinks I'm crazy, he won't work with me. My work is important, Kathy. I don't do it just for the money. Mark needs me, God's truth. I just keep getting stuck in these horrible situations."

"Mark isn't here, Susan."

Susan snorted. "You sure that son of a bitch ain't home?" she said with a little laugh. "You're alone just like me—we're by ourselves while the big man is out making a name for himself." Kathy sighed, lit a cigarette, and settled in for the duration.

"I know he just wants to forget all about me. Mark thinks I can't do nothing for him anymore, I know he does. It don't matter to him about the danger I was in, it don't matter that I could have got killed, just as long as he's got his reputation and his big government job. I'm the one has to worry about these people up here. They all know that I'm an

informer. I tell you one thing, Kathy: Mark, he don't know
the information I could give still. And I might not help him
again, ever. All he cares about is that job; he don't even
care about me getting hurt, or you stuck at home with the
babies. You know, you're the stupid one!''

At once, Kathy became alert. Quickly, she said, "Susan,
where's Kenneth?"

"Gone. He hit me and took the car. I don't even have a
car!"

"All right. What about the kids? Susan, are the kids
okay?"

Susan mumbled that they were. "Brady's in bed. Miranda was running when I called you, but she'll tire out and
curl up somewhere. Kathy, he's started to hit me in front of
the kids, and they cry. I just can't deal with this no more."

"The first thing is, you have to calm down, Susan. Are
you messed up now, or can you listen?"

Susan insisted that she was straight.

"Tell me what happened, Susan."

"He hit me in front of the *kids*."

"Did he hit the kids?"

"No."

"Are you hurt badly? Do you need to go to a hospital?"

"No, I'm okay."

"Why did he hit you?"

"Oh, Lord, he was all fucked up, and accusing me of
having money. Money that he didn't know about. And why
wasn't he getting any of the money. He said that I was
spending too much time with Mark and not getting anything
out of it. I told him Mark and me has to spend a lot of time
together, it's my work. I *told* him you knew all about it.
You don't object, so why should someone who's my ex-
husband? When I talk about Mark, it gets him furious. He
just loses it. And I told him, I said sometimes me and Mark
go to motel rooms and all—"

"You told him what?"

"I told him that, about motels—" Quickly, she added,
"—Which ain't true. You know I ain't sleeping with Ken-

neth no more, and he's real jealous. I tell him about my feelings for Mark, what a gentleman Mark is. I said, Mark cares about me as a person. I can't help my feelings for Mark, Kathy! Mark would never do me like Kenneth does. He's just like the devil, Kenneth is. He started slapping me and hitting me, and Miranda was crying—''

"Susan, you have to realize, when Kenneth is like that and the two of you start fighting, you can't antagonize him, Susan! It only makes matters worse for yourself—''

"I know, I know. I don't want to make things worse. I'm so sick, Kathy. I don't want him hurting me, I just want him out of here. I wish I never knew him.''

Kathy stubbed out her cigarette and lit another. "Susan, how many times do I have to tell you? *You are better than this*, Susan! You have to take charge of your own life! You know that you're smart enough to get you and those kids away from this! But you have to care enough about yourself first. All those children have is you. Do you want them growing up like this? You have got to give those children a chance at a decent life, Susan, by getting yourself and those kids out of there.''

Calculating her position, Susan said, "There's something I didn't tell you about. I signed custody of Miranda to Kenneth. I had left and I signed her to Kenneth. I don't have rights where she is concerned. If I left, he could get her back. I think about what happens if I leave, and I can't. The kids all dirty and without shoes—not like your kids. Mark don't care about anything that's happened to me—' ''

"Susan, you have got to start taking responsibility for yourself.''

"I *have* decided, Kathy.''

"If you're sure you really want to do something, I will try to help you. But you have to take charge of yourself.''

"I want that, Kathy. You're a friend to me; I can't talk to no one else.''

Kathy sensed this was going nowhere. She said, "What are you going to do now?''

"I don't know. I did look at a couple of apartments,

though. One was real nice. I got to be far away from where he is.''

"You can do anything you set your mind to, Susan.''

"Why couldn't Mark just tell the court to fix it for me? He can do stuff like that if he wants to.''

"No, he can't, Susan. That has absolutely nothing to do with Mark or the FBI.''

"It don't matter because Mark won't fix nothing for me anyway because there's nothing in it for him, no big case for him to show off to his supervisor.''

With exasperation, Kathy said, "Susan, that's the point. You can't expect everybody to fix things for you. You have to take responsibility—''

Susan slammed the phone down.

Whatever its social risks, informing for the FBI at least paid well, especially for people, such as Susan and Charlie Trotter, who were otherwise unemployed.

Shortly after the raid on the chop-shop site, Mark had counted out $5,000 in hundred-dollar bills for Charlie's work—bringing his total to $11,000 to date—with more to come after indictments and a trial. Yet Charlie was already broke and calling regularly, clamoring for more. He told Mark he had spent most of the money on prostitutes and cocaine.

Susan, however, had lost hers to Kenneth, with whom she was still trying to live. In the fall, Mark had given her another $4,000, which he said was payment for assisting Poole on his drug cases, as well as for the work on the Phelps bank robbery. In reality, the $4,000 was more of a charity gesture. Kathy had been pleading Susan's case— Susan was afraid of Kenneth, she needed to find a place to live—and Mark knew there would be no problem getting the bureau to approve another $4,000. But Susan didn't use the money to move out. Instead, soon after she got it, she phoned Kathy to say that Kenneth had claimed half of it, for drug debts he said she owed. The other half had gone to a used car—Kathy thought it was interesting that the car was a Dodge Diplomat, similar to Mark's bureau-issue vehicle. Kenneth had promptly taken possession of that, too.

"I bought that car as an investment," Susan told her. Kathy wondered if it was hopeless.

Mark insisted that it was. Yet he had no stomach for the scene that Susan would undoubtedly make if he tried to break the connection cleanly. For a cop, Mark had an unusual aversion to confrontation. Trying to foist her off on Poole wasn't going to solve the problem, either. Poole was obviously interested in continuing to work with Susan—in fact, she'd told Kathy that he had expressed his interest in her more than once. But she hated working with him and said so. On paper, Susan's cooperation continued to look good, but Mark was seriously worried about the lengths to which she would go to ensure her usefulness. The Phelps bank robbery was a case in point. Susan had helped solve the case for the FBI, but the fact was, she had also helped to *plan* the robbery, entrapping Cat Eyes' uncle. The entrapment had been clever, almost brilliant. What, Mark worried, would she think of next?

But he was busy elsewhere, mostly over in Letcher County. There, while working the chop-shop investigation, he was trying to position himself to make inroads into official corruption that would dovetail with the secret corruption investigation he'd learned about. Letcher County, where anything (and, it was said, anyone) could be bought, was an excellent place to do that.

He wasn't aware of the fabulous new stories Susan had been circulating in the Tug Valley. Unable so far to interest him in her sexually—and Susan was a woman for whom sexual attention was crucial—she had simply wished it true, as she had wished so many other things in her life. And characteristically, her wishes had become grand. To hear Susan tell it—her sister Shelby was hearing all of the details now as Susan spent many nights at her house—Mark had fallen deeply in love with her. They had gone to motels,

even to his house (Kathy, she said, was often in Connecticut), where they had sexual romps that lasted until dawn.
Susan told people that she had already been pregnant by
him, but lost the baby in a miscarriage. Still, there was
plenty of time for more. There was a lifetime, in fact, since
Susan maintained that he was going to divorce Kathy to
marry her. Furthermore, Mark had appointed her, Susan
Smith, to a special position as a U.S. informant, fully protected from assault by federal law, she said, ''just the same
as a clerk in the post office.''

In Freeburn, people knew Susan well enough to assume
that only about half of what she said was true. But there was
at least a suspicion that *some* of it was true. Shelby was
furious at Susan's imprudence and warned her to forget
about the FBI man and stay away from Pikeville. Kenneth
also showed his disapproval, but less benignly. As Susan
had already made clear to Kathy, without fully explaining
why, he beat her.

Alarmed, unable to turn her back on Susan, Kathy cham-
pioned her cause more avidly to Mark, urging him to do
whatever he could to help her out.

Late one afternoon at the end of October, Susan called
Kathy to tell her she was in the hospital. At first, Kathy was
afraid she'd been beaten again, but Susan assured her she
was in only ''for tests'' for a few days because she was
''run-down'' and exhausted and needed to ''build myself up
because I lost too much weight.'' Kathy was considering
telling her what she really thought, which was that she
needed to cut out the pills and cocaine, when Susan suddenly burst into tears. ''Nobody has been out to see me
since I got here,'' she whimpered. ''I haven't even heard
from my family.''

Kathy bought a get-well card, signed it, had Danielle
write her name on it in her big child's scrawl, and handed
it to Mark when he got in that night. He didn't want to sign
it. He was even less happy when Kathy suggested that he
deliver it personally. Kathy insisted, ''That girl has led a

tough life, and you owe her, Mark. Aren't you going to go visit her?"

"Absolutely not. No way. This is business, not personal."

"Well, I think you should, Mark. That girl has helped you out. You've kind of put her out front with those people where she lives. A lot of them won't even speak to her now because of what she did for you. I think you owe it to her to at least go see her."

He acquiesced, not wanting to get into it with Kathy. But he was annoyed at her interference. Yes, he felt sorry for Susan. Yes, her work had put a feather in his cap—she had delivered, no argument. She had also been paid well. As far as he was concerned, it was time to move on.

Susan was in a hospital in Williamson. Unhappily, Mark drove out to the Tug Valley, where he found her alone in a double room, pale and thin, but animated. She giggled over the card when he gave it to her. Then she put it on the nightstand. Tugging at his hand, she said, "Why don't you climb into bed with me? Ain't nobody else in this room. The door shuts."

"Susan, cut it out."

She stuck her chin out raffishly. "Right here, right now. Nobody would ever know. What do you say, Mark?"

"Come on, cut the crap."

She stared brightly at him.

"Susan, that would be a major mistake. You know that."

She knew no such thing. "Not if nobody ever found out," she said, and smiled. "And they won't."

He managed to change the subject. But on the drive back home, he found himself reflecting on the offer. She made it sound so simple. *Pure submission*, he thought. In his cranky, beleaguered frame of mind, it had a certain appealing lack of ambiguity. Quickly, he put Susan out of his mind and forced himself to think about his troubles, as if by way of penance.

He had come to see, with some bitterness, that the career

potential in the chop-shop case could cut both ways. The U.S. Attorney's office in Lexington, exercising particular caution in assembling the case because of its possible use as a springboard for bigger things down the road, hadn't yet come up with the indictments of the Mullins gang. In Letcher County, the delay was being read differently. On the one-year anniversary of the raid, noting that no suspects had been charged, although everyone knew who they were, a Letcher County newspaper had even printed a story suggesting that not only certain local police officers, but the "federal boys" as well, had been paid off for protection. There was no doubt in anyone's mind, least of all Mark's, whom that referred to. He was infuriated by the story, and he took it very personally, since it was the first time in his life that he had ever been accused, however elliptically, of wrongdoing. He was convinced that the insinuation had compromised his reputation in the area. Yet he never mentioned it to anyone, not even his wife.

The pilfering of material from the site was so routine now that it had become a local joke that the stuff was cheaper now than it was when Vernon Mullins and the boys were selling it. Mark was convinced, though he had no evidence, that at least one of the local cops was involved. This gnawed at him constantly. He didn't know whom he could trust, and so he trusted no one.

He left the house early one morning and saw that all four tires of the Olds had been flattened in the driveway. That was the first warning that the line between work and home had been erased.

Another came when he was working in the driveway one Sunday afternoon, furiously chopping firewood for the stove, working up a comforting sweat. He was interrupted by the light tapping of a car horn. At the curb, Poole had pulled up in the Bronco, with Susan beside him in the front seat. They waved and looked as if they were going to get out to talk, but Mark turned his back and strode into the house.

He confronted Poole in the office the next morning.

"Why in hell did you bring her to my house, Ron?"

His partner had a look of innocent surprise. "We were out for a drive and she only wanted to see where you live, old buddy. That's all."

Mark's face was so red that Poole thought for a second that he might throw a punch. "Don't you *ever* bring a fucking informant to my house. Do you hear me, Ron? Don't ever do that again." Poole muttered that he'd meant no harm.

Mark warned Kathy to be careful. He wasn't the only one. One day she was out front picking up Danielle's toys in the driveway when a woman who lived across the street, and who hadn't been particularly friendly in the past, came over.

"I know your husband's got that case in Letcher," the neighbor said, crossing her arms against a chilly wind knifing down through the hills. "You should tell him to be very careful up there, that's probably the worst county there is." As she left, she added, "My brother was shot and killed up there."

At the end of the day, Kathy was standing at the kitchen sink pouring milk into the baby's bottle when she happened to glance at the window. She was startled to see a man looking directly at her. He grinned, showing missing front teeth. He wore a knit cap over stringy, greasy hair. She dropped the milk carton into the sink and in a panic grabbed the .357 that Mark kept on the top pantry shelf. She glanced at Mark Junior, eleven months old, amusing himself in the playpen, then checked to see that the gun was loaded.

Feeling her throat constrict, she moved toward the front door and yelled up at Danielle, "Stay in your room, okay, honey?"

A small voice came down. "I'm just playing. I'm the mommy and Amanda is the baby."

"Just stay in your room!"

Kathy slipped outside, trying to remember what Mark

had taught her about the gun—defensive tactics, how to round a corner, confront a suspect. You keep the gun down, not up by your head like the goddamn cop shows. Try to stay sideways to your opponent to present a smaller target. She took a breath and edged around the corner of the house—and promptly forget everything. She faced the intruder clutching the gun with both hands in front of her face, just like on the cop shows.

"Don't you move!" she ordered.

Shocked, the stranger raised his hands as high as he could, just as he had seen in the cop shows. "Okay, lady! Okay!" he said, practically choking on the words. From the corner of her eye, she saw a figure flee behind the bushes next door.

"What are you doing looking in my window? You're in my backyard looking in my window!" she shrieked.

His eyes were wide. "Okay, okay, lady! We was just a-fixing the cable wire, putting in new wire. The cable tv?"

His hands fell to his side and he turned to look for his partner, who was now peeking from the corner of the house.

"I said don't move!" she shouted. But then she saw the spool of heavy wire on the ground beside the patio.

Seeing that she wasn't going to shoot, the cable man forced a tight smile that had the effect of making her angrier. "I was just looking in to see was anybody home," he said in a high-pitched voice. "Let you know we was working back here."

She lowered the gun to her side. On the man's shirt was the logo of the local cable television company. She felt more foolish than she ever had, but she let loose on him. "You dumb hillbilly!"

He shrugged and looked askance.

"Why didn't you simply ring the doorbell and let me know you were out here? Looking into windows. How stupid can you be?" She felt like a bully, which only made her madder. "I almost shot your ass, do you know that?"

"Yes, ma'am," he said, glad for the opportunity to provide an answer this madwoman would accept.

Just then, Mark's car pulled into the driveway. They watched him approach quickly.

"What's going on here, Kat?"

"This idiot. I almost shot him. He was looking in the window!" Her heart was thumping; she felt like a schoolgirl. She also realized how easily she could have pulled the trigger if the man had made the wrong move.

Scowling, Mark realized that his wife had threatened to shoot an innocent laborer. He thought fast. The best way to diffuse the situation—he didn't want Kathy to have to explain herself to the local police—was with an effective offense. No point in letting the guy see himself as a victim, he decided. Let him think he's getting off easily. Mark flashed his badge at the stranger, who looked it over carefully and nodded approvingly. "What's going on here, friend?" Mark asked in an accusatory tone, while casually taking the gun from his wife.

The cable man yammered like a schoolboy to a teacher breaking up a fight, "I'm just a-fixing the wires, mister, and she comes out wanting to shoot me! I didn't do nothing!"

Mark asked for some identification, which the man dug nervously out of his pants pocket.

"Don't you think it might be a little better to go the front door and knock instead of looking in the window?"

"Yes, sir, buddy. We should of thought of that."

"Next time you will, right?"

"Sure will." Mark gave him his identification card back like a state trooper letting a speeder off with a warning.

When the cable truck pulled away, Mark marched Kathy into the house and sat her down at the kitchen table. She felt her face burning. He tried to make a joke out of it: "Hey, Kat—I know they raised the rates, but you can't be holding the cable company at gunpoint, you know."

She was not amused. "You bastard!"

"Me? Hey, you're the one who almost shot the guy for Christ's sake! What the hell did you think you were doing?"

He went upstairs, pointedly taking the .357 with him.

Hearing him laughing with Danielle as if nothing had happened, she banged around in the kitchen in a rage. How could her marriage come to this? Had the power shifted so decisively? How had she become so ridiculously afraid?

He trotted back downstairs and stood there stretching, cocky and smug in his gray sweats, ready for his run before dinner. Outside, the mountain in back of the house loomed dark against the twilight sky.

She snapped on the kitchen light and fumed, unwilling to speak. "Come on, don't you think you're overreacting a little?" he said with an attempt at cool reassurance, patting her behind and trying to hug her. But she pushed him away and said sharply, "Don't patronize me, goddammit!"

His expression darkened. "You knew what we were getting into from the beginning, Kat. I thought you had what it takes. You took this on, Kathy."

"I didn't take *this* on," she said, flinging a gesture toward the window. "I was always there for you. I did my best, Mark. But I didn't bargain for this. This, Mark, is too much to ask!"

"*What* is? Pull yourself together, Kathy." He was shouting. Mark never shouted.

That did it. She threw down the fork she'd been using to fix Danielle's plate, brushed past her daughter, ignored the baby's wailing, grabbed her coat and her keys, and rushed for the door in tears. As she backed out of the driveway, she screamed at the face of the woman next door peering from her window.

A few miles out of town on Route 23, she acknowledged that she had nowhere to go. She stopped at a convenience store for cigarettes. On her way back home, she pulled off in the dark near the sway bridge over the Levisa and sat there smoking, waiting for her heart to stop pounding. She forced herself to think of the last really happy time she could remember, in Myrtle Beach: sunlight on the faces of her husband and children, a startling blue sky, the surf breaking in clean white curls at their backs. Amusement-park lights twinkling on black; dinner, walks in cool night sand. When the kids were in bed in the next room, she'd put on a silky teddy and they'd nibbled cheese and crackers and sipped red wine while they talked. She'd given him a massage with lotion heated in the baby's bottle warmer. They'd made love in the dark, smelling of the sea and suntan oil.

As she calmed down, she told herself she was overreacting. She remembered the lectures they gave for agents' wives who came to the orientation session at the academy before their husbands started training. *Know what you are getting into: The pressures of a cop's life are intense. Marriages fail. Keeping them working requires constant vigilance.* For some reason, she thought of a much earlier time in their life together. He was still a clerk waiting to get into the FBI; she'd had six FBI most-wanted posters framed and hung them in the hall as a joke. He loved them. The "Putnam collection," he'd called them when showing them to friends.

A car rattling over the bridge made her look up. Feeling the chill, she turned on the engine and went home.

But the warmth of the house seemed artificial, the colors too bright. In her cotton Strawberry Shortcake nightgown, Danielle bared tiny white teeth to show that she'd brushed them; Mark played with the baby, who tottered into a castle of plastic blocks his father had built. "Okay, buddy, knock it down, go ahead." And young Mark kicked the castle blocks down. "Okay, buddy, you want to play, you got to pay, help to pick it up." The children and their father lay on the floor.

"Gonna get you!" she heard him say with a laugh, pretending to chase the kids up the steps.

Breathing shallowly, she sat back. The phone rang.

"Hello, Susan, how are you?" Kathy said in a monotone.

Mark caught her eye, shaking his head.

"Sure, Susan, he's right here. Just a minute." She slammed the phone into his chest. Wordlessly, she went upstairs to check on the kids.

Mark was still on the phone when she came down, speaking in the intimate tone a man uses with his wife. "I know that Susan. . . . I know. I *know*. Susan, don't say that. You know that's not true."

When Kathy stepped into his sight, his tone became firmer. "Susan, if you don't want to work with Ron, just tell him. It's that simple, just tell him."

Mark put the phone down with a shrug. "She hung up," he said, coming into the kitchen where Kathy was busy with the dishes.

"What's wrong with her now?" she asked in a flat voice.

"You know, I really feel sorry for her, really bad for her. She's a good kid. She's just so screwed up. If she'd get the hell out of here, she'd be okay."

"Wouldn't we all."

He went on about Susan's problems and was surprised to see his wife's face show disgust.

"You are too close to her," she snapped as if she herself hadn't been encouraging Susan's persistence. "What's she doing for you now? You're finished with her, Mark. I thought you wanted to get her off the books. She doesn't want to let go, I can see the way she's working you. Everybody knows her game. You know how naïve you can be."

"Naïve? Hey, who almost shot off the cable television man's ass today?"

"Shit!" she shouted.

Calmly, he picked up the leather billfold with his badge from the counter and tossed it onto the kitchen table in front of her.

"Hey, you know so fucking much, the job's yours. Put on the badge. Why don't you show me how it's done."

He slammed the door and went out for a run.

While he was gone, the phone rang again. This time it was Ron Poole, who heard her sniffles and asked what was wrong. Grateful for the sympathy, she blurted out her misery.

Poole lectured her sternly. "How many times have I told

you? You guys don't have to put up with this. What are you waiting for, shots through the window? You've had threats. Those boys in Letcher County play hardball. Who do you think let the air out of your tires? That was just a little warning.''

"Mark says—"

"*Listen to me!* All that husband of yours has to do is talk to Terry about the threats. Tell them you're scared. They'll get you out. I mean it. I'll back you up. I'm telling you, you'll be gone in a heartbeat.''

"Mark says there's not enough of a real threat—"

"Fuck, Mark says! What the fuck does he know, a rookie worried about his boss? *You're* smart. You do not have to stay here. You know how it works!''

When Mark came back, he found his wife taking a hot bath, deep in thought. She asked him to close the door and leave her alone.

7

Kathy had come to the conclusion that Poole was right. The threat she felt to the safety of her family was genuine, no matter how amplified it was by her personal anguish about having to remain in Pikeville, perhaps indefinitely, as her marriage drifted away from its moorings.

Mark didn't see it that way. Yet he himself, deeply disturbed by the insidious way he had allowed his work to penetrate into his home, had felt strongly enough about it to warn her repeatedly about the calls from Charlie Trotter, some of which—like Poole's—she hadn't even told him about. "Just don't mess with him," he said flatly. "Take a message and hang up. I'm the one that went to the academy, Kathy. I mean it, don't get involved. These are dangerous people."

Kathy's position on that was, if they're so dangerous, why not ask for a transfer on the grounds that his family's safety was being compromised? She knew the answer without asking. Mark thought he could handle it, without endangering anyone, which she in fact knew was probably true. And besides, he was adamant about not wanting to look like a quitter.

So Poole's advice to take matters into her own hands made sense to her, even though she was savvy enough to see that it was offered mostly to serve his own agenda. Poole disliked Mark, which figured. Mark was intensely competitive, and determined to shine in the estimation of his superiors, which couldn't help but make Poole look bad. Furthermore, Poole's interest in Susan was obvious—he'd made that clear not just to Susan, but to Kathy as well. But poor misguided Susan was in love with Mark, as she had told both Kathy and Poole on several occasions.

The situation was crazy. They'd paid their dues. She'd intervened before when her husband was mired in inertia and doubt. It was time to do so again, for the sake of her husband, their children, and her marriage. It was time to get them out. The problem was, she didn't know how to do it without driving her husband farther away.

An odd opportunity to force the issue presented itself quite unexpectedly in the second week of November, when Kathy's sister, Chris, flew up from Florida to visit for a week and offered to baby-sit to allow Kathy and Mark a rare Saturday night out. They were delighted for the chance to be together somewhere other than at home. They went out to dinner at a restaurant called the Showboat. Afterward, they stopped for a drink at the cocktail lounge of the Land-mark motel, the most popular nightspot in Pikeville.

As they entered the crowded lounge, they edged through a small group of people dancing woodenly to a blaring rock band. Through a haze of cigarette smoke that clung to the room, Mark saw a familiar face at a nearby table.

"That's the guy I pointed out on television," he whispered, trying to ignore the man's wave.

Kathy squinted to recognize a local politician from a forlorn coal town in Letcher County. Mark knew him through one of his informants. When the official had been interviewed by the local media about a minor story out of Letcher County, Mark had pointed him out to Kathy as a man involved in cocaine dealing, saying, "That's one of the guys I'd like to get talking."

There were no vacant tables in sight, and the man kept beckoning. "We'll stop for a minute and leave," Mark muttered. "What's up?" he said as the politician scraped to his feet, practically sweeping Kathy onto a stool with a broad gesture of hospitality. Kathy was wearing a low-cut sweater and a skirt that was shorter than most people in Pikeville were used to seeing. She was uncomfortably aware that their new companion was staring at her thighs.

The man seemed delighted by the company. "Why don't you sit down and let me buy you a drink?" he offered, flashing Mark a quizzical look that said, *Wife or girlfriend?*

Mark explained, "This is my wife, Kathy."

The official was planning to go home soon and suggested they take the table when he left. But first, they should have a drink. A round was ordered. The two men spoke for a few minutes about something of more than passing interest to them both, the delay in making arrests in the chop-shop case. Everybody in Letcher County was talking about it. Their companion pursed his lips. "Well, you ain't come up with any indictments yet. I hear some of the property is disappearing. Problems?"

This was a sore point, and Mark tried not to show his concern. He sipped a beer and said in a measured tone, knowing that the conversation would be repeated, "We're very methodical. We always get our guy." Looking him directly in the eye, he said, "Why don't you tell me something about the case that I don't already know."

This elicited a boisterous laugh. The politician wiped some beer from his chin. "I don't know anything about that, man. Nothing."

Mark had spotted a local businessman he wanted to talk to at the bar and excused himself for a few minutes. He kept an eye on the table, though, and noticed with some amusement that the official had edged closer to Kathy. She, meanwhile, was trying to think. She nodded pleasantly at her companion. Watching him light his cigarette with a practiced flourish, she reconsidered Poole's advice—*Get involved in something. I'll help get you all out of here.* She wondered if she was looking at opportunity leering at her across the table, trying to get a peek down the front of her sweater. His voice was oddly high-pitched. "And what about you, little lady? Do you just sit there looking pretty or do you say something?"

She concealed annoyance at being patronized. "When I have something to say, I say it," she said, glancing across the room to show that she could see that her husband was out of earshot.

He had moved close enough on the high stool to press his thigh against her. She flinched, but covered by saying, "You know, I saw you on television."

This had its effect. "And did you like what you saw?"

"Actually, yes. I remember telling my husband, now this man is a *politician*. You had on just that casual shirt. Not like the windbags in fancy suits that we have back east."

He exhaled cigarette smoke in a leisurely curl. His leg was rubbing against hers. "Why do you sleep with a cop?" he said, deciding to be blunt.

"I married him." She had her swizzle stick between her lips and ran her tongue languidly around its tip, not believing what she was doing. He looked at it, transfixed. "Honey, I don't get much from my wife either," he said.

At that point, Kathy pressed her leg conclusively against his, which caused him to reappraise things. Now he looked startled. Boldly, he said, "Honey, your husband don't know what he's got, does he? You're a hot little bitch, ain't you."

She smiled beautifully and led him on inexorably, telling him, finally, that she was bored, miserable, lonely, and looking for some fun. "It's been a long time," she said. "My husband is always working, and I think he finds what he needs somewhere else, if you know what I mean." He did. Soon, Kathy had deftly brought the subject around to cocaine. "It's a lot better when you do coke first," she said with a small sigh.

"Hell, you didn't never touch no coke."

"Sure I did, back east. But now I'm an agent's wife. There aren't many chances to make a connection these days."

"Hell, that ain't no problem around here."

They stopped talking and looked up innocently as Mark approached the table with another round of beers. Kathy had a gleam in her eye. When the politician got up to go to the men's room, she had a mischievous look. "Mark, this guy is doing a lot of talking. I could find out anything I want from this guy.''

Mark wasn't quite sure what she had been up to, but he knew she was pumping the politician for information. Knowing Kathy, he guessed that she would get some. The prospect was enticing, but he was cautious. "Don't say a word to him. If he wants to talk, let him talk.'' She winked.

"Believe me, Kat,'' Mark said sternly. "He's smarter than he looks. When he comes back from the john, I'll walk away again. Let him talk. But watch yourself. Just listen.''

Kathy shot him a sharp glare and said, "Just get out of my goddamned face, Mark!'' He stiffened, but then felt their companion looming behind his shoulder. Frowning, Mark made another excuse to leave. He placed himself in a group of people, almost out of sight of the table, where he could keep a discerning watch on the man, who was grinning like someone who thought his ship was about to come in. After a few minutes, Mark saw him get up and leave Kathy alone at the table. Then he came back. In a moment, Kathy sat bolt upright and the two shook hands. With a quick glance around the room, the Letcher County politician walked out.

Mark raced back. She was already putting her coat on and handed him his. "What's going on?'' Mark said, hurrying out the door behind her. It was well after midnight, and time to go home anyway.

"We got talking about drugs,'' Kathy said when they reached the car.

"I kind of thought you would.''

"Well, I kind of told him that I like to party a little bit. But I can't because of my husband being who he is. I told him everything has to be discreet.''

"What did he say?''

"He said, 'Well, you can do coke anywhere,' And I said, 'Yeah, that's true, but I don't know anybody, and I can't trust anybody.' ''

"And he said?''

She took a gulp and giggled, imitating the official's twang. " 'You can trust me, sweet thang. You sit tight for a minute, and I'll be right back.' "

"And?"

"And this." Eyes wide, she opened her pocketbook and showed him a wrinkled plastic bag on top. "Mark, he put a gram of coke in my pocketbook. He said there was more, anytime I was interested."

"What! Are you sure? Jesus, do you know how bad we want this guy?" Then he stiffened, glancing furtively around the darkened parking lot, suddenly afraid that she had been set up. How would he explain this if he and Kathy got busted then and there with a gram of coke in her purse? "Don't touch it!" he ordered. "Let's get out of here."

Despite the hour, they drove to the office a few blocks away, where Mark got on the phone and woke up Terry Hulse in Covington. Hulse took it in stride, if a bit groggily. His instructions were to phone Poole and have him come down immediately to witness Mark securing the cocaine in the office safe. Mark offered to take Kathy to the emergency room for blood and urine tests to show that she had not used any of it, "just for the record."

That wasn't necessary, Hulse said reassuringly. "Just make sure the stuff is locked up." Hulse said that he would want to interview Kathy himself "to see if this leads us anywhere."

When Poole arrived, unhappy to have been called out of bed, Mark locked up the cocaine, which was in fact two grams, along with a cocktail napkin on which the Letcher County politician had written his phone number for Kathy.

It was after three by the time they got home. They talked a little about the implications of her stunt, with Mark bristling at her insistence on following up on the politician's offer to supply more coke. Mark wanted no part of that. Entrapping a local politician certainly had allure—once a man with connections started talking, there was no telling where the lines could lead in the tangle of coalfield politics.

Yet he was irritated by his wife's impetuous intervention. This was a dangerous game, and he wanted her out of it immediately. He figured that Kathy could make her statement for the record. Beyond that, he wasn't prepared for any further involvement by his wife. He drifted off to sleep.

Kathy stayed awake with her mind churning. She hadn't boasted about it to Mark, but she was proud of her skill in inducing a presumably crafty politician to pass two grams of coke to an FBI agent's wife—with the agent himself not twenty-five feet away. Now *that* was undercover work. Additionally, the encounter had shown her what she recognized as an opening—there was just enough danger inherent in it. If she could follow up, if she could involve herself in an actual police sting, wouldn't that be the key to a transfer? She figured she knew what she was doing. All she needed was the chance to work it out.

It appeared as if she was going to get it, too. On Monday morning, Hulse and another agent from Covington drove down to Pikeville to take her statement. They came right to the house, without Mark, who was instructed to wait in the office. Kathy supposed they were there as a formality, to interview her and file it away. But their interest sharpened as she described what she had done and insisted that she could do it again.

"I can get this guy," she told them, quite sure of herself. "He told me he would get together whenever I want. I know you guys want this man, and I can get him without any problem." Enthused by their deferential attention, she plunged ahead, telling them, "The only thing is, I have to call my shot soon, one way or the other, so he doesn't smell a setup. I'm already in this, you know." They didn't chuckle condescendingly, as she had feared they would. Instead, they spoke quietly and earnestly of the wisdom of allowing an agent's wife to participate in what would be a significant drug bust.

Seeing that she had them, Kathy offered to take a drug test, to establish for the record that she was not a user herself. That wouldn't be necessary, Hulse repeated with a smile and a nod toward Danielle and little Mark playing in the next room. Saying he would be back in touch, Hulse left with his colleague.

Mark was furious when Hulse told him about the conversation with Kathy. He said, in a testy tone that he never thought he would take with his boss, "We've got two small kids, for Christ's sake. I'm not letting my wife get involved in this kind of thing. Would you let *your* wife get involved in something like this?"

Hulse shook his head understandingly. "Yeah, I see your point."

But Kathy kept at it until Mark relented and called Hulse to say that she was available to take the next step, which would be to make what the bureau called a "controlled call" to the official from their home, to set up a meeting, with Mark and Poole on hand as witnesses. Under bureau orders, Poole came to their house with a tape recorder to supervise the call, which was made from the upstairs telephone in the hall outside their bedroom.

"That coke was really good," Kathy said during the short conversation, practically purring into the phone. The man was smart enough not to incriminate himself on the phone. But he did say he would be glad to meet her somewhere. She told him she'd call when she knew she could get away.

The ball was in the bureau's court. Hulse told them he would have to notify the U.S. Attorney's office in Lexington. Meanwhile, Kathy was instructed to avoid any contact with the target. The long Thanksgiving weekend was coming up, and a decision about pursuing the matter had to wait.

Kathy was feeling a lot better now that she had at least taken some initiative, no matter what came of it, and she found herself looking forward to the holiday. She always liked to cook a big dinner for Thanksgiving, which was something of a problem in Pikeville because their social

circle was small. The men Mark knew at the courthouse and
state police post all had their own family obligations, and
none of them had been anything more than casual work
acquaintances anyway. The Putnams really hadn't had much
time to develop friends. But Kathy had a thought. She
hadn't spoken to Susan for several days, and she was hoping Susan had made some progress in her so-far futile attempts to leave Kenneth and start looking for a new place to
live. When Mark came home from work, she suggested
impulsively, "Why don't we invite Susan and her kids for
Thanksgiving dinner?"

Mark felt the hair on the back of his neck bristle. "Wait
a minute," he said. "I don't want an informant in this
house. Do you understand? All I want is a day off to be with
my family. I don't even want the phone to ring."

As it happened, Susan called that night, but the talk
wasn't about Thanksgiving or finding a place to live. It was
about the encounter with the man from Letcher County.
Kathy was astonished to hear her rattling off most of the
details of the possible sting operation, including the controlled call from their home.

"Susan, how did you find out about that?" Kathy said
with some alarm.

"Oh," Susan said, off-hand. "Ron Poole told me."

Kathy was flabbergasted. Without telling Mark, she
called Poole at home and demanded to know why he had
given such sensitive information to a woman who had the
biggest mouth in eastern Kentucky. Poole was in no mood
to be challenged. He exploded in anger, "I didn't tell her
anything. Your fucking *husband* probably did. You listen to
me, nobody fucks with me like that! Don't you *ever* fucking
talk to me like that. I'll tell you something else, Kathy.
Your fucking husband has been fucking me over on two of
my cases. Tell him he better smarten up."

Kathy didn't know what to say. It was obvious to her that
Mark wouldn't have told Susan, who had no reason to lie
about that at least. But she was stunned to hear what

sounded very much like a threat from her husband's partner.

Into this turmoil came a disturbing phone call on a night when Mark was working late. "The boys in Letcher understand that you like to party," said a man obviously disguising his voice. If so, the caller said, Vernon Mullins would be happy to arrange it. All he wanted in return was a look at Mark's investigative file on the chop-shop case. Shaking, Kathy had a sudden suspicion that the anonymous caller was Charlie Trotter. She replied brashly, "Vernon has to deal directly with me, Charlie. Got that?"

There was an appreciative chuckle on the phone. "You really are one holy bitch, ain't you. You just be careful not to screw me over. Just remember, I got the FBI behind me anytime I need it." The caller laughed uproariously and hung up.

The week after Thanksgiving, Mark got a call from the U.S. Attorney's office asking him and Kathy to come to a meeting to discuss the drug sting. They argued about it all the way to Lexington, where they met with the U.S. Attorney, Louis DeFalaise, and two of his assistants. Terry Hulse was also there. It was readily apparent that the men had discussed the idea thoroughly and liked it. Mark was appalled and especially peeved at the way Kathy kept addressing her appeals directly to DeFalaise.

"You guys are nuts," Mark said with distaste when they asked him if he would leave the room for a moment so they could talk to Kathy alone. In the receptionist's office, he thought, *That woman is going to sell them on this! They're going to deputize her ass right in there.*

He was right. When he was asked to come back in, it was apparent from their faces that they were convinced. "I know you guys want this man," Kathy was saying, "and I can get him."

Mark tried to suggest that, rather than Kathy, they use a regular informant. He mentioned Susan, but even he knew that wouldn't work. Finally, he threw up his hands in disgust. Quickly, it was decided that Kathy would be authorized to call and arrange a buy. Extraordinary precautions would be in place. The meeting was to be in a car in the K Mart parking lot in Pikeville—a safe, logical place for a drug dealer to meet a housewife. There would be agents and cops hiding in nearby cars. When the cocaine was passed, dozens of cops would leap out and make the arrest before the perpetrator knew what hit him. Details were to be worked out in the coming week.

After the meeting, Hulse, who had quietly begun to share Mark's misgivings but was reluctant to dampen the enthusiasm in the federal prosecutor's office, sent a Teletype message to FBI headquarters in Washington summarizing the plan and requesting authorization for an agent's wife to go undercover. The Drug Enforcement Administration was also notified.

The Putnams were hardly back home when they got the word. A reply to Hulse's Teletype message had rocketed back from Washington with flames coming off it. No one in Washington had ever heard of such a lamebrained idea. Chastised but also relieved, Hulse ordered it called off immediately.

Out of the hospital and back with Kenneth, Susan needed money. More than that, she needed attention from Mark. Sadly aware that she had exhausted—or alienated—the sources of information she had used in the Tug, where no one trusted her at all after she double-crossed Cat Eyes's uncle, she knew that she had to develop a new forte to rejuvenate her career as an informant for Mark.

Poole suggested that if nothing in Pike County was working, she might look to her past, specifically her drug connections up north. She'd mentioned a cop she and Kenneth had gotten to know when they lived in Cicero, Illinois—a cop heavily into drug traffic who could line up a fairly big deal if the money was there. That was worth considering, Poole said. Mark's disdain for drug cases might be overcome, he speculated, if he knew that a cop was involved.

Susan figured it was worth a try since she didn't know what else to do. First she made a call to Cicero to ascertain from an old contact that the cop was still active. He was. She then called Mark to tell him she had important information on a new case.

She met him at McDonald's, where he said he didn't have time to take her for a ride. They sat in the car in the parking lot while she described the scenario she had in mind, which involved infiltrating a major urban cocaine and crack operation and drawing its connections to the Tug Valley. Mark looked bored.

"The guy that runs it?" she said.

Impatiently, he said, "Yeah?"

"Well, he's a cop."

He took out a notebook.

It was apparent, however, that she didn't have a lot to offer so far. Susan hadn't had much contact with the Cicero crowd since well before Cat Eyes showed up at the house. Actually, on those increasingly infrequent occasions when Susan would manage to put together enough cash to make a drug deal, she and Kenneth usually scored out of Cincinnati, closer to home.

Susan told him that she had already discussed the situation with Poole. That was fine, Mark said. Poole knew the Chicago drug scene. When Mark mentioned to his partner what Susan was considering, Poole brightened at the prospect of joining them on such a case. They decided it could work—if Susan was able to back up what she said and deliver a crooked cop engaged in interstate drug trafficking. It would involve undercover activity—Poole figured he could pose as her boyfriend and help her to infiltrate the operation. Cops seldom worked alone—it was likely other officers were involved if one was. What's more, cracking this kind of a drug operation out of Pikeville had a special appeal; the bureau brass would love to see the imperious Chicago office tweaked by two agents out of the hills of

Kentucky. Poole, in particular, savored the prospect of a triumph over his former colleagues. It was, he maintained, a "win-win situation."

There was a problem, however. Susan still didn't want to work with Poole.

A week before Christmas, Mark drove her into the hills north of Pikeville to a place where they had stopped to talk often in the past, a clearing just off an abandoned coal-mine road, twenty minutes out of town. Mark had been brooding about his difficulties, professional and personal. Nothing was working out; nothing was being resolved.

It was late afternoon, not yet dusk, but the sun had dropped behind the mountains and the air was cold. He let the engine run, taking notes disconsolately while Susan talked. Then he felt Susan's hand resting lightly on his shoulder.

"Is there something wrong? You seem way out in left field, honey."

She had not called him that before.

"Oh, you know, everybody's got problems, Susan."

"I know there's problems at home because Kathy tells me about them."

He was not happy to hear that. How often did Kathy and Susan talk? He really had no idea.

"She's feeling as bad as you are, honey, but there isn't anything you can do about that right now. You have got to have somebody, and maybe for right now, I'm that person for you. Whatever I can do to help you feel better about yourself, I intend to do. Like I always say, you are real different. You care about people. You listen to me. You helped me a lot. A lot. Now it's your turn for attention."

As she leaned toward him, he noticed the gold chain with a tiny cross she wore. She was rubbing his neck now, and he rolled his head to feel it.

"God, are you tense."

"I just need some time off. That or a good ten-mile run to sort everything out."

"Well, you can't run here. Look at me, Mark. You know how I feel about you."

He said, "Yeah, I know."

"Any time you need a release, I'm around."

"I appreciate that, Susan. But I don't think that would accomplish anything. It would just dig me in deeper, you know? I'm already in pretty deep." He didn't know exactly what he was trying to tell her.

"Mark, sometimes you have got to look past that and take care of yourself. You've been looking terrible lately. Real ragged."

She moved close to him, kissed him, stroked the inside of his thigh, and studied his face with a smile. "I think you should make love to me right now, Mark."

"I don't think that would be a good idea, Susan."

"I think it's too late for that, honey. Just relax."

Jesus, he thought. *Why the hell not? Why the holy hell not?*

He didn't see her for a few days afterward. He told himself it had been nothing. Quick, passionless, detached, as if he weren't even a part of it. He told himself, *It's like a pickup in a bar at college. You see a girl you know will do it. It's over and forgotten before you know it. No sweat. That's the last you think of it.*

Of course, that wasn't true.

And he knew what a fraud he was a few days after that when he drove her out to the place again, like a horny teenager. Afterward, he said he would take her home to Freeburn.

"You seem pretty upset," she said as they drove back onto the main road.

"I am. I'm pissed off at myself, not at you." He stroked her hair lightly, caught his reflection momentarily in the rearview mirror, and said, "I betrayed myself, my wife, my kids, and my job."

She laughed at his gloom. "Mark, honey, you take yourself entirely too seriously. It wasn't no—any—big deal. It was just a fuck in a car.''

Years later, Mark would insist that they had sex no more than five times over a two-week period, always in his car. Then, aghast at his carelessness and disgusted with himself as he had never been before, he broke off the relationship. Characteristically, instead of confronting Susan he chose to avoid her, leaving her to wonder what had happened.

Kathy never suspected that her husband was having an affair, however brief. Nevertheless, around Christmastime, she detected a palpable change in Susan's attitude. She wasn't calling as much as before, and when she did call, she didn't want to talk much. She was cordial and correct—''she seemed like she was on top of the world, for once,'' Kathy would later recall. Her self-esteem seemed to have undergone repair. Kathy was heartened by the improvement. Maybe Susan had finally decided to take control of her own destiny. At least, Kathy thought, *something* seemed to be getting better.

She wished she could say the same about her own situation, which had deteriorated rapidly. Later, she would struggle to analyze the breakdown, trying to sort out its causes. What parts were depression and paranoia, and what parts were a reasonable psychological response to real threats? How much fault lay in her unreasonable expectations, Mark's overbearing pride, the bureau's indifference and stupidity, the manipulations of Poole, Susan, Trotter, and others who might have hidden agendas?

This much was sure: there were deliberate attempts to frighten her. The most terrifying came in the middle of January, with Mark out of town for the night on a bureau training session. The phone rang around midnight. Picking it up tentatively, Kathy heard a voice growl, ''We ain't sure whose side who is on no more. We think you been sleeping with cops too long. You're alone with them babies tonight, ain't you?'' Frantically, she grabbed the .357 from the shelf and stormed around the house snapping off lights. She spent the night on the living room floor in the dark, with the gun aimed at the door.

On February 2, there was another late-night call, this one at four-thirty in the morning. Kathy would remember the date precisely because she filed away her calendars, and on this date, next to the note *Kids portrait Sears 9 A.M.*, she'd scrawled, *Kenneth called A.M. ???*

She had never spoken to the man before. All she knew about him was what Susan had told her, which of course was terrible. Kenneth wasted no time on social niceties with her.

"Kathy, this is Kenneth. You listening?"

"Kenneth?" she said huskily, standing in the dark upstairs hallway in her nightgown. For some reason, the previous owners of their house had installed only one phone jack on the second floor. Mark had been promising to run one into their bedroom for over a year. It was one of the several dozen chores he hadn't yet got around to. Instead, they had made do with a long extension cord. Carrying the phone, she made her way into the bedroom and sat on the floor beside the bed, gesturing to Mark in the dim glow of the night-light.

She heard scuffling. It was the old Susan, crying hysterically, who grabbed the phone. Gasping, she said, "Kathy, I'm so sorry that he did this. He doesn't understand! Kenneth, *quit it!*" There was more struggling, and the sound of a sudden crash. Near the phone, Kenneth cursed his ex-wife as a slut and a whore. Kathy rested her head against the side of the mattress and pushed Mark's arm away as he reached down to take the phone, telling him, "It's Susan—and Kenneth. It's *all right*." Kenneth got on again. She could hear Susan fighting for the phone, but Kenneth held on long enough to blurt out the astonishing declaration that Susan was pregnant—by Mark. "Is that all right with you, Kathy!" Kenneth shouted. "Is that fucking all right with you, lady?" His message delivered, he apparently voluntarily handed the phone to Susan, who stammered, through sobs, "He found out I was pregnant and lost it last month, and he says it was Mark's baby! It ain't true, I swear it, Kathy! I told you how jealous he is!"

Kathy was sitting cross-legged on the floor, trying to clear her head. Mark, sprawled across the bed, was looking at her apprehensively. Kathy heard Kenneth shout something about a private detective, about pictures of Mark and Susan coming out of a motel, before Mark took the phone from his wife's hand and said, sharply but with a measure of stern control, "Kenneth, get your shit together, man. You can't call people up raving like this." Mark listened quietly for a moment more and said, "Kenneth, I am just not going to listen to this." He dropped the receiver into its cradle on the floor.

They got back into bed, but Kathy was worried about Susan and wondered whether Mark should call the state police.

"Look, I'm not Susan's baby-sitter," Mark said, turning over with a sigh of disgust. "I'm tired of these games with her. They're both nuts. I can't deal with this anymore, Kathy."

They were silent for a full minute while she listened to him breathe.

"Mark?" she said, listening for his grunt. "I thought she said she couldn't have any more kids."

He exhaled heavily and leaned on an elbow to look at her. "What are you talking about?"

"She told me there were complications with the last one. That she couldn't have any more."

"That's what she said. So what's your point?" There was a touch of wariness in his voice.

"Well, now she says she was pregnant last month and lost it."

Mark was silent.

"Mark? Kenneth said it was your baby."

"Jesus Christ," he said in a tone of exasperation.

She was nursing a brief doubt, but discounted it as a reaction to being awakened in the middle of the night by a frightening phone call. She had already considered the possibility that Mark might have slept with Susan and dismissed it as ridiculous. So what if Susan said that she loved him. Lots of women found Mark attractive and let him— and her—know it. She had asked him in the fall, point-blank, "You didn't have sex with this woman, did you?" His reply had made her feel both foolish and slightly disloyal. "Of course not, Kathy. How well do you know me?" She didn't see a need to ask him again.

Still, there was Susan's newfound air of assurance. She was less desperate in her need to know everything she could glean about Mark from Kathy, as if she already knew all she wanted to. If she didn't know better, Kathy would have described her manner as *possessive* of him.

"Mark?"

"Kathy, you don't learn, do you? Leave it alone," he said. "Okay? They're both nuts. It's not even worth discussing. They're both whapped out on drugs."

He pulled the blanket over his shoulder and went to sleep.

And then, astonishingly, it was over before Kathy realized what had happened.

After well over a year, the indictments in the chop-shop case were finally handed up in February. Vernon Mullins, his nephew Charles Edward Tackett, his son, Michael, and four other Letcher County men were charged with conspiracy to violate federal law by receiving, possessing, concealing, storing, and altering the identification numbers on stolen motor vehicles and equipment that had crossed interstate boundaries. They all pleaded not guilty.

In early March, a detention hearing was held in the federal courthouse in Pikeville. Tom Self, the assistant U.S. attorney who would prosecute the case, asked that the men be held without bail and specified that Vernon Mullins and Charles Tackett presented a threat to the community.

Almost frantically, with Poole whispering encouragement in her ear in phone calls that Mark still didn't know about, Kathy began to apply fierce pressure on her husband to make his own case in court. With less reluctance now than he would have had before the indictments were in place, but still uneasy because he believed he was stretching the facts, Mark testified at the detention hearing that the defendants presented a danger to his family. He alluded to information from Charlie Trotter that some of the defendants had made veiled threats against him, his wife, and his children. "I do not feel safe," he told federal magistrate Joe Hood. "I have a gut feeling that given the opportunity, some harm could come to myself or my family."

The judge allowed the men to go free on bail after warning them not to have any contact with Mark or his family.

But the implied threat was enough for Hulse, who seemed to have become deeply sympathetic to the Putnams' plight in Pikeville. After the hearing, Hulse sent a memo to his supervisor in the Lexington office to request that Mark and his family be transferred. It was clear from what Hulse wrote that the situation had become severely tangled not only for the Putnams but for the bureau itself. Hulse described Mullins as "a very arrogant individual," previously convicted for other stolen-vehicles operations, who "has allegedly been paying off state and local law enforcement personnel to protect his operation over the past years."

Noting the threats conveyed to Mark, Hulse added in his message to the Lexington supervisors that Judge Hood had told the defendants in court "that they better pray to God that nothing happens to any potential witness" and ordered them to stay away from the Putnams. Hulse said that Trotter had been working "both sides of the fence" and had told Mark that Mullins knew "where Putnam lives and what bedroom Mark and his wife sleep in, as well as his daughter." Hulse said that Trotter had been threatening to take back information about payoffs of state and local cops and threats to the Putnams "unless we pay him more money."

Noted Hulse, "We have paid the source approximately eleven thousand dollars over the past two years."

Moreover, Hulse pointed out, a Kentucky state police officer whom Mullins claimed to have paid off had potentially embarrassing information. Along with Trotter and Mullins, the dishonest cop was fully aware of the drug transaction with Kathy Putnam and the politician from Letcher County.

Hulse added that a local newspaper had run an article on the hearing that mentioned the threats to Putnam, and that "the neighbors on Putnam's street told them that they did not want their children at the Putnams' house for fear of something happening to them." Hulse had spoken with Mark and believed it to be "in his and his family's best interest to move him as soon as reasonably possible. . . . You and I have previously talked about a Miami transfer, but Putnam understands that he can go anywhere."

In a follow-up memo, explaining the transfer to the FBI director, a supervisor in Louisville referred to Mark as a "highly motivated, dedicated, competent, and aggressive agent who has spent over the last two years in an area that borders on qualifying as a hardship assignment, and at best could be described as undesirable."

The memo argued that Pikeville "is recognized as an area of extensive criminal activity where individuals, groups, and entire families accept violence as a way of life, routinely carry firearms, and have little regard for law and order." Because of that, the memo recommended, "an agent with previous law-enforcement experience be selected" to replace Mark—who'd had none himself before he came to Pikeville.

The transfer orders arrived within days. Kathy barely had time to pack. The bureau sent the movers in and ordered her and the children to leave, with Mark to follow in a few weeks. They were going to Miami.

Kathy thought it was like hitting the lottery.

8

With Mark gone, Susan was more disposed to return the attentions of Ron Poole, a circumstance that gratified the beefy FBI agent. With Susan, he could have an attractive woman at his side, as well as the possibility of undercover assistance that could lead him into action, and out of Mark's shadow. Mark had warned Poole not to underestimate Susan; as Poole himself had discovered, sometimes she actually delivered. If the drug operation in Cicero panned out, all the better. Even if it didn't, it would entail some undercover duty on his old turf, and perhaps dinners in Chicago and ball games at Wrigley Field after work, instead of Big Macs out on the Pikeville four-lane. After a year and a half in Pikeville, a break in the monotony would be welcome.

Besides, Poole liked being around Susan. He told Mark so in a phone call shortly after Mark arrived in Florida. "There's something about that girl," he said, looking for encouragement. Mark, weary of Poole's jealous needling about Susan, replied with some relief, "Go for it, buddy."

Susan had her own agenda, but it fit Poole's, too. She was lonely, afraid, and destitute. He offered friendship, protection, status of sorts—and income. She understood the game well enough to know that she needed to provide sufficient information to establish her credentials. Then she would be back in business.

But this was no easy thing to accomplish deep in the remote hills of southern Appalachia. The serious drug business was city-based. Marijuana was just a mountain-grown weed, a modest crop scarcely more subject to outside market forces than turnips. Cocaine was another matter, a complicated industry involving financing, manufacture, import, wholesale distribution, and retailing. Only the end of the process had any appreciable base in a sparsely populated rural area; the Tug Valley was not exactly prime territory. It had been a long time since Susan and Kenneth ran with the city crowd; most of their friends had forgotten her. Susan tried to rewire her connections. But in the urban drug business, Susan Smith of Freeburn, Kentucky, wasn't a high priority.

By spring, her sense of rejection was nearly total. She had been measuring her days with fantasies about Mark, with whatever drugs she could obtain, and with self-destructive visits to Kenneth. One or two nights a week, saying that her children needed her, she drove across the river to stay with him and be with her children. Usually, she slept on the couch. She and Kenneth fought constantly; she got the worst of it, but she always came back.

The rest of the time, she was living with Shelby and her husband Ike in Freeburn, where the three formed a tense triangle in the little house alongside the Tug. Susan watched television incessantly, while guarding the telephone like a jilted teenager. Shelby was distressed that Susan's favorite television program was "Miami Vice," the police drama that featured handsome cops fighting crime in stylized subtropical settings of Florida.

Susan's brothers were no happier with her. They had welcomed Mark's departure as a way to erase the stigma, not to mention peril, of having a government informant in the family. But now, laughing off their warnings, she had teamed up with Ron Poole.

Susan and Poole made quite a pair, the sassy young woman from Freeburn and the corpulent, middle-aged agent whom she referred to teasingly as Jethro. In April, Poole took her to Hillbilly Days in Pikeville, an annual festival that is the high point of the town's sparse social calendar. For three days, the tiny business district is overwhelmed with a carnival that takes as its theme the Hatfield-McCoy feud. The main event of the festival is a parade in which townspeople, the occasional front tooth blackened with greasepaint, wear big, comic straw hats and bib overalls and behave the way hillbillies are thought to behave. Hooting and hollering, they parade through town in "hillbilly mobiles," cars and pick-ups festooned with signs, washboards, and other mountain claptrap, while the real hillbillies come into town to look on. There is much food and drink, and when the mountain music gets going, clogging breaks out spontaneously among the old coal miners and other spectators.

Susan did not like to think of herself as a hillbilly except during Hillbilly Days, when she dressed like a city girl come home for a visit. She looked beautiful and took many pictures. Poole beamed at her side.

But the joy disappeared when he brought her back over the mountain to the ramshackle jumble of Freeburn. In the gray gloom of reality, she retreated into fantasies. Her romance with Mark had been more than a couple of quick tumbles in a car on a strip-mine road with a good-looking man having troubles at home. No! They had been happy lovers for two years. He had brought her home, to his house. It was only a matter of time until they would be together; even now, he was down in Miami making the *arrangements* to leave his wife and marry her. As was her habit, Susan shared this fantasy with anyone who would listen.

What's more, she was pregnant with his child, she told people. Why, they even had names for the baby she carried: Mark, if it was a boy; Markella, for a girl. It did not seem to matter, and no one really had the heart to point out, that Mark already had a namesake. In Florida, it would all work out. It might be complicated, though, given her activities as an undercover informant on major drug cases. Susan even suggested to a few people that they should not worry if she disappeared without a trace. That was how the federal wit-ness protection program worked.

Just how embroidered her tales were, and how threadbare the truth, not even those who knew her well were aware. Among her vivid repertoire of stories of her glamorous life as an informant was one that would later be repeated as gospel by some, about Mark Putnam's parrot. A woman who had known Susan for many years in Freeburn remembered the story clearly years later because she had never heard of such a thing in Pike County.

"A parrot? What's he doing with a parrot?" the woman asked when Susan told her about it.

"He keeps it in his house, of course. It's in a big old cage in the living room, but sometimes he lets it set on his shoulder, like a pirate."

"Does it talk?"

Susan rolled her big brown eyes. "Oh, it don't ever shut up! In fact, I was afraid that stupid parrot was going to get us in terrible trouble back when I was living with him, when his wife was up in Connecticut that time? One morning, a deliveryman come to the door and I had to scrunch down behind the couch so he wouldn't see me in there. I thought that parrot was going to give me away. But all it said was, 'Hello! Hello!' "

Susan laughed and laughed, savoring the tale, firmly fixed in her mind, in which Danielle's pet parakeet, which Kathy had casually mentioned in a phone call, had metamorphosed into a radiant creature with feathers as red as the stripes on the flag, as blue as the sky in Florida.

Susan told some of her stories at a beauty shop on the road beside the river in Freeburn, not far from the foot of the Barrenshea. Being in a house, the beauty shop offered the informality and camaraderie of a coffee klatch. Many of the customers had known Susan all her life, and overlooked the odd, stilted enunciation she had developed to disguise her hillbilly twang as she chattered on about the life she imagined for herself far from the Tug Valley. It did not matter that she had gone away before and come home desperate. Dreams required no plans; they happened haphazardly, like everything else she had ever known in life. All she had to do was be there and hope for the best.

Susan did not know that the older women eventually

came to look at her with pity. Once her girlish audacity and brassy boasts had been a diversion, but now she seemed shrill, desperate, and somehow past her prime. Now she insisted on not just attention but deference, which was something a girl from the head of a holler was not about to get in Freeburn, not with that act.

The women talked among themselves about how different she had become with her children, on whom she once doted, seven-year-old Miranda especially. Now they got slaps across the face for interrupting, and they had learned to wait for her silently in the beauty parlor, their eyes watchful.

Susan talked of going to Florida, but instead she went to Kenneth, and that was inevitable, too. "All that boy ever has to do is promise that he is going to straighten out, and Susie gets down and kisses the ground in front of him," one woman said. She had been a teenager when Susan was a little girl and had once thought that Susan's irrepressible nature would let her beat the odds. As she watched Susan in the beauty shop, she was saddened to see the pallor under Susan's tanning-parlor bronze, the dark puffy half-circles under her eyes, the tight lines at the corners of her mouth. She tried to remember the sassy little girl in a white cotton dress, skipping along the road beside the Tug as if she always had someplace to go. What had happened to that child? As if alerted, Susan turned and met the woman's distracted gaze defiantly before resuming her monologue about being a "bonded informant" on a mission for the FBI.

"It's a top-secret operation," Susan said, addressing the room at large.

"If it's top secret, Susie, you probably shouldn't be talking so much about it," someone suggested gently.

"Shoot. It don't matter. It don't have nothing to do with this place," Susan replied, shifting her eyes to the window and the shabby old town outside. "Besides, I'm fully protected. Nobody dares do nothing to me."

When she left, they talked about her, not unkindly, but with general disappointment. "That must be some protection,'' one of them said. "My husband saw the poor thing sleeping in her car the other night.''

Early in May, Susan filed charges with the police against her ex-husband. She said that in one of his rages, Kenneth had tied her up and dragged her through the house in West Virginia. He had accused her of being an informant and betraying her own people, she said. He called her a whore from his car outside Shelby's house, and when she got in to settle him down, he drove off, shoving her out the door a few blocks away. She said that he threatened to shoot her.

Kenneth retaliated by reporting her to the West Virginia welfare office for receiving benefits from two states. As a result, she lost her West Virginia check and was left with the $249 a month from Kentucky. Meanwhile, Susan was finding it difficult to score cocaine and pills just when she needed them most. Since she had announced all over the valley that she was on a top-secret undercover drug mission for the FBI, all of her local sources had dried up. Desperate for cash and drugs, she turned to Pikeville.

Almost every Thursday night, she took a room in a motel at the crest of a hill behind a strip mall on the four-lane out of Pikeville, not far down the highway from the country-western bar where she had once dreamed about the singer who would take her away to Nashville. A clerk who worked nights at the motel would later recall that Susan Smith was working as a prostitute.

"She was annoying, demanding, and arrogant and expected to be treated like a queen," the woman said. "She had this attitude that, no matter what she did, she was untouchable. It was obvious what she was doing—she was always with a different man. You'd be surprised at what goes on in this small town.''

Adrift, frightened, strung out on whatever cocaine and amphetamines she could scrounge, Susan saw danger everywhere she looked. Here fantasy collided with paranoia and reality; but to those who knew her, there was a sense that Susan was coming perilously close to the end of the line.

Again, there was public trouble. In the middle of May, Susan was beaten up by Sherri Justice, Cat Eyes Lockhart's girlfriend, who threatened to kill her. According to Shelby, the beating was witnessed by Kenneth, Susan's brother Tennis, and Tennis's girlfriend.

Confused and battered, Susan sought protection from the FBI man who was still in her life, Ron Poole. As she did, she focused the blame for her problems on the one who had walked out of it, Mark Putnam.

In April, in a telephone call to Mark in the Fort Lauderdale hotel where the bureau had put the Putnams up while they found a new place to live, Susan told him that she was pregnant and asked what he intended to do about it. Stunned, Mark asked her if she was sure. She said she was. He was due to come back to Pikeville to finish up work on the chop-shop trial. They would talk then, he promised.

The call from Susan shattered any illusions he had about leaving Pikeville behind. He had convinced himself that the affair with Susan, disturbing as it was to his notion of himself, was a mistake that he had gotten away with. All he could do, he decided, was keep the trouble to himself and find a way to work it out, alone.

Mark was actually scheduled for two trips back to Pikeville for pretrial hearings on the chop-shop case. During the first, a stay of only a few days, he managed to avoid seeing Susan, who didn't find out he had been back in Kentucky until after he left. When he went back to Florida, Mark concealed his despair. Kathy, annoyed that Susan was still calling, but unaware of why, thought that in time, once the trial was over and they were settled into a new home, he would cut his ties.

Shelby had been pressing her sister to confront Mark about the pregnancy, but Susan had been afraid. After she found out that he had come to town and gone, Susan lied to Shelby, saying that she had seen him. They'd argued and he had tried to push her out of a car, just as Kenneth had done, she told Shelby.

The next time Mark was scheduled to return to Pikeville,

this time for a few weeks of work, Ron Poole made sure that Susan was forewarned. He telephoned her at Shelby's house and told her that Mark was due in on June 5. Shelby would later tell investigators that she was relieved that her sister would finally have the opportunity to confront Mark about the baby.

On Tuesday, May 30, Susan went to the public health center in Pikeville to have a pregnancy test and get a report confirming it. She explained to the physician that she needed the confirmation to apply for state welfare benefits, although in fact she was already receiving them. Based on what she said, the doctor who interviewed her gave her an estimated due date of November 19—indicating that the date of conception had been near the end of February. The doctor also noted that Susan had had a miscarriage and a D&C on January 2.

Susan took the report to Poole, who made a photocopy of it. That weekend, Susan visited her children at Kenneth's place. It was the last time they would see her.

On June 4, Mark Putnam, full of dread, boarded a flight in Fort Lauderdale. The chop-shop investigation that had consumed him for eighteen months, and on which he had staked his personal reputation, was nearly ready for trial, and the U.S. Attorney prosecuting the case had conveyed his nervousness to Mark. And waiting for him in Pikeville was a woman threatening to expose him as a fraud and an adulterer. He had no idea how he would control the damage.

On the plane, looking out across the vast dark mat of the Everglades, he wondered how he had blown it all so easily and with so little thought to the consequences. He shut his eyes and considered how he had disgraced himself, his family, and his badge, perhaps that most of all.

Years later, he would describe what went through his mind on that flight: "Kathy and I were finally in an environment where we could thrive, in Florida. And I threw it away. What did I swear to? Fidelity, bravery, integrity, character beyond reproach—the things that got me into the bureau. As soon as I had the affair, I knew I wasn't equal to my peers, even if some of them were up to their own things. I wasn't upholding my own standards. Yes, I put a lot of pressure on myself. I had to be the best person I could be. And I failed. In Florida, I was in a new competitive environment now with three hundred smart agents, and I knew they'd see that I was a flash in the pan. The only way I got into the bureau in the first place was pure audacity—and a wife who fought for me. I sure did find a nice way to thank her for that.''

In gusts of memory, he denigrated his accomplishments. Soccer star, baseball journeyman, good student working hard to keep up his grades, loyal husband, and devoted father—all now seemed to be thin veneer on cheap wood. He'd always feared his father's disdain, and now he knew why. He wasn't good enough, not then, not now, and the truth was about to come out.

As the airplane leveled out at cruising speed over the Florida panhandle, his mind wandered back to his freshman year in high school, when he was hopelessly in love with a pretty girl. There was a dance at the school; she led him outside on a warm spring night, much like this one, to join some friends who had a private party going near the track—booze and marijuana, people acting sloppy. In a panic, he fled, leaving the gorgeous new girlfriend behind with a can of beer in her hand. He literally ran the three miles home.

In high school, in college, and later in marriage and parenthood, those closest to him knew that Mark Putnam insisted on having an unsullied record. He had to keep it that way, without ever asking the question, Who says?

A man who couldn't tolerate small failings in himself was staggered by a big one. How could he possibly explain it when they came to him with the proof? With a female informant, he had compromised the bureau. There would be a scandal. Was resigning the only way? Could he simply tell the bureau, ''Look, guys, I screwed this up. I'm sorry. Give me my punishment. I won't mess up again. But there is nothing you can do to me that would be worse than what I have done to myself. Let me work it out. I promise you I will suffer''? No, he could not.

He did not consider discussing this problem with the person who knew him best and loved him unconditionally, his wife. He was in a terrible jam, but he would face it, and somehow overcome it, alone. Having never, ever, been in trouble before, Mark Putnam simply did not know how to ask for help.

In Huntington, West Virginia, which has the closest commercial airport to Pikeville, a hundred miles away through the mountains, he rented a Ford Tempo, in the standard bureau class, and told the clerk that he expected to keep it for about three weeks. It was a long and tedious two-hour trip south through the hills to Pikeville, on a road that narrows to two lanes as it climbs, with a constant barrage of coal trucks barreling north out of the hills toward the Ohio River.

As Mark drove gloomily south, Ron Poole hurried out to Freeburn to meet Susan at their usual place, the post office across the road from Shelby's house. He had already arranged a room for her at the Landmark, which he guaranteed with his American Express card. Another person was already at the motel on the FBI's tab. Charlie Trotter, the nervous star witness in the chop-shop case, had been salted away there for weeks, to keep him out of trouble. Mark knew he was going to see Charlie at the Landmark. Susan would be a surprise.

After a restless night, Mark walked into the FBI office in downtown Pikeville and found Ron Poole on the phone. "Hey, guess who's here!" Poole boomed into the phone. Mark's heart sank. Winking, Poole handed over the receiver as if he were doing Mark a favor.

Susan's voice had a brittle edge. "We are going to get together, aren't we?"

Mark tried to keep his voice down, though he could see

that Poole was listening. "Susan, I'll be here for at least three weeks. We'll hook up, I promise you."

"It'd better be soon, goddammit. I'm sick of this. You fucked me over."

The hostility surprised him as much as the crudity. Susan had always tried to be civil and "proper" in front of Mark, even when she was in a fury about something. That pretense was gone. Watching Poole, who was feigning interest in a file, Mark wondered just what had been going on between the two of them, but he didn't want to get into it any further with her, not here.

"Yes," he said patiently. "We'll talk, Susan."

Poole tossed him a sly smile when he hung up and said, "Hey, buddy, look there on the desk, would you? Hand me that piece of yellow paper there?"

Mark picked up the document, which lay next to a pamphlet about prenatal care. It was dated May 30; on the top was Susan's childish signature, and at the bottom, that of a technician at the Pike County Health Center. It read, in part:

> I fully understand that if the pregnancy test reading is NEGATIVE, it does not necessarily mean than I am not pregnant. . . . I also fully understand that if the pregnancy test reading is POSITIVE, this does not necessarily mean that I am pregnant. False positive readings can occur for such reasons as misinterpretation of results, undiagnosed medical problems (Aldomet, marijuana, methadone, aspirin in large doses, phenothirazine, antidepressants, antiparkinsonian, and anticonvulsants). . . . I have been informed that in order to lessen the chance of serious problems it is my responsibility to have the test results confirmed by a physician before considering myself pregnant or nonpregnant.

At the bottom was the notation: TEST RESULTS POSITIVE.

Mark felt sick. He glared at his ex-partner. Why was

Poole involved in this? How many other people had he shown the report to? Clearly, this problem was already out of control. She was pregnant, sure enough. And he was the father, she said. Given the proof of one premise, he accepted the other.

"Doing anything this afternoon?" Poole asked. He invited Mark along on a drive to Letcher County, where he had to do an interview. Mark, who wasn't due in Lexington until the next day, agreed to go, but on the long trip down through the depressing coal towns, along a mountain highway with road signs that said, like a bad joke, THE TRAIL OF THE LONESOME PINE, he regretted that he had. Susan didn't come up. They gossiped about cases and discussed the possibility of reactivating Charlie Trotter as a working informant once the chop-shop trial was over. It was an awkward trip and Mark was glad to get back to the motel in the early evening. He went down for something to eat, called Kathy and the kids, and climbed into bed to watch television. After a while the phone rang. Susan.

"Where are you?" he said. The connection from Freeburn was usually slightly fuzzy; now it sounded as if she were next door.

Which was about right. "I'm in the motel," she said.

"*This* motel? When did you get here?"

"I need to talk to you."

"Susan, I'm beat to hell. I have to get some rest because I have to be up at five to drive up to Lexington. I promise you, we'll talk when I get back tomorrow."

"We are going to talk about this, goddammit. Don't think we're not!" She abruptly ended the conversation.

He was up before dawn. He did not look forward to the three-hour drive over the mountains to the federal building in Lexington, where Tom Self, a prosecutor known for being methodical, wanted to conduct intensive reviews of the evidence before the trial, which was scheduled to begin in late June.

Mark was there at nine and felt greatly put out to learn

that Self had been called to court. Tired and ornery, he cooled his heels for six hours in the U.S. Attorney's office, brooding about his troubles. When Self came bustling in around three, he only had a few minutes to talk. He asked Mark to come back the next day.

On the endless drive back over the mountains, Mark thought about his ex-partner. "What the hell are you doing putting her up in the motel when you know I'm going to be there, Ron?" he said aloud, watching the rearview mirror as an eighteen-wheeler loomed bigger, tailgated menacingly for a few seconds, swerved into the passing lane, and roared on out of sight.

No sooner was he back at the motel, showered and trying to relax, when there was banging on the door. Susan stormed in, and her mood clearly hadn't improved any. Her eyes were bloodshot, and he wondered which chemicals were at work.

"You're avoiding me," she said.

"Hello to you, too, Susan. How are you?"

"Don't give me that shit. We are going to *talk*."

"Listen, I promise I'll set some time aside this weekend. Susan, I am beat to hell. I just can't do it now."

"That's just like you. You put everything before me! I should have killed them all when I had the chance."

He had no idea what she was talking about. "Killed who?"

She shrugged. It didn't matter.

It was obvious that Susan was high. Afraid of a commotion that he wasn't prepared to handle, he asked her if she wanted to go out to McDonald's for something to eat. With that, an amazing transformation occurred—the old Susan came back. They ate in the car and talked. Crying now, she poured out her misery. She was afraid someone was going to kill her. She described the beatings by Kenneth, by Sherri Justice. Shelby and Ike were threatening to turn her out. She had no money. Kenneth was keeping her children away from her. Poole was pressuring her to work for him, and she didn't know if she could do it. And he, Mark, a man she had trusted as no other, had gotten her pregnant and abandoned her to all that.

"Would you consider having an abortion?" he asked.

She most certainly would not. The fury came back. He could see no solution. As he took her back to the motel, he glanced at the woman sitting stiffly beside him in shorts and a T-shirt and thought, *If this is my kid, she's five months pregnant. The last time was before January. Shouldn't she be showing? Maybe the drugs keep it small.* But he dismissed the thought as craven and wishful. She went back to her room petulantly, without replying when he said he would find more time to discuss it next week.

Mark found Charlie Trotter sitting by himself in a lawn chair outside the room where Poole had installed him a month earlier. Living temporarily at the Landmark was an arrangement Charlie liked just fine, and not only for the security it offered. Charlie had robbed a motel or two, but he was not in the habit of actually staying in them; he considered it the height of luxury to be able to pick up the phone, order a sirloin and a six-pack, and when it came, sign a piece of paper saying the U.S. government was buying.

But Charlie, the toughest man on the mountain, had gone jittery. He told Mark that he was afraid the "Letcher County boys" had located him and were watching. A couple of them, he thought, had been driving by every night.

"They know where I am, Mark," he said with grave eyes.

"Christ, Charlie, do you want to change rooms with me? We can change motels if you want."

Charlie thought it over and said he would be okay. The FBI payment for his work was to come at the end of the trial. It would be substantial—in fact, it was going to be $30,000, on top of the $15,000 he'd got to date. Charlie said he would stick it out.

"We've been through a lot on this one, Charlie," Mark said as he left. "We can't let the case go down the tubes now, buddy."

Mark was deeply troubled, not only by the possibility of Charlie's backing out, but by the implications of using this man, who had been a friend, and then leaving him to fend for himself. It did not matter much to Mark that Charlie worked both sides of the fence; that was the way the game was played. In another couple of weeks, assuming he could work his way through all of this, Mark knew he would drive over the hills and drop the rented car at the airport. A few hours later, he'd be back in the sunshine of south Florida, with the loving wife and beautiful children and the three-bedroom town house with beige walls and palmettos out front, with neighbors on either side who did not know each other's names. But Charlie could call nowhere else home. After the trial, if he testified, he would have the big check in his pocket, with a pat on the back for a job well done. Charlie would be flush, though he'd piss that away on women and cocaine soon enough. But always, when he woke up in the morning, Charlie would be in these hills where the boys never forget an insult and always settle a score.

These were the ethical compromises inherent in using informants like Charlie and Susan. Truth to tell, keeping them active, as the bureau insisted, was a monumental headache. God, they wore him down. He was exhausted by the months of whining and crying, the nearly infantile dependence. Give them a thousand bucks, and they wanted two thousand more. Cultivating informants, keeping them happy and productive, required a huge and often debilitating personal effort: phone calls at three o'clock in the morning, paranoia, scheming, and double-crossing all came with the territory. He had seen how utterly different the FBI could be in a place like Miami, where the rules were clear-cut, the supervisors were on the scene, the work was dispersed among a large number of agents, and everybody had room to spread out: you weren't looking at the same damn faces everywhere you turned. All he wanted to do was get this case finished, control the damage with Susan, leave these hills for good. Why was that so much to ask?

*   *   *

The next day, he again made the drive to Lexington, wasted more time waiting for a meeting that he thought could just as well have been handled on the phone, and made the long trip back. When he got to his room, it was nearly nine o'clock; the only thing he had eaten all day was a glazed doughnut that a secretary had given him while he waited. But he was too tired to get in the car and drive out to a fast-food joint, or even to go down to the dining room, and room service had even less appeal. Instead, he pulled down the bedspread and lay on the bed studying water stains on the ceiling and wondering idly what would remove them. Finally he fumbled backhanded to snap off the forty-watt bulb in the lamp on the nightstand. His eyelids drooped and closed. His body felt light; at last the weight of trouble fell away and he relaxed.

He had been asleep for about a half hour when the phone went off like a firehouse bell in his ear.

"Hello!" he barked, more forcefully than he had intended.

"Heeeeeey." Oh, sweet Jesus, Mark thought, recognizing his ex-partner's signature greeting. The man had the unique ability to raise Mark's blood pressure just by entering his consciousness. "How's it going, buddy?" Poole asked.

Trying to conceal his annoyance, Mark said evenly, "We're all set to go with the trial, Ron."

But Poole hadn't called for a legal report. "You talked the stuff over with Susan?"

"Stuff?"

"You know what I mean, old buddy."

"No, not really, Ron," Mark replied warily. "I've been too preoccupied with this case."

"Well, I can understand that. I'll bet you can't wait to be done with that and get out of here, huh, buddy?"

"Yeah, I'm anxious to get back to Miami."

"Talk to you later," Poole said abruptly, and hung up.

Mark was annoyed at his own cordiality. Why didn't he just tell Poole to take a hike? They were no longer partners; even given the bureau's insistence on agent-to-agent bonhomie, Mark saw no good reason to extend courtesy to a man who always let you know he had a little something on you, then had the nerve to press for acknowledgment of that fact.

Mark thought back to Kathy's warnings about Poole, which he had largely written off to her desperation to get out of Pikeville. "You're naïve," she had said. "This guy has his eye on Susan, and he thinks you're in his way. This guy will do you harm."

He'd replied, with dismissive assurance, "An FBI agent wouldn't deliberately try to screw another FBI agent." He still had no idea how much Kathy had talked to Poole as she plotted to get them out of Pikeville.

Again Mark had fallen into a deep sleep, this time dreaming of the beach, the happy shrieks of his children over the crash of surf, when the insistent ringing of a telephone again broke through. He ordered himself awake. The voice on the phone was Susan's. It was eleven-thirty, she reported in a slurred voice, and asked, shrilly, "Sleeping? You sleeping son of a bitch."

The vehemence surprised him. "Susan, would you shut up and let me get some sleep?"

She banged the phone down. His anger was raw now with rudely dislocated sleep. He hated Susan, wished he had never recruited her, used her, paid her, encouraged her, comforted her, depended on her, and finally, stupidly, dropped his guard enough to have sex with her on the front seat of a car amid the sorrowful debris of an abandoned strip mine on a Kentucky mountain. That, finally, was where she had him, pregnant with his child or not, and they both knew it.

That was his abject ruin, the mortal sin for which absolution could not be had. And grievous sin was not a simple matter; with its commission came the torture of ambivalence and ambiguity. The fact was, as he knew very well, Susan had been there when he needed her, and Susan cared greatly for him. She had accepted this outsider when a lot of people hadn't. Later, she helped get him on the map. Working cases, she was as patient with Mark as he had to be with her. It was a weird balance. He pitied her circumstances and her upbringing. Like Kathy, he wished he could help her. They had always tacitly maintained the fiction of her un-sullied reputation, and in a funny way, between them it was true. She had offered herself not only in desperation and desire, but out of deep and simple trust. Their passion hadn't been devoid of love, no matter how flickering and transient. Furthermore, she had shown physical and even moral courage, beyond the lure of the money, to turn against people he knew she would have to face for the rest of her life, people who knew her parents, her aunts and uncles, her siblings, and her kids. Susan was brave, she had guts; in her own defiant way she was as loyal as a sister. Susan had put her ass on the line for him. Mark knew that his sacred career had benefited—directly, immediately, and substantially. She was an indelible part of his record.

He thought back on the first time he and Susan had had sex, steaming up the car windows like adolescents, the gear-shift knob jabbing at shifting limbs. He had always felt nothing but contempt for cops who kept framed pictures of their wives on their desks and meanwhile screwed anything that didn't resist. And now he had done worse. As a civil matter, becoming sexually involved with an informant was a fireable offense. Morally, it was unforgivable.

Now she was charging hard at him, hostile, impatient, unreasonable, and dangerous. She wouldn't give him time. It was going to be like working the bomb squad; disarming her would be tricky, especially with Poole lurking in the background. It could blow up in his face at any time.

He thought of what she had said the other night: "I'm going to be a thorn in your ass, Mark. I'm coming down to Florida to make sure you don't forget me."

9

He had pulled the motel room curtains tight the night before, but they did not fit the window well and the gloom seeped in with the dawn. When he opened his eyes, he looked at the dingy stains on the ceiling.

At least it was June. By noon, the sun was high enough in the sky that the light came over the hilltops. The trees were full and green on the mountains. People were ashamed when the hills lost their cover, exposing the deep gashes from the strip mines, the giant conveyer machines trellised over stepped ridges of blasted sandstone and slate, the sallow streams and tumbledown shacks. Winter was not a good time to sell a house in Pikeville, although now spring was over and still their place on Cedar Creek remained unsold. Tending to the house was another of the unwelcome chores Mark had to do before he could go home.

He turned over and pressed his face into the pillow, imagining south Florida, Danielle hopping off her bike to run to him in the front yard when he got in from work, Kathy happy again and making plans to complete her degree, little Mark bright and mischievous, a miniature image of his old man. It had taken a lot to get there; all he wanted now was to get back. The bathroom faucet dislodged another drop of water that hit the sink with a resonant *plonk*. Kicking off the thin blanket and stiff bedspread, Mark sat up naked on the edge of the bed, feeling sore and dizzy. He thought, *I've got to start eating and sleeping better than this. Cut back on the hours, loosen up, work out more*. In a few weeks, he hoped, Ron Poole, Tom Self, the bureau supervisors in Lexington, the Hatfields, McCoys, and everybody else in Pikeville,

Susan especially, could then do him a great favor by losing his phone number.

His head rested on his chest. The date was June 8, his father's birthday. His father had been dead for ten years, but he still thought of him without fail every day. If the old man had been around, Mark wondered if he would have gone to him and said, *Look, Dad, I'm jammed up here. I messed this thing up bad, and I don't know how to get out of it.* Mark tried to imagine his father's face when it was strong, but what he recalled instead was a familiar sad photograph of a man in his late forties, gaunt and defeated, with a month left to live.

Wishing that he had inherited his father's equanimity in the same measure as his introspection, Mark made his way to the bathroom, where he scowled at his face in the mirror and gingerly pressed at the puffiness under his eyes. In the shower, the spray was weak, but at least the water was hot and soothing against the tight muscles of his shoulders. He closed his eyes and let the water beat on his face.

There was a pounding on the door as he was drying off on the tacky blue rug. He wrapped a towel around his waist and had barely pulled back the dime-store bolt when Susan pushed her way in, red-eyed and looking as if she'd slept in her car.

"Don't you look nice," she said smiling broadly and tugging at the towel till it came off. "Is that your new 'Miami Vice' outfit?"

"Hello, Susan," Mark said wearily. "You're up early."

She brushed past him and went to the bed, but he continued to face the door, not willing to acknowledge her possession of his room. *Christ, not now,* he thought. This was business for tomorrow, maybe. Not now.

"I've got to leave for Lexington in five minutes, Susan. I'm going to be tied up there all day." With resignation, he turned to face her, trying not to show the disgust he felt with himself. She didn't look pregnant in her little shorts and

University of Kentucky T-shirt. When had Kathy started to show? He couldn't recall.

"Are you avoiding me again, Mark?" Susan demanded, planting herself on the bed. "We got to talk. How many times do you and those guys need to meet, anyway? Why didn't you just get a room up in Lexington?"

"Because I wanted to straighten out some problems here, Susan," he said pointedly. The shoulder muscles had tightened up again. He felt sweat building under his arms; a rivulet began a jerky path down his back.

"Don't give me that bull, Mark. Don't fuck with me."

"If I didn't do that, we wouldn't be in this mess, would we," he said, but he regretted the juvenile crack immediately. He didn't want her riled. All he wanted was for her to let him get out of there. He walked over to put a hand on her thin shoulder and was surprised to feel her flinch. "We'll talk this weekend, okay?" he said.

"I always take a backseat to the precious FBI, don't I?" she said petulantly. He'd heard that before, of course. And the reply, had he chosen to give it to her, would have been: *Yes, dammit. Everything else takes a backseat.* Why was that so hard for people to understand?

Instead, he said, "I've got to get dressed and get out of here." When he came out of the bathroom, she was still sitting on the edge of the bed.

"I've got to go, Susan."

"Wait, wait. I need to use your phone to call my sister, and I need to borrow a pair of shorts," she said, sounding plaintive.

"For what?"

"I didn't bring enough clothes with me. I just want to borrow them. You'll get them back, Mark."

"But why do you need to use my phone? Use the phone in your room."

"I have to call my sister, and I don't want Ron to know I did because it's about him."

This didn't make any sense, but he wasn't in the mood to argue.

He grabbed his bulging files off the top of the television and caught her injured look in the dingy mirror. "Okay, make your call, grab your shorts, and close the door when you leave," he called back as he left, hooking his thumb at the table where his suitcase lay open.

As he shut the door, he heard her mutter, "Bastard."

In the rented Ford, he wondered for a moment about Susan borrowing his clothes, but she was always borrowing somebody's clothes. He deliberately put her out of his mind as he negotiated the high pass that cut through the mountain north of town.

In Lexington, he was once again kept waiting until well after lunch. He and Tom Self finally met late in the afternoon, spending less than an hour going over details of trial strategy. Though Mark resented having his time wasted, he regarded Self as one of the few mentors he could name during his time in eastern Kentucky. Trying to please Tom Self during a prosecution was like trying to get an A from a particularly exacting teacher. Mark thought of him with grudging respect as a "ball buster" who insisted that every flap in a case be nailed down tight before he took it to trial. Often, he would ask Mark to go back and reinterview people he had already talked to, fill in more detail. Self was never confident and never let investigators relax until the jury adjourned.

The chop-shop case was solid and ready to go, assuming Charlie Trotter didn't bolt. Charlie seemed to have steadied the last time they spoke on the phone; Mark hoped he could keep him that way. Still, it was never a sure thing with a mountain jury. Cases got lost simply because jurors didn't like the idea of outsiders coming down on a local boy living hard, making do. Mark never forgot his first trial, when witness after witness ostentatiously crossed their fingers as they swore on a Bible while the judge pretended not to notice, the jury's eyes widened, and spectators nudged one another.

He also knew that the bureau was watching this case carefully—after all the time and trouble, after the emergency transfer out of town, he knew that he had to bring a clean conviction to the table, especially if Susan persisted with her threat of going to his superiors.

Feeling that he had wasted another day, he started back into the hills around five o'clock, as the afternoon sun edged the ragged mountains and cast deep shadows over the valleys. He realized that he needed a vacation. The past two and a half years had caught up with him—everything, even his nightly three-mile run, seemed to take extra effort. In a month, he would be thirty. He no longer felt young.

Susan, determined to force the confrontation that Poole and Shelby had been insisting she have, waited all afternoon for Mark to return. Every fifteen minutes after four o'clock, she left her room to look for his car. Anyone who glanced at the pretty, brown-haired young woman standing on her tiptoes on the balcony of the motel might have taken her for a mountain bride on a honeymoon waiting for her husband to come back from the store. She would look, see nothing, smile wanly, and with studied dignity return to her room.

Mark saw her at the railing when he turned into the parking lot. She did not acknowledge him except to glance his way, steadily but without apparent interest. At the end of a long drive and a frustrating day, he was furious to know that the next thing he could expect was a confrontation. He turned off the engine, braced his arms against the steering wheel, put his head down, and muttered, "Shit, shit, shit, shit, just leave me alone for five minutes." All he wanted to do was read the paper and have dinner. But he forced a look of nonchalance and went up to his room with Susan hard on his heels.

She followed him inside and stood silently by the door until he came out of the bathroom. She had changed into his gray gym shorts and T-shirt since their encounter that morning.

"Are we going to talk about your baby now?" she said. He could tell she had been drinking, and by this time of the day there would be some pills at work, too.

"Not tonight, Susan. Please. I have some calls to make, and I need to spend some time with Charlie."

She snorted. "Your job again."

But he was surprised when she sauntered out without a commotion.

Alone, Mark made a few local calls and then walked down a floor to talk with Charlie Trotter, again installed in his lawn chair, again wavering. "It's going to be tough looking them boys in the eye when I'm on the stand," Charlie said, reaching for the can of beer at his side. He dragged hard on the nub of a Marlboro that was barely visible under his black mustache, then flipped the butt over the railing and folded his hands on a prodigious belly.

From where the two men sat, they could see the single bulb shining in the gathering twilight from atop the cupola of the Pike County Court House, repository of challenged deeds, ancient threats, and tenuously adjudicated brawls.

Having to look the boys in the eye was the curse of this land, of course. But Charlie's testimony was important, if not crucial. Without it, the case could well collapse.

Mark sighed. Charlie slumped in the lawn chair, his powerful hands now tightly clenched between his knees, as if in combat. He turned slightly away, which Mark recognized as a telling shift in alignment, a sign of inner conflict signaling a potential for deceit. *Give empathy, not sympathy,* he recalled from his classes on psychological manipulation of informants and suspects.

"Charlie, I'm not going to blow smoke up your ass," he said, choosing his words deliberately. "I won't even try to understand what you're going through right now. Just do the best you can, man. You're a stand-up guy. Remember all the bullshit these clowns put you through. Remember what they did to you, Charlie." He stood up and clapped Charlie on the leg. "What do you say we grab something to eat and have a few beers? Uncle Sam's buying."

"Already et," Charlie said, sitting back to nurse his beer.

*   *   *

A little later, Susan thumped pathetically at Mark's door. She stood at the threshold with her arms crossed over her breasts, smiling unevenly. Again, he knew she was high. She lunged at him the moment he shut the door behind her, slapping him hard across the cheek with her right palm. She was wide-eyed and crying.

"You're avoiding me, you son of a bitch! I'm sick of this, Mark! High-and-mighty FBI—I'll see you burn in hell!"

He knew better than to aggravate one of Susan's tantrums, and he was astonished to see it directed at him. She had never acted this way with him before. Spit flecked the corners of her mouth. Her hair was unkempt; she looked as if she had fallen off the back of a truck. Another forty pounds and another ten years, he thought, and this was a woman framed in defeat in the doorway of a mobile home, yelling at the kids.

She screamed at him, "My life has been fucked up since I met you!" He resisted the impulse to point out that it had been that way before she met him, too. At least now she was on the right side of the law more often than not.

"Now you are going to pay for it!" she vowed. Her lips trembled. He wasn't sure what she meant, but he looked around quickly to make sure his gun was in the bureau drawer. He remembered: he had put it in beside the Gideon Bible.

"I'm not having no abortion," she repeated.

He wanted to reason with her, and the drug rage was complicating that. He felt shaky. He wished her no harm. All he wanted was for her to be out of his life. "Susan, I understand about the abortion," he said, struggling to control the situation. "If this is my baby, I don't want you to bring up that child. Kathy and I would raise it."

He had not anticipated making such a suggestion; immediately, he regretted the hurt the words caused.

Susan was sobbing. "I am a good mother. This is your baby, Mark. You insinuate that I been fucking everybody in Pikeville, but this is yours!"

"Susan, I didn't insinuate anything like that. Please keep it down. I don't want the neighbors to know our business."

That let her regain the offensive. She stamped her foot. "The damn neighbors? You're so concerned with your reputation? Your reputation ain't nothing now, Miami Vice!"

Her pupils were dilated. Whatever was going on, he wanted to change the physical location and negate her ability to threaten him with a public scene. Exhaling loudly, he suggested, "Look, let's go for a ride and cool off." She surprised him by taking his hand as if he had asked for a date.

They drove deep into the mountains on steep and familiar roads, talking but getting nowhere. Again and again, he asked her what she expected him to do. When she managed to connect her sentences, Susan's replies were threats. She insisted that the baby was his, and that she would tell the FBI, his wife, and his children about it. But unless it was to renounce everything else and stay with her forever, he could not figure out what she expected him to do. He thought about the two miserable years working grueling hours in Pikeville, the phone calls at three in the morning, the threats, the corruption he saw everywhere he looked, the stress of the impending trial, Charlie Trotter wavering in his motel room. Back home, the strained marriage still not free of the bonds of Pikeville, the phone calls from Poole, the need to establish a new reputation in the tough, competitive, high-profile Miami bureau. And now, beside him, Susan, still shrieking that she was pregnant with his child, and everybody in his fragile world was going to hear about it.

"Ron says they'll fire you when they find out," Susan said.

He bristled at that. "What about Ron?"

But she backed off. "Nothing. He didn't say nothing. They will fire you, though, Mr. FBI."

He kept quiet, but he believed that what she said was true—that was the real threat.

He had instinctively driven out Route 23, where the big coal trucks hit cruising speed at night on the long haul up the valley, and turned off onto the seclusion of Route 119, the only good road east into the Tug Valley. At Meta, he turned right onto Route 194, a narrow two-lane that winds southeast along Johns Creek into the rugged hills that border the Tug Valley. Once in the hills, the only turnoffs are narrow gravel roads dug in by mine companies, who move on down the ridge, leaving behind shattered rocks and rutted roads, after the thickest veins of coal have been clawed out and hauled away.

He did not notice, but the closer they got to Freeburn and Barrenshea Hollow, the more distraught Susan became. As they approached the crest of Peter Creek Mountain, she suddenly lunged across the seat at him, slapping him with both hands. Fighting to keep control of the car, he made out the contours of one of the coal-road turnoffs in his headlights and made a right turn onto it. The stones rattled under the car as he drove about fifty yards up the road. He shut off the engine and the lights, and silence fell with the darkness, as if tumbling down from the mountain itself. Where the sky showed above the ridge, it was filled with stars. Mark rolled the window down and felt the air cool his hot cheeks and burning eyes. He listened, as if trying to extract from the gloom any sound other than Susan's short panting, raw with spite.

Placing his hand on her shoulder, he said, "Let's try and work this out instead of acting like a couple of idiots." This was exactly the kind of setting that had led to sex on other occasions, but even the intimation of affection now caused Susan to recoil in revulsion and slap his hand away.

"What's gotten into you, Susan?"

The question set her off again. "What do you mean *me?* You're messing with me, Mark! I know that now. I don't know why I didn't see it before. I'll be goddamned if I'm going to let you prance down to Florida with your little wife and your spoiled kids to resume your wonderful life. You owe me, buddy!"

He had the sense that these were lines someone else had given her. Susan was a verbal chameleon. *Buddy* wasn't a word she normally used, and Mark thought he knew where she had picked it up.

"Susan, I've given you everything I could. Leave Kathy and my kids out of this." She looked down indignantly, and he realized he had been using his index finger to poke at her chest for emphasis.

"You sure did give me everything you got," Susan said, and patted her belly. He watched this, thinking again that she did not look pregnant, but not having any good recollection of how a woman looked at five months.

"And now I'm going to have a little Mark Jr.," Susan went on. "I'm going to bring this baby down to Florida and knock on your door and put the little bastard right into your precious daughter's arms. Your son is going to want to know why the baby's name is Mark Jr., the same as him. I can't wait to see the look in your wife's eyes! Then you know what I'm going to do? I'm going right on down to your FBI 'Miami Vice' office and tell your new friends there how you solved your cases by fucking an informant and leaving her pregnant and barefoot to look after herself in Kentucky. I own you, Putnam! I own you and your precious job!"

She was determined. "I own you! Own you! Ron says they'll fire you and Kathy will leave you!"

"Ron again?" She laughed at his pique.

"Susan, just tell me what you want from me. From day one, all you've done is bitch and feel sorry for yourself. Now please just tell me straight, what do you want from me?" His heart was pounding.

Suddenly, at last, Susan was all business. "We are going to have this baby. You *will* be there when it's born and sign the birth certificate as its daddy. Second, you will leave that whore Kathy and those spoiled kids and marry me. If you don't, I'll ruin your life." She smiled triumphantly.

Mark, never a negotiator, went for the immediate opening. Kathy hadn't done any injury to Susan. Far from it. Kathy had been Susan's friend, her confessor, and even her role model. When Mark wasn't in the mood, which had been very often during their last months in Pikeville, Kathy had been the stalwart who patiently endured Susan's crying jags on the phone; Kathy had been the one to assure Susan that she had value, that she was better than she believed. "Hold it, dammit. If you ever call my wife a whore again, I'll smack the shit out of you, Susan." And he meant it. He jammed his right hand under his leg.

"You don't have the balls to hit me, Mark. You're a pussy with no balls! For someone so smart, we played with you so bad. I don't even know why I let you fuck me—you're no man! I've had real men before, and you're nothing—you're nothing but a spoiled rich kid!"

This floored him. He thought of his father, taking on odd jobs to scrape together the thousand dollars a year that wasn't covered by his scholarship at Pomfret. The insult infuriated him. He smacked Susan across the face with the back of the fingers on his right hand. The blow barely fazed her. As if welcoming it, she let out a yelp of satisfaction.

"Well, the little boy has the balls to hit a woman! That's the first real emotion I ever seen in you! I hope I didn't hurt your delicate little hand!"

He was breathing in gulps and close to hyperventilating. Sweat burned his eyes. She kept at him. "The only reason I worked with you in the first place was because I saw how pitiful you really were. Seen how they sent a pretty little Yankee boy down here with real men. Maybe your precious FBI wanted to toughen you up, but it didn't work. All the cops used to make fun of the pretty Yankee boy who wanted to work all the time." Delighted to have found a vein, she stabbed at it: "They laughed at you behind your back!"

He tried to make out her face in the darkness. Her voice was cold and strange.

"I own you, little boy! Now I'm going to have two little Putnam boys sucking at my tits."

"You're a fucking bitch, Susan, you know that?" he said quietly, desperate to control the quiver in his voice, afraid that he was about to cry.

"Oh, the great one spoke out! My hero spoke! Did it hurt to swear, Mr. Perfect?" Her breath was sour on his face. "Your life sure ain't so perfect now, is it, honey?"

He tried reasoning again. "Okay, Susan. This is what I think about our problem—"

"*Our* problem? Oh, no, Mark. *Your* problem. I've never been happier myself. I told all my friends I'm going to have an FBI baby. I can't wait to see Kathy's face when I show her our baby."

He resisted the urge to hit her again. His training told him to stay on track, be professional, avoid emotionalism and direct challenge, summarize frequently, maintain aplomb.

"Since you won't have an abortion, after the baby's born I'll come back and take a blood test to establish paternity."

She screamed. "I ain't no whore like your wife! I haven't fucked nobody except you! How dare you say that!"

"Well, that isn't what I heard, Susan. I heard your sister threw you out of her house—"

"That's not true!"

Sensing advantage, he bored in, impulsively brandishing the option he had not yet even considered discussing with his wife: "If the baby is mine, Kathy and I will adopt it. *We* will adopt it. You've proven what kind of a mother you are by signing over custody of your kids to that drunken ex-husband of yours. I'll be damned if I'd let any kid of mine grow up here with you."

Humiliation overcame her spite. Shrieking, she slammed into him, slapping and scratching wildly, like a child having a tantrum. Mark realized what Bertie Hatfield had meant when he said that Susan could fight like a rained-on rooster.

"I won't let that whore raise my kid!"

"She's a better mother than you'll ever be!" Mark retorted, pushing her away roughly with an exaggerated and hurtful show of disdain in the cramped confines of the car. This made her hysterical. She was on top of him, pounding down with her fists. He couldn't get his arms free to shield his face.

"Susan, cut . . . the . . . shit." He struggled into a dom-
inant position, working to pin her arms. Her screaming
appalled him. Fogged by their breath, the windows were as
opaque as if covered by snow.

"You bastard!" Susan shrieked, flailing at him. "I
should have killed your kids." With a guttural moan, she
dug a long fingernail at his eye. Stunned by the sudden pain,
he swung at her, this time with a fist. But he missed. His
hand slammed into metal on the dashboard.

"Fuck you to hell!" she cried as the punch flew past.

Blood oozed from the gash across his knuckles. She saw
the bleeding hand and bit it, with her feet pressed stiffly
against the windshield. The pain was astonishing. She
hissed through her teeth. He needed silence. *Shut up!* he
thought, wrenching his hand free and grabbing her neck
with both hands. He held her that way, pressing for silence
until her fury and his abated. He let out his breath steadily
while she struggled weakly and then submitted to his grasp.
"Relax, Susan, relax," he said, almost as if he were giving
her a massage. When his breath was fully exhaled, his grip
relaxed. The tension drained from his arms, which fell
heavily to his side.

Susan was quiet. He opened his eyes and inhaled unsteadily, not knowing whether ten minutes or ten seconds
had passed. His face stung from the slaps. She was a fighter,
all right. But now she was leaning against him, the fight
gone. He stroked her damp brown hair, wondering why she
was not breathing heavily after struggling so hard.

"Susan, are you going to take it easy now?" he said,
nudging her gently, as if to wake her up. He regretted the
insults. His lips brushed the top of her head. His shirt was
soaked; his right hand ached, the knuckles were wet with
blood. He'd never felt more physically exhausted. "Susan,
let's go."

The night had grown chilly; he thought of starting the car
to get the heater going. Freeburn was still ten miles around
the mountain. Sullenly he said, "I'll drive you home."

She slumped forward when he removed his arm. As he tried to ease her gently off the console and into the passenger seat, her neck craned at a grotesque angle.

He blinked and said, "Oh, my God. Oh, shit. Oh, my God." He shook her. He sat her back and pounded on her chest. "Susan! Susan! Oh, my God!" He tried blowing air into her mouth, but her lips were cool and unyielding. He pounded on her chest and felt frantically for a pulse.

His first thought was that it was a coincidence, a tragic heart attack, perhaps exacerbated by the excitement. He certainly hadn't *killed* her, not that easily. There would be some explaining to do, but . . . Then he knew that she was dead, and he had killed her.

He cradled her head and rocked back and forth, sobbing, staring in disbelief at her face, very white and composed in the chill glow. *I have killed this person*, he thought. *A mother of two children. This woman in my arms*.

Trembling uncontrollably, he got out of the car as if to stalk away from it. The door slammed and the sound reverberated from black-faced mountain walls. He screamed; that came back, too, with the same empty echo. He fell back against the car, hearing only his breathing and the grunts of bullfrogs in the brush, and in the distance the splash of water spilling off a slate ridge like a broken spigot.

He tried to arrange his thoughts. A steady wind rushed through the trees on the mountaintop, like the roar of a stadium. Foolishly he looked around in the dark, as if for a pay phone. He got back in the car and replayed the scene in his mind, looking for excuses—the threats, the fury, the tears, the blows and flailing arms. He went over the story he would tell to the state police or, better yet, to Bertie Hatfield at his place on the Tug, just beside the bridge.

He would expect no special treatment, beyond a certain professional courtesy, a cop-to-cop understanding that this girl had got run over just as surely as if she stood in the middle of a mountain road shaking her little fist at a twenty-ton coal truck rumbling out of the switchback. It was strictly his fault, of course. He would take his medicine. Bertie would be heartsick; Bertie would know what to do. He would tell him how to break it to Kathy. Kathy would tell the kids.

Another image crept into his mind, that of Danielle as an infant, three or four weeks old. It was the time of their marriage when he and Kathy were happiest—he was working hellish hours, the day job clerking in a liquor store, nights clerking at the FBI in Hartford, praying for an opening at the academy. When he came home after work at one o'clock one morning, the baby lay curled in her crib. Gently, he woke her and she smiled at him sleepily. He scooped her tiny, sweet-smelling body into his arms, held her to his chest, and whispered hoarsely, ''I promise you: I am going to be the best father I can be. You will always be proud of me. And you will always be able to come to me, with anything. I promise you that, Danielle.''

One life was destroyed. Why destroy the rest? He was on a lonely mountain road. Not a single car had passed in the time they had been parked there arguing and fighting. Furthermore, they hadn't seen anyone else when they left the motel. Chances were, no one even knew that he and Susan had gone out together.

Susan's body was losing its warmth to the night. Absurdly, he reached over to roll up the window for her. Looking at her blankly, he considered suicide, but he didn't have his gun along. Then another thought broke through the guilt and terror: he could fake a car accident. He was hurt, she was dead. This he quickly dismissed, however. People don't get strangled in car wrecks.

He got out and walked around the car several times, as if to encircle the problem and confine it, but he couldn't, no matter how hard he walked. *All of my life,* he thought, *I stayed out of trouble. I was the one who got the other guys out of jams in college! I kept my nose clean.* But he was the one alone now on a mountaintop with the body of a woman he had killed. What would his father say to that?

He ran to the passenger door and struggled to lift her out,

astonished at how heavy she was. He had eased the body almost out of the car when it abruptly toppled to the ground, the head hitting the gravel with a whack. Mark screamed in fright, as if he had injured her anew. He fell to his knees and vomited, bile burning his throat. He cradled her head, rocking on his heels, praying, *She is not dead, she is badly injured, in a terrible coma.* It would be horrible, there would be some jail time, but she would be alive and maybe, someday, she would forgive him.

A light drizzle materialized from the mist. He stared at his hands. A mosquito landed on his arm. He watched it take its fill but was unable to swat it. The rain became heavier; rivulets of water splashed from the high escarpments into crevices and hollows and creeks, the rain beating hard on the rocks and leaves as it fell over the Cumberland Plateau, from the watershed where the Tug starts down from the hills to the flatlands where Susan once thought she had seen her future.

He saw the lights of a vehicle coming up the mountain road from far away, blurred through the rain. He watched, squatting beside his darkened car. A big yellow bulldozer lumbered into sight and passed by, emergency lights throbbing. It emitted an insistent beeping sound that changed pitch as it climbed the mountain and disappeared over the crest of the road.

At some point, the rain stopped. Mark was cold and his clothes were drenched; he had no idea how much time had passed. With the end of the rain, the sky was full of stars.

It was time to go. Shakily, his muscles aching, he managed to lift Susan's body into the trunk of the rental car. His degradation was total. Laying a hand on her small breast, he said, "Susan, Susan, how did we ever let this happen?"

10

The headlamps probed the fog that lay in the valley where Johns Creek makes its run off the Pikeville side of the mountain toward the Levisa. Mark drove with both hands locked on top of the steering wheel. Ahead the fog reddened with the lights of the Kentucky Carbon Company's Johns Creek loading site, deserted as he passed the tipples and the lines of conveyors descending down the ridge like the monorails of hell. Beyond, at the base of a hill to the west, the trapezoid-shaped cars of a night coal train rolled along the Norfolk and Western spur line.

Mark had decided to go back to his motel and wait. He wasn't sure what he would wait for, but he needed time to consider whether there were any options beyond the single judgment that blared in his mind: *You are done, pal. You are done!*

There was the service revolver, of course. It lay in the motel room drawer where he had left it. He diverted himself for a moment with the idea of putting the barrel in his mouth and pulling the trigger, but it was not a real consideration. He took inventory, standing at the mirror like a suspect in a lineup. He had wrapped a towel around his damaged hand. The index finger throbbed more than the rest of the hand. He figured it was broken. Susan had fought hard, and those long nails were effective: he could see scratches on his arms, and some on his jaw and neck. He certainly looked as if he had been in a fight.

It was almost three o'clock. He took a shower, dressed, walked across the road to the all-night Super American convenience store and bought some Band-Aids and antiseptic. He dressed the cut and got into bed with the light on

Kathy Putnam.

Mark Putnam at his graduation from
the FBI academy.

Pikeville,
Kentucky.

Main
Street,
Pikeville.

Mark Putnam as
a child, with his
father, Walter.

Mark, Kathy, and Danielle.

Susan in her seventh-grade
yearbook.

Susan Smith. (AP/Wide
World Photos)

Barrenshea Hollow in Freeburn, where
Susan grew up.

Mark with Danielle and Mark, Jr., in Florida.

Det. Richard Ray at the site where Susan's body was found.

Commonwealth Attorney John Paul Runyon.

Susan's father, Sid, and her sister, Shelby Ward, at the second burial in 1991. (AP/Wide World Photos)

Mark Putnam at his sentencing in Pikeville, June 1990.
(AP/Wide World Photos)

because he was afraid to turn it out. For the rest of the night, he stayed awake and alert. He couldn't think of anything to do except to go on with the day and see what happened. He had no idea what he would do about the body.

In the morning, he forced himself out of bed, and an hour later he was surprised to find himself in the car, dressed and shaved, his briefcase on the seat beside him, holding it steady at fifty-five on the Mountain Parkway into Lexington. The sun was shining brightly through the dirty windshield. For the first time, he noticed the long crack in the windshield on the passenger side. As he changed lanes, easing to the right on one of those stretches where a car can pass, he thought about Susan in the trunk.

This time, the meeting with the U.S. Attorney was long and detailed. Somehow he got through it. Around lunchtime, Tom Self sat back and asked him what had happened to his hand, and to his amazement, Mark heard himself saying spontaneously, "I was out to our old house in Pikeville taking care of a mess in the garage, and I ripped it on a nail."

He watched Self's reaction carefully, and it didn't show anything other than friendly concern. Was it that easy to lie? As a kid, any time he had told a lie, no matter how inconsequential, his red face had always given him away. Now that he was a killer, had it become easy? Was this what he had never understood about crime until now?

Self kept him occupied all day with the minutiae of the chop-shop case, which Mark now knew by heart. If Self noticed the scratches on Mark's neck, he did not mention them. In fact, Self seemed completely comfortable with him, even at the few points when Mark had to choke back the dry heaves. *He thinks I'm hung over,* Mark decided. He even stopped worrying about the trembling of his hands until lunch at a corner restaurant, when he thought to order a sandwich so he wouldn't have to hold a fork. Self was expansive and optimistic about the trial. Mark realized that people, even those with sharp police instincts, can overlook a lot when their guard is down.

By the time Self turned him loose, it was after four o'clock. Mark still had no plans. From the courthouse steps he spotted his car. The courthouse workers had bolted for theirs at the crack of four, leaving his alone on a side street in the deep shadow of a sycamore.

Off and on during the day, he had wondered about the smell, figuring that if someone noticed and called the cops, that would be it. There would be nothing for him to decide. They'd cuff him and it would be done. But it hadn't happened. He approached the car uneasily, with his nostrils flared. Amazingly, there was no smell yet; the trunk was tight. He dug in a pocket for his keys, thinking, *something is on my side here*. For an instant, he considered opening the trunk and looking inside, to make sure she was still there, but he came to his senses with a quick shudder. Best to drive off, into the hills. He wondered how long his heart could pound like this.

It was not yet seven o'clock when he got back to town. He found himself sitting behind the wheel of the car, engine off, in a parking slot in front of the Pikeville state police barracks, his mind as blank as a man's coming out of a stupor. He had no idea how he'd got there. For a long time he sat, listening to the hum of traffic on the grade below the cut-through. Numbly, he stared at the lighted windows. Inside, a dispatcher would be at the switchboard in front, trying to cope with the phones; there would still be a sergeant and a couple of troopers from the day shift at their desks in back. Someone he knew would be on duty, diddling on the phone. Lt. Paul Maynard, the supervisor of the post's overworked detective squad, usually stayed late. Maynard was a friend. Maynard would hear him out, at least, and maybe he'd have some advice to offer before he had to put the cuffs on.

Mark's head throbbed, but the shock had diminished and he could see things more clearly now. He forced himself to think through the contempt and rage that seeped into his consciousness. *Okay, hotshot, here you are with a body in the trunk. Now what?* Without realizing it, he was mouthing the words, as if addressing himself from nearby. *But nobody caught you yet. Nobody knows yet, asshole. Why not wait and see what happens?* He argued with himself for a while, then started the car and drove off.

He took the four-lane north out of town. A few miles past the strip mall where the K Mart was, just down the road from Marlow Tackett's country-western bar, where he and Kathy had often stopped for a drink, he turned right onto Harmons Branch, a side road that followed the property line of a brick house whose lawn was bordered with a white paddock fence. The car kicked up gravel; a man in shorts pulling weeds in the waning sunlight on his lawn paused to watch him pass. Mark's heart raced; his jaw set, he drove slowly, painfully extending his throbbing right hand along the top of the passenger seat in an effort to look casual. It was a road he and Susan had taken before. If you drove all the way up, past the strip-mine equipment shed, you came to some bungalows set back in the trees from the foot of a high hollow. But he wasn't going that far. He watched in the rearview mirror through the dust until he saw the man go back to his weeds. About a half mile up was the first mine road, now unused, which went up a few hundred yards into the ridge. Beside that was a ravine with a small creek at the bottom, thick with weeds. The car thumped, its bottom scraping the ruts gouged into the road by coal trucks. In this part of eastern Kentucky, once you got off a main road, the terrain was honeycombed with hollows and veins of creeks, mostly dry now that the spring runoff was finished. The area wasn't isolated, but he knew that not many cars used the road, especially at night. He could see some trailers on a clearing a quarter-mile off through the trees, across a hollow that had another road in and out.

When he turned in to the spot he knew and stopped the car, he could hear the brittle noise of dirt bikes, kids racing up and down in the soft dirt on one of the mine roads. He couldn't see them, but they were not far away. He rolled down the window and felt the breeze of the late-spring night. This was where he would put her, at the edge of a ravine thick with brush and saplings. This, he figured, was where she would be found.

The body was heavy. His arms trembled; it was impossible to be gentle. He lugged her out, listening for the sound of an approaching vehicle, hearing nothing but the wind in the trees and the croak of the bullfrogs and the incessant whine of the dirt bikes. Using his legs for leverage, he dragged the body a little way down the ravine, just out of sight from the road. The slope was steep, and bristles scraped his arms as he struggled clumsily. His feet got tangled in roots; he stumbled and fell with a shout. He began to cry. Then, getting a better hold under her arms, he pulled her down the hill as far as he could. They were about fifteen feet below the roadbed now, and this is where she would stay, barely concealed, like his guilt. Kneeling beside the body, his weight on his knees against stiff bushes like a prayer stool, he cried, stroking her face, and said, "I'm sorry." Carefully, he removed the clothes, tugging the T-shirt off. His shorts, thirty-two-inch waist, slid off easily. Susan never wore underwear in warm weather. He did not think about whether she looked pregnant. She was barefoot; the sandals had come off in the trunk. He gathered the clothes under his arm and left her behind in the branches and leaves.

When he struggled up to the top of the ravine, he found himself looking into the eyes of a dark-haired young woman astride a chestnut quarter horse. She stared implacably, with just a hint of a raised eyebrow, at the good-looking young man climbing up from the bushes.

Mark was stunned, but he thought fast enough to tug at his fly, flash a boyish grin, and say, "Nature."

The woman kicked her spurs and trotted off.

It rained again that night. Great muddy sheets of water lashed at the hills. Holed up in his motel, Mark managed to call his wife and children, though he could not remember what he said to them. Afterward, he was very hungry. He got himself together to drive out in the rain to the Log Cabin, on Route 23, where he ate a steak and drank a beer.

It was here that he had his first real scare.

Myra Chico, the local radio reporter, had a part-time job tending bar there on weekend nights. Mark had known her for years and had even tried to recruit her for the FBI. He and Poole had arranged an interview for her at the bureau office in Lexington, where the supervisors had liked her well enough to invite her to apply. But she decided she couldn't leave Pikeville.

She came by his table and said that she had to talk to him. "It's very important, Mark. Can you meet me after work? I've got to talk to you about Susan."

The beer and food had worked on him, and he was dead tired. He studied her pleasant expression and asked, "What time do you get off?"

"A half hour. Come on over to my place for some coffee."

He followed her home in his car, anxious and miserable, but strangely glad for the company.

He wanted a glass of 7-Up, not coffee, and when she had brought it, they sat cross-legged on either end of her couch and talked.

"What about Susan?" he asked tentatively.

"Do you know where she is?"

"No. Why?"

"Ron Poole told me she left the Landmark sometime yesterday and didn't go home."

"You know Susan."

"Listen, you got a problem, do you know that?"

He waited.

"She's pregnant. Ron showed me the test. He says you know."

"She told me."

"She says you're the father."

"Ron tell you that, too?"

"She's telling everybody you're the father."

"You believe it?"

"No."

"I never touched her."

"Ron asked me to ask you—he wants to stay out of it—where Susan went to."

"I don't know where Susan is."

Myra had no reason not to believe him, and none even to question him. They talked about other things. He seemed very tired, a little emotional, perhaps. She figured it was the strain. As a friend, she understood.

The motel was as quiet as a dormitory settled down for the night. At the front desk, a groggy clerk said that there were no messages and didn't seem to wonder why anybody would want to know at that hour. Mark's room had been made up, but wasn't otherwise disturbed. It smelled faintly of disinfectant and cheap soap. He fell into bed, exhausted enough at least to try to sleep.

He switched off the lamp and tried to force everything that was bad out of his mind; after a while, with much effort, he succeeded. He remembered when they put Cat Eyes in jail. That had been their best time together, the time he wished he could freeze in place forever. God, it had seemed as clever as a spring caper. Who would have thought it would graft Susan onto his life? When they taught you about informants in the academy, they didn't explain that you bought not only a piece of their time, but a part of their history, too. He hadn't understood that in order to renounce her past, Susan had found it necessary to affirm a future with him.

You made me a hero, Susan.

But not without a price, of course. The frantic phone calls at home at night, as if her problems were now immutably his: "Mark, would you come and get me out of here please? Kenneth beat me up. Could you put me up someplace?"

The bad thoughts rushed back. He turned the light on to wait out the rest of the night.

The next thing he knew, it was after nine o'clock. He awoke in a nauseous sweat with the bedsheet knotted around his feet. He hurried down to get a Lexington newspaper out of the box by the service elevator. On his way, he pushed the plastic bag holding Susan's clothes into a trash receptacle. He scanned the headlines as he walked back to the room. There was nothing. Not today.

Numbly, he pressed on with his work. A subpoena in the chop-shop case had to be delivered to a man out in Magoffin County, which took a good part of the day. When he got back into town, it was late afternoon and he had begun to think more clearly. The condition of the car was on his mind. He went to a service station on Route 23 and in the car-wash area vacuumed the interior of the Ford. He found an earring on the floor and fed it into the vacuum hose. Using a bottle of kitchen cleaner he had bought, he carefully washed his bloodstains from the dashboard and console. He bent down to look at the rubber floor mat on the passenger side and noticed what looked like dried mucus. He was afraid to throw out the mat in the gas station, where he could be clearly seen.

Kathy had told him to make sure he stopped by the house on Cedar Creek to check things over. As he'd told Self, the garage needed straightening. On his way over, he dropped the floor mat out of the car into a trash-strewn ditch beside the high school track where he used to run after work.

At the house, he ran into a neighbor, Cecilia Fish, who had noticed the car in the drive and wandered over. She looked at his cut hand. He had lost the bandage and it had begun to bleed again. He explained that he had ripped it on a nail, and she gave him a new bandage.

The next day, having cleaned the car, he got rid of it. He drove back up to the Huntington airport a hundred miles away and said that the windshield had been cracked by a chunk of coal falling off a speeding coal truck. They gave him another Ford Tempo without any problem.

Coming back, he wondered why he hadn't heard from Poole. Usually, Poole was as alert as a burglar when it came to Susan and Mark. He had to know she wasn't in the motel, and he'd probably already called Shelby looking for her.

But Poole did not call. That night, Mark fell asleep while talking to Kathy on the phone.

On Monday, three days after he'd left Susan's body in the ravine, Mark took another decisive step. He made a phone call to Shelby Jean Ward in Freeburn and asked, calmly and deliberately, whether she had heard from Susan.

"No, I haven't heard, and I'm worried. It ain't like her," Shelby said tentatively, not wanting to show any courtesy to a man she believed had used her sister, gotten her pregnant, and abandoned her. Shelby thought that Mark Putnam had monumental nerve expressing concern for Susan at this point. Ron Poole had kept Shelby well posted on Mark's evasiveness.

Mark said, "Listen, I'm worried, too. She told me she was going to meet—"

"Ain't nobody seen her for three days, after she was out to the Landmark," Shelby interrupted coolly.

"I was thinking that if you don't hear from her, you should probably file a missing person's report."

"I know that. I already thought of that. Somebody already told me I should do that."

Mark didn't need to ask who that might be.

After talking to Shelby, Mark called the Pikeville state police and spoke with Paul Maynard. Mark told Maynard that he was worried about Susan. He said she had left the motel on Thursday or Friday and not returned to her sister's house. He made sure to mention that Susan had told him she was planning to meet some of her drug contacts from up north on Saturday, when they came through West Virginia on their way south. He also told Maynard that he had called Shelby and advised her to make a missing person's report. "She thinks something might have happened to her sister."

"Mark," said Maynard, "this girl has a habit of taking off. You know that."

Aware that Poole had already told people about his problem with Susan, Mark anticipated Maynard's next thought. "Well, I've known her pretty well for two and a half years. If you need any help on this, send a couple of the boys over to talk to me."

Shelby also phoned the state police that day. The initial report summarized her call succinctly:

SHELBY WARD of Freeburn, Kentucky, telephoned Post to report that her sister SUSAN SMITH of Freeburn, Kentucky, was missing.

Victim was brought to Pikeville by the FBI and left at the Landmark motel. She arrived on June 5, 1989, and stayed until June 8, 1989, when she left the motel for unknown reasons. She left a few articles of clothing and makeup in the room. Her sister talked to her last about noon on June 8, 1989. FBI agents state that they do not know where she went.

A report of this kind is routine, filed as an alert for possible reference in case an unidentified body is found in a highway wreck or some other mishap. It is not regarded as an indication of a crime. The police assume that an adult is free to disappear if he or she wishes and does not break the law in the process. The standard police procedure is to wait seventy-two hours before initiating an investigation, by which time most missing people either return home, call, or turn up dead.

Susan Smith had done none of those things by the time that period expired. When Det. Richard Ray came to work on Friday morning, he found her missing person's report on his desk. On it was a note from his boss, Lieutenant Maynard, instructing him to get in touch with the woman's sister Shelby Jean Ward and see if anything had turned up.

The detective called Shelby and took down the information quietly and politely, his big fingers thumping at a keyboard to enter into the state and national law enforcement data networks the facts of the missing woman's existence, as stated by her sister: Susan Daniels Smith; white female; twenty-seven years old; short brown hair; five feet five inches tall; 130 pounds; tanned complexion; no occupation. Address, Freeburn, Kentucky, lives with sister, Shelby Ward; missing as of June 8. Sister last saw her wearing white shorts, blue University of Kentucky "Wildcats" T-shirt, gold necklace with gold cross.

Ray looked this information over. He was the kind of detective who notices the wayward rustle of a curtain or the dent on a car even when he is not working, and he detected in Shelby's voice an angry undertone. He asked her a few questions, listening intently to the answers. Then he told her he would be out to see her.

At the age of fifty-four, Richard Ray was the most experienced detective in the Pikeville post, a distinction that gave him more leeway than most other detectives, who complained that they had to get permission for virtually every move they made away from their desks. Understaffed and chronically underfunded in a state where politicians were historically uneasy about having an independent-minded law enforcement network on hand, the Kentucky State Police tended to keep its detectives on a short leash and off-balance. A detective with decades of experience could find himself starting a murder case in the morning, unable to follow up in the afternoon because he was switched to highway patrol—and unable to find an empty desk or a free telephone when he got back to the office.

In Pike County, where the per capita felony statistics always came in near the top among the state's 120 counties, the workload was especially fierce. A detective might handle 130 or more cases a year and report to a boss who had spent most of his career in the driver's license department. As a result, case coverage tended to be, as one detective said, "forty miles wide and one inch deep." In fact, Ray had already decided that he'd had it with the state police. He was planning to put in his retirement papers the next year.

Freeburn was a forty-five-minute drive away, but Ray was glad that he took the time to indulge himself on a hunch. It seemed that the missing woman had enemies. She had worked as an informant and put one local boy in the penitentiary. Yes, she had run off before, but she always called to check on her two small children, who were with their father. He was also interested to hear that the missing woman had been over to the Health Center behind the courthouse a couple of weeks earlier for a pregnancy test—and had named as the father FBI special agent Mark Putnam. The sister evidently hated Putnam, from what Ray could tell, even though she had only spoken to him on the phone. Shelby explained that the other Pikeville FBI man, Ron Poole, had checked Susan into the Landmark motel so that she could confront Putnam with the bad news. And then she had disappeared.

Ray was a taciturn man, with eyes that betrayed no surprise, a man who saw no need to punctuate conversation with anything more than a nod. He took down Shelby's information, thanked her, and said he would be back in touch.

Ray knew Mark Putnam slightly. He thought of him mostly as a typical FBI man who had been taught never to trust the local cops. On the other hand, he had run into him on enough major investigations to regard him, if only grudgingly, as a hard worker who wasn't afraid to get his hands dirty. If he had to sum Putnam up in one word, from what little he knew at that point, the word would have been *overzealous*. But then that was how he would have described himself when he'd first started out as a state cop in Harlan County more than thirty years earlier.

On Monday, Mark was out of town serving a subpoena. The next day, Ray and another state police detective, Kenneth Sloan, found him at the federal building for a pretrial hearing on the case. During lunch break, they borrowed an empty office and spoke informally for about an hour.

Ray gave Mark a copy of the missing persons report. Mark read it quickly and saw that the document had only routine information—vital statistics, the fact that Shelby had last seen Susan in Freeburn on June 5 (that would have been the night before she first came to his room), that her dental and medical records were available, and where. In the space beside the words *Tattoos or Deformities,* he saw that Ray had printed *None* but added, between tactful parentheses, *5 months pregnant.*

Watching him, Ray thought that Mark was nervous but cooperative—a little too cooperative. He was all over the field, and the detective had to scribble fast to get everything down:

> Agent Putnam told me . . . he knew Susan Smith and that she was a witness against Carl "Cat Eyes" Lockhart in the bank robbery trial. He said that Lockhart's girlfriend, Sherri Justice, had beaten up Susan while Susan's brother watched. Putnam said that he had talked to Susan's husband, Kenneth Smith, about being an informant against Lockhart. He said that Kenneth demanded money and probation on a drug charge and he would not deal with him. Susan had been paid money for being a witness. Putnam said that Kenneth came for Susan's $200 one day and he ran him off as Susan had said not to give it to Kenneth. Susan was paid about $9,000 for being a witness and an informant.

According to Ray's report, Mark told him that "Kenneth would call me and complain about how we used Susan. Kenneth called my wife and told her I was fucking Susan. Susan talked to my wife and denied it. Susan was trying to help Agent Ron Poole with some drug buys."

Mark described to the two state detectives Susan's dependency on him and Kathy. He said that the last significant work Susan had done for him was in the fall, but that they had stayed in touch afterward and had spoken on the telephone a few times after he went to Florida.

Mark also told the detective that he had spoken with Susan at the Landmark several times during the week before she disappeared—once in his room—about "her problems." He said they discussed the possibility of her having an abortion, and that he had offered to help her find the money for it. She did not want to have an abortion, Mark said.

He said that the last time he spoke with Susan was about ten-thirty on Wednesday night when she phoned his room after he got back from his meeting in Lexington and asked him to join her in the lounge for a drink. He told her he was too tired and had to be up early. She then told him about a "strange phone call" she had received about a meeting in West Virginia in a few days with drug contacts, "some guys from Chicago, the amigos," she called them. She described one as a "Spanish cop" from Cicero. Mark said that she declined his offer to follow her to the meeting "in case of trouble."

Why was Susan at the motel in the first place? Mark told the detectives that Poole brought her there "to do some undercover work" for him.

Did Mark know she was pregnant? He knew she was saying so, he said, because she had told him herself just before he transferred to Florida. Had she told him that he was the father? No, he replied. Furthermore, he wondered if Susan really was pregnant, since she didn't appear to be showing. "I tried to feel her stomach at the motel, but she jumped away," he said. Did she ever tell him who the father was? "No," said Mark. "She wouldn't tell me."

So he hadn't seen her after the Wednesday-night phone call? No, Mark said. Charlie Trotter told him that Susan had checked out of the motel at the end of the week. He hadn't heard from her since, although he knew that Ron Poole was making inquiries, trying to find her. Mark offered to do whatever he could to help.

Mark sensed Ray's antagonism, but that was nothing especially remarkable. The detective had always been cool toward him, and Mark guessed that Shelby had amply filled Ray in on Susan's claims about their relationship.

Trying to be helpful, Mark described his whereabouts not only on the night Susan left the motel but on the following night, Friday, when he said he had gone to the movies.

"What did you see?" Ray asked with casual interest.

With equal casualness, Mark replied, "Something called *Road House* or *Rock House,* something like that. Patrick Swayze was in it."

When Ray made a few more notes at the end of their conversation, Mark cast a quick glance and saw that the detective had jotted down the name of the movie.

The conversation with Putnam gave Detective Ray a lot to consider, not the least of which was the extent to which Susan had been dependent on the largess of the FBI. Everybody in Pike County knew that the FBI had money to pay for information, but Ray was surprised to hear Mark confirm that Susan had received at least $9,000. In fact, he was disgusted. Here was the FBI man—with a salary roughly equivalent to a state police captain's—peeling off big bills to coddle informants while he, a state police detective often working the same cases, had to go hat in hand to his boss for permission to put a couple of hundred extra miles a week on his police vehicle, even when he was working the extra hours on his own time.

For his part, Mark was puzzled by what he regarded as diffident questioning on the part of the detectives. He fretted over the encounter, unable to decide what he would have done if they had asked him directly, "Did you have anything to do with this girl's disappearance?"

He thought that his answer might have been, "Yes."

What if they had then asked, "Did you kill her?" He tried to be honest with himself, but his mind was swimming with thoughts of guilt and survival. Before he fell into a feverish sleep, he decided that his answer, then and there, might have been, "Yes; yes, I did." But perhaps he was deceiving himself. At any rate, they hadn't asked.

Mark flew back to Florida a few days later. Then a coal-mine strike in Pike County turned violent, with gunshots fired at trucks, and Ray was barely able to keep track of the Susan Smith case. On June 23, he managed to get a few hours free to sit down with Ron Poole at a sandwich shop on Main Street. Curiously, Poole claimed that he had been concerned about Susan's assertions that she felt threatened by both her ex-husband and outlaws in the Tug Valley, vowing retribution for her work as an informant, and had thought that registering her at the Landmark would be a good way to look after her. But he said that his main reason for putting her in the motel was to give her and his ex-partner the opportunity to discuss this business about her being pregnant. Poole said he had hoped they could "work this out," because, frankly, he was "tired of hearing about it" in Pikeville from Susan while Mark enjoyed the good life in Florida.

Poole, too, seemed to be excessively helpful. He even suggested that Mark would come back to Pikeville to take a polygraph test "whenever we need him to." That struck the detective as a fine idea.

After his brief conversation with Poole, Ray studied his notes. It was possible that the two agents simply saw the situation differently, and of course there was the sensitive matter of the pregnancy and the bureau's well-known proclivity for protecting its ass, not to mention the ill-defined undercover operation that Susan was apparently talking about to everybody she knew. Local cops never expected to hear the full story from the FBI. Maybe they had stashed her in the witness protection program, although Ray couldn't imagine that this particular source had information momentous enough to earn that kind of treatment. What's more, Poole had denied it.

Another complication was Susan's reputation. Even Shelby, worried as she plainly was, conceded that Susan was a loose cannon, a woman who had run off in the past without telling anyone where she was going.

Yet Ray couldn't put out of his mind how effusively helpful Putnam had been in providing details of his activities. *Too many details.* He wondered if he would have the time to see which of them didn't check out.

Ray found the maid who had worked the second floor of the Landmark that week. She told him that the woman in

Room 224 had kept mostly to her room, watching television all day with the door bolted. She had not seen her with anyone. Her checkout bill, which Poole had paid with his American Express card, showed that she ordered room service and ate in her room. Nothing extravagant—$9 one day, $10 another—certainly nothing to indicate that she was entertaining visitors. There were a couple of short local calls, and three long-distance calls to her sister in Freeburn, two of them on the morning she disappeared, just as the sister had said. The maid had collected a few of Susan's clothes, her purse, and some makeup that she had left behind and taken them down to the lobby. The fat FBI man took them with him when he paid the bill, which came to $251.46.

Ray finally raised his concerns with his superiors in July, nagged by the worry that he was missing something obvious, and frustrated by his inability to spend any time on the case. He was convinced it was time to formally question Putnam with regard to what he knew about Susan's disappearance. But he was told that there were probably better things he could be doing with his time as an investigator. Putnam had long since left town; there would be no state-police junkets authorized to Miami, of all places, not without a good goddamned reason. Besides, wasn't the bureau itself looking into it? Wasn't Poole making his own investigation? Why waste time on a routine missing person case?

The girl was wild, Ray was told again and again when he asked questions out on Peter Creek. So what if an FBI agent or two had screwed her? Hadn't she run away before? Hadn't she always turned up? And if she was double-crossing a drug operation, she'd turn up for sure—in the morgue in Cincinnati or Chicago.

Yes, he thought. That much was probably true.

By August, she still hadn't turned up. But Ray still had only speculation, innuendo, and instinct to go on. If there had been any sort of unpleasant confrontation between the missing woman and either of the FBI men, he could find no one at the Landmark who knew about it. No one had seen Susan and Putnam together on either the day she disappeared or the day before; moreover, Charlie Trotter and another man staying at the motel who talked to Putnam that week said that Mark had made it clear he was doing everything he could to avoid her. Reasonable enough, Ray thought, since she was accusing him of getting her pregnant and running off. Furthermore, if they *did* have a confrontation—and from what Shelby had said, Susan was looking for one—Ray had found no one who saw or heard it.

The complications troubled him. He tried to separate what little he actually knew from the nagging suspicion that something was very wrong. A poor mountain girl who has been on the FBI payroll as an informant—something near $10,000, maybe more—turns up missing. From the way it looks, she and this FBI man were involved; she gets knocked up, he's gone to Florida with the wife and kids. He comes back to town on government business, the FBI sets her up in the same motel. *The FBI sets her up in the same motel with this guy who doesn't have any further government business with her?* And she turns up missing.

But the FBI man isn't the only one this girl has been involved with. To hear people tell it, she gets around pretty good. She is also a wildcat who fights at the drop of a hat, and just before her disappearance, she gets coldcocked by the girlfriend of the bank robber that she sent to the penitentiary. She turns up missing.

Furthermore, he thought, this is a girl messed up bad on drugs, whose ex-husband beats her up, not to mention the other enemies she has obviously made, being an informant out on Peter Creek where mountain people tend to frown on such things. Besides that, she has been known to run with a bad crowd out of Cincinnati and Chicago in the past and has supposedly been in contact with some of that crowd recently. And her sister Shelby Jean, who has had her own run-ins with Susan, and who is nervous about her working as an informant, takes a phone message for the girl while she's in the Pikeville motel at the FBI's expense. The message is that she is supposed to meet some drug dealers on Saturday at a rendezvous in West Virginia. On Friday, she turns up missing.

Assuming something bad happened to her, Ray thought, that made for a fair number of suspects. Even in normal circumstances, the first suspect was always the husband or ex-husband or boyfriend. And here was an ex-husband who abused her and whom she keeps going back to. That made one prime suspect. Then there were the drug dealers she was supposedly going to see. Add the bank robber's girlfriend, the bank robber's buddies, any *other* outlaws she'd informed on—not to mention Poole, the sister herself, and maybe even some still-unidentified pillar of the Pikeville community whom she'd tried to shake down in a motel. Hell, even without Putnam, that was already a regular damn Las Vegas chorus line of star suspects—assuming she hadn't just run away.

And Ray had to assume first that she had, in fact, merely left town on her own. What Ray couldn't quite understand was why, given that, given all of the other likely suspects if foul play was actually the case, the earnest, well-chiseled face of Mark Putnam stayed in his mind as if it were painted there.

Besides his bosses at the state police post, the only other person Ray confided his suspicions to was Myra Chico, who was friends with most of the cops in town. One night when Myra was tending bar at the Log Cabin, they were talking about Susan Smith's disappearance, and Ray surprised her by saying, "I think Mark Putnam had something to do with it."

Myra laughed and said, "Richard, you're nuts!"

Ray didn't often say things twice. He shrugged and changed the subject.

11

The change from Pikeville to Miami had been abrupt. Overnight they'd traded the black and gray of an Appalachian late winter for the sudden Technicolor blare of southern Florida in spring.

"Daddy, you can see the sky all over," Danielle had exclaimed with childish delight from beside the pool of the residence hotel where the bureau had installed them while they looked for a new house. At four, she was already learning to read and write. Mark Jr., at sixteen months beginning to exhibit his father's dark good looks, showed his appreciation for the improvement in scenery in a way that reminded Kathy of her husband—he'd simply hurl himself onto the thick rich grass beside the pool and roll around in it like a pooch freed from its kennel.

Kathy felt like a woman awakening from a trance. She thought of the joke about pounding your head against the wall because it feels so good when you stop. At once, she was renewed; she felt young again, not haggard and ashen as she had been in the last months in Kentucky. The troubles in Pikeville swirled out of mind.

Only the phone calls intruded, and these she accepted with the mild annoyance of someone fending off telephone sales solicitations. Soon after they left, whenever Susan called for Mark, as she did several times a week, Kathy exchanged a few arm's-length pleasantries, handed the phone to Mark, and walked away to do other things.

There was plenty to do. It fell largely to her to settle her family into a new home, a task that she threw herself into with verve. Mark had a new job to acclimate himself to, and old business in Kentucky to finish. She figured that after the chop-shop trial, Pikeville and all that went with it, not the least of which was Susan, would be history, to be filed away with her old calendars.

For the first time, she felt like part of the "FBI family" that she had read about in orientation brochures from the academy. Mark finally had bosses, colleagues, and a support system at work. With help from the bureau's relocation office, she quickly found a house, a three-bedroom condominium in a new subdivision beside a canal. The town, Sunrise, lay at the western edge of the coastal sprawl, on the fringes of the Everglades, but still only a forty-five-minute commute from the FBI office in North Miami Beach.

And then, in June, the phone calls from Susan had stopped. With so much emotional and physical distance between them, Kathy accepted the news of her disappearance impassively. She had done her best with Susan, who never listened. If Susan had taken off for Chicago or Cincinnati, as Kathy assumed she had, the futility of what she had tried to do was another unpleasant memory to forget about and write off to experience.

So eager was she to embrace a new life that Kathy failed to calculate the emotional distance that still separated her from Mark. He was the more sensitive, introspective one, and the one who had shouldered most of the burden; she figured he required more time to rejuvenate than she did. In her elation, she discounted a number of signs that her husband was deeply troubled in the summer of 1989. He wasn't sleeping or eating normally. Sometimes she would wake in the night aware that he lay beside her motionless and alert. He was losing weight, and he had developed a nervous habit of scratching at his chest, to the point where a raw patch of skin appeared on his sternum.

These symptoms she attributed partly to Mark's anxiety about establishing himself in a new job in a competitive and hierarchical work environment. And the echoes from Pikeville hadn't totally ceased with the end of Susan's calls. Poole still checked in, usually with word that nothing had been heard of Susan. Myra Chico also called from time to time to pass on Pikeville gossip, but Kathy made it clear to Mark that she had little interest in it.

One night in the summer, after speaking with Poole, Mark abruptly mentioned to Kathy that Susan had been saying that she was pregnant right before she disappeared. "So who's the father?" Kathy said with a trace of sarcasm. Mark shrugged his shoulders.

She found his diffidence irritating. "When are you going to put that behind you?" she demanded. "Forget about Susan. She isn't your problem anymore."

"How can I?" he said almost plaintively.

"Look, if she's still missing, the next thing you know, Mark, you could be pulled into this. She could be lying dead somewhere."

His face darkened and he replied quietly, without meeting her eyes, "Don't ever say that."

Kathy believed that, Mark's sluggish recovery aside, they had settled in happily. The cost of living in south Florida was higher than Kentucky; with Mark earning $33,000 a year, a little more with overtime, they had to make the money stretch, which Kathy always knew how to do. To put a little aside for their next summer vacation, she took a part-time job on Saturday and Sunday mornings, waiting tables at an International House of Pancakes near Fort Lauderdale. One of the waitresses she met there was a woman with two children and a husband in prison. When Kathy told Mark how sorry she felt for her, he looked away and changed the subject.

For Mark, there were many such moments as he contemplated the calamity that he knew lay ahead. In retrospect, he would wonder how he managed to fool anybody during that time as he waited for what he knew was the inevitable moment when he would either be caught or give up. "My insides were frazzled," he recalled.

Outwardly, he projected a sense of purpose. It helped that the work in the Miami bureau was nearly as fast-paced as it

had been in Pikeville, with the huge difference that he was
not off on his own. The new environment offered both the
collegiality of a large group of fellow cops and the reassurance, at least in those unguarded moments when he focused
on the job and not on his secret, of being adequately supervised. For once, Mark felt he didn't have to make it up as
he went along. He appreciated his circumstances with a
sense of poignancy, aware that they would last only until he
was exposed.

Nevertheless, he impressed his bosses. Without excep-
tion, his supervisors in Miami regarded him as likable, tal-
ented, and extraordinarily hardworking. In many ways, with
his steady demeanor, polished manners, physical bravery,
and good looks, Mark represented the FBI's image of itself,
and in retrospect, it would help to explain why the bureau
would be almost the last to believe the worst about him. In
Miami, it was obvious to everyone except Mark himself that
the young agent had a bright future in the FBI.

At several times during the year Mark believed his time was
up.

Not long after he got back from Pikeville, on July 5, the
day after his thirtieth birthday, he was summoned to the
office of the top man in the Miami bureau, the special agent
in charge, William Gavin. But instead of arresting him,
Gavin slid a memo across the desk from Louis DeFalaise,
the U.S. Attorney for eastern Kentucky. It read in part:

> I want to formally express to you our thanks and
> appreciation for the work and assistance of Special
> Agent Mark Putnam of your Miami office. Special
> Agent Putnam, prior to assignment to your office, was
> in the Federal Bureau of Investigation office in
> Pikeville, Kentucky. While that was his first office
> assignment, you would not know it.
>
> While he was there only two years, his reputation
> for hard and diligent work left its mark in the area.

Our office had the pleasure of working closely with him during his tenure and I can say confidently that he is a unique Special Agent whose career with the bureau will be long and fruitful.

I want to specifically call your attention to the excellent job he just completed leading up to the successful conviction of seven defendants in the case of *U.S. v. Vernon Andrew Mullins et al.* . . . Special Agent Putnam was involved from its inception in the investigation of a multistate ''chop-shop'' operation centered in a remote section of eastern Kentucky. Following the execution of a state search warrant which uncovered the remains of millions of dollars of trucks and truck parts, Mark worked with one of our assistants in identifying the vehicles, tracking down the owners and ownership documents and preparing the case for trial. As stated, all seven defendants were convicted on a thirty-eight-count indictment. . . . Special Agent Putnam's in-depth knowledge of the case was primarily responsible for the government being successful in its case. He worked long hours and weekends assisting our office in preparing and presenting this case. Without his hard work and dedication, the result would not have been so satisfactory.

Special Agent Putnam's departure has left a real void which will be hard to replace. You have gained a topflight agent in Miami in Mark Putnam, one who exemplifies the dedication and professionalism of a fine Special Agent. Please convey to him our devout appreciation for his service to eastern Kentucky and to our office.

Not long afterward, in August, Mark had another scare when he answered his beeper on the street and got a message to contact his supervisor immediately.

Feeling sick, he found a pay phone and called the office. But his immediate supervisor, an agent named Roy Tubergen, came on the line laughing. "Hey, you know two good old boys named Hatfield and McCoy?"

"Yeah, I know them."

"That really their names?"

Mark sighed with great relief. "Yeah. Like the feud. Why? What did they do?"

"Well, they stopped by here to see you. I'll tell them you're on your way in."

Paul Hatfield and Fred McCoy, eyes wide with sleeplessness, had driven all night to get to Florida. For months, they'd been working together to expose corruption in the Pike County sheriff's office. As part of their investigation, they had spent days at work wearing hidden recorders, taping literally everything that was said. For good measure, they had also videotaped each other reading long statements about county funds being misused to buy campaign hats and badges.

In Pikeville, with their evidence stacked up like the Watergate transcripts, they had called a press conference to denounce the sheriff's department as "a small Mafia" and the sheriff himself, a man named Fuzzee Kessee, as "the godfather." A few days later, Hatfield and McCoy were summarily fired. Announcing that they feared for their lives, the two then boxed up their tapes and drove straight through to Miami, where they had never been before.

"You're the only one we can trust with this material, Mark," said Hatfield, pulling at a long beard.

"Wait a minute," Mark said, not wanting even temporary custody of their cache of evidence. "I don't have responsibility for that stuff anymore!"

While they waited, their eyes darting anxiously around the bustling Miami FBI office, Mark called Tom Self in Lexington to ask for advice.

"Tom, you're not going to believe this. Paul Hatfield and Fred McCoy—"

"Tell me they're not down there," Self groaned.

"They're here. With a suitcase full of tapes that I don't want to listen to and I don't even want to touch."

Self told him to send the material to Lexington.

Hatfield and McCoy drove back home immediately to follow up.

Mark's fellow agents hooted and razzed him about the episode, and the following day, when he came in to work, one of them had on a big straw hat with a corncob pipe between his teeth. Mark chuckled in a good-natured way, but it bothered him. He had worked hard to fit in in eastern Kentucky, and he had succeeded. Hatfield and McCoy and the others were more than caricatures to him; even *hillbilly* had an ugly sting to it, like *dago* or *spic*.

In September, Mark and a colleague from Miami were sent to New York City for a few days to trade information on an undercover case with agents in the Manhattan office. After going to a Yankees game with a group of agents after work one night, Mark returned to his hotel and found an urgent message to call Lou DeFalaise at home "no matter what the time." Figuring that this was it, with a shaking finger Mark tapped out the phone number for the U.S. Attorney in eastern Kentucky. As he heard the phone ringing, he steeled himself. *It's all over. He wants to tell me as a courtesy that I'm about to be arrested.*

DaFalaise was plainly agitated. "Mark, what the hell is going on? All hell is breaking loose here."

Mark felt tears well in his eyes, until he realized that the federal prosecutor wasn't talking about Susan Smith. He was talking about Hatfield and McCoy, who had called another press conference—this time to accuse the U.S. Attorney's office of covering up their investigation.

Still shaking, Mark gave DeFalaise his assessment of the situation, which was that as diligent as Hatfield and McCoy were in tape-recording everything spoken, they really didn't have a case. And authorities apparently concurred because no action was taken against the sheriff. DeFalaise thanked him cordially. Mark put the phone down and slumped in his chair.

*   *   *

While there was a new camaraderie in Mark's work life, there were no close friendships. He declined invitations to dinner, cookouts, and drinks after work. He was afraid to make friends. His time was running out, and he did not want to embarrass any other agent who might have the misfortune to be close to him when the end came. As a consequence, some of his new colleagues in Miami saw him as aloof. To others, he was quiet, diligent, careful, and dependable—a good team player, a man who could be trusted in all circumstances, but still, a hard man to get to know.

One of the agents who worked with him on a five-person undercover operation against a ring of property thieves tried to get close and failed. In fact, Mark liked this agent enormously—for his honesty, tenacity, and sense of humor. On several occasions, most notably on an all-night surveillance job when he relaxed enough to regale his companion with stories of Kentucky law and order, Mark had to restrain the impulse to confide in him about Susan. Bitterly, he withdrew from the incipient friendship, thinking, *Can I put him in that position, being a friend to the guy who's about to be a pariah? Do I even have the right to have a friend?*

The year was full of painful irony. Once, he and Kathy invited a young agent from the office who was having personal difficulties to dinner at their house. Warmed by the glow of affection and security he had felt in the Putnam household, unaware of just how fragile it was, the agent told everybody he saw in the office the next day what a wonderful time he'd had.

"This guy has everything—a beautiful wife, good looks, two beautiful kids, a great job," he told a group of colleagues, clapping a hand on Mark's shoulder when he came by. "What more could a man want?"

Mark's heart sank. "Everybody has their problems, John," he said, smiling wanly.

If only they knew, he thought. He had lost fifteen pounds since the summer. Nearly every day he had diarrhea. Nights were worse. He was afraid to go to sleep. He did not know if or when he would confess. He always assumed they would find Susan and arrest him, and he was bewildered that so much time was passing without any indication that an end was in sight. Again and again, he replayed the scenario until he was convinced that he believed it. They would come to him and ask, *"Did you do this?"* In his mind, he always gave them the same reply, without hesitation: "Yes."

In the winter of 1990, Kathy's younger sister, Chris, who had been living near Miami, came to stay with the Putnams temporarily while she was going through a divorce. Chris, as easygoing and laconic as Kathy was intense and expressive, admired Mark very much. He had helped her to find a job as an officer with the Florida Marine Patrol. She regarded him as an ideal husband and father who had become almost a big brother to her. When she'd visited Mark and Kathy in Pikeville, she had known that their life was difficult and stressful. In Florida, she didn't notice anything alarming about the way Mark was behaving.

As she later recalled, "Mark was kind of hyper anyway, not in an odd sense, but just a real active guy. He ran every night without fail. If he was watching television, he was also reading a book at the same time. When he and my sister first got together, he always had two jobs. All the time I knew him, he was always working. The only thing unusual in Florida was he had developed this nervous habit, this scratching at his chest. I thought he was like anxious to get back to work."

One other thing she noticed was that he bought several newspapers a day and flipped through them methodically, as if looking for something small—always first checking the pages that had state-by-state news items in *USA Today*.

"Why's he read all those papers?" Chris asked Kathy once with a laugh. "Don't they all have the same news in them?"

Passing time burnished Mark's nerve. He wondered how long he could wait. He still heard from Poole often, but Poole had his own anxieties about Susan, who had told people that she slept with him, too. Baffled as to what had happened to Susan, perhaps suspecting that Mark knew more than he let on, Poole told Mark of Richard Ray's request, unsuccessful so far, that the two of them be given polygraph tests.

"Ron, I don't care," Mark said boldly. "I'll take their polygraph."

Poole replied, "I'll take one, too. I don't give a shit what these hillbillies do." And he added, "Well, buddy, you and I got to stick together on this thing."

What thing? Mark thought contemptuously. What did his ex-partner feel he had to hide? It was almost amusing to think that Poole was worried. For the first time, Mark felt that he had the advantage in these verbal jousts. If Susan turned up dead, whose problem was it going to be?

Still, Mark resisted the urge to probe for information on the investigation that he knew was going on in Pikeville. He did not know much about it and didn't ask, preferring to be seen not as disinterested but as disengaged. With Myra Chico he remained circumspect, afraid that if he gave any indication that he was worried, that anxiety would be conveyed to the state police.

Had they found the body? That was the main thing he didn't know. Stubbornly, he didn't ask. Still, how could it *not* have been found, lying there just out of sight in a place where people came by on horses and trucks, where kids ran their dirt bikes up and down the ridge? Maybe they had found the body and were keeping it quiet, building their case. Every time the phone rang, he jumped.

He did not expect any respite from the obsession. Susan was the first thing he thought of every day: she flashed into his mind as if a switch were thrown the moment he awoke, and she stayed there until he managed to fall asleep at night. To live with himself, he had settled on a term to describe what had happened, as if supplying the kicker to a headline: *tragic accident.*

There were frequent reminders of what he had already

lost. The most painful came when Tubergen took him aside one afternoon to ask if he would consider a transfer to a smaller office elsewhere in Florida, where he would be promoted to a supervisory rank. It was an invitation onto the management track. But what would have been fabulous news to the man who had dreamed about a career in the FBI since high school now had a bitter sting. Mark mentioned the overture to Kathy, but told her that he had turned it down because they had just gotten settled and the kids were thriving in their new home. He said he didn't want to see his family uprooted again so soon. In his mind, he knew that he was protecting the bureau from the further public disgrace of having a supervisor led away in cuffs.

While he waited for time to pass, he thought often of the father he had revered. The man had exuded dignity, even during a tragic and prolonged death from cancer in middle age. In a way that he could not quite articulate, Mark had believed it was his responsibility to ratify his father's memory. But, instead, as he had always secretly feared he would, he had disgraced it forever.

There had been times during the year when he had edged toward confession and pulled back. As early as September, he had told Tubergen about the rumors in Kentucky that he had been sexually involved with an informant who was now listed as missing. Mark asked Tubergen if he would contact OPR, the Office of Professional Responsibility, the Justice Department's internal affairs unit with supervision over the FBI, and request them to investigate the disappearance of Susan Smith to "clear up" the ambiguities associated with his relationship to the missing woman.

Literally, he was told not to make a federal case out of it. A missing person case was a state police matter. The rumors had already filtered down to Miami through the FBI grapevine, where discreet inquiries had been made to assure supervisors that Susan Smith was the sort of woman who ran with a dangerous crowd and had gone off before. Mark was seen as naïve and excessively punctilious, a young man who had been through a tough tour of duty in a rough place and had acquitted himself with honor and distinction, even if he had stupidly become involved with an informant. He was a man above suspicion.

Besides, Mark was told, he was due for a promotion in grade, which would mean a higher salary. An open OPR investigation, no matter how pro forma, would put that on hold.

Once, while leaving for work, Mark looked up to see his daughter gazing at him from her bedroom window. She met his eyes and held them in her gaze, and he thought then that she knew something was very wrong.

He thought, *How can I face her day after day, year after year, knowing what I know? What kind of a father can I be to her?*

Sometimes, he would pretend that it had not happened. He would place himself ten or fifteen years into the future. He would still be in Florida, a good, solid, low-profile agent who knew all the ropes. He would be at his desk reading a case file, the family portrait propped beside the phone. Danielle, a young woman now, as pretty and smart as her mother, would pop in unexpectedly to ask him to lunch as his colleagues watched with envy.

Or he'd spend the day with little Mark, an adolescent now, allowing him to play hooky from high school on the opening day of spring training. In the bleachers, they would feel the hot sun on their necks as they argued about the new crop of pitchers.

Or he thought of himself with Kathy, middle-aged and still in love, strolling south Miami Beach. In a gentle ocean breeze they would hold hands and look at the lights strung along the low-roofed art deco hotels on the strand. He would guide her body toward his. They'd mold perfectly, as they always had. Their lips would meet, their tongues touch. He'd feel her breasts against his chest. She'd arch her long back slightly in his arms as they looked for a deserted place on the beach.

Relentlessly, he supervised these three daydreams like a movie director who is never satisfied with the take. Again and again he replayed the same scenes in his head, varying the nuance and inflection, as if he needed to get them perfect before fixing them in his mind.

Running was a way to pass through time without thinking. For a while, he hadn't been able to do even that. "When I got back to Florida after Susan's death, I stopped running for a while," Mark would later recall. "I was afraid to go out, to be alone. Especially at night. I was even afraid of a dark room."

In time, he forced himself to overcome his fear and go out to run every night. The wind blew away everything but the churning of the legs, the pumping of the arms and lungs. His regular nightly route took him along a remote stretch of road, beyond a canal at the edge of swampland. On that stretch one night, he tripped and fell. Scraped and bruised, he sat on the ground, arms clenching his knees, and cried.

"The day of reckoning is coming, Susan," he said aloud to the black sky. "It is. I promise."

By the winter, he reached the point where he realized his guilt was diminishing his effectiveness as an agent.

He had been investigating a major organized theft ring operating out of the Port of Miami, a bazaar of criminal activity. Laboriously working informants and poring over insurance records, he made inroads until finally he had a suspect in a major insurance-fraud case, a businessman named Tito who was as arrogant as he was crafty. If he broke, Tito would lead to bigger fish, Mark knew.

Mark stopped at Tito's computer-parts business in Miami one day and told him, "Listen, pal, I'm on to your sorry ass, and I'm going to see you again."

"No problem," Tito said in his singsong voice.

Finally Mark had enough evidence to nail the man, who was just arrogant enough to try to bluff his way through a polygraph and take questions afterward.

"Listen, I've got you by the short hairs on this thing,

man,'' Mark said as they sat alone at a conference table in the office. ''I've got documents here, with your fingerprints on the documents. You took a lie detector test and flunked it. That's not admissible, I'll give you that, but it's important because it confirms to me that you are lying. The people who receive my report will know that you did it, and continuing to lie to me will only make it worse.''

Insulted, Tito insisted that he had not lied. The machine may have lied, but he never did.

Assuming the frown of a suspicious tax auditor, Mark opened his thick folder and turned pages slowly, occasionally grunting at something he pretended to read. Out of the corner of his eye, he noticed Tito was unconsciously telegraphing the classic signs of a worried man—clearing his throat, squirming, brushing imaginary dust from the table, swinging his feet slightly but hastily, as if they would propel him right out the door if they touched the rug.

Mark heard the telltale sound of a sniffle and looked up expectantly. Tito met his eyes and said, arrogance now gone, ''I got a business, man. I got a wife and kid. You know how those guys down the Port are. They can lean on you pretty good.''

''I know what you're going through,'' Mark said sympathetically, thinking how nice it was to actually have a textbook example of what they taught in the academy about how to usher a wavering suspect into a confession:

You aren't the typical criminal. You seem like a man under terrible pressure. Nobody is perfect—if the perfect person walks into this conference room, we will both get down on our knees. This is probably the first time you have done something like this. You can stop with this. Did you know that eighty-five percent of people who deal with merchandise steal something at some point? You seem to be basically an honest man, a man like you said, with a wife and kid that you obviously love. You've probably been dealt a pretty bad hand. I've always been curious about what motivates a person to do something they do not feel is right.

What caused you to do something so dumb? You're an intelligent man, you got in a jam. But could you put your arm around your kid right now and feel right? You can make this right. Ever since the pencil was invented there have been erasers on it.

Tito started crying.

Mark looked at him with disgust that slowly curled inward as he thought, *I'm busting this guy's ass for some lousy computers. Who the hell am I? I killed somebody. There's a body out there with the bugs and snakes and whatever else is in those hills. There are two kids who don't know where their mother is because of me.*

"Tito, get the fuck out of here. I don't want to see you again," Mark said abruptly, standing up.

Tito was stunned. "What do you mean, man?"

"Tito, go home. I don't give a shit what you do. Just leave me the hell alone."

Tito's feet found the floor. He backed out of the office like a court attendant and practically ran to his car in the lot.

Later that day, an agent Mark passed in the hall said by way of greeting, "How you behaving, Mark?"

"Above reproach," he said quietly.

Each day he awoke more secure in his assumption that the body had not been found, and despising himself more for his cowardice. The diarrhea persisted. His urine had blood in it. He was haggard and sour. This could not go on, and yet it did.

One morning, Kathy heard him muttering in the bathroom. She called from the bedroom, "What did you say, honey?"

Standing at the mirror, he replied, "I said, 'Good morning, killer.' "

12

No one looking for Susan Smith could have anticipated how many tiny threads of her life she had left tangled.

One of the first calls Richard Ray made when he began his investigation was to the man who was the source of the mysterious phone message for Susan at the Landmark. This man was not in fact the drug contact from Cicero that she had been telling Mark and Poole about. It was another one, an old contact, a man from Milwaukee.

No, he told the detective, he had not met Susan the weekend after she disappeared. In fact, she never returned his phone call. The man said that Kenneth had called him the next week, looking for her. Then an FBI man also called.

Ray ventured a guess. "Poole? Ron Poole?"

"Yeah, something like that. FBI."

"Not Putnam?"

"No, the other one you said. Poole."

This should have been an indication that the FBI was investigating, but like everything else in this case, the answers were ambiguous. The FBI generally declines to confirm or deny whether it is investigating, but Ray had determined informally that there was no "active" investigation into the case.

What then was Poole doing? The way Shelby told it, Mark Putnam's ex-partner was persistent and involved. She told Ray that she had been talking to Poole almost every day. She said Poole told her that while Susan was at the motel, he took her with him one day to serve warrants. Shelby also said that Susan had mentioned that she might be spending a day with Mark in Virginia, also serving warrants.

And then there was Susan's brother, Bo, who appeared to

be running his own independent investigation, questioning people who knew Susan, even trailing people he thought looked suspicious across the Tug into West Virginia. Bo wasn't sure what had happened. When pressed, he couldn't even say for sure that there had been a sexual relationship between his sister and Mark.

"They would keep it secret," he would later explain to authorities. "She was coming out here in front and calling him, and he was meeting her out back at the parking lot. And they would go and stay gone for two or three hours at a time."

What, Ray had to wonder, was *Bo* up to?

Ray worked quietly and moved easily among a great range of ordinary people: motel clerks, librarians, secretaries, truckers, drifters, outlaws behaving themselves between felonies—all felt comfortable with him because he didn't come on like a cop or a reporter. Gossiping with people outside a lunch counter, usually saying little himself, he kept track of the social undercurrents of the Peter Creek communities. Usually, he could get a fairly good line on current events.

Susan Smith was a tough one, though, because there were so many conflicting opinions about her. Everyone in Freeburn knew that she'd fight at the drop of a hat, that she was a heavy drug user, that she had a mouth on her, that she did outrageous things such as the time she went over to the car lot and mooned Bertie and his friends. He also heard about the time she'd gone to the federal courthouse and lifted up her shirt to flash her boobs at the boys in the marshal's office.

But there was another side to this woman that took a little more patience and trouble to find. She seemed also to be someone who always picked up a phone and called when she was away. Up the hollow at Barrenshea, Susan's mother, Tracy, said that Susan never forgot to send a birthday card, Christmas card, Mother's Day card—"no matter where she was living." In Phelps, the high school principal, Beth Compton, had known Susan since she was in sixth grade at the old Freeburn school. She described her as "a young girl who fought her way through life. She had to struggle for everything she ever had in a world where a girl's greatest ambition was to get married and have children." But she also recalled a transformation in Susan when she came back home after those years living in the city. Then, she said, "Susie had suddenly developed into a strikingly attractive young woman who projected poise." And, at least when Compton saw her with her two children, Susan appeared to be "an interested and concerned mother."

Something was not adding up.

The rumor mill of Peter Creek, which had ground along chronically malfunctioning since the days of the Hatfield-McCoy feud, also made it difficult to sort out information. Every time it appeared as if Susan Smith was indeed missing, and possibly dead, another rumor seemed to pop up to throw the theory out of whack. Almost weekly, Ray drove out Peter Creek to check out the latest hearsay. Much of it was difficult to evaluate. Among the things he heard, from Shelby and others, was Susan's apocryphal tale of the Putnams' parrot. He also had to consider Shelby's speculations. Perhaps, she mused once, Susan had followed Mark down to Florida and was simply lying low, waiting for him. Or maybe she had gone off to hide out with another sister, who lived in Texas.

A man in Turkey Creek named David Blankenship, whose deceased brother had been married to that sister, said that he, too, thought that might be where Susan was "because she was close to her sister and missed her." But he also reported that Kenneth had informed him that Susan "took off with a detective." Moreover, Blankenship said, he had heard that Susan recently went up to Cicero to get drugs and came home bragging that "she could sell all the drugs she wanted and not get busted" because the FBI was protecting her.

*   *   *

On August 8, Ray had called Shelby to get an update on the case, and she told him that a Phelps man named Johnny Stump had gotten a phone call from Susan. But when Ray drove out to see the man, that turned out not to have been the case. Stump explained Susan had once bought a 1979 Ford LTD from him and had not made the payments. He had filed a judgment against her, and she had failed to appear in court when the case came up two weeks earlier. He complained about her, but he said he hadn't told anybody he'd heard from her.

Meanwhile, Shelby's husband, Ike, said that he had heard Susan say, on the night Ron Poole picked her up to take her to the Landmark, that she was actually going to stay for a few days at the house of a former sister-in-law, though he believed this to be another of Susan's stories.

Bewildered, Ray decided that Shelby ought to take a polygraph test, ''to see if it was some kind of plot, if she knew where her sister was at.'' Shelby was insulted, but she complied. On August 22, she took the test and passed. The results showed that she didn't know where Susan was and that she was ''very concerned, very worried about her.'' Moreover, she insisted that the people they ought to be strapping to the polygraph machine were Kenneth Smith and Mark Putnam.

This proved to be no easy chore. Ray and Paul Maynard went to Capt. Gary Rose, the commander of the Pikeville state police post, who in turn called Terry Hulse, Mark's former supervisor in Covington. But word came back that while the FBI would of course cooperate in any investigation to the extent it saw necessary, it saw no reason to involve an agent. ''Polygraph the ex-husband,'' Captain Rose said he was told. ''Maybe he had something to do with it.''

Later, Maynard would express the frustration the state police experienced in those first six or seven months after Susan was reported missing. ''We had information that she had been in different parts of the country, and we had contacted different police agencies to request assistance and try to locate her—and all the leads turned up to be dead ends. We couldn't locate her.'' The difficulties were compounded by the reports that Susan was involved with a drug gang. However, aside from Susan's own apparent exaggerations as she tried to get herself reactivated as an FBI informant after Mark was transferred, there was no indication that she was involved in anything but petty local drug deals. ''She was a known drug user and would on occasion sell drugs to support her own habit,'' Maynard said.

Meanwhile, Ray would later recall, ''The FBI people just kept putting us off.'' Apparently they had talked to Mark about the investigation and had come to believe that ''this is a plot by the people up there to discredit him, to cause him trouble.'' What Ray did not know was that in Miami, Mark Putnam had already approached his superiors and volunteered to take a lie detector test to clear up the matter, and they had told him he was being silly.

Meanwhile, Kenneth Smith, who Susan had claimed had actually caused physical harm to her in the past, turned up in custody—his own. In October, Kenneth was sentenced to thirty days in jail for a series of motor vehicle violations. Because he was the sole guardian of the two children, seven-year-old Miranda and four-year-old Brady, the judge allowed him to serve an alternate ninety-day incarceration at his place in Freeburn. With an electronic device strapped to his leg to monitor his movements, Kenneth wasn't available to come to Pikeville to be polygraphed until January.

By then, Kenneth declared that he was making an effort to straighten himself out and provide a decent home for the children. He had a job as a night watchman at a strip-mining company. On January 12, Ray and Bertie Hatfield called on Kenneth, who told them what they already knew, that he had been married to Susan for three and a half years until they were divorced six years ago, and that they had lived together off and on since then for the sake of the kids. According to Ray's notes, Kenneth said that Susan had been going to Pikeville frequently to see Mark and also, at times, to buy drugs.

Kenneth said that Susan "told me that she loved Mark and he loved her. I called Mark's wife and told her about it. Susan said she hoped Kathy would find out so she would leave Mark." In early June, he went on, "Susan spent a night with me and the kids. The next night she was at Shelby's, and around midnight, the FBI came and got her. I have not seen her since. . . . Susan told me she was pregnant about three weeks before she left. She said she had discussed it with Mark and that he had agreed to help keep the baby up."

Asked if he had any idea where Susan was, Kenneth replied, "I think she is in Florida with Mark Putnam."

Ray suggested to Kenneth that he accompany them to Pikeville to take a lie detector test, and Kenneth readily agreed. Actually administering it successfully proved problematic, however. On January 16, Kenneth took the first polygraph test at the state police post in Pikeville. The operator, Charles Hines, believed that Kenneth was telling the truth when he said he knew nothing about what had happened to Susan, but it was difficult to get a good reading because of the chemicals in Kenneth's system.

"He's pretty bad hooked on drugs and we had a hard time," Ray reported afterward. After two inconclusive tests on successive days, Kenneth was kept overnight in a Pikeville motel under state police guard, "to try to straighten him up" for the next day's test. That test was not much more conclusive. Finally, Ray concluded what the machine could not. Kenneth apparently didn't have a clue.

And then it seemed again that Susan Smith had surfaced. In January, Shelby phoned Captain Rose at the state police barracks and said happily, "You can stop looking for Susan now."

"What do you mean?" said Rose.

"Josie Thorpe has gotten a call from her," Shelby declared. Thorpe was a fifty-two-year-old distant cousin whose rusted trailer sat on a wedge of land hacked into the low ridge on the road into Freeburn. Susan occasionally went to visit her and bring clothes.

Ray hurried out to Peter Creek, where Shelby had already spread the word that her sister had turned up. As usual, the detective stopped by Bertie Hatfield's little car lot, and Bertie went with him to talk to Josie. The door was open, though it was the dead of winter. When they rattled the screen door, which was missing one of its hinges, there was a muffled commotion just inside, followed by silence, and then the unmistakable click of a shotgun. Ray looked at Bertie and thought, *Someone is going to shoot me.*

Hastily they called out, identifying themselves. A voice responded, inviting them in. As they edged inside the doorway, a younger woman in a housedress tore past them and ran down the hill toward the road shrieking, "The law! The law!"

Inside, an older woman put down a shotgun and eyed the intruders warily from the couch. "Well, what do you want?" she said evenly.

Bertie introduced Ray to Josie and started to explain their business. As he did, Ray glanced curiously at the cast-iron stove that was radiating a wall of heat from the corner. He was wondering about the dark yellow smoke that seeped from under the lid when something inside the stove exploded with a great boom that caused both men to experience something akin to cardiac arrest.

"Damn girl!" their hostess said with well-worn exasperation. While the smoke cleared, she apologized for the cherry bomb.

The ice having been broken, they persuaded Josie to describe her telephone contact with Susan Smith. Shelby had said that Josie told her she had in fact received two or three calls from Susan, and that she was all right. Josie quickly confirmed the report.

But Ray's relief dissipated like the yellow smoke from

the stove when Josie added, "At least, she *said* she was her. Now, I had never talked to her by phone before, but it sounded like her. She would only talk a couple of minutes and hang up. She said she had left a sweater and fingernail polish at Shelby's and that I could have them."

Josie looked at them sweetly and jabbered on, describing how Susan, or whoever it was on the phone, she wasn't at all sure now, told her to make sure to take her medicine. "It could have been a tape recording or a prank," the woman suggested. "I take a lot of medicine and am not well. I don't know why she would call me, and I don't remember her saying she was Susie Smith. Besides, my number is unlisted."

The two officers looked at each other and got up, thanking the woman for her time.

Poole, Ray discovered, had already supplied Josie Thorpe with a tape recorder to record future phone calls from Susan, but Josie did not report any further contact.

Not long afterward, Ray tracked down Charlie Trotter at his home in McRoberts, far up in the hills of Letcher County. Charlie confirmed that he had stayed at the Landmark, on the FBI tab, for nearly five months, including the week Susan and Mark were there in June. After testifying successfully in the chop-shop trial, the nervous star witness had checked out in August. Soon afterward, he got his final payment of $30,000 from the FBI.

Charlie said that he hadn't seen anything at the motel to indicate any problem between Mark and Susan Smith. He said that Mark was usually gone most of the day during that week, not getting back till late at night. He seemed perfectly normal, Charlie said, other than complaining that the U.S. Attorney's office was "jerking him around" in Lexington all day when he really needed to spend more time preparing his witness to testify. Charlie didn't think Mark saw Susan for more than a few minutes during that week.

"Why do you think that?"

"Well, I saw her come out on the balcony a couple of

times looking for Mark. He would park in the lot under the balcony. She gave me the impression that she was coming on to Mark, and he would hide in his car and try to dodge her, like she was after him or something. I don't think Mark was fooling with her.''

How did he learn that Susan was missing?

"Ron Poole told me about the girl being gone," said Charlie. "I never saw anyone talk to her except Mark Putnam and Ron Poole.

Charlie also said, "She was rougher looking than the picture you showed me.''

By January, Richard Ray figured he had chased every goose and run down every lead. The holidays were past, and Susan hadn't contacted a soul since the day she disappeared. He went to his boss and told him it was time to get tough with the FBI. Assuming something untoward had happened to Susan Smith—and that was precisely what he was assuming by now—there was at least one easy-to-find suspect who hadn't been eliminated yet. It was time, Ray said, to demand that the FBI have a talk with its agent Mark Putnam, preferably with a polygraph machine strapped to his arm.

The supervisors in the FBI's main regional office in Lexington once again responded civilly but firmly to the entreaties from Pikeville. They were not prepared to produce a federal agent for questioning by Kentucky cops just because the state police were unable to find Susan Smith.

The reasoning behind their attitude was logical. First, there was no evidence that a crime had even been committed. Furthermore, there was plenty to suggest that the missing woman, a reputed small-time drug dealer with an abusive ex-husband and a passel of enemies, had simply gone off somewhere. Yes, there was speculation, but there was always speculation in places like Tug Valley. The agent whose name was being bandied around, Mark Putnam, had compiled a distinguished record fighting crime in eastern Kentucky, speculation about his personal relationship with the woman aside.

Shelby was furious about the rebuff she got from Terry Hulse when she'd phoned to demand that the FBI question Mark. "He acted like she didn't need to be found," Shelby would later say. She claimed that Hulse told her that Susan would undoubtedly turn up alive, at which time "we'll do a pregnancy test to determine if it was Putnam's baby or not. But from what I've heard, your sister fooled around with everything in Pikeville." Shelby was bristling. "They just talked to me like I was dirt under their feet," she said. "It is impossible for me to understand why they would feel that this was a problem for the Kentucky State Police when we all knew Susan was a paid informant for the FBI and had testified and given information about several potentially dangerous people."

Of course, part of the difficulty was that although Shelby never wavered in her insistence that Mark Putnam had been personally involved with her sister, she herself had given investigators various theories about her sister's disappearance, with no evidence for any of them. All she knew was what she said Susan had told her.

But Ray had sorted through the various accounts and come back down the blind alleys. He was certain that Mark Putnam knew more than he said about what had happened to Susan Smith. Convinced now that the woman was dead, stymied by bureaucratic lethargy within a state police hierarchy that was reluctant to incur the ire of the FBI, he decided to go outside channels. Early in January, he stopped by the downtown office of the county prosecutor, Commonwealth Attorney John Paul Runyon, to ask for advice.

Ray told the prosecutor that he thought the FBI's refusal to take any role in the investigation was inexcusable, Mark Putnam aside. The woman had *worked* for them, after all. She had put herself in danger for them. "They don't seem to understand that they have a special responsibility to this girl," he said.

Once he had heard the detective's description of the dilemma, Runyon readily agreed. He himself had long been troubled by what he regarded as the cavalier way the FBI used its money to buy informants. He thought it was basically a cynical system that encouraged a kind of outlaw welfare state, with little genuine long-term law enforcement benefit.

This seemed to be a perfect example, he decided. A poor mountain girl disappears; the federal agent who has put her in danger pulls up stakes and goes off to Florida. Didn't the FBI owe her family at least the courtesy of an active investigation? Missing persons' cases were not under FBI jurisdiction, but tampering with a federal witness sure as hell was. Besides, as Ray brusquely pointed out, the FBI had always managed in the past to find a way to insert itself into a local investigation when it felt like it, especially if the case looked as if it might yield some glory. Where was the bureau now?

Runyon told the detective he would make it his business to find out.

Kentucky's county-based commonwealth attorneys perform the function of district attorneys, prosecuting felonies. But in the state's unusual political structure, where power is concentrated intensely within the county courthouses, a commonwealth attorney wields significant influence over a wide swath of civic life, especially in poor rural areas such as Pike County. Now in his sixties, approaching the end of his fifth term in office, John Paul Runyon was the dean of Kentucky commonwealth attorneys, a man both widely admired and feared in Pike County.

He also happened to be an occasional hunting buddy of Richard Ray's, and he respected the veteran detective's levelheaded comprehension of the societal currents in isolated regions such as Peter Creek. An athletic man, six feet four, with thick white hair and chiseled features, Runyon prided himself on his accessibility. His storefront office on a side street in downtown Pikeville was the kind of place where a man with a grievance could come in, stroll back to the prosecutor himself, sit down at his desk, and say, ''John Paul, you sent my cousin to the penitentiary five years ago, and he always told me you was fair . . .''

Runyon was also acutely aware of his public image. His predecessor as commonwealth attorney, a blustery coal tycoon named Thomas B. Ratliff, had attracted the ridicule of the national news media in 1967 by leading a posse in a midnight raid on the farmhouse of a couple who were active with Vista, the federal antipoverty group then calling attention to the destitution of southern Appalachia. Ratliff announced the discovery of a cache of "communist propaganda" in the house—actually, he'd found a handful of newspaper clippings about civil rights marches in Alabama—and successfully prosecuted the bewildered couple for sedition. By 1972, when the case was overturned by the U.S. Supreme Court, Pikeville had more important things on its mind, such as the giant mountain Cut-Through, one of the largest earthmoving projects in U.S. history. It allowed Route 23 to be rerouted and the flood-prone Levisa Fork to be diverted, freeing Pikeville's downtown for new development.

Runyon, a county official previously credited with bringing new state roads through the mountains, personified the desire of Pikeville to present itself as a progressive and vibrant commercial center, not a backwater hillbilly hamlet. He was first elected commonwealth attorney in 1972 and had been reelected, with increasingly wide margins ever since, resisting blandishments to run for statewide office. He liked to tell the story of a man he knew who had once run hard in a Democratic primary for governor and had unexpectedly gone down to decisive defeat. "You got beat because you didn't want to *be* governor badly enough," Runyon had told him. "Unless you wake up in the middle of the night in a cold sweat screaming, 'If I don't get elected governor, I'll *die!* I'll *die!*' you are simply not going to be governor. I could see you didn't have that."

His own aspirations were clear. In 1990, he was planning to round out his career with election to one last term as commonwealth attorney the following year. He wanted to win it without opposition—hell, by *acclamation*, if possible. And his acute small-town political instincts told him that the Putnam case, with its undertones of exploitation, cover-up, and official betrayal, was a booby trap. He did not intend to stumble into it blindly.

While Ray sat in his office, Runyon picked up the phone and called Lou DeFalaise in Lexington. The U.S. Attorney told the prosecutor that he happened to be on his way to the Justice Department in Washington.

"Well, kick somebody there and get them working on this, will you, Louie?" Runyon said.

Runyon also got together with Captain Rose, who recounted his own frustration in dealing with the FBI. He was especially unhappy since the state police had now heard, from Poole and other sources, that Mark Putnam had already said in Florida that he would agree to take a polygraph test. Yet every time the state police tried to take Putnam up on the supposed offer, the bureau stalled and finally, in early February, said flatly no.

Rose said that Putnam was now the "main suspect" in Susan Smith's disappearance and strongly suggested that Runyon meet with Shelby Jean Ward, who, he warned, was threatening to call a press conference to charge that law enforcement authorities were engaged in a cover-up of the murder of her sister, a federal informant.

On February 9, a very unhappy Shelby Ward met with Runyon and state police officials in the prosecutor's office.

Shelby was quite serious about her threat, and it had some weight. National tabloid television programs would quite probably be interested in the story, which had all the right ingredients: the poor coal miner's daughter; the dashing prep-school FBI man; treachery, cover-up, intrigue, and, of course, illicit sex.

While he figured only a federal investigation would get to the truth, Runyon knew that putting Mark Putnam on a polygraph machine, even if he could get Putnam to agree, was not building a criminal case. Polygraphs are inadmissible as evidence in court. Essentially, there was no case without evidence that a crime had been committed. And there was a conspicuous absence of evidence in the one at hand.

Shelby, as the state police had found, could offer the prosecutor little more than anger and speculation. "Is your sister the type of person who would just up and leave like that, maybe go off and stay in an apartment or something with Mark Putnam?" Runyon asked her.

"It's possible," she said.

"Or leave with somebody else?"

"That's possible, too," Shelby allowed.

Explaining that he had no significant involvement in the investigation yet, and that no solid information had been developed, Runyon asked Shelby to consider that if the FBI man was in fact involved in her sister's disappearance, premature publicity could "run Putnam to ground" and let him escape. They knew where Putnam was, and he wasn't going anywhere. Runyon asked Shelby to stay quiet for "two or three weeks to see if I can build a fire and get this thing moving."

Reluctantly, Shelby agreed.

When she left, the prosecutor, now believing that a full-scale federal investigation was the only way to "shake this thing loose," called Terry Hulse and suggested strongly that the FBI should get involved in the case, if only to clear their own man's name, which was being dragged through the mud in Pike County.

Hulse prudently made some calls. In Washington, the bureaucracy stirred. There was a request from the Justice Department for Richard Ray's case file.

A month passed. The case was reported "under review." In April, two federal officials visited Pikeville for a briefing on the case. They were Sarah Pickard, a supervisory special agent with the FBI, and David P. Bobzien, an assistant counsel with the Justice Department. Hulse drove down from Covington to participate in the meeting.

The federal agents conceded to Runyon and the state police that there was no current investigation, either professional or criminal, into the allegations against Mark Putnam. If Poole had been investigating, he was working on his own.

"I can't believe that you people don't have *any* kind of

investigation going on into Mark Putnam,'' Runyon
snapped.

Ray would later recall, "After talking to them, I had a little
hope. They read my report. They weren't really aware of
what we had here; they seemed pretty concerned. They assured us that once they got back to Washington, this case
would take a little higher priority than what it had been before, which was apparently none. I think some of the FBI
people had heard about it, and they didn't think it was very
serious or something. They figured that probably this woman
would show up somewhere. Which I knew she wouldn't.''

A few weeks later, Captain Rose called Runyon. He had
heard back from the Justice Department. The message, essentially, was, "We're not interested. You handle it.''

Runyon sighed impatiently and told Rose, "That's a serious mistake. To start with, you don't have the resources.
You don't have the jurisdiction—the boy you need to talk to
is in Florida. And you can't talk to him without permission
from the Justice Department. Let me see what I can do.''

This time he was less delicate in his approach to the FBI.
"Listen,'' he said angrily, "you people got a problem. You
people are in this up to your eyeballs. You threw this young
girl to the wolves, and if you don't get off your ass, I'm
going to have Geraldo Rivera breaking down your office
door sticking a camera in your face, and saying, 'Where is
your missing informant?' ''

13

With twenty-three years in the bureau, supervisory special agent Jim Huggins had seen his share of hotshot rookie agents roar out of the academy in a blaze of energy, thinking they were the greatest thing to happen to federal law enforcement since Eliot Ness, and burn out before they qualified for their second week's vacation.

Not so, he thought, with this Putnam. Huggins had run into him only a few times when Mark came up to Lexington for gun training, but he knew enough about his reputation down in Pikeville, where the kid was practically a one-man band, to regard him as one of the best young agents he had ever encountered. Huggins believed fervently that the future of his beloved FBI depended on a steady supply of dedicated young agents just like Mark Putnam.

Like every other senior agent in the Lexington bureau, Huggins had heard the scuttlebutt that Putnam "had some problems" because of a personal relationship with a female informant who had disappeared. That would be a damn shame if it was true. Getting caught with your pants down, especially with an informant, was a definite career-damaging problem in the FBI. The kid would spend a few years atoning for it. But J. Edgar Hoover and his priggish ways were long gone. In time, if Putnam kept his nose clean, he could get back on the track.

On May 1, Huggins was called in to see Terry O'Connor, the special agent in charge of the Lexington office. O'Connor told him he was being dispatched immediately, with four other agents, to head a special squad that would get to the bottom of the allegations about the disappearance of Susan Smith. It would be a "joint investigation" with the

state police, who had been on the case since June and had
come up with "nothing." The commonwealth attorney
down there was "bouncing off the wall" and threatening a
media circus. Washington was demanding to know what the
hell was going on. The questions "needed to be resolved."

Resolving them would turn out to be the most unhappy
experience of Huggins's career.

From the beginning, Huggins and the other agents who
were sent down to Pikeville—there would soon be ten of
them in all—believed that they were looking into a situation
that had been thoroughly mishandled by the state cops. Not
that the bureau was totally clean. It was clear that Putnam
had a lot of explaining to do. And there was the delicate
underlying problem, "the Pikeville horror story," as one
agent put it, of an office out of control and apparently run
amok—a rookie agent doing the work of four people in
partnership with a veteran who'd been moved out of the
mainstream and sent to Pikeville. Clearly, the Pikeville office had been trouble waiting to happen. Now that it apparently had, the bureau's vaunted public image, which every
agent was trained to protect at all costs, was in peril.

Huggins met first with Captain Rose, who, he said,
"made available all of the resources of the post." These
resources consisted primarily of Det. Richard Ray, who was
somewhat resentful at being assigned to escort the newly
arrived FBI agents as they essentially duplicated his own
investigation. It was clear to him that the FBI's elite squad
thought they had been sent down to straighten out the mess
that the hillbilly cops had made. Their attitude, he thought,
was, "Let's do a thorough job, clear our guy, and find the
guy that really did it"—assuming "it" had been done at all.
He was supposed to play tour guide, driving the agents—
most of whom knew nothing about mountain people and
had never seen Pikeville before—on their rounds as they
checked off the likely suspects.

Not having the detective's firm intuition about what had

happened to Susan Smith, the agents quickly got mired in the muddled theories, half-baked speculation, and false leads that had confounded Ray for many months. They, too, soon gathered plenty of indications that Susan was unreliable and disreputable, a drug user with outlaw friends—and enemies. Informants often—almost inevitably—became disgruntled. Agents were routinely falsely accused by unhappy former informants cut loose from the gravy train. If this woman had been harmed, Mark Putnam did not even make first cut on the list of likely suspects.

For example, David Blankenship told them that Susan's brother Bo had told him that *he* believed Kenneth had killed Susan. According to the FBI's investigative file, Blankenship said that Susan claimed she had been paid $12,000 for her work on the Cat Eyes case and described to him the way she had subsequently set up Cat's uncle in another bank robbery. Susan "feared for her life because people had threatened her," he told them.

A few days later, Ray drove FBI agents Claude Adams and William Welsh across the Tug to Vulcan, West Virginia, to talk to Ronnie Mounts, one of the old friends who used to sit around the kitchen table for hours on end with Kenneth and Susan, drinking beer and playing cards.

Mounts said Susan frequently used drugs. She was mainly a "pill popper," he recalled. He told the investigators that, while he had no idea where Susan was, he had heard reports that she had gone off to Chicago. But he had also heard she might be staying with her sister in Texas. On the other hand, Kenneth had told him that he thought Susan was somewhere in Florida—though he hadn't seen Kenneth in weeks and thought he was "on the run," too. He said that he knew Kenneth had accused his ex-wife of "going with Mark Putnam." Mounts said he hoped they found her soon.

Why? he was asked.

"Because she owes me sixty-five dollars."

*   *   *

Just as Ray had found, the FBI discovered that the people who knew Susan Smith had a variety of theories to explain her disappearance. Most mentioned her drug use and drug connections. Mark Putnam's name came up, but always in the context of secondhand information.

Pam Daniels, a thirty-year-old former neighbor on Barrenshea Hollow, was among those who told agents that Susan had a "bad drug habit." She claimed Susan had come to her house in the spring after being "run off" by Shelby and her husband during an argument over her relationship with Mark Putnam. She also said that Susan told her that if Mark did not give her enough money to support the baby, she was going to "set him up," which Pam Daniels interpreted as a threat to tell Kathy about the affair.

According to another bureau report, Ike Ward described Susan as "the type of person who would make stories up and make statements that she knew who was involved in a criminal act when, in fact, she would have no idea who committed the crime." He also told agents that Susan was a heavy cocaine user who would take any kind of drugs except marijuana and would do "anything" to obtain them, although that had become difficult for her because of her reputation as an FBI informant. Personally, he said, he thought that Susan was dead, "possibly killed by drug dealers or someone she testified against."

Ike reported that Susan had told everyone who would listen that she worked for the FBI and was "bonded." It was Ike's impression that "Susan felt superior to other people by running around with FBI agents." He had never observed Mark with Susan, although he had once seen Poole pick her up at the car lot. Still, Susan was "in love" with Mark, Ike said, and would have done anything for him. Although he noted that he seldom believed anything Susan said, he did believe she had an affair with Mark and was pregnant by him.

Ike also told the agents about the beating Susan had received just before she disappeared from Sherri Justice, who, he said, "threatened to kill her." Further clouding the picture, he confirmed that while Susan was at the Landmark, Shelby had relayed the phone message from a contact of Susan's who was believed to be a drug dealer. He added that Susan had said in the past that the man and his family "would keep her" if she was in town and needed a place to live.

The agents' report on their interview with Ike Ward concluded: "Ward advised that he was not trying to get anyone in trouble and would not swear against Mark Putnam or Ron Poole because all the information he has is hearsay and that Susan was a cheat and a liar."

Shelby herself was more specific on the relationship between her sister and Putnam, but her account, too, lent support to the notion that Susan had a lot of enemies. According to the agents' report:

Shelby stated that Susan, Kenneth Smith, and Tennis Daniels went to the Pikeville FBI office to pick up the money for testifying, and supposedly later in the day, Kenneth stole the money from Susan, who later got the money back. Shelby does not know what Susan did with the money, because Susan and Kenneth were both heavily on drugs at the time.

The money was supposed to be for Susan to get out of the area, because Susan was getting a lot of threats from Sherri Justice . . . and Cat Eyes, who said if he ever got out of prison, he would have her killed. . . .

About the first part of May 1989, Sherri Justice beat up Susan, causing cuts and bruises, and also smashed out a window in Susan's car. Justice swore she would kill Susan. . . . Shelby stated that she and Susan would often talk about the threats made against Susan, inasmuch as Susan was very afraid of Sherri Justice and Cat Eyes and wanted to get away. . . . Shelby advised that during the two-year period Susan worked for Putnam, Susan and Kenneth fought continuously, with Kenneth getting physical with Susan.

Kenneth was very jealous over anyone. . . . Shelby advised that Susan was on cocaine bad enough that she had to have it, and that was Susan's reason not to completely stay away from Kenneth. . . . Shelby further added that Susan lied a lot. However, she told the truth a lot also.

. . . On Thursday morning June 8, 1989, Shelby received a phone call from Susan. Susan seemed real happy, being with Putnam and talking about the baby, and laughed about Putnam not giving her money, and that Putnam would send her money when he got back to Florida and got straightened out. Susan was going to get Poole or Putnam to bring her back to Shelby's. Susan was not upset and was laughing.

About two hours later on Thursday morning, Susan called again, and her attitude changed. She was not happy. Susan wished there was some place she could go with the kids and be away from Kenneth. Shelby wanted Susan to come home, and Susan told her that she loved her, but could not stand to be around Kenneth and could not take it anymore.

Shelby advised it was very unusual for Susan to say she loved her. Shelby stated if someone would have given Susan money, she would have left. Shelby advised this phone call on Thursday was the last time she had heard from Susan.

Meanwhile, there was a new wrinkle in the FBI investigation. The agents had come across a witness who had actually heard from Susan Smith five months after she had supposedly disappeared.

They had found Josie Thorpe.

The official report of the FBI interview with Josie Thorpe read as a classic example of investigative objectivity. Anyone reviewing it at a desk far away in Lexington or Washington would have had cause to wonder just what the fuss over Susan was about:

Josie Thorpe, date of birth December 19, 1937, Freeburn, Kentucky, advised that she knew Susan Smith
and Susan would visit with her on occasion. Thorpe
stated that sometime after Susan's disappearance she
got several telephone calls from her. . . . During one
call, Susan inquired as to how Thorpe was getting
along and if she was still taking her medicine. Susan
also inquired about her own children and told Thorpe
that she (Susan) had a dark blue sweater and orange
fingernail polish that she had left at her sister Shelby's
house and that Thorpe could have them.

During the last telephone call, Susan inquired about
her children, Miranda and Brady. Thorpe stated that
the telephone call had to be after Thanksgiving, since
she told Susan that her ex-husband, Kenneth Smith,
and the children ate Thanksgiving dinner with her and
that she served spaghetti. Thorpe stated that she told
Susan that people were worried about her and looking
for her and that she should call her sister Shelby.
Thorpe also told Susan that Ron Poole, Federal Bureau of Investigation, had also interviewed her regarding Susan's telephone calls. Susan told Thorpe not to
tell anyone that she had called or she would not call
anymore.

Thorpe stated she believes the person she was talking to was Susan and that Susan was alive. Thorpe
stated that she has had her telephone number changed
and that Susan had called her on the old number,
which she could not recall.

What the Huggins task force had come up with, in short,
was the same snarl of conflicting information that Richard
Ray had uncovered in his many months of investigation.
The FBI agents seemed thoroughly confounded by the per-
plexities of the case. Like Ray, they concluded that Putnam's role required further elaboration. But they had an
advantage that the state police lacked: *they* could ask Mark

Putnam himself about it. To Ray's great relief, Huggins
returned to Lexington with his squad determined to take
Putnam up on those offers he had been making to explain
himself.

Mark was aware of what had happened in Pikeville because
both Poole and Myra had called to say that Huggins and his
men were in the area retracing the state police investigation.
Mark received the information with an odd mixture of dread
and relief. In a month, Susan would be dead for a year.
Mark was intensely aware—the thought, he later said, never
left him—that she had been out there in the woods all that
time. When he looked at his own two children, he often
thought of hers, a little girl and a little boy who had no idea
where their mother was.

In early May, feeling close to the abyss as Huggins's
team was starting its work in Pikeville, Mark had gone in to
see Roy Tubergen once again, repeating his request for an
OPR investigation "into the allegations against me."

"No way," the supervisor said flatly, aware of the damage this could do to an innocent man's career. But, he
asked, "if the Kentucky state cops want you to go on the
box, would you do it?"

"Yes," Mark said, not certain in his own mind whether
this reply was motivated by a desire to confess or to appear
eager to deal decisively with the situation and get it behind
him. Later, he would understand that it had been both.

A week went by without further mention of the situation.
Then, at the end of a workday, Tubergen took Mark aside
and mentioned that Jim Huggins and a couple of state police
detectives wanted to come to Miami to talk to him.

"It's strictly your call," Tubergen said.

Mark felt a coldness in his toes and fingertips. He forced
himself to be steady. "I have no problem whatsoever with
that," he said.

He needed a little time, he thought, to draw a deep breath
and brace himself. He had been overwhelmed with work

lately, on a major undercover theft investigation. His unit had rented an apartment in Fort Lauderdale to set up a sting. It had been a heady experience, almost like the thrill of the chop-shop case, except that this time he was part of a well-oiled unit, not a lone wolf, a professional among professionals, all prepared to go the extra mile for one another. He could see himself now, however transiently, as the agent he had always wanted to be.

He had achieved that, at least. He savored it briefly, through secret fear, shame, remorse, resignation, submission, mental exhaustion, and oddly, an occasional gust of elation. He worked with a massive headache that never eased.

Okay, he thought, *I'm ready*. But he wasn't about to simply surrender. The outcome was inevitable—he would lose it all, and soon—but he wouldn't just give it up, not after all of the decent things he had done to earn it. They were going to have to take it away, he thought. *And then that's it*.

He struggled to stop from thinking about what was about to happen to Kathy and the children. It was as if he were watching his family from afar as they were about to drive off a cliff—he could see the deadly hidden turn in the road, the car accelerating, the coal truck bearing down—but there was nothing he could do. Shouting would be futile.

On the afternoon of May 15, he left the office, telling the receptionist that he had an interview to do. Knowing he would be alone, he drove to the apartment they had rented for the sting. He sat on the couch, in the orange slats of late-afternoon sunlight. In his hand was his bureau-issue Smith & Wesson .357, which he studied as if he had never seen it before. He could smell the oil. He thought, *Would this work?* The gun metal was cool in his hand. He raised the barrel and pressed it hard against the perfectly squared sideburn at his right temple. How would it look? Who would find the mess? Would there be pictures? He lowered the gun and tapped the barrel thoughtfully on the palm of his left hand, probing his feelings as if poking at a broken filling with his tongue. He tried to cut through the bullshit: *If I do this, who benefits?*

He lowered the gun. Had he just spared his life? Or was this an exercise, another step he had to take to face his fate like a man? Again, the fragment of a headline came to mind: *tragic accident.*

He was cop enough to know they didn't have much of a case. He had the case all in his head. Had the flurry of FBI activity in Pikeville meant that they had found the body? If so, why hadn't they simply arrested him? Why talk now? If they had the body, they still obviously didn't have any other evidence. Did this mean that he could make his inner peace with himself and with Susan, whatever the cost for the rest of his life, and brazen his way through the rest for the sake of his family? All trouble got easier over time. Why not this?

He left the apartment utterly unable to decide. He stopped back at the office to check out and head home. Roy Tubergen spotted him at his desk.

"They're coming down tomorrow," Roy said.

All Mark remembered driving home was looking down to see the speedometer needle edge past ninety on I-95 out of North Miami Beach. He let up fast on the accelerator and checked the rearview mirror for a sign of a police car light-rack in the line of cars strung out behind. Queasy with guilt, he imagined that a Florida highway cop who pulled him over for speeding would easily guess the rest. He could see the cop's impassive face at the window, his nostrils sniffing the panic sweat, his hand at his gun.

Mark found himself turning into the driveway, his temples throbbing. It was almost six o'clock, the usual time. The kids tackled him at the door. Little Mark tottered off into the playroom while Danielle wrapped her arms around his legs and held on, chattering about her day. But when he only stood there silently for a minute, she stopped talking and looked into her father's eyes, and he thought that she read there a deep and sudden sorrow. He knew then that he was going to prison for a long time, and that when he was a part of her life again, she would be grown.

At dinner, Kathy hung back, sensing that something was very wrong. She guessed it was Pikeville again. After the kids were in bed, they talked for a while in the screened-in porch outside the kitchen. Was everything okay? No problem, he said. Just work. He got up and went out for his run.

The night was muggy and warm, the dark sky streaked with milky clouds. He started out easily, feeling the energy build as he picked it up. He was at about the halfway point, two miles, on a stretch of county farm road, when a car full of teenagers roared by. *Fucking asshole!* he heard. An empty beer can sailed by his head and clattered onto the asphalt. He stopped, panting, and watched the taillights on the road. Joy-riding was just the kind of thing he had avoided assiduously as a teenager, so worried about his ''record'' that he ran like a rabbit from a girl with a can of beer. Snorting, he circled back behind the beer can lying on the road. Picking up his pace, he kicked it in stride, watching it rise through the air and bounce ahead. Breathing evenly now, he quickened his stride, adjusting his step as he approached to boot the can again. It sailed away in a perfect arc and clattered down twenty feet ahead. The wind gathering force through trees on either side of the road sounded like the roar of a stadium. Again he approached the can, shifted stride, and met it with a powerful stroke of his right foot. The roar was deafening now. He could see the American flag on its staff high above the stadium, a postage stamp stuck on the corner of a bright blue sky. Again, he came up fast on the can and booted it in a fury. It sailed out of sight. He heard it clank to rest somewhere ahead in the dark.

Winded, he tripped and fell, sprawling nearly spread-eagle on the asphalt. He crawled to the side of the road and sat in the wet grass beside an irrigation ditch, scraped and bruised. He looked into the sky, lighter in the east with Miami's cold glow, falling off to darkness to the west, where the Everglades covered the land eighty miles wide.

*   *   *

He dreamed of Susan again that night. She was closer to
him now. He knew that he had called out her name because
the sound of his voice woke him. Kathy slept on gently. He
looked at her beside him and groped for the right emotion.
Was love even possible, with what he had done to her and
what more was to come? Would remorse ever be enough?
He kissed her arm lightly, careful not to awaken her, and
slipped out of bed.

At work, he busied himself with papers on his desk,
avoiding the phone, until he saw them come in. As he had
expected, Richard Ray was there. Paul Maynard came in
with him. Jim Huggins, whom he recognized from the Lexington bureau, led the way.

At eleven o'clock sharp, he was called into the conference room adjacent to the office of the assistant special
agent in charge, Larry Torrence, who immediately excused
himself. Mark took a place at the table. Huggins nodded at
him diffidently. Maynard and Ray avoided eye contact.
Each of his interrogators had files and a legal pad before
him on the table.

Huggins cleared his throat and advised Mark of his rights
as an employee of the Justice Department to answer questions voluntarily. Huggins nodded to Maynard, who looked
directly at Mark and recited words that startled him with
their familiarity:

"You have the right to remain silent. Anything you say
can and will be used against you in court. You have the
right to talk to a lawyer for advice . . ."

Mark closed his eyes.

"You're sure about the lawyer, Mark?" Huggins's voice
intruded into a serenity that had settled briefly over him.

Mark looked up. "Positive. I don't want a lawyer. I'm
ready."

He was asked to provide a detailed day-by-day account of
what he remembered about the week during which Susan
Smith had disappeared. But Mark was not going to make it

that easy for them. He would confess, but he had decided he would make them sweat for it. They wanted details? They'd get them, but let them show what kind of cops they really were. *Gentlemen,* he thought, *make yourselves comfortable, because we're going to be here for a while.* A good detective knows that a suspect who recites details, one after the other, hour by hour, probably has something to hide. On the other hand, a good detective—and nobody would dispute that, no matter what else was said, Putnam could claim to be that—is one who instinctively collects the minutiae, sifting it endlessly in search of a tiny nugget. It was all in the details, he thought. Let them figure it out.

Speaking slowly, Mark went over his career in Pikeville, incident by incident, as it reflected his association with the missing woman. He described how Bertie Hatfield introduced him to Kenneth Smith and Susan in the summer of 1987. Literally from that point, he explained, from the first time he met with the woman in a car parked in plain view of a restaurant where Kenneth, Bertie, and Tennis waited and fumed, the relationship between agent and informer was dogged with "ridiculous" rumors that he was having a sexual relationship with Susan. Susan herself was one of those who spread the rumors, he said.

As he listened, Richard Ray perked up. After all the roadblocks that had been thrown in his way, he had not been confident that this session, under FBI auspices, would result in anything but more obfuscation. But even in denying it, Putnam had already introduced the subject of his sexual relationship with the woman. Ray wondered what Mark was up to; did he sense that Ray was the only other man at the table who knew that he had killed Susan? Was the agent toying with them, aware that they couldn't prove a thing unless he slipped up? Why talk on at length, then? Why not just answer each question carefully and succinctly and wait for the next? Without changing his facial expression, which reflected nothing more than bored disdain, Ray took careful note of every nuance in the account, aware that Mark had no

way of knowing which blanks Ray still needed to fill in. He
watched and listened for false clues.

Mark did not wander from the subject, the way most
guilty suspects would. He kept the focus on himself and
Susan. The payments to Susan for informing on Cat Eyes
and others. Susan's clamoring for more money, for protection from threats. His and Kathy's attempts to help her find
a new life away from Kenneth. The gifts Susan pressed on
him. The intimations about a drug operation she had resumed contact with involving the policeman in Cicero, Illinois, and Poole's interest in that.

By early 1989, when he was about to be transferred to
Miami, Susan was desperate for money and heavily involved in drugs, Mark said. "From her conversations, I got
the impression she was selling drugs and also involved in
prostitution."

He recounted the four-thirty A.M. phone call in early
February, in which Kenneth had told Kathy that Susan and
Mark had had an affair. "He was extremely jealous of me
because of the informant relationship with Susan," Mark
said, effectively highlighting the potential motive of another
suspect. "Sometime during January of 1989, Susan advised
me that Kenneth had hired a private investigator and had
photographs of Susan and me in a car, and also coming out
of a motel. After one alleged beating of Susan by Kenneth,
just before Christmas, 1988, I got her a motel room at the
Goldenrod Motel in Pikeville. I registered in my name and
told her I had a room there so she could get away from
Kenneth. . . . I paid in cash." Similar arrangements were
made on two other occasions in January or February of
1989, he said. He didn't need to add that haphazard utili-
zation of informants, motels, and government money had
become standard practice, actively encouraged by the bureau in its zeal to keep undercover investigations active and
statistically fruitful, not to mention private.

As for Susan, "she had a reputation around Pikeville for
telling people that she was having sex with various individuals in the Pikeville area."

When had he first heard that Susan was pregnant? Maynard asked, narrowing the focus.

"Sometime around the middle of April 1989," Mark said. He had received his transfer orders to Miami; Susan called to discuss her wretched personal problems; she was broke, strung out, battered, afraid, and forlorn. In that context, he said, she mentioned that she was pregnant. "I asked her who the father was, and she said it was none of my business."

Later, in Miami, there were odd telephone calls from Poole, reporting on Susan's despair and imploring him to call her and try to help. When he did, Mark said, "she started crying and told me that I was leaving her out in the cold. She told me she was feeling bad, and that she had been beat up by Sherri Justice. I asked her what I could do to help, and she said, 'Fuck you. You don't give a shit about me.' "

Painstakingly, barely saying a word, Ray sorted Mark's words into mental files: what he knew for a fact; what he strongly supposed; what he simply did not know.

Two hours had passed since Mark started talking. Ray could sense the agent's mind racing as the chronology moved inexorably toward that final week in June of 1989. He thought, *This guy is going to slip up. He's just too cocky.*

Mark described his return to Pikeville, in June, and recalled his surprise at finding Susan at the motel when he checked in. How had she known he was coming? "I assume Poole told her," he said. He said Susan came to his room to talk about her troubles. That was news to both Ray and Huggins. It was a detail that no one had turned up, relevant only, Ray knew, in that Mark had seen a need to mention it.

What did they talk about in his room? "Again, she never accused me of being the father of her child," Mark said.

Ray watched him with hooded eyes, wondering if he had caught a whiff of panic.

"I got upset with her." He paused. *Upset?* Mark couldn't believe he had used such a stupid word! His heart beating fast, he went on evenly, and made another mistake. "During this conversation, I raised my voice and grabbed her by the arm, but did not in any way hurt her."

The cops at the table, Mark included, felt this tactical blunder like a tiny electrical shock. No glances were exchanged. Mark's mind flashed urgent warnings about the "indicators of deceit" that every good cop knew to watch for in a suspect who was about to cave in. He took instant stock of how he was projecting his mental state. Body language: Do not shift position. Do not move! He glanced at his hands resting casually on the table and resisted the overpowering impulse to touch them together, form a blockade with his arms. Keep your voice at the same pitch. Do not lick your dry lips. Do not sigh or yawn. *Do not swallow!*

He imagined that he was on a small rubber raft, in fast water now, listening for the low thunder of the waterfall ahead.

He knew that if any one of them had stood up and pointed a finger at him at that moment, he would have admitted everything. He was ready to take his punishment and be done with the lies and the shame. The impulse to confess was crushing, yet the need to go on was overpowering. No one looked at him. No one rose to denounce him for murdering Susan Smith. Grimly, he drifted on.

He explained that he flew into the airport in Huntington, West Virginia, "because it was closer than Lexington, which was the next-closest major airport, and I believed at that time that most of my work would be in Pikeville." Eyes downcast, he took a breath, not wanting to meet a gaze at the table. "At Huntington, I rented a car—"

Huggins interrupted him: "Hold it, hold it. You rented a *car?* What kind of a car?"

Mark shot an incredulous look at his fellow agent. Was this a bluff to knock him off-balance? How could they not have known about something as basic and obvious as the rental car? How the hell did they think he got around town that week, drove back and forth to Lexington? The question surprised and even exasperated him, but he tried to sort out the ramifications before answering. They seemed to be unaware of the car. But what kind of an investigation had they conducted, if they hadn't found the car, hadn't even *known* about the damn thing! There were rental records, expense vouchers—easy-to-check, routine stuff! Mark considered Ray a first-rate detective: methodical, perceptive, tenacious, smart. Had the FBI thrown that many roadblocks in his way? Were the state police brass so afraid of going against the FBI and being wrong? How hard had they *really pushed* here? To a man who had thought he was cornered and was merely playing for time—Mark was calculating days, not even weeks, by this point—the implications were breathtaking. He paused for an instant, sifting possibilities, wondering almost playfully if the hole was big enough to kick a ball through. *They didn't even know about the car! What had they been doing all year? What* else *didn't they know?*

He paused for a moment to collect his thoughts. He had always believed that Susan would eventually be found, that he would be confronted, and that he would confess and put her soul and his to rest. It was only a matter of time. In the past few weeks, as they closed in on him, he had assumed that they had new evidence, that perhaps they finally had the body. Now, looking around at his questioners' faces, suddenly blank with the realization that they had overlooked the *car,* he knew for certain that they had not found her.

"Yes, I rented a car, a blue Ford Tempo," he said calmly.

"Go on."

He was thinking, *Can I bullshit my way out of this?* The prospect unsettled him deeply because it required more introspection and there was no time for that. In a weary voice, he went on, lying with confidence now about his activities on the day Susan disappeared and the days that followed. He felt like a man lifting a barbell, muscles trembling with tension and pain, desperate to put it down, determined to press just a few more.

Ray detected the change in Mark's tone and watched him carefully. Was that a glint of sweat on the man's upper lip? Covering his vigilance with a sigh, the Kentucky detective waited for signs that Mark was ready to break.

But Mark forced himself to keep going, methodically

touching on each of the points of the chronology that he assumed they had already established. Checking into the motel and discovering that Susan was there, too. His talks with Charlie Trotter. His trips to Lexington, with arrival and departure times. His several encounters with Susan (he was careful to mention the phone message she said she received from Shelby about supposedly meeting her drug-dealer friend). The perplexing calls from Ron Poole, checking on Susan. His routine on the night she was last seen.

Uninterrupted, he went on, describing his trip to Lexington the next morning for another meeting with the assistant U.S. attorney. Dinner at the Log Cabin, followed by the friendly talk long into the night with Myra Chico.

So far, it checked out as well as the evidence could support, Ray knew. But Mark was going too fast, layering in too much detail. He had passed over the critical time, the hours during which Ray believed he had killed Susan Smith, but there was something he seemed impatient to explain.

On Saturday, June 10, two days after Susan disappeared, Mark said that he left the motel at about eight-thirty A.M. and drove out of town to serve a trial subpoena on a witness. "I returned to Pikeville around noon," he said. "I then went to my old house, which still had not been sold and still had some personal belongings in the garage. I pulled my car in the garage, checked out the house, and went back to the garage to discard some old paint cans that were stored under a workbench. Reaching under a shelf, I cut my right hand on a nail that was protruding from the shelf. The wound began bleeding very heavily; I got in the passenger side of the rental car and started slinging my hand up and down, causing blood to splatter on the passenger seat and on the dash. I wrapped my hand in a towel to stop the bleeding."

Mark paused. They didn't even know about the car! Why was he blurting out something else that they never knew about? Besides, the blood was his, not hers! He thought about the cracked windshield and struggled mindlessly to explain it: "While sitting in the front passenger seat of the car, I was extremely angry over cutting my hand; in an act of frustration, I kicked the front windshield with my right foot. It caused the windshield to slightly shatter in the area of the middle of the right side between the mirror and the right post.''

If Richard Ray had had any doubts, he now knew for certain that Mark Putnam had killed her. Only a guilty man in his last shrieking ride down the chute would babble on, providing new information about something like that without prompting. Whom did he think he was kidding? Ray felt a strong urge to stand up and arrest the suspect immediately, not only for murder but for insulting the intelligence of a police officer. But he remained silent as Mark went on and on: How he took the car with the cracked windshield back to the rental agency in West Virginia, blamed the damage on a chunk of coal flying off a truck, and got a replacement car—"I lied about the damage because I didn't want to have to pay for the windshield." How he had lent Susan his gym shorts and shirt. How Susan had told him about rebuffing Poole. How she "may have met up with the group from Illinois on a drug deal" and come to harm. Or how "her ex-husband, Kenneth Smith, could have harmed her, since he had beat her up on numerous occasions in the past."

He was exhausted, morally and physically. "I have no idea where Susan Smith is at the present time," he said. "Both Ron Poole and I cared about her very much and are concerned as to what happened to her. I certainly did not kill her intentionally or accidentally, because I could never do anything like that."

Ray stared at him with a calculated look of malice. The signs were clear. Mark had bowed his head. He was perspiring and seemed to be fighting back tears. Ray shot a glance at Maynard, who nodded almost imperceptibly in reply. The detective reached into a folder in front of him and slid out an eight-by-ten photograph of Susan Smith. When Mark looked back up, Ray was prepared to fling it right across the table at him and demand, finally, "Man, where did you put her body!"

Mark was braced for it, too.

But a chair scraped. Huggins stood up, his face pale.

"That's enough for today," he said, staggered by what he had just realized.

Afterward, Ray was furious. It was one of those times a cop knows—*He's breaking. He is going to tell me what I want to know.* Sensing the detective's quiet outrage, Huggins told him, as he and Maynard collected their things to return to their motel, that he had just taken Mark aside and asked him to take a polygraph test at FBI headquarters in Washington, to "clear this thing up." Mark had requested time to think about it overnight. He would let them know the next day. They'd done all anybody could do.

It was little consolation. The Kentucky detectives, bound to a meager expense authorization, had to fly home the next morning. Ray was convinced that the opportunity was lost, that the FBI had thwarted him once again, and Mark would once more be untouchable.

"What are they going to let us do next?" Ray asked his colleague.

"It's out of our hands," Maynard said.

14

Kathy was in the kitchen making dinner, absently monitoring the noises of the kids playing out back near the screened-in porch. From the canal two blocks away, a breeze drifted over neat lawns deep green from spring rains.

Absently, she glanced up and saw her husband standing mutely on the other side of the breakfast counter, his shoulders slumped and his tie undone. As he peeled off his suit coat and dropped it on a chair, he sagged with weariness. He tugged at his holster and took out the .357, and, to her annoyance, laid it on the breakfast counter. They had an inviolate policy about that gun. It belonged high up, usually on the upper shelf of the bedroom closet, in the back. She scowled at him and placed the gun pointedly atop the refrigerator. When she turned, he was standing right beside her. He took her in his arms and kissed her clumsily.

"You know I love you."

She did, but she hadn't been hearing it much lately and was curious about why she was hearing it now, with a pot lid rattling on the stove. Laughing uneasily, she moved away and studied his face. His eyes looked sunken; he was pale, as if he hadn't seen the sun in a year.

"What's the matter with you? You look awful."

He looked drunk, in fact, but Mark seldom drank, and never more than two beers, and never before coming home from work.

He sat her down and tried to guide her into a channel he knew was soon going to become deep and fast. "They came down to interview me today. It went on for a long time, all morning and after lunch. I'm a little worried."

Susan, again. So they'd finally come down. She and

Mark had discussed the possibility that he would be questioned, especially with the first anniversary of Susan's disappearance approaching. Cops got nervous when anniversaries passed without results. Poole had been passing on the play-by-play every week or so. Kathy wouldn't talk to him, but she could tell by Mark's clouded expression when Poole was discussing Susan's being missing. Kathy knew that Shelby was on the warpath. Fine, she thought. She was sick of the gossip. She had warned Mark that Susan was trouble; there was no satisfaction in being right. All she wanted was for Susan to be out of her life.

"The thing with Susan?" she asked warily.

"Yeah."

"Has she turned up?"

"No. That's what they wanted to interview me about."

"Mark, who came to interview you?"

They had gone in to sit on the couch in the living room. "The FBI's been getting into the investigation," he said. "A guy named Jim Huggins from the Lexington office. He came down, and so did Richard Ray and Paul Maynard." She could see he was holding back.

She had met Richard Ray. He was always on the big cases. She also knew that Ray would lock up his granny if he had evidence, and she did not like the idea that the Kentucky State Police, who were so cheap that a man on a stakeout couldn't even put in for a cheap motel room and was expected to catch a nap in his car, had sent detectives all the way to Florida for what should have been a mere formality of a phone interview.

Kathy felt her anger rise. In fact, if it hadn't been after office hours, she would have got into the car and gone right to Miami to let Mark's boss have a piece of her mind over what she regarded as an example of stupid and unnecessary harassment of an officer who had done his job well under difficult circumstances and deserved to be left alone. The bureau questioning Mark was one thing. She welcomed that as a way to finally clear the air and put Pikeville behind them. But the Kentucky State Police? What business was this of theirs?

She said in a tone of exasperation, "*Richard Ray* is handling this investigation?"

"Yeah." Mark got up unsteadily and trudged up the stairs to change. She thought it odd that he hadn't gone out back first to spend time with the kids before they ate.

Later, after watching Mark talk to them with forced animation and pick listlessly at dinner, she put Danielle and little Mark to bed and came down feeling it was time for her to step in and put an end to the nonsense. She had, in fact, already spoken with Terry Hulse about what she regarded as the whining in Pikeville over Mark's deeply misunderstood relationship with Susan. The more she thought about it, the more insulted she was at the idea that her husband should be put in the humiliating position of being questioned by a pair of hillbillies from the Kentucky State Police who couldn't find a missing person. Whose problem was that?

They had finally achieved what they wanted. Their marriage, she felt, had begun to come back on track in Florida, despite the lingering distraction from Pikeville. Mark had been asked to become a supervisor. Things should be going beautifully. Too much was at stake for her to let them continue pushing him around.

"Mark, you are just too trusting," she said in the sternly reproachful tone she used when she thought his good nature overwhelmed his good sense. "Tomorrow morning, I want you to call in and tell them you'll be a few hours late. You stay with the kids. I'm going down to the office first thing in the morning. They're going to hear me out before this goes on any further."

He didn't object. And he didn't ask her what she was going to say. She figured he was so beaten down from it that he didn't care.

He went out to run. When he returned, he found her out back smoking in the darkness of the porch. He pulled up a lawn chair and sat facing her.

She pressed her palms against his cheeks, which were hot.

"Is there anything you haven't told me about, Mark? No matter what, we'll work it out."

He felt tears again. He broke eye contact.

He tried to force himself to tell her everything.

"No," he said. "There's nothing else." Across the stockade fence, the neighbors' electronic bug-zapper crackled and went quiet.

"Do you remember when the windshield broke in the rental car?" he asked.

"Mark, what does that have to do with it?"

"Well, if they ask you any questions about that, I just wanted you to know that it wasn't a piece of coal that fell off a truck and broke that window. Remember that's what I told you?"

She only vaguely remembered. It was nearly a year ago, after all. He had phoned from Pikeville, worried that the car rental company was going to make him pay for the goddamned windshield, cracked by a chunk of coal bouncing off a truck, a common enough occurrence on the mountain highways. The kind of Boy Scout earnestness Mark conveyed in that phone call was one of the few things that truly irritated Kathy about her husband. Here he was, a G-man, worried that a rental agency would yell at him for an accident. She had suggested to him that he simply return the car and tell them how the windshield got cracked. The insurance would cover it. It was the last she'd thought of the matter until now.

"I just wanted you to know that that's not how that happened," Mark said, pressing on. "The windshield didn't break the way I told you it did."

"What does that have to do with anything?" she said, gesturing impatiently, as if to dismiss the topic.

"Do you remember when I smashed my hand?"

That was the same trip. Cleaning the garage, a nail. Two weeks later, when he got back to Florida, his hand was badly swollen, gashed across the knuckles. He thought he'd broken a finger, but it was healing. Mark was always banging something up. Of course she remembered.

"Well, I said it was a piece of coal off a truck because I was worried about what you would say," Mark continued deliberately. "The truth is, I was working in the garage, and after I snagged my hand, I got mad and kicked the windshield of the car. That's how it really got cut. I didn't want to tell you that because you would think, how could he be so stupid? What if the insurance company makes us pay for the damage? I didn't want you to worry. If you go down there tomorrow, they'll probably ask you some questions about the windshield, and I want you to know what really happened."

A warning bell went off in Kathy's head. She realized that she was not the first person today to hear this incidental piece of information from Mark, this *adjustment*. "Did you tell them that when they interviewed you today?" she asked sharply.

Uneasily, he replied, "Yeah, I did."

"Jesus, Mark! What are you telling them about something like that for? Why did you even mention the damn windshield? Don't you realize how that makes you look? How could you be so stupid? What does that have to do with *anything?*" She folded her arms, simmering.

"Because Kathy, they think I had Susan in the car and I took her head and smashed it into the windshield."

The bluntness of the statement stunned her. Not even Shelby was saying anything quite like that. Kathy tried to analyze the situation. If, God forbid, Susan was dead, if she had actually turned up dead, it would be a reasonable move for the authorities to question Mark, since he had been so close to her. *Fine,* she thought. *He should tell them what he knows and that will be the end of it.* Why was he compounding the equation? Why in the world was he babbling about the windshield?

He got up to pace, and she knew he was looking not at her but somewhere out into the darkness. "They wanted to know about my activities that week," he explained wanly. "I have to tell them everything that happened as it happened." He explained that after the meeting with Ray and

Maynard, he dug the car rental agreement out of his travel voucher file and gave it to Huggins.

"This is totally out of hand!" Kathy shouted. "You're fueling this yourself now!" She stormed into the house, letting the screen door slam behind her.

An hour later, she was awake when he climbed into bed. She lay pointedly on the far side of her half of the mattress, so their bodies did not touch. They lay awake for a long time, but neither of them spoke.

Grinding her teeth, Kathy thought, *I am goddamned if this is going to continue. We worked hard to get where we wanted to be—the nightmare was supposed to be behind us.* Finally, still without acknowledging her husband's presence, she drifted off to sleep.

Brimming with righteousness, early the next morning Kathy gulped down a cup of coffee and drove to the FBI offices, which were housed in a nondescript modern office building just off the interstate in North Miami Beach. Even agents' wives are required to show identification, so she brusquely dropped her driver's license on the reception desk and stated her business with a cool succinctness that struck the receptionist as arrogance. "I'm Kathy Putnam, Special Agent Mark Putnam's wife. And I'm here to see Mr. Huggins." The receptionist picked up a phone, murmured a few words into it, and asked Kathy to take a seat.

As she waited, she studied the agency's seal on the wall between the two mahogany doors leading into the inner offices and snorted quietly at the slogan depicted on a banner beneath the scales of justice: FIDELITY—BRAVERY—INTEGRITY. We'll see about that, she thought. Above the seal, a video surveillance camera peered obtrusively into the reception area, recording on a tape that no one would ever watch the image of a bored, quietly affronted secretary tapping at a keyboard, studiously ignoring the young woman in a neat business suit who sat nearby. In their mutually exclusive piques, both women wished they could smoke a cigarette.

After a few minutes, the door to the left opened and a man who looked to be in his fifties appeared with a hand extended and one foot planted on the reception-area rug. He introduced himself as Roy Tubergen and asked her in with a cordial flourish. It was the first time they had met. Kathy shook his hand briskly, then got right to the point. She saw no need under the circumstances to play the role of the primly careerist wife or waste time with a man who probably didn't have a clue about what had gone on in Kentucky.

"I don't mean to be rude, Mr. Tubergen, but I came here to see Jim Huggins. I want to see Huggins, and I want to see that state trooper from Kentucky."

The FBI official had repaired behind his desk, an immense glass-topped expanse on which were displayed a brown leather out basket, a spray of miniature flags in a planter, and Tubergen's hands, folded casually beneath parchment-stiff cuffs squarely fastened with shiny silver links. Teeth gleaming, he smiled benevolently at his visitor, who sat erect in a chair placed carefully just to the side of the desk. A plush dark carpet and billowing tropical plants on either side of the shiny desk required only the accompaniment of a lazy wood-blade ceiling fan to complete the impression of a concierge station at a first-class Moroccan hotel.

"I know you're upset, and I know Mark's upset," he said with studied sympathy. "Why don't you tell me what's going on."

But Kathy had left the little-girl manners behind. "Listen. I want to talk to them, not to you. As far as I'm concerned, the bureau owes me right now. I went through hell in Kentucky. I slept with a *gun* for this agency. And I'll be damned if I'm going to be jerked around or let you do what you're trying to do to my husband. I'm sorry!"

"I'm really sorry that you're upset like this," Tubergen said, assuming that tears were about to arrive. His hand brushed absently at the handkerchief peeping out from his breast pocket.

But her brown eyes flashed anger instead. "No, you don't seem to understand. This is not a matter of my being upset.

When an agent's name—*Mark's* name—is thrown out in the way it obviously has been in Kentucky, the FBI should have been all over it before it escalated to the point where my husband's integrity is on the line. I have never seen my husband like this. And now they are *questioning* him? I am here with information that should have been included in this investigation a long time ago, and I want it straightened out. I demand to be interviewed. The FBI is going to hear me.'' Her chin was set.

Tubergen had had only a few hours to prepare himself for the prospect of an agent under his supervision being the possible target of a criminal investigation. He had taken no time at all to anticipate an assault from that agent's wife. However, a career in the federal bureaucracy had prepared him with the requisite etiquette for such uncertain circumstances. "Let me get Mr. Huggins for you," he said, lifting the phone with palpable relief.

Tubergen vacated his office gratefully, and Huggins took his place behind the same desk. Huggins was a soft-spoken man, but Kathy could see the distress in his eyes. He had no desire to cause any further grief to a woman whose fierce loyalty he found heartbreaking.

Before he could say anything, she let him know she was in no mood for social chatter. "Where is Richard Ray?"

Huggins's bushy eyebrows went up. "He's on a plane. He left early this morning."

This was a major disappointment. She had wanted the Kentucky cops there when she said her piece. Yearning to comfort her, Huggins heard himself giving assurance to Kathy's obvious belief that the investigation was routine, a technicality perhaps muddled by police ham-handedness. He told her that the FBI was only investigating the matter of a possible kidnaping. He did not feel a need to point out that kidnaping—a federal crime—was a way for the FBI to gain jurisdiction in a homicide, which is a state crime. Nor did he mention his own reactions to the previous day's questioning.

"I understand why you're angry," Huggins said, hoping to take control of the conversation. "Look, all I can do is explain to you what the FBI is doing. We are officially involved now in the investigation, and we're going to see to it that this thing is taken care of, once and for all. There are questions that need to be answered—you know as well as I do the kinds of allegations that are flying around in Pikeville. Well, now the big guys are involved." He smiled benignly. "The bureau is on the case, and we're going to get to the bottom of it, no fooling around now. Everything's going to be fine once the air is cleared."

Kathy relaxed a bit, satisfied that she had at least staked out a defense of Mark's honor. She figured the investigation would get the questions answered—Mark would take a few lumps, of course. He had been sloppy with informants such as Susan, who should have been closed out long before she disappeared. But it wasn't Mark's fault the FBI had let that office get out of control, and besides, Mark had plenty of credit in the bank. He was one of the bureau's fair-haired boys. Police work was never neat. You got kicked in the teeth at times; he'd recover. And besides, Kathy wasn't about to let her husband take the heat alone—she remained determined to make the bureau confront and concede its own culpability, sending a rookie agent to a hellhole like Pikeville with all of sixteen weeks' training, including a *two-hour* class in working with informants, and no daily supervision. And then compounding the error by stashing Poole there, too. Dick Tracy would have had a hard time under such circumstances.

"Mr. Huggins," she said calmly, "it's no secret that we went through a terrible ordeal. I don't know how far you've looked into what was going on in Pikeville, but they've used me and Mark. My family was almost destroyed because of what happened down there. As I said, I don't understand when Mark's name was thrown out initially why the FBI wasn't all over this thing." This time there actually were tears in her eyes. "Where were you? Nearly a year has

gone by since Susan supposedly disappeared and all of this
talk started. Mark is *distraught* over this thing. When he
came home last night, I've never seen him like that. And
it's his own people doing this now. We left Pikeville behind, but it keeps coming back to haunt us. And Mark's
own former partner is up there taking part in the whispering
campaign. That has to stop!''

"Kathy, I hear what you're saying. Mark is one of the
finest young agents in the bureau. That's why we're involved now. Why don't you tell me what's on your mind."
Huggins took out a yellow legal pad to make notes.

She obliged, launching into an indictment that she had
mentally prepared for months, honed the night before, and
rehearsed on the drive down from Fort Lauderdale. Right
off, she threw in the person she held almost as responsible
for Mark's difficulties as Susan was.

"As far as Mr. Poole is concerned, I have absolutely no
respect for that man. He's got no business carrying a badge.
If you want to talk to somebody who's had a relationship
with Susan, don't forget Poole. From what Susan told me,
Poole spent an awful lot of time trying to get her to go to
bed with him.''

"Poole?'' Huggins scribbled some notes, realizing that
this could get complicated. One by one, Kathy spelled out
her grievances about the Pikeville office, impressing him
with her command of details about FBI business in an operation that had clearly gone badly out of control. Informants tripping over each other and making secret, often
conflicting deals. Crossed signals. Huggins's pencil
worked furiously trying to keep up. He hadn't known
about the abortive drug sting; he'd never heard of an
agent's wife being encouraged to risk her neck like that.
That alone was very, very irregular. And then, Kathy's
allegation that Mark's partner leaked it to an *informant?*
To a man who took great pride in the professionalism of
the FBI, what Kathy told him constituted a disturbing indictment.

Clearly, Putnam was not the only one who needed to come up with some answers. And whatever happened with him, there would still be the fury of Kathy Putnam to contend with. This was not a woman who tended to stay in the background. And while he realized that Kathy was projecting some of her anger and frustration onto Mark's former partner, she was also obviously prepared to hold forth in some detail on matters that would add complications that this investigation, highly touchy to begin with, did not need right now.

When she wound down, Huggins sat back and exhaled loudly. "I can't believe what went on down there," he said, then asked, "You don't think Poole killed her, do you?"

"No," Kathy replied, sitting back and smoothing her skirt over her knees. The fact was, she didn't even believe Susan was dead. Had Huggins invited her to make a guess, she would have guessed the same thing the authorities in Pikeville had assumed, that Susan was hiding out somewhere, lying low because she had shot off her big mouth once too often and someone was threatening to shut her up permanently. That was Susan.

Huggins cleared his throat and thanked her for coming. "We're going to see to it that we check all these things out, and that this is resolved as quickly as possible."

That sounded vague but promising to Kathy, who drove home with a degree of satisfaction that she had at least laid out the outlines of the Pikeville problem—given them enough information to investigate properly, make their report, and let Mark get on with his career and them with their lives. So confident was she that things were moving along in the proper direction that she welcomed Huggins's seemingly offhand suggestion, delivered as she was leaving, that Mark might want to take a polygraph test—just for the record. Mark had been ridiculously eager to cooperate anyway. "Oh," she had said with an airy wave of her hand, "he'll have no problem with that."

*   *   *

She was glad to find Mark out back watching Danielle and little Mark splashing in the inflated wading pool. She could tell he was nervous by the tentative way he asked her how it went.

"Everything's going to be fine," she said. "You've got to relax. I gave them enough information to clear this thing up. If anybody has anything to worry about now, it's Poole."

"Well, I don't know about that."

She wished he would just let her handle it. "Mark, you don't realize the kinds of thing an investigation like this can uncover." Hardly incidental to her concern was a desire that Mark not realize the extent to which she had confided in Poole during the winter about getting them transferred out of Pikeville. She knew that Mark would not appreciate some of her secret dealings with his former partner.

Yet Mark remained as apprehensive as he had been the night before. "Well, I'm going to get dressed and go to the office." He kissed the kids and turned to go in the house. "I just want you to know how much I appreciate your going to bat for me."

"We're in this together."

He didn't say so, but Mark knew that was absolutely no longer true.

Friday morning, Mark entered the office on feet that felt as if they had ten-pound jogging weights strapped to them. The level of chatter fell noticeably. So they know, he thought, heading straight for the conference room. Inside, Huggins was alone, unable or unwilling to look at him directly.

Huggins said in a measured tone, "Mark, there's a couple of things that I'm a little confused about. To clear this whole thing up, how about taking that polygraph?"

"Well, Jim, you know, a polygraph indicates guilt, that you think I'm guilty."

"No, it's just a tool for us to gauge."

"Well, let me think about it a little, okay?"

Mark had already decided he was going to take the test. It was the next step, and it would probably be the big one. A polygraph operator was not going to worry about insulting his professionalism. A polygraph operator would look at him coldly and ask, at last, *Did you kill this girl?* He wasn't sure how he would reply. But he knew the rules of the game would change at that point. Huggins had little else to say. Mark spent the rest of the morning on paperwork.

As lunchtime approached, Mark took Huggins aside.

"Okay, I'll go on the box. Let's get this over with."

Huggins told the agent in charge, Gavin, who phoned FBI headquarters in Washington. Very quickly, it was arranged for Mark and Huggins to fly to Washington that night. The test would be administered the next morning.

Mark went home early to pack. After much wavering in his mind, he was now certain that they didn't have a body. No one had found Susan. No one could prove that she was dead. But again, he had to think, *She has been out there for a year.* Wasn't it time to bring her in?

Now he was measuring his time in hours. He felt like a man desperate to extend a vacation. Would there be one more night with the kids? He did not know. He did know that very soon, it would be out of his hands.

Kathy had hoped to see a glimmer of optimism in her husband, but he looked worse than ever. With more resignation than she thought appropriate, Mark told her that he had decided he had to take the polygraph, though Huggins and Tubergen had assured him it was strictly voluntary. To get it over with, he was planning to fly to Washington that night. The test was the next morning. She watched him stuffing underwear in an overnight bag.

"Do you want to do this?" she asked, frowning at his mechanical motions.

"It's to clear my name," he said without much conviction, turning to her with a look of helplessness. "Do you think I should or not?"

Kathy took a deep breath and exhaled slowly. To her, the important thing was to get this behind them. After thinking for a moment, she accepted his decision. "I guess it makes sense for you to take the polygraph and straighten this out. Calm down. You're making this into a bigger problem than it has to be. This is going to work itself out. How could it not work itself out? I don't understand why you're so upset."

"You're right." He seemed to brighten.

Kathy made an early dinner. Mark didn't eat much, and he barely noticed the kids at the table. Before he left for his flight, he went through his usual ritual of reading the kids their bedtime story. Kathy lingered in the hall and looked at the three of them on the bed, a tableau of familial trust, fatherly love, childlike devotion, framed in the doorway of Danielle's room. Kathy unconsciously hung it like a photograph in her mind. Then she went out back to smoke and think.

Her afternoon courage faded with the daylight; with a sick feeling, she considered what she should have realized a long time ago, the likelihood that her husband had had an affair with Susan. Nothing else that she knew of could explain his prolonged agitation, and what she now recognized as his abiding guilt. She despised the thought, threw it against the wall of reason, but it bounced back. He had. The son of a bitch had.

If that was true, agreeing to the polygraph was a mistake. When he came out to say good-bye, she said, "Look, Mark, something's obviously wrong." She was thinking fast, trying to review the options realistically through her growing pain. "Whatever it is, you've got to know by now, with everything we've been through together, that we'll work it out. If there's something you have to tell me about, about you and Susan, or whatever, tell me now before you go and do this thing tomorrow. If there's something that you're hiding when you take this polygraph, it's just going to make you look guilty. Whatever it is, you can tell me. Tell me what it is now and we can get through this, Mark. If we got through Pikeville together, we can get through this.'' Desperately, she wanted an admission before he left her alone in the night with her thoughts.

He didn't comply. "Well, what would you think if I had?"

She didn't want to say, "Had what?" Instead, she tried to hurtle forward in time, forgive him, and start the healing. "Mark, we'll work it out. If something happened between you and her, we'll deal with it. There isn't anything you can't tell me—"

"What if I had—"

"—*nothing*, Mark," she repeated, fighting tears as the truth displayed itself.

"I want you to understand something. I have to take the polygraph tomorrow. I have to do it. And then I'll tell you everything. And you'll understand."

And then he left.

On the plane, he and Huggins spoke uneasily, quickly exhausting bureau gossip. Each gratefully grabbed a magazine when the flight attendant came by. Pretending to read *Sports Illustrated*, Mark sensed Huggins's distress and was deeply sorry for being the cause of it. He felt as if he had a ton of iron on his shoulders.

It was late when they got in to Washington National Airport. Mark remembered arriving there in 1986, a new agent in training, on top of the world. On their way to Quantico, the thirty-five rookies in the FBI class checked each other out for what they could spot: attitudes, guts, brains, physique. Looking for the edge. Hoping they'd make it. Wondering who among them would not.

At the same airport on Thanksgiving weekend, on a three-day leave from the academy, he was met by Kathy and two-year-old Danielle, all dressed up. They stayed at the Crystal City Marriott and visited the monuments with the happy tenacity of Japanese tourists. Would the baby remember the sense of proprietorship her old man felt when he showed her the Capitol, the Lincoln Memorial, the White House? Would she ever think of her father as a federal agent, in this city, that wonderful time, the three of them in love?

He and Huggins took a cab to the hotel. Huggins went his own way. Mark put his things in his room and went back out to wander the empty streets of the capital. In a while, he managed to straighten up a bit as he walked. He was still an agent of the government he was sworn to protect. A damned fine agent, one of the goddamned best. Hardworking, focused, a self-starter, a guy you only had to tell once. He wasn't the smartest or the best educated or the craftiest. He was naïve. But he was ethical and honest, and he would match his dedication against anybody's. Briefly, he savored that.

He thought of getting rip-roaring drunk, but quickly ruled that out. He walked for hours. God, he had wanted to belong. This is where he belonged, in this meticulously dignified capital with its monuments like alabaster tablets forced on the sky by floodlight.

He turned back to the hotel. As he walked, he spoke with her. "Well, Susan, my time is up. I don't know how you're feeling about this, but it's time to get this thing squared away. It's time to get you back home."

He went to bed amazingly at peace.

His wife had no peace that night, nor any other that followed. Kathy went to bed crippled with injury. Okay, she thought. He did it. Yes, the bastard slept with Susan. *Susan!* She cringed to recall how pathetic she had found Susan at the time. But it was true! She closed her eyes and thought hard, as if to summon the unknowable: When and how did they do it? Where did they do it? How did they keep it from her? *They.*

Susan blabbed about everything else—how could she have kept her mouth shut about a such a coup? For that alone, Kathy hated her, for mocking her so effortlessly. Did they laugh about it together?

But her imagination recoiled. No, she decided abruptly,

it was not true. Mark never lied to her. It had never happened. Oh, it *almost* happened, probably, but it never got that far. He had better sense than that. Her heart flooded with love and gratitude for the loyalty her husband had shown, at a time when their marriage was strained; she cherished him for the guilt he must have felt, at what he almost did to her—and to Danielle, his sweetheart, to dapper little Mark . . .

She kicked off the covers and lay there, wide awake, her thoughts spinning. Nothing stayed in place long enough to make sense. She steadied her impressions, fixed on them one at a time, ran down a mental checklist. The hazard lights were flashing again. Come *on,* she told herself brutally. There was something seriously wrong with Mark, and there had been all year. She could see it now. A man who was never sick, suddenly always complaining about diarrhea. That scratching at his chest, to the point where he had to go to the doctor to get medicine for the rash. Mr. Easygoing, now so distracted he couldn't brush his teeth without moaning. What the hell was wrong with him?

And that rental car! The cracked windshield, his bandaged hand. Why had he lied about it? Why had he gone to so much trouble to bring it up when she had pretty much forgotten about it, would never have given it another thought? She could see his boyish face, lying as brazenly and haplessly as a child. And Susan throwing her head back with that shrill laugh. How foolish she must have sounded: *Susan, you are an intelligent, attractive, and worthwhile woman. Mark is not the only man in the world. You can have what I have, Susan. Don't sell yourself short.* Susan! Susan always looked for the easy way. Susan was a thief. She took what she wanted when she knew she could get away with it. Of course she took Mark. Of course she did! What idiot wouldn't see that!

She burrowed into the covers, feeling desperately alone. *You can have what I have, Susan. You have to set goals and work toward them.* How delicious that must have seemed to

her lying in Mark's arms, against his body. And she had;
Kathy now knew it as surely as she knew her children's
names. Susan had slept with her husband.

Dammit, she was closer to Susan than Mark was! Susan
was *her* friend! She'd been the one to teach that slut how to
behave like a lady! She knew all of Susan's tricks, all of her
brittle fears, her inadequacies, and unfocused ambitions.
Susan was pretty, if you liked the Daisy Mae type, but she
was dumb as a doorknob. Kathy and Mark used to make
cruel jokes about her! For a fleeting, righteous instant,
Kathy resented her husband deeply for the contempt he had
shown Susan, her friend and admirer. Hadn't Susan even
started dressing like her, *talking* like her, for God's sake?
Hadn't she begun to say *you,* not *y'all?* Susan had told her
she loved Mark, that Mark was "gorgeous." Kathy merely
shrugged that off.

Kathy began to probe the wound again, fixing on the
moment of betrayal, when he unzipped his pants. She tor-
tured herself cruelly with the image. She looked at Mark's
pillow, demanding an accounting. Details, goddammit!
Chapter and verse, buddy boy! When? How many times?
What were you wearing? What did she do that I don't do?
How many times, Mark? Did she come? Did she squeal?
Did you kiss her precious little face, hold her precious little
hand, walk in the precious goddamn woods? Did you! What
did you say to her? Did you laugh about me? What did you
tell her about me! What did you say! *Why didn't I know
about this!*

How stupid she felt. Of course she should have seen it. But
a worse fear was overwhelming her merciless insistence: the
ramifications of the affair, not the least of which was the possibility that the rumor she'd dismissed as ridiculous—that
Susan had been pregnant with Mark's child—might also be
true. That there could be a baby—her husband's baby—
Danielle and little Mark's half brother or half sister! Kathy
struck her clenched fist on the mattress with each word:
"That's why this had such an impact on him."

The only sensible thing to do was to divorce him. But marriage is not often sensible. She groped through doubts: Can I live with this? We have two children. Do I throw away eight years, especially knowing what I know about Pikeville, who Susan was, and where she came from? She meant nothing! They would never see her again! Then it struck her anew: if he had had an affair with her and he was trying to cover it up, it was going to make him look guilty if Susan really was dead. She thought of the damaged hand, the disjointed comments, the phone calls and brooding looks of the past year. *What if he* did *know something about her being missing?* What *about* the lies about that windshield? There were too many lies now, leering like hobgoblins in the shadows.

At last her mind began working like a cop's. Okay, they are in the car. They make love in the car. (How tacky, Mark! The car?) He has a short affair with her, and one night they are in the car and they get in an accident. She's hurt, hurt bad—he panics and leaves her. That could explain the cracked windshield.

No, Mark would never leave Susan lying somewhere, injured and helpless. But was there any other way Mark could have been involved in Susan's death—assuming Susan was dead? Say they skid off the road, hit a tree. Yes, Susan dies, she's dead. Mark panics and then leaves her in the mountains somewhere. No, that would mean there would have been more damage to the car than just a broken windshield. But how about, they're having an affair; okay, they have a fight when they're in the car. There's a big argument, Mark gets pissed off, punches the windshield, Susan storms out of the car and wanders away . . . and later, one of these *other* things happens to her, like that scummy ex-husband catches her and beats her once too often, or one of those other lowlifes she knows kills her, one of the drug dealers or bank robbers who always seem to be in the wings of her life. So Susan is dead, and Mark is indirectly involved. This is possible.

Hellish images rage through her mind. His bandaged

hand, their faces gazing at each other; Susan's inane giggle, countless casual comments now swollen with cruel irony. The way Mark brooded when they discussed Susan's disappearance, his reaction that time when Kathy mused, "She could be lying dead somewhere," now startling in hindsight: *"Don't ever say that!"*

Kathy weighed her own role. She was a big girl, a child of the 1970s, an honors graduate of the sexual revolution. So he had a tumble with someone else, big deal. He came home to his wife, didn't he? It wasn't the end of the world; affairs happened to the best of people in the worst of times. They can be shrugged off in time, even laughed off in time. But why did it hurt like this? She'd found the false base on her life, that's why. Her husband, once a part of her being, suddenly seemed as alien as the man in the next car at a red light. She felt foolish and exposed. She had never measured up. She heard ghostly laughter rise in chorus, from a grade school in Manchester, over fog-chilled hollows of a Kentucky night.

She opened her eyes to a dull headache. The sun warmed the bed, flooded the room. Downstairs, she could hear Danielle lecturing her brother on the proper way to pour cereal into a bowl.

In the kitchen, as she banged the kettle down on the stove, the phone rang. It was Mark. His voice was shaky. She pressed her eyes shut against the sunlight, knowing that the nightmare hadn't ended.

"I just wanted you to know that this is not going to go well today. I'm really scared about this. I don't know if you're going to understand," he said.

An artery in her neck throbbed. "I'm glad you called. Don't do this! I want to talk to you first." First, she wanted to hear the truth in his own words, even if this was a situation she could no longer control. He said, "I told you I have to do this. But be prepared." His voice broke.

She thought fast and said, "Whatever happens, whatever the results of the polygraph, don't talk to them until you talk to me. Don't give them a statement or any information. You don't have to do that, Mark."

He was noncommittal. "I'll talk to you afterward."

The test was in FBI headquarters, the J. Edgar Hoover building. Huggins introduced Mark to the polygraph technician. Huggins and an FBI supervisor watched the test on a closed-circuit television from an adjoining room. The questions were short. The technician paused between each to read the machine and make notes. He asked about kids, college, cases. Finally, he asked about Susan.

"Did you ever have any sexual relationship with Susan Smith?"

"No," Mark said.

"Did you cause the disappearance of Susan Smith?"

"No."

"Do you know, was she wearing your clothes at the time of her disappearance?"

"No, not that I know."

Afterward, the technician told Mark that his voice had dropped perceptibly in pitch on the questions on which he had lied. "The real Mark Putnam told the truth about college and his family and the cases he worked. But he lied about Susan, didn't he?"

Mark knew that it was over, and so did Huggins, who looked at him sadly. "Mark, we have some problems."

"Yeah, I know you got some problems," Mark said, almost with a sneer.

"Why don't you talk about it with me?"

"No. I want to go home and talk to my wife about it first. I need to talk to my wife. And then after I've done that, I'll do whatever you want to get this thing squared away."

Huggins said he could call after he talked over the results some more.

"I want to go back to Florida and tell her in person. I need to talk to her," Mark insisted.

They said he could call.

"How did it go?" Kathy asked.

"Not very well. Things are bad." Mark said he was calling directly from the interrogation room.

She was trembling. "Are they holding you there?" Her words sounded muffled and disconnected, like a television playing through the wall of an apartment.

"No, they're not keeping me but they want me to talk to you over the phone. They have a stenographer here to take down whatever I say."

"No! Mark! Mark? Don't say anything! If they'll let you come home, come home and we'll talk about it here. Don't say anything else. You don't have to. Do you hear me? Come home."

"Okay. I'll try."

So now he at least knew. When they came to him and asked point-blank, he had lied.

He sensed a flurry of activity around him as he spoke to Kathy. Someone on another phone, papers being shuffled. A different process being set into motion. He remained outwardly calm, but his mind raced. It was quite clear that the rules had changed. Much of the professional courtesy was gone. He felt it as surely as if they had slapped the cuffs on him. They wanted to know everything, and he said they would have it, but he insisted he had to see his wife first.

"Can I go home?" He figured this would be his last time there. "Then I'll tell you everything."

There was a hurried conference out of his earshot. Obviously, there was no evidence except his confession. There was some concern about suicide. He was asked if he had brought his gun. He had not. Finally, they agreed. He was allowed to fly back to Fort Lauderdale. It was understood that he would also see a lawyer.

His flight was the last one into Fort Lauderdale airport that night. An after-hours glare harshly lit the faces of the stragglers shuffling past the darkened shops, barricaded cafés, and unattended ticket counters. Kathy found Mark waiting alone at the far end of a wide, empty corridor.

He started to speak, but she held up her hand and said, "Just—don't—talk—yet."

In the car, she suggested that they stop at a Holiday Inn near the airport for a drink. It was a conversation neither of them wanted to have at home, where Kathy's sister, Chris, was still living with them. Kathy looked straight ahead and lit a cigarette in the car, something she hadn't had the nerve to do in many years.

It was nearly one o'clock when they walked into the Holiday Inn lounge. At the bar, Kathy ordered a double Black Russian for herself and a beer for Mark. Carrying the drinks, she led him silently to a table in the darkness. Across the room, a four-piece band was playing heavy metal; couples in their twenties, the last gasp of the fading Fort Lauderdale beach scene, danced under lights that flashed like those on a patrol car.

Defiantly, Kathy lit another cigarette and blew the smoke at a point just over Mark's shoulder. She moved her glass to the side and looked directly at him for the first time that night. She waited.

"This is really serious," he sputtered.

Damn right, she thought. In a cold fury, she smoked and waited.

"I'm sorry—"

Get on with it, she thought angrily.

"It's—"

"Look," she said in the sarcastic tone of a prosecutor trying to dismiss the ridiculous before homing in on the self-evident. "Did you *kill* her?" She spat out the words with a street swagger she hadn't used since she was a teenager.

"Yes."

This was not an answer she had anticipated. She had been expecting a nervous chuckle, a "Come *on,* Kathy!" before she probed the painful details and watched him squirm. She blinked slowly, her mind two beats behind the words.

"So you slept with her!"

"Yeah, I did."

"And this could have been your baby." She flung the sentence across the table.

"Kat—"

"Don't talk to me! . . . How did this happen?"

Confused, he did not answer right away. He kept crying. Briefly, she indulged her contempt, then demanded, "Was there a car accident?"

"No."

This elicited a furious, thin stream of smoke. "It wasn't a car accident. Did you *shoot* her?" Her voice was rising. Out of the corner of her eye, she noticed a middle-aged man in a business suit drinking alone at a table a few feet away. He had been casually watching them, with his eye on her. Now he stiffened at what he overheard.

"No. I choked her." Mark made a feeble little choking motion.

"You choked her," she said in a flat tone. Then her voice rose, her face contorted with sarcasm, and she made an exaggerated choking motion, as if to show him how it was done. "You *strangled* her?" With that, the eavesdropper at the next table abandoned any pretext of indifference. He got up, slapped a twenty-dollar bill on his table, and scuttled away.

She waited until the man was gone. "How do you know she was dead? If you left her, are you sure she was dead? Are you sure, Mark! They haven't found the body. She was unconscious. Maybe she just got up and walked away."

"I thought that a million times. She was dead. I know she was."

Mark had regained some control. His eyes were smarting from the smoke, which she was making no effort whatsoever to direct away from him.

"I want to explain—"

"All right," she said abruptly. "Tell me how it happened."

He said that he hadn't lied to her when she first asked him about Susan, back when Susan was shooting her mouth off about Mark. He had laughed it off as absurd. And it was—he hadn't slept with her then. That happened later, but except for the night Kenneth called, the subject hadn't come up again until now.

All of the pieces fell together with a deafening thud. There was another round of drinks that was brought by a waitress wearing a thong bikini bottom and a lacy push-up bra under a little red jacket. Kathy was dimly aware of her trying to make eye contact with Mark. Her mind careened through uncertain frames of time: Mark and Susan drive into the mountains; they park, argue some more, suddenly she's screaming, hitting—and he loses it. It's over in sixty seconds. He pulls her out onto the ground, desperate, but she won't breathe. Like that, she's dead. She's wearing his shorts and T-shirt, for some reason that Kathy forgets. He puts her in the trunk of the car and goes back to the motel. And then drives to a meeting in Lexington the next day and parks the car out front with Susan's body in the trunk. *He drives around with a dead woman locked in the trunk of his car, like a gym bag?*

"You have to remember, she was screaming at me, Kat. I was afraid that everyone else in the hotel would hear about it."

He succumbed to wrenching tears just as the reality of what Kathy was hearing slammed finally into consciousness. In a flash of contempt, she walloped him, smacked him so hard her arm resonated with pain. He tried to duck the blow, which caught him forcefully on the right side of his face. As he dodged, he lost his balance and fell to the floor, one hand grasping the little table on which the drinks had spilled. He was crying like a three-year-old when he came back up. She had never seen Mark shed more than a few sentimental tears and watched the spectacle with the detached interest of a motorist passing an accident scene.

"I want to get out of here. Kathy, please let's get out of

here and go home and talk. I don't want the neighbors knowing our business.''

She wasn't budging. ''No, I'm not moving and you're not moving. I'm simply not ready to get up yet.'' She had mustered a degree of haughtiness now and caught the eye of the waitress, who had wandered over expectantly when she saw Mark fall. Kathy regarded the waitress contemptuously in her skimpy costume, ready to wallop her, too.

''Another beer?'' the waitress asked Mark, and added with a look at Kathy, ''Another double Black Russian?''

''Yeah, another double. And he'll have a beer.''

Kathy turned back to Mark, but the conversation had begun to blur. Several surreal rounds of drinks later, she and the man she had long loved and respected, the father of her children, had explored every facet of the fact that he had killed Susan Smith.

In the car, Kathy lay back and blamed herself: ''I could have stopped this if I had been paying attention.''

''Hey, I did what I did. Nothing you did could have prevented this.''

''Yes, I could have! I could have! You don't know what I know!'' She was nearly hysterical.

She recalled making a few clumsy thrusts: ''You bastard, how could you do this to us?'' and ''Why did you *tell* me! Now that I know, I can't lie for you!'' She remembered him wordlessly and gently undressing her in their bedroom and taking his place in bed beside her. She sat up and shouted, ''What am I going to do with the kids while their father is in *prison*, Mark! Did you think of *that* when you killed her?''

15

She slept for less than an hour. With her mind instantly reeling again, she bolted up in bed, sensing Mark lying beside her with his eyes open. She squinted at the glowing red numerals on the alarm clock. It was five-thirty. She was due at her part-time waitressing job at the International House of Pancakes at seven, to get ready for the first wave of the Sunday-morning church crowd. Her first cogent thought was that she needed to phone her manager to say that she wasn't coming in, in time for him to bring in a substitute. But it was still too early to call. She remembered that Mark had told her he had to be in the office at ten, to talk to the special agent in charge. She wanted to go with him.

Not knowing exactly what to do, she dressed quickly and walked down the hallway to Danielle's bedroom, where the sight of Chris, asleep in the spare bed, vaguely irritated her. *How could you be sleeping at a time like this?* she thought, shaking her sister until her eyes were open. "Wake up! I need you!"

"What in the world is wrong?" Chris asked sleepily.

Kathy was put out, as if Chris should somehow know that a calamity had occurred. "I can't believe he did that!"

"Did *what*, for God's sake?"

"Mark killed that woman!" Kathy hissed like a madwoman.

Chris, fully awake now, gasped, "What woman?"

Kathy began to cry with frustration, sensing that this was only the start of the pestilence of explaining that lay ahead of her. "The one in Kentucky!"

Chris's own police instincts snapped into place. Full ex-

planations could come later. "Should I get you and the kids
out of here?"

"What for? No! He's fine!" Kathy sobbed, afraid of
awakening Danielle, who slept on with her face turned to
the wall.

"What do you want me to do?"

Kathy threw her hands up. "Leave me alone!" she said
in a shrill whisper, and stormed into the bathroom, where
she mechanically brushed her teeth. Absently, she fumbled
in the medicine chest for her makeup and dabbed it at her
face.

There was no protocol for starting such a day. The closest
parallel was a sudden death in the family, but Kathy had not
even had any adult experience with that—she was only
thirty years old; her own parents were relatively young;
even three of *their* parents were still alive. She found herself
in the kitchen, staring in bafflement at the wall phone in her
hand. She put it to her ear and heard it ringing at the other
end.

Her father answered huskily. Why *him?* she thought furiously; why couldn't *she* have picked it up? Her voice
quavering, she managed to say, "It's Kathy. It's serious. I
need you guys to come down here right away," but that was
all she could get out. Sensing Mark's presence behind her,
she slammed the receiver down on the breakfast counter.

"I'll handle it," Mark said, rushing back upstairs. Wordlessly, she put the phone to her ear, listening to her father's
labored breathing. When Mark picked up the extension in
the bedroom, she heard her husband say, "Ray, it's Mark.
There's something I have to talk to you about . . ." With a
trembling index finger, she pressed the button down and
placed the phone into the cradle.

By now it was after six; little Mark had wandered into the
bedroom, waking Danielle. Chris took charge of the kids
and didn't ask questions. Once she had decided that no one
was in any danger, she figured the best she could do was to

keep the kids occupied and not worry about clarifications until Kathy and Mark sorted out whatever had occurred. She made a deliberate decision not even to speculate, beyond supposing that an accident of some kind had happened involving Mark and someone else when he was in Kentucky. She was vaguely aware of the problems they had experienced in Pikeville, especially of Kathy's misery there just before they left. She had heard something, during the time she had been living with them in Florida, about an informant being missing. But she figured these were just normal headaches of FBI life.

When she brought the kids down for breakfast, Chris spotted Mark on the couch watching her with a stricken and questioning look. She ventured a cheerful "Good morning."

"Hey," he said very softly, forcing a grim smile. "How's it going, Chris?"

During the six years she had known him, Chris had come to respect her brother-in-law for his equanimity and his steady good sense. She thought, without any question, that Mark was the best thing that had ever happened to Kathy. The months she had spent living with them had only reinforced that assessment. If Mark was in control, how bad could it be? She had never even heard the man raise his voice. Kathy, the volatile one, was out in the kitchen making coffee, which was reassuring in itself, although Chris did observe that her sister had spilled the grounds in a small heap on the counter and had not poured any water into the machine. Furthermore, Kathy's makeup, usually light, appeared to have been jabbed on with a paintbrush, and her outfit looked as if it had been assembled in the dark. Chris took over the coffee-making and said nothing.

Kathy broke down again when she called her boss at the restaurant. As gently as he could, Mark took the phone and explained that a family emergency had come up and she wouldn't be in. The manager was considerate and concerned. To Mark's relief, he didn't pry for details.

They had to leave around nine for the drive to the office to talk with Gavin, the special agent in charge of the Miami FBI bureau, who had kept in touch with Huggins in Washington the previous day. It was a meeting both men dreaded.

At some point before they left the house, Mark telephoned his mother. Kathy could not imagine what he said to her.

A janitor let them in a side door. Gavin was already waiting in his office. A large, affable man who supervised more than three hundred agents in one of the FBI's most important and sensitive bureaus, he had been fully apprised of a situation that was, as far as anyone could tell, unprecedented in the eighty-three-year history of the FBI: an agent—one of his people—appeared to be facing a charge of criminal homicide. While Putnam had not confessed, he had badly failed the polygraph—and he wasn't exactly protesting his innocence. Making the situation even worse, for veteran FBI men such as Gavin and Huggins, men who had seen it all and remained true to the faith, was that the offender wasn't some rogue cowboy on some drug-addled flame-out. Of all of the eight thousand agents in the bureau, it had to be *this* guy—this walking personification of the goddamn Boy Scout code, this earnest, likable, gifted, indefatigable young man who seemed not only to avow, but to actually *project,* every virtue that the bureau still imagined itself as representing. The guy they would have put on a recruiting poster now qualified for a wanted poster.

Gavin greeted them in jeans and a short-sleeved shirt, which made him look like an interloper behind his massive mahogany desk. He was accompanied in the office by his second-in-command, the assistant special agent in charge, Larry Torrence, who had on a suit and tie. Gavin apologized gamely for the stifling atmosphere in the building and sent Torrence out to see if he could find someone to turn on the air-conditioning. He asked if they were comfortable, if they wanted coffee. All Kathy wanted was to smoke; seeing her desperation, Gavin went out himself to find an ashtray.

The social preliminaries were excruciating for Kathy. She was mortified to find herself shaking with fright, which she knew was not over the confrontation at hand, but over what would follow. The fact was, she and Mark had not yet been able to have a rational discussion about their future. Sitting there trying to get her body movements under control, she was suddenly afraid that her husband might not even make it home with her. She tried mightily to order her thoughts.

Grateful for both the ashtray and the consideration Gavin showed in holding a match to her cigarette, she drew in great gulps of smoke, exhaling furiously between racking sobs, while Torrence returned and the two supervisors persisted in discussing the air-conditioning. "No dice on the AC," she heard Torrence say. "It takes four hours for the building to cool down on a weekend." Kathy was afraid she would scream, but she only cried quietly, painfully aware that if either Gavin or Torrence had any question at all about whether Mark was guilty, one look at the state of his wife would give them their answer.

Trying to pull herself together, she asked where the ladies' room was. Gavin invited her to use his private bathroom. She cupped water on her face and stood at the sink trying to steady herself. Overcome by dizziness, she sat down. This was what Mark could have had one day: an office with a private bathroom. There was a vanity in there, with shaving things arranged neatly on it, and an extra tie folded carefully over a hanger. She put her head between her legs to stop it from spinning and saw a cockroach scurry across the floor.

When she rejoined the men, she heard Mark apologizing for the disgrace he had brought on the bureau. She followed the uneasy conversation between Mark and the two supervisors only in phrases that pierced her staggered consciousness. "I can't believe this has happened," someone said. "The FBI family" was invoked several times. She heard "worst-case scenario" mentioned. She struggled to focus.

On the sofa beside her, Mark was bowed, repentant, and she saw with a mounting sense of alarm, *compliant*.

She fought to resist the allure of the empathy that wafted over the desk of the supervisor, aware that while so far they had talked *around* any specific mention of the awful event itself, the parameters of the discussion were slowly constricting. She heard phrases that sounded familiar from somewhere: *Stress of a cop's job . . . We've all been there. Things can happen in a flash . . .* She looked anew at the three men—the chief, brimming with concern and sympathy; his affable sidekick murmuring affirmations; the contrite, mortified suspect, abjectly grateful for small kindnesses—as if peering from an apartment window at a scene far below on the street, aware only that the participants were going through certain predetermined motions. Then she heard Mark utter the words, "I would like to take care of this and clear the air," and she saw the trapdoor at his feet, triggered to spring open. Her husband was about to confess to a capital crime.

"No!" she said, the force of her protest causing the three men to stop, shift their positions, and fix her with surprised stares. "Mark," she said with a glaring look, "we have to talk."

The interruption broke the momentum. Kathy now saw that Gavin was less assured about the process than she had supposed. There was a small bend in his tone; an opportunity for reflection crept in. Of course, if Mark wished to take care of this thing, he could make a statement now. A stenographer would be called in, he could lay it out, get it over with. He would be treated with respect and consideration. Kathy was now evaluating each word. Of course, on the *other* hand, she heard, perhaps Mark and Kathy wanted to discuss it privately. Maybe they wanted to think about getting a lawyer. Gavin said that it was not his role to recommend a course of action. Seeking legal counsel was a decision only Mark could make. Nevertheless, names of good defense attorneys could be provided, if Mark wished.

"Could we talk privately?" Kathy asked.

Mark had the look of a man who has no choice but to acquiesce to his wife's wishes. "No disrespect, sir," he stammered.

Gavin told them to go into an adjacent office and talk it over.

Jumping up, Kathy marched her husband next door. Just as she thought, Mark wanted to spill his guts. "I have to take care of this thing," he protested. "It's time."

Time? He could talk about time? She thought about time: How much did they really have? A day ago, to her, it was a lifetime; now what was it—days, *hours,* before they hustled him off to prison? Mark tried weakly to protest. "This is the *FBI.* They'll treat me right," he insisted. But she shook her head violently. "Those men are *cops!* They will *do their jobs!*" she told him, not caring that she had begun to shout.

The unspoken arrangement in their marriage was that on certain occasions, one partner could invoke an ex cathedra privilege and demand that the other shut up and comply. It worked both ways, which was why it worked. Now Mark listened, although sulkily. "They can *arrest* you and put you in jail *today!*" she said. "We haven't even told the kids!"

For the first time, they talked soberly about what would happen after he confessed. He had not given it any real thought. Thirty years? Life in prison? *Execution?* Neither of them really knew. In all the time that he had been obsessed with his guilt, over the entire year since he had killed Susan, Mark had never thought through his options. It had simply never occurred to him that he had any, except to confess, to "put things right" and accept disgrace and whatever punishment the authorities saw fit to impose. It was as if the problem were strictly an intensely personal crisis of conscience, with consequences so overwhelming that no single person could affect the outcome in any way. Kathy suddenly understood that she had been omitted from that estimation. Her eyes flashed with resentment.

*   *   *

While the Putnams were talking, Gavin contacted Lou De-Falaise, the federal prosecutor in Kentucky, for advice. DeFalaise told him that since there was no outstanding state or federal arrest warrant, Putnam would be free to leave the office, even if he gave a statement, pending the filing of charges once any statement he gave was corroborated.

When he and Kathy came back in, Mark apologized for not being able to give his statement immediately. He asked for the names of some lawyers. Torrence made a phone call to a Fort Lauderdale defense attorney who had previously been an assistant U.S. attorney in Miami. In the upside-down world into which the Putnams had tumbled, this was good, because former prosecutors were "cops' lawyers." Mark and Kathy retreated again to the privacy of the spare office, where he picked up the phone. "Don't say another word until you see me," the lawyer ordered.

Long after that day, Kathy would refer to the calendar she kept for 1990 to try to sort out the chronology. She had made notes in big blocks of space on each page, next to the "Sesame Street" characters. It surprised her to see how compressed the events had been, how quickly things had happened, one after the other. At the time, it had seemed that they had neither beginning nor end.

At home, the household did not become a shambles, though Kathy thought it had. Chris soon pieced the story together, although she didn't yet grasp the consequences. "Kathy was looking at me for a reaction, and I was, like, is he going to be *demoted* at work?" she would later say. The house was immaculate. When she wasn't crying, Kathy was cleaning.

Yet she moved through a mental fog. Late Sunday afternoon, she found herself at the airport, unable to understand why she was waiting at a gate, in what she noticed for the first time were mismatched clothes, her eyes swollen, hold-

ing her husband's hand tightly. She saw her mother and
father hurrying up the corridor toward them.

"I don't know how he's going to react," she heard herself say. "Don't be surprised if he hits you."

"I hope he does."

Instead her father shook his hand. She collapsed on top of
her mother. She felt safer and more vulnerable than ever.

Back home, practical matters had to be dealt with. Mark
was on vacation time, but that would end; the $600-a-week
paycheck would stop. Kathy's pay at the pancake house
wouldn't keep the household afloat, not with child-care ex-
penses. Lives were shattered, but the mortgage was due,
with no grace period for calamity. Mark was going to
prison, perhaps for the rest of his life. She had two young
children. Flaming wreckage lay everywhere. The idea of
simply soldiering on was staggering.

There were moments of respite. She remembered having
a drink and smoking a cigarette Sunday night with her parents on the back porch, the cool air coming in through the
screens, lulling her into consideration of a future without
Mark.

She was focused well enough to discuss plans. She knew
she could go home, but the idea of asking for her father's
sanctuary again caused her deep anguish. Father and daughter faced each other from well-marked emotional positions.

She broached the subject of moving back to Connecticut.
She could work, finish college, get her life together. Her
mother listened stoically as her father's mind leaped forward to control the damage. He was anxious to have his
daughter and grandchildren close by, but he couldn't stop
himself from glancing with disapproval at the drink she had
in her hand.

"I am going to help you," he said, and Kathy stiffened.
"If you want to go wherever Mark is going, I understand
that—"

She exploded. "Sure, anything to get me and the kids out
of sight!" Her father's mouth was agape. She rushed out,

thrusting the screen door behind her. Even more infuriate
that it would not slam, she stormed into the garage an
rummaged frantically for something expendable. She picke
up little Mark's lightweight stroller and smashed it agai
and again on the concrete floor until it was twisted and ber
like an umbrella in a windstorm.

The appointment with the lawyer was scheduled for Tues
day. On Monday, they decided to see a child psychologist
Huddled together in their bedroom, with Kathy's parent
and sister in the house and Mark's mother on her way dow
to Florida, having no idea what anyone would say, or eve
where everyone would sleep, they had struggled with th
need to tell Danielle that her father had killed someone an
was going to prison for a time that would outlast her child
hood. Danielle, alerted by the activity in the house, th
houseguests, the urgent verbal reassurances and muffle
cries through bedroom walls, knew that something terribl
had happened. They knew that she was waiting to see wha
it was.

"What do we tell her? 'You've always been Daddy'
little girl, but now Daddy's leaving?'" Kathy said. "How
do we not destroy her?"

Mark didn't have an answer. Kathy went down a list o
psychologists in the yellow pages and made an appointmen
with the first one who was available that day. As soon a
they saw her, they realized how impossible it was to explai
their situation coherently to a total stranger. But the psy
chologist surprised them by restating the problem suc
cinctly: "Your husband is going to jail for killing someone
and it is a total shock. You are both loving parents. How d
you explain this to your daughter, who is five years old an
loves her daddy?" She suggested practical ways to begi
sorting out the situation for both Danielle and little Mark
Find a previous example of how the child had handled ad
versity well, explain it, and hold it up as a way to approac
the current situation. Offer love and as much stability a
possible. Above all, hear the child out.

*   *   *

That night, Kathy told Mark to wait upstairs until she brought Danielle. Sitting on the bed, he said, "I don't know if I can handle this."

"Just get yourself together. I'm going to bring her in and we'll do it together, just the way we discussed this afternoon."

Kathy brought Danielle in. She scampered onto the center of their bed between her parents and asked her father why he was crying. He got up and went into the bathroom, where they could hear him sobbing loudly.

Kathy told her to wait. She returned with Mark leaning on her. Danielle watched quietly.

"Danielle, Daddy is so very sorry," he said, unable to go on. They both looked at Kathy.

She held her daughter. "Listen, do you remember when a couple of weeks ago, you were in the kitchen and Mommy was by the sink making supper, and dinner was cooking on the stove, and little Mark went over to the stove and he was going to reach up and maybe get burned? And you pushed him away and he fell and bumped his head, and he cried? And Mommy only saw you push him, she didn't see him reaching up for the stove?"

"Yeah, I remember it."

"And do you remember how you felt when I yelled at you?"

"I felt bad."

"But you really shouldn't have pushed him so hard?"

"I know."

Drawing a deep breath, Kathy explained that another bad thing had happened. Her father had done something impulsively. It was wrong, he had not meant to do it. A lady in Kentucky had been hurt very badly, there had been a fight, and Daddy had to be punished. The psychologist had stressed the need to explain that Mark was not bad, that the situation was. Moral nuances could be explored in years to come. "It wasn't as though Daddy had time to think about anything," Kathy said. "He reacted quickly, just like you did. Daddy had to tell the truth about what happened, but because of what happened, it was wrong. It was a terrible mistake. He's going to have to go away for a long time.''

Danielle started to cry. She looked at her father and said, ''Is that why you're crying, Daddy?''

Then she jumped into his arms and said, ''If you're telling the truth, why do you have to go away?''

''Because what Daddy did was very wrong.''

He told her that he would always love her, that he was proud of her, that she was a big girl, and he wanted her to be brave. ''Can you do that for me?''

She said she could.

Kathy asked Danielle if she had any questions.

She didn't. She said, ''Me and Mommy can take care of things.'' She told her father not to cry. ''You're making your nose all red.'' And Danielle left the room.

Mark was shaking violently. Kathy put her arms around him and rested her head on his chest.

''I can't believe I did this to you and the kids,'' he said.

She left him there and went downstairs to the sounds of life. Danielle was outside playing. Kathy's mother was in the kitchen, making dinner. A storm had come up fast over the Everglades. Mark stood at the upstairs window and watched the Florida downpour, which continued steadily for two days.

16

The commonwealth attorney's office started moving on the prosecution of Mark Putnam the day after the state police detectives got back to Pikeville. Capt. Gary Rose had called John Paul Runyon at home on Saturday to tell him that Mark had just taken the FBI polygraph and failed it, and that he was going to be questioned the next day by supervisors in Miami. Runyon supposed this meant that Putnam either already had a lawyer or would soon be getting one.

On Monday, Runyon held a meeting with the state police, the FBI's representative from Lexington, Terry O'Connor, and the U.S. Attorney, Lou DeFalaise, to discuss the options. The men gathered in the prosecutor's office knew that all they had on Mark at this point was that he had made false statements in an interview and during a polygraph test. Failing a lie detector test was not a crime, nor a legal indication of one. There had been no admission of guilt. They believed that he had killed Susan, but he hadn't yet admitted it, and there was still no way yet of proving it in a courtroom. There wasn't even enough to file a charge.

Runyon insisted that they evaluate the potential criminal case: In the absence of a confession, what did they have independently? Well, they could establish that Mark had a motive to cause Susan Smith harm. Several witnesses, Shelby most notable among them, would testify that Susan had said she was pregnant by Mark and had threatened to hound him until he met her terms, whatever they were. However, no one had actually heard her say these things to him. The motive was weak but at least presentable.

Furthermore, Mark had had the opportunity to commit

the crime. His presence in Pikeville at the time Susan disappeared could easily be established; the two had been registered at the same motel. However, no one had been found who actually saw them together.

That, stripped down to its bare essentials, was their "case," Runyon acknowledged morosely. The major problem, obviously, was the absence of any proof that a crime had been committed. The investigation had run its course, they knew that. After a year, they still had no physical evidence, no witness to a threat—and no body. All they could do was wait for the killer's next move.

Runyon, who had prosecuted hundreds of homicides during his career, was a formidable opponent for any defense lawyer. Not only was he smart, he was *convincing*, which is often more useful in dealing with a jury. He had the unusual ability to cry real tears when summing up a case that particularly moved him. A performance of this distinguished white-haired servant of the people in front of a jury, literally crying for justice, was one that lawyers took time off to witness. After one trial, a judge had questioned the prosecutor about his remarkable theatrics. "Judge," Runyon replied apologetically in a slow drawl, "it is a strategy I never use unless I feel that it is absolutely necessary." To which the judge had snorted, "Hell, John Paul, in my opinion any lawyer has that ability and *doesn't* use it is guilty of malpractice."

Runyon knew that if he could get Mark Putnam indicted and in the dock in a Pike County courtroom, obtaining a conviction would be no great problem. He was already lying awake at night, rehearsing his summation to a jury of mountain people: "This slick prep-school boy from *Connecticut,* a college graduate"—here a knowing glance at the jury—"this highly trained *criminologist* for the Federal Bureau of Investigation who murdered, *in cold blood,* a poor, ignorant, pregnant mountain girl, a mother of two little children . . ."

But it was an exercise in fantasy. No matter how he shuffled the cards, he knew he did not have enough evidence to indict Putnam. And he worried that Putnam and his lawyer knew the same thing.

Runyon waited impatiently to hear from that lawyer, whoever it was. Monday passed without a word. Runyon was bewildered.

Finally, late on Tuesday afternoon, he received a phone call from a Fort Lauderdale attorney who introduced himself as Bruce Zimet, a former assistant U.S. attorney, now in private practice, representing Mark Putnam.

Runyon said he knew the name.

Zimet wanted to talk hypothetically. But first he needed to invoke Rule 11 of the federal rules of criminal procedure. The prosecutor had been expecting that. Rule 11 is a standard procedure that basically enables a guilty party to discuss a plea to a lesser charge, without being subject to criminal liability for anything that is divulged during those discussions. Under Rule 11, true statements "made in the course of any proceedings under this rule" are inadmissible if the plea is ultimately rejected or withdrawn. Prosecutors with a solid case do not agree to hold discussions under Rule 11.

Carefully, Runyon told Mark's lawyer to go on.

Speaking hypothetically, Zimet explained that while a client might be willing to confess, he was not willing to take the maximum penalty for a charge on which the state apparently had no evidence.

Two weeks of negotiations had commenced.

Runyon and his assistants researched their dilemma as the talks got under way. Their central problem was that, even in the unlikely event that evidence that Mark Putnam killed Susan Smith could be produced independent of a confession, an indictment for murder would be almost impossible to support in Kentucky, where state criminal law divides "criminal homicide" into four possible charges: murder, first-degree manslaughter, second-degree manslaughter, and reckless homicide. The requirements for a charge of murder clearly reflected the historical realities of justice in a frontier state. Only cold-blooded homicides really fit the definition:

> A person is guilty of murder when, with intent to cause the death of another person, he causes the death of such person or of a third person, except that in any prosecution a person shall not be guilty under this subsection if he acted under the influence of extreme emotional disturbance for which there was a reasonable explanation or excuse, the reasonableness of which is to be determined from the viewpoint of a person in the defendant's situation under the circumstances as the defendant believed them to be.

Even with a body and independent evidence linking Mark to the killing, the requirement for intent would have been difficult to meet. Moreover, even with a riled-up jury, a prosecutor would have a difficult time countering the defense that Mark's state of mind, reflected in facts that no one disputed, was consistent with "extreme emotional disturbance," which was defined under Kentucky law as "a temporary state of mind so enraged, inflamed or disturbed as to overcome judgment and to cause one to act uncontrollably from its impelling force, rather than from evil or malicious purposes." It would not have taken Clarence Darrow for the defense to establish that Putnam met those criteria.

If this was a homicide case, it appeared to meet the definition of first-degree manslaughter:

> A person is guilty of manslaughter in the first degree when: (a) With intent to cause serious physical injury to another person, he causes the death of such person or of a third person; or (b) With intent to cause the

death of another person, he causes the death of such person or of a third person under circumstances which do not constitute murder because he acts under extreme emotional disturbance.

Still, manslaughter was a major crime, carrying a maximum penalty of twenty years in the penitentiary. But even in a cut-and-dried case—with the perpetrator found standing over the body holding a smoking gun—twenty years was an ambitious goal for a prosecutor. Runyon had his staff research the court statistics on homicides in Pike County during the 1980s. The average sentence for all homicides (murder and manslaughter) was 7.6 years. For manslaughter alone, the average sentence was about half that. Nationally, the average time actually served for these crimes was nowhere near twenty years. A national study of homicide cases from 1976 to 1987 in eight states—California, Georgia, Montana, New Jersey, New York, Ohio, Washington, and Wisconsin—found that the median length of confinement for defendants found guilty of murder was five years.

Aware that he would have to vigorously defend whatever verdict he obtained on the Putnam case, Runyon was determined to hold out for the stiffest sentence he could manage. But he had to be careful how he did it. As both a sportsman and a politician, Runyon knew well that hooking a fish took a lot less skill than bringing it in. He spent restless nights deconstructing his problem, not knowing—not even able to eyeball—his quarry circling at the far end of a telephone line. Yet Runyon knew instinctively that in the churn of mountain politics, a prosecutor who lost a case like this—the case of an outsider, a *federal agent* who killed a poor coal miner's daughter, dumped her body, and left her there for a year—would be vulnerable not only to defeat, but equally bad, to derision and scorn. And he knew very well that this case *could* be lost. The killer could manage to wriggle off the hook, even if he conceded doing it, on the *technicalities*—he could practically hear the word curling from the lip of an as-yet-unknown political opponent, some Pikeville populist grabbing the opportunity to bring down the invincible John Paul Runyon.

If Mark Putnam walked, it would not matter politically that the state police and the FBI between them had not managed to produce a shred of evidence that a crime had even been committed, even though the brass from both agencies were now busy clapping themselves on the back for cracking the case. All that would matter would be that the prosecutor had let a murderer slip off the hook.

The prosecutor had no way of knowing that Mark Putnam was grimly determined to throw himself into the boat.

Down in Florida, Mark insisted that he was going to prison for thirty or forty years. "I killed somebody, Kathy. I've got to go to prison for a long, long time. You and the kids need to cut your ties to me," he told her in conversations that started at dawn and continued until they fell asleep exhausted at night.

His fortitude confounded his lawyer. Zimet had been stunned by the story that Mark and Kathy told him when they came to his office in Fort Lauderdale on Tuesday morning, but he immediately saw the advantages his client had in negotiating a deal. It did not make sense that Mark wasn't interested in negotiating. In fact, when Kathy stepped out for a minute to have a cigarette, Zimet asked Mark whether he was actually protecting someone else, such as his wife.

A suspicion of misguided gallantry was perhaps reasonable for someone who did not know the Putnams. Not many criminal suspects begin their case stipulating that they are guilty, even to their lawyers. Fewer still insist that they intend to admit to their crime. It took a while for Zimet to understand that Mark Putnam meant everything he said. Mark had been anticipating this reckoning for a year, focused entirely on the guilt that crushed him and the confession he needed to make.

It also took Zimet some time to see that, stricken as she

appeared to be, struggling to keep her hand steady enough to sip coffee from the china cup in which it was served by a secretary, Kathy Putnam could be a strong force on her husband's will. For Kathy, the disaster had just happened. She was like an earthquake victim crawling out of flaming rubble. But as she got her bearings and began to look ahead, she tried to impress on Mark the idea that assuaging his conscience was not the only consideration. There was also the fate of his family, and any hope they had of putting a life together at some point, no matter how far in the future. She worked hard to persuade him that he did not have the luxury of acting unilaterally. He owed it to his family, if not to himself, to begin thinking like a defendant. She realized that without Mark's confession, the authorities did not have a good case—if they had one, they would obviously have made it by now.

On Wednesday, when she and Mark returned to Zimet's office to hear his assessment after his initial conversation with Runyon, Kathy had already identified a number of options, the most sensible of which, she had decided, was to deny everything. Let them make their case and prove it in court.

Though he was uneasy dealing with a spouse who had positioned herself squarely between him and his client, Zimet had come to the same conclusion.

"You don't want to plead out on this," Zimet told Mark. "You won't have to do a day. They just don't have enough of a case. They don't even have enough to indict you."

But Mark wanted to put an end to the ordeal. He refused to elaborate on his reasoning, but he knew that it had much to do with guilt and pride and little with legal strategy. If he could avoid it, Mark had no intention of letting a Pike County prosecutor put him on trial. He would rather prosecute himself by pleading guilty. Furthermore, he had been tormented for a year knowing that he had abandoned Susan in a mountain ravine. Even while he had delayed it as long as he could, he had always known that there could be only one resolution. Susan would have to be found, and he would have to confess to killing her. There was no other way he could live with himself.

"It wouldn't be right to try to beat it," Mark explained darkly. "I tried it for a year. Look at me." The lawyer had no way to compare, but Mark had by now lost over thirty pounds, and his face had the drawn, sallow look of a deeply troubled man. Besides, he argued, a trial could badly damage the all-important image of the bureau. A single agent pleading out on a homicide was one thing. In a trial, the whole sorry mess—systemic abuses of informants, shoddy procedures, indifferent supervision of agents—was likely to come out. He was not willing, he said, to cause further damage.

Invariably he returned to the bottom line: "I killed somebody. I did it. There is no excuse for what I did."

Zimet suggested that Mark and Kathy go out to lunch to talk it over.

At a restaurant across the street, Kathy tried to breach the wall he had erected around his guilt. "What do they really have, Mark? You're going to give them everything. I understand that. I accept it. But you can get some concessions in return. You don't have to spend the rest of your life in prison. *Think* about what you're doing to us, Mark."

He repeated his mantra. "Kathy, I killed that girl."

"Mark, if you go to jail in Kentucky, they'll kill you."

Overhearing this, a busboy who had been clearing the booth behind them dropped a plate. The crash brought a look of recognition to Mark's face.

Kathy went on. "Mark, you have to think clearly. Think of Danielle and Mark and me. You have some power in this." She was imploring him as she never had before. Finally, his mind managed to move past the word *deal*. By the time they went back, he had agreed to let his lawyer negotiate one.

Back in Pikeville, the prosecutor had guessed at Putnam's rationale. A more cynical man might have scoffed at the notion, but Runyon finally sensed that Mark was being impelled, step by step, not by his lawyer but by his conscience. Runyon didn't know how long that situation would last—consciences can fade when things get tough. He had no idea how far he could push.

In what quickly evolved into a high-stakes poker game, the phone calls flew back and forth between Kentucky and Florida every day for two weeks. Runyon told his associates at the onset of the plea negotiations, ''I can never be sure when I hang up the phone today whether he's going to be talking to me tomorrow.''

The prosecutor presided over a small group of people who had an interest in the case and whose judgment he trusted. They gathered daily around the conference table in the windowless second-floor library of Runyon's office, where the speakerphone provided a disembodied link to the suspect in Florida. Always on hand were Richard Ray and Rick Bartley, the assistant commonwealth attorney. At various times they were joined by Lou DeFalaise, Terry O'Connor, Jim Huggins, Gary Rose, and Paul Maynard.

DeFalaise had more than a passing interest in the homicide investigation against Mark Putnam, which was a state matter. As the U.S. Attorney's office in Lexington entered the initial phase of its long-planned investigation into political corruption throughout eastern Kentucky, it was evident that several of the cases that had been developed in the Pikeville office, both by Putnam and by Poole, could be part of the interlocked framework on which that federal initiative would have to rest. There was concern about what might come out in a trial of Mark Putnam. No one knew what to expect.

At the initial gathering, Runyon laid out the dilemma: ''We know the boy did it—but gentlemen, we can't prove that in a court of law. We can't even prove that a crime has been committed.''

What if Putnam backed out?

Runyon didn't like to consider that possibility: ''We've got to turn up the heat as high as we can.''

Richard Ray huffed and puffed at the notion that Putnam

might be able to cop a plea, but he was a good enough detective to know that there was probably no other choice. "We have no way of locating her body," Ray conceded.

Runyon went around the table, polling each participant individually. None of them disagreed with the plan to negotiate the best plea agreement possible under the circumstances.

"You going to hold his feet to the fire?" Ray asked morosely.

"You bet I am," Runyon replied, though he was not at all certain that he would be able to deliver on the boast. "I'm not going to take anything less than a twelve-year sentence."

There was a low whistle. Someone said, "Good luck, John Paul."

Under instructions from the Putnams to proceed on plea negotiations, Zimet had laid out the broad outlines of what he anticipated. A prison term was inevitable. The only question was how long. And with a defendant determined to plead guilty, that seemed to be a matter largely in the hands of the prosecutor.

"I wanted ten years," Zimet told them at the end of the first week of negotiations while Mark listened in stony silence. "If this had happened in Florida, there is no way you'd serve more than four. But Runyon says he won't sleep with less than sixteen."

Mark surprised them by engaging in speculation for the first time. "What do they really have? I told them about the car, so I guess they can find the car, but I checked it over pretty carefully. The floor mat is long gone. Of course, if they want your ass in Pike County, they can find anybody to testify to anything. But really, only that girl on the horse can put me on the scene."

Startled, Kathy asked, "What girl?"

Mark looked at her blankly. *The one on the horse!* The young woman who had ridden off without giving a second thought to the dark-haired young man she had encountered climbing up out of the ravine—the woman whose knowing face, fleetingly as he had seen it, had not left his mind for a single day in the past year. The one who could put him at the scene! He couldn't believe they didn't know whom he was talking about.

The men gathered around Runyon's conference table were making grim bets on whether the talks would collapse.

"You think they're going to back out today?" someone invariably asked.

"Not today," said the prosecutor. He never knew about tomorrow.

Early the following week, Zimet made a formal offer: Mark would plead guilty to first-degree manslaughter in exchange for a guarantee of an eight-year sentence.

"I couldn't live with myself at that," Runyon said, digging in hard with a bluff. "It's got to be eighteen."

As he talked, Runyon doodled abstractly on a yellow legal pad. Later, he would see that he had put down the number *18* but crossed it out. Beside it, he had written *16* and underlined it in hard black strokes, with an arrow drawn right at it. But the fact was, he was prepared to take twelve.

The next day, Zimet had a new gambit. If Mark pleaded guilty to whatever sentence they agreed on, he wanted to serve his time in a federal prison, not a Kentucky penitentiary.

Richard Ray felt he had to object strenuously to this, as a matter of principle. "What if I did this?" he asked. "What would happen to me? Could I serve my time in a federal prison?" He would never actually say it, but he felt the responsibility of speaking for Susan Smith, and maybe for generations of other poor, ignorant mountain people. But he knew that if this was the major concession they needed to make to get a stiff sentence, and if Runyon was ready to take the inevitable heat for making it, it should be made.

In fact, the cops, Ray included, were the most worried

among the group that gathered in Runyon's office. Collectively, they had seen too many defense lawyers wreck too many criminal prosecutions, and they understood that this one could collapse in a minute if Putnam bolted out the door of Zimet's office. As Runyon himself had pointed out in amazement when he realized Putnam was willing to talk, "any defense lawyer in Pike County would tape that boy's mouth shut and tell him to take a long vacation until his conscience stopped bothering him."

Runyon replied that he was willing to go along with the federal prison. On June 1, the Kentucky Department of Corrections tentatively agreed not to object to Putnam's serving his sentence in a federal facility. This handed Runyon his last card to play.

"Runyon won't go for twelve," Zimet told the Putnams when they came in that day. "It's got to be sixteen." He broke it down. "Sixteen years. You won't do more than twelve; you're eligible for parole after eight, and it's in a federal facility."

Mark looked uneasily at his wife, who nodded shakily. "Let's go," he said.

Runyon's letter spelling out the plea agreement was drafted and faxed back and forth until both sides signed off on the final language. It was dated June 1. The key portions of it read as follows, with italics representing the additions Zimet insisted on:

This will confirm our conversations with regard to your client, Mark Putnam. As a result of these conversations it is agreed by and between the Commonwealth of Kentucky and Mr. Putnam as follows:

An investigation into the disappearance and possible killing of Susan Smith is being conducted by the Kentucky State Police and the Federal Bureau of Investigation.

Mr. Putnam will be completely forthright and truthful with this office and federal and state law enforcement agents with regard to all inquiries made of him regarding Susan Smith. Mr. Putnam will give signed and sworn statements if same are deemed necessary. In any interviews conducted pursuant to this agreement, Mr. Putnam may have counsel present if he desires. *These statements will be exclusively made pursuant to this agreement. If this agreement is not fully consummated for any reason, these statements cannot be used against Mr. Putnam.*

It is anticipated that evidence obtained from Mr. Putnam as well as evidence obtained by law enforcement investigators will be presented to the Pike County Grand Jury and that an indictment will be sought against Mr. Putnam *on or before June 11, 1990,* charging him with *manslaughter in the first degree relating to Susan Smith.*

In the event that Mr. Putnam is indicted for murder for his role in the killing of Susan Smith, the Commonwealth of Kentucky, by and through John Paul Runyon, 35th Judicial Circuit Commonwealth Attorney, agrees to amend the charge to manslaughter in the first degree. If the grand jury returns an indictment charging Mr. Putnam with first-degree manslaughter, no amendment to said charge will be recommended by the Commonwealth.

Mr. Putnam will plead guilty to the charge of first-degree manslaughter *on June 12, 1990, or within ten days thereafter. Mr. Putnam may voluntarily appear for his guilty plea.*

The maximum penalty to which Mr. Putnam will be exposed by virtue of his guilty plea is imprisonment for a term of 20 years and the minimum penalty will be imprisonment for a term of 10 years. Kentucky law does not provide for the imposition of a fine for this charge. Court costs of $57.50 and a $10.00 payment to the Crime Victims Compensation Fund will be paid in full on the date Mr. Putnam is sentenced.

The Commonwealth will recommend that Mr. Putnam will be sentenced to a 16-year term of imprisonment following his guilty plea.

Acknowledging that sentencing is "within the sole discretion of the court," the agreement letter nevertheless stipulated:

In the event the Court rejects this plea agreement *or refuses to follow the 16-year recommendation of the Commonwealth* and Mr. Putnam refuses to plead guilty or withdraws his guilty plea, pursuant to Kentucky Criminal Rule 8.10, nothing contained in any statement or testimony given by Mr. Putnam pursuant to this agreement or any evidence developed therefrom will be used against him in any further criminal prosecutions.

Only a few loose ends remained. Zimet wanted assurance that Mark would not face a related charge over the death of a fetus if it was indeed true that Susan had been pregnant, and in the unlikely possibility that an autopsy on a body that had lain exposed for over eleven months would still show evidence of it. Kentucky law was clear on that point. The state Supreme Court in 1983 had held in the case of a man who killed his wife while attempting also to kill her unborn baby that a "fetus was not a 'person,' as that word is used in context of criminal homicide statutes, and could not have status as victim of criminal homicide."

Negotiations concluded with that. On Monday morning, June 4, Paul Maynard and Jim Huggins got on a plane and flew to Florida. A state police unit was ordered to stand by to recover the body of Susan Smith.

*   *   *

Maynard and Huggins arrived at Zimet's well-appointed office in Fort Lauderdale just after five o'clock. Mark had asked Kathy to stay home. He was ready this time when Maynard read him his Miranda rights.

Speaking softly, Mark confessed that he had killed Susan Smith and told where to find her body.

The directions he gave were so simple that the officers standing by in Pikeville didn't believe him. He said the body was in a ravine on the left side of a gravel road on Harmons Branch, five miles from the center of Pikeville, not even a mile off Route 23, a few hundred yards from a cleared area with a big shed where the mine company stored big earth-moving equipment and parked coal trucks. Just before the ravine, also on the left, was a slope back through the trees where kids rode their dirt bikes.

It sounded preposterous. "There's no way she could be laying there," Ray scoffed to Maynard over the phone. "Somebody would have found her."

When this was repeated to him, Mark muttered that that was the point. He thought they would have, long before now.

With a scrawled map and the directions, Ray drove a small and gravely dubious group of searchers up the rutted mine road on the low ridge above Harmons Branch. Accompanying him, in two vehicles, were state police lieutenant Ed Shemelya; two FBI agents, Sam Smith and Tim Adams; and Fred Davidson, a state police officer who had brought along his excitable German shepherd, which he called a "body dog."

Driving slowly over the deep ruts, Ray spotted the clearing where it was obvious that dirt bikes had clawed into the loose soil on a hill. Above, a high black ridge went on for miles, blocking out most of the thin sunlight. Ray found the turnoff and stopped the car on a mud-caked siding beside a narrow and bumpy coal-truck road that climbed sharply up to the strip-mine cut. With the light fading, they wouldn't have much time.

Mounds of fresh dirt and debris were pushed up at the side of the road, on the lip of the ravine. It appeared to be rubble from the strip mine, pushed down from above by bulldozers. They climbed over it and peered into the ravine, which was thick with undergrowth. After the first ten yards, the ground fell off sharply. They used ropes tied to the truck to ease down, one by one, lurching for the nearest bush or an occasional sapling for support. The dog thrashed ahead. The trickle of a small creek could be heard coming from the bottom of the ravine, but it was difficult to see through the brush. About halfway down, the way was blocked by a weed-covered pile of dirt and trash, remnants of tangled wire-mesh fencing, rotted mine timbers, and moldering trash bags. The rubble appeared to have been pushed down from the roadbed some time ago.

The dog was making a commotion somewhere below, but it scrambled back toward them, whimpering. Ray had no faith in the dog anyway. He had never known it to find anything before. It climbed on up toward the road, peed on a bush, and barked at the searchers stumbling downward.

Ray heard a shout from the brush about ten feet below. "Hey, it looks like there's some bones here!"

Ray stumbled and slid down to where Tim Adams had braced himself between two bushes and was staring down at the bones, which appeared to be from a skeleton that had come apart. At first, Ray thought they looked like the bones of a child. A flashlight glinted off metal; prodded with a stick through the dried mud and matted leaves, it proved to be a thin gold chain with a tiny cross.

Shaking his head, Ray squinted back toward the top of the ravine. The remains of Susan Smith lay not fifty feet from the road.

A radio transmission was made back from the scene to the state police post in Pikeville, where the message was relayed to the small group in the lawyer's office in Fort Lauderdale. Maynard put down the phone and said, acknowledging Mark's distressed look, "They found her just where you said."

Mark took a few minutes to collect himself. Then he continued talking as a stenographer took down the rest of his confession.

It was dark by now. The cops who had found the body waited until another state police vehicle arrived with two officers who would remain to guard the scene through the night.

Just before eight o'clock the next morning, a police car and a pickup truck lumbered up to the site. A man from the state medical examiner's office, a forensic anthropologist named David J. Wolf, got out to supervise the removal of the remains.

Complaining about the difficult climb down, Wolf worked slowly, taking copious notes. Some of the bones were entangled in the wire mesh, as if tugged at by animals. "Evidence of scavenger activity was visible," Wolf wrote.

To Ray, who had returned to the scene with Wolf and some other officers, Mark Putnam's claim that he had placed the body near the top of the ravine seemed plausible in the bright daylight. The hill was too steep for a man to have carried a body down that far, where anyone standing at the side of the road would have had to look hard to see it. Wolf's report described the scenario:

> Though heavily vegetated with briars, weeds and grasses, the embankment had very few trees closely spaced that could impede a body rolling down the steep incline. . . . Based upon the topography, it became obvious that the body rolled down the embankment from the crest of the brim alongside the road until it became entangled in the wire mesh fencing which stopped its further progress downhill. Due to the steepness of the slope, the unevenness of the slope, the vegetative cover, as well as the quantity of wire mesh fencing, it would have required a truly herculean effort for one person to have carried the body to the site where it was found and deposited it among the flattened coils of the wire mesh.

As a police photographer took pictures, Wolf supervised the collection of the bones and the loose soil on which they were scattered. He reported: "During the troweling activity, small bones (wrist, ankle, finger, etc.) were observed but were not individually collected at that time."

Annoyed by Wolf's officious direction, the state cops removed the material and placed it in ten-gallon coal buckets. They used wire cutters to cut away the pieces of fencing. According to Wolf's inventory, "several dark human hairs, a gold-colored chain with crucifix attached, and several fingernails as well as toenails that had been painted with red polish" were found in the debris along with the bones. "Flecks of nail polish that had exfoliated from the nails were observed. No other physical evidence (e.g., clothing, jewelry or personal effects) were observed on the surface at the scene."

Holding on to ropes tied around trees near the road, they passed up the buckets containing the loose soil and bones. When they were finished, a worker from the mining company drove up in a truck and asked when they would be finished.

Wolf said they were finished now.

When Ray asked the man why he wanted to know, the driver explained that the mining company was planning to bulldoze the mounds of backfill into the ravine. Within days, Susan Smith's remains would have been buried under sixty feet of strip-mine debris.

The detective felt a little better about the plea agreement with Putnam. That eliminated the nagging thought that perhaps the body would have been found by chance. It meant that the only other potential physical evidence was the car in which the crime had taken place—the rental car that Putnam had told them about when they questioned him.

The FBI, in fact, had already located the car. The rental agency had long since sold it to a man in Virginia who lived, coincidentally, not far from the bureau's renowned forensic laboratory in Quantico, Virginia. There, bureau technicians tore the car apart piece by piece and finally discovered a tiny speck of human blood between two layers of foam inside a front-seat cushion. Jim Huggins would later say that this discovery showed the bureau at "its truly most impressive combination of dogged searching and use of technology." But Ray didn't see much ground for boasting since the blood sample didn't match either Susan's or Mark's. The FBI technicians concluded that it must have come from an assembler in the factory where the car was built. There had been no physical evidence at all linking the killer to the crime.

On Friday, June 8, Mark Putnam's brief career with the FBI officially came to an end. He had typed out a short letter of resignation, just a few sentences, which he planned to take to the office personally. But he was no longer welcome at the office. Instead, Gavin and Torrence said they would come by his house in Sunrise.

When they arrived at the front door, the two supervisors asked Mark if he had any bureau property in the house besides his gun and credentials. He did not. Wanting to find a neutral site, they suggested a short ride. Mark and Kathy accompanied the two agents in their car, Mark in the front passenger seat, Kathy in the back. They drove in silence to a location cops tend to feel comfortable in, a McDonald's a few blocks from their house, not far from the Florida turnpike, at a place where the suburbs of Fort Lauderdale and Miami expire beside the Everglades.

Torrence went inside to get two cups of coffee. Mark and Kathy passed.

It had started out proudly in a crisp ceremony at the FBI academy in Quantico. Now it was ending with three cops and a grieving woman parked outside a fast-food joint, ruefully watching children at play on bright plastic playground equipment, their mothers on guard at tiny white tables.

"I'm sorry it has to be like this. Doing it this way is in the best interest of the bureau," Gavin explained.

"I understand," said Mark.

While they waited for the coffee, Kathy thought of a day that seemed further in the past than it was. On a cool October morning in 1986, the letter they had been expecting for many months finally arrived in the mail at their apartment in Connecticut, in a long envelope bearing the return address, "U.S. Department of Justice, Federal Bureau of Investigation." Their future was inside.

Neither of them had had the nerve to rip it open, so afraid were they that it would say, "No, thanks." They left it unopened on an end table. Mark plunked one-year-old Danielle into the stroller for a hasty walk around the block. Kathy ran into the bedroom.

When Mark got back, Kathy heard him opening it. "Just tell me what it says!" she squealed. He slipped it under the door, faceup, and she would never forget the joy and sense of accomplishment that she felt, for both of them, when she looked down and read:

Dear Mr. Putnam:

You are offered a probationary appointment in the Federal Bureau of Investigation, United States Department of Justice, as a Special Agent . . .

They laughed and cried; at dinner they drank wine, and at bedtime they made love. And the next day, while Mark was at work, it had all almost come undone. She'd received a phone call from a personnel clerk at the bureau, apologizing that a mistake had been made. The letter was in error; an overlooked review of Mark's medical records had turned up the 1985 shoulder surgery to correct the old soccer injury; the FBI regretted that it could not accept the potential liability this presented. Horrified, Kathy didn't even call Mark to tell him. Instead, she just refused to take no for an answer. For hours, she worked the phone, calling office after office at the Justice Department, until she reached someone in FBI personnel who heard her out. "Please listen to me," she said. "We've been around FBI agents for four years, and frankly, a lot of them are fat guys who couldn't run two blocks if they had to. This man is a perfect physical specimen, I'm telling you. I swear to you, I absolutely *guarantee* you that my husband will have no problem with agent training; we'll sign whatever waiver you want for your liability. You *have* to do this."

And, unbelievably, they did. She'd talked him back in. The next week, Mark, as happy as she had ever seen him, was on his way to Quantico, marveling at the tenacity of the woman he loved.

Now that they had their coffee, the agents were ready to get back to the office. Numbly, Kathy watched her husband pass his credentials, his gun and his holster, his pager, and bureau keys to Gavin. He then handed over his letter of resignation.

Gavin cast a look back to Kathy. "I want you to know, if there is anything we can do for you, we'll be there for you." It was a nice thing to say. She knew it had no meaning.

And that was the end of the bureau business. Susan had been found. Mark had confessed. His resignation was official. The rest was up to the State of Kentucky. Mark and Kathy didn't want a ride back. They got out of the car and walked home silently along the sandy shoulder of the road.

17

Shelby Jean Ward knew that Susan had been found when she got a call from John Paul Runyon late Monday, asking if she could come to his office the next morning at nine o'clock. He wouldn't say why, but she could tell from the tone of his voice.

Runyon and Captain Rose from the state police were already there when she arrived, shaken and subdued. They told her that Susan's remains had been found and tentatively identified.

"Mark Putnam?" she asked.

"Mark Putnam," Runyon replied. "He confessed last night." Knowing how sensitive the matter was, Runyon tried to explain the necessity of a plea arrangement.

"Why, it's cold-blooded murder, John Paul," she protested.

Rose read her Putnam's confession. Runyon then went over the main points of the prosecution's case, which came down, he said, to the fact that there was no evidence without that confession. He said that a sixteen-year sentence was substantial, far in excess of the average for manslaughter.

Shelby wasn't buying it. She left his office in a tearful fury, and Runyon knew he had a problem on his hands even before he got the grand jury into session to prepare the indictment. But he didn't know what else he could do. On Tuesday, June 12, Mark Putnam would be brought to Pikeville to plead guilty. He would be in prison that night. Until then, Runyon hoped that the situation could be kept quiet.

The Wednesday-morning edition of the *Williamson* (W. Va.) *Daily News*, the paper that circulated in the Tug

Valley, carried a small story with the headline "Unidentified Body Found Near Pikeville." The story didn't identify the body and said only that the state police and the FBI were involved in the investigation.

Shelby and her brother Billy Joe filled in the details for anyone who wanted to know. By Wednesday, the news that an FBI agent had been implicated in the death of a young woman was moving on the Associated Press wire out of Pikeville.

"It's cold-blooded murder to me. My family's all upset about this," Shelby told a reporter from the *Miami Herald*, which had been alerted to the story because it involved an agent assigned to the Miami FBI bureau. "What was so bad is when he took the body and dumped it over the hill like it was nothing," Shelby said.

"Like some dog," said Billy Joe.

Other reporters soon gathered details of the sordid relationship between Susan Smith and Mark Putnam. "She was possessed by him, madly in love with him," Shelby said. "We tried to get her to date other people, but she didn't even want to talk about it. She swore that it was his baby. She wouldn't even have had that baby if it belonged to somebody else. She was even going to name it after him if it was a boy." Shelby described how she had warned Susan to "quit threatening" Mark about the baby. "She wanted him to leave his wife. She was threatening to tell his wife about the baby and he was scared to death."

On Monday, June 11, when she came to the courthouse to testify to the grand jury, Shelby was surrounded by reporters and cameras. "Because he was a big FBI, famous and everything, they don't want him to get justice," she said, denouncing the plea agreement, which had not yet been publicly disclosed. "I don't care what the clique in there says. To me it was brutal murder. Brutal, brutal murder."

*   *   *

Grand juries are pliant tools of the prosecutor, but there is
no law that says a grand jury can't get something into its
head and refuse to go along, especially with the media
going full tilt on Shelby's impassioned denunciation of the
deal as a miscarriage of justice, a cover-up orchestrated by
the feds, in collusion with the prosecutor. It was hard to
argue reasonably in so overheated an atmosphere, especially given the public sympathy flowing toward the victim's tearful sister and other family members. It was highly
unlikely, but Runyon knew that if grand jury members decided they were being bamboozled, they did have the legal
authority to defy the commonwealth attorney, ignore the
practical realities, dig in their heels, and return a murder
indictment. That would present Runyon with the worst of
all possible scenarios—not only would the plea agreement
be null and void, but he would have to prosecute a case on
which he had no evidence, on a charge he could not support. Politically, it would be a debacle.

Runyon and his staff had worked diligently all week to
prepare a presentation designed to foreclose that possibility.
When the grand jury opened its session Monday morning,
Runyon called Richard Ray as the first witness. He had the
state police detective describe his long and frustrating investigation, beginning with his bewilderment over the FBI's
role in delivering Susan Smith to the Landmark motel in the
first place, and his uncertainty about the activities of Ron
Poole after she was reported missing. Ray said he was surprised to learn that Poole "was doing this more or less on
his own—he didn't have an official investigation going."

"At the time that you determined that she was at the
Landmark motel, did you find anyone that actually saw him
[Mark] with her?" Runyon asked.

"No, we didn't. We couldn't find anybody that saw them
together, nobody at all."

Turning to the plea agreement, Runyon asked, "Up until
the time that he openly was Mirandized and waived his
rights on June fourth, 1990 . . . did you have any admis-

sible evidence or evidence that you could obtain a criminal charge against Mark Putnam?''

"No, we didn't."

"You didn't have a body then?"

"Didn't have the body. I suspected that she was probably over in the Freeburn area somewhere, and I was pretty sure that she was dead, but didn't have any information that we could have charged him with."

In his testimony, Jim Huggins reiterated that point. The plea bargain, he stressed, was the only viable option. "We had no choice whatsoever, or Mr. Runyon didn't. If he hadn't entered into this agreement, we wouldn't be here today. We would have an unsolved homicide, or would have worse than that—an unsolved homicide where we know who did it, but we would not have a body."

Much to the annoyance of the state police, Huggins took the opportunity to give the FBI credit for solving the case, saying he wished the bureau had gotten involved sooner, "but unfortunately we didn't enter it as a joint investigation until the first of May, and we had the case solved in two weeks."

A juror asked Huggins pointedly what had taken the FBI so long to get involved.

"I think the girl's history as being a runaway, and a lot of questions about her past, would indicate to the agents or the detective at the time that maybe she ran away with some other group, she's going to show up in a few months. I don't believe that initially it was taken as serious—no one really wanted to believe that an FBI agent committed a murder, in my opinion."

Captain Rose testified that, without the agreement, "that fellow would have walked. He would never have pulled one day in the penitentiary." On the question of premeditation, Rose added, "I personally do not believe that he intended to kill her. He didn't know she was going to be at the motel. He came back here for court, and there she was. The evi-

dence that we obtained during the investigation was that he
actually tried to avoid her during the week. I believe, as
somebody said, had he actually planned to do it, he would
have done a lot better job than the job he done.''

Since she had been the main source of pressure on the
police throughout the year that her sister was missing,
Shelby Jean Ward was an important witness. But it was
clear that she had no evidence that gave legal weight to her
insistence on a murder indictment. The grand jury quickly
saw that her knowledge of the relationship between Susan
and Mark was strictly hearsay. Shelby conceded that all she
knew about Mark was what Susan was telling her.

''Did she tell you that she would come to Pikeville and
see Mark Putnam?''

''Yes.''

''You don't have personal knowledge, I take it, that she
did, but that she told you she did—you weren't over there
when she met with him?''

''No, she told me she did. And also Ron Poole, an FBI
agent working along with Mark, he said that Susan was
coming there and seeing Mark and going out with him on
dates, and he said that he knew—she would set and tell him
about, you know, that she was pregnant by him. They talked
about it. But I never did see them together. I've never seen
the guy. I've talked to him on the phone. He called my
house several times wanting to know if she was there, and
sometimes I would tell him she wasn't when she was because I didn't want her fooling with him.''

''But you didn't have any personal knowledge of whether
they met or didn't, or what their relationship was, other than
what she advised you of?''

''No. She would get ready and come over here [to
Pikeville] and see him, and she told me they would go out
on dates.''

Before dismissing Shelby, Runyon wanted her firmly on
the record about whether she understood and agreed with
the plea arrangement. ''Incidentally,'' he said, ''I doubt

you are aware that all the officers that have testified, even Richard Ray, have testified that we had no choice, that if we had not done this, he would be walking free today without any punishment—without any. Do you understand it and accept it as being the thing that had to be done, but not the desirable thing from the standpoint of our wishes or our likes?''

"Yes," Shelby replied.

"That until he confessed and revealed where the body was, that we had no evidence on which to even base the charge—have you been advised about that?''

"Well, he took a polygraph test and he failed that, you know, but they say you can't use that in court. . . ."

"That's right. . . . Well, if you felt that without this plea agreement, we have no charge at all, would you agree that this is the best we could do?''

"Yes."

After working well into the night and early the next morning, the day Mark was coming to court, the grand jury handed up the indictment in the form Runyon had wanted. It read, in part:

Detective Ray's initial investigation into Susan Smith's disappearance produced no hard evidence regarding her whereabouts. . . . Because a body had not been located, the case remained an investigation into a missing person. . . .

The Kentucky State Police, the Federal Bureau of Investigation, the United States Attorney and the Commonwealth's Attorney . . . discussed that although Mark Steven Putnam had a motive and the opportunity to kill Susan Smith, and although circumstantial evidence indicated he had, no eyewitnesses were available, and no physical evidence existed sufficient to support a criminal charge against him. Most importantly, no homicide charge could be supported because no body had been found and no other evidence of the killing existed. It was decided and agreed upon by all concerned that further investigation would be unlikely to reveal the location of the body or other evidence conclusively linking Putnam to the killing. A decision was made to enter into negotiations with Putnam through his attorney.

. . . In return for the complete disclosure of the location of the body of Susan Smith and the manner in which she died, the Commonwealth agreed to recommend a 16-year term of imprisonment if Putnam would agree to plead guilty to first-degree manslaughter.

. . . The Grand Jury during this investigation had made available to it various legal principles and the constraints that they placed upon this investigation, and under which the law enforcement officers and the prosecutors were compelled to operate. . . . On the case at hand, all of the information necessary to establish the legal requirement [for the charge] was furnished by the defendant only after he had been assured as to the recommendations of the Commonwealth.

The Grand Jury was further informed that these plea negotiations were entered into under the limitations and constraints imposed by Rule 11 of the Criminal Rules of Procedure, which provide that any statements, admissions or incriminating facts that are disclosed during the negotiations cannot be used against the accused unless a plea agreement is ultimately reached and finally consummated. . . .

It is our opinion that the plea agreement should be ratified and accepted by the court.

The Grand Jury is not unmindful that a death has occurred. However, we are also not unmindful of the fact that without the cooperation of Putnam and his attorney, most probably the body of Susan Smith would never have been found and the case would never have been solved.

The Grand Jury invited the sister of the victim, to wit, Shelby Ward . . . [who] concluded by acknowledging that although the punishment to be received by the accused does not satisfy her, she now fully understands that without the accused's voluntary confession and disclosure of where the body was left, no charge whatsoever could be brought against the accused. She is satisfied that this is the most that can be achieved by this Grand Jury.

The Grand Jury is also aware of the Commonwealth Attorney's concern for the family of Susan Smith and the desire at all times to be able to bring this matter to a conclusion for their peace of mind. The decision of how best to proceed when faced with the facts and the circumstances which John Paul Runyon and the investigators were given was most difficult. The decision made, without question, was correct, appropriate, and in the best interest of the family and the citizens of this Commonwealth.

It is the Grand Jury's opinion that the charge of manslaughter and the recommendation of 16 years in prison reflect the realities of this case. Obviously, Putnam would not cooperate with the investigators and reveal the location of the body without assurances that the Commonwealth would recommend less than the maximum possible sentence. The information given by Putnam and his plea of guilty have two positive results. First, the family of Susan Smith can now know her fate and can begin to adjust and reconstruct their lives with this painful knowledge. Second, a guilty man will be punished for his crime.

The Grand Jury sincerely hopes that this inquiry by a duly assembled and randomly selected Grand Jury of 12 impartial Pike County citizens will help to clear up some of the erroneous, irresponsible and seemingly deliberate false statements disseminated by the media.

On her way into the courtroom to hear Mark's plea, Shelby got caught with a loaded .38 in her purse, wrapped in a thick cotton sock. It set off the metal detector when she passed through. "I just plumb forgot I had that gun," she explained. She was promptly disarmed and two state troopers accompanied her to her seat.

Up front, waiting for the judge, Runyon rolled his eyes when he was told what had caused the commotion in the back of the courtroom. Mark, waiting with his lawyer in the witness room, didn't know anything about it. A few cops milled around in the jury room, and Mark caught the eye of Bertie Hatfield and tried a feeble joke that he regretted immediately: "You remember when you told me that girl was trouble?" Bertie winked and made a small clicking noise with his tongue.

"There's a lot of media out there," a court marshal said apologetically, explaining to Mark that he would have to handcuff him after the plea for the benefit of the cameras from the Lexington television stations. Mark appreciated the consideration of being told what to expect.

He considered his court appearance a technicality, since in his own mind the verdict had already been given and the sentence was in place. This allowed him to brace himself for the ordeal with a measure of concealed contempt. Had things worked out for him in Pikeville, Mark had expected to be a key investigator in the federal probe of political and judicial corruption in eastern Kentucky. He had to accept the cruel irony of standing there, accused and guilty under the scornful gaze of several people whom he had once anticipated he would help indict.

It was the first time he had ever appeared in court dressed in anything other than a neat business suit. Instead, he wore blue jeans, sneakers, a white shirt unbuttoned at the collar. Only the fact that his shirt was wet with sweat and clinging to his back betrayed the deeply conflicting emotions he felt as he stood at the defense table. The room smelled of fresh paint. Every seat in the little courtroom was taken, and spectators were crowded at the entrance, straining to see inside. He could hear whispers and titters. Whenever he turned his head, he saw faces hidden by cameras. The still cameras made nervous fluttering sounds; the television cameras were silent and watchful.

Court was called into session. Pike circuit judge Bayard Collier opened the proceedings with a soliloquy on the majesty of the law. Drifting out of time and place, Mark thought about bracelets. At the academy, they called handcuffs "silver bracelets." They had explained that the bracelets had both practical and psychological functions: one to disable a prisoner, the other, sometimes equally important, to humiliate him. Mark rubbed his wrists together, wondering how they would feel.

"It was sixteen years or nothing at all," Judge Collier was intoning from the bench, calling Mark back to attention. "If I had not accepted, or expected to deny, the motion to accept the plea, then according to the law I would have had to tell Putnam and his attorney that in advance. At that point, he simply would have withdrawn his confession and we would have been back to square one." The judge peered down portentously at the cameras. "No evidence, no case." Shutters chattered in response.

The judge looked at Mark and asked if he was in agreement with the terms of the plea arrangement.

Mark forced himself not to clear his throat and said, firmly and loudly, "Yes, sir, I am." The judge didn't meet his stare. He appeared to Mark as if he were at the end of a long tunnel.

A voice whispered in Mark's ear to put his hands behind his back. A drop of sweat collected on his eyebrow just at the top of his vision. The cuffs snapped on with the resonance of a car door slamming. The cameras clucked with satisfaction. The judge imposed the sentence. The whole thing was over in less than a half hour. Having no idea where he was going, Mark said good-bye to his lawyer and was led out of the courtroom by two marshals.

* * *

A few days before the court session, Runyon, unable to
convince Shelby that he had negotiated the best deal he
could get, had advised her, "Hell, Shelby, if you don't
understand what I'm telling you, go get you a lawyer, somebody you trust, to explain it for you."

The next day, Runyon had received a phone call from
Larry Webster, a tough-talking young Pikeville lawyer
whose business cards depict a bungalow set in a mountain
holler. Webster often defended hill people in criminal cases.
Runyon distrusted him with grave wariness, believing that
he harbored political ambitions. But Runyon at least credited him for having a modicum of intelligence, and he
thought Webster would have set Shelby straight.

"Look, Larry, explain it to her," Runyon said.

But Webster was staking out a new claim. "Well, the
FBI could have done more."

"Larry, I'm in a position now where that's immaterial.
They *didn't*. We're beyond that point."

The morning of Mark's court appearance, Webster, representing Shelby and other members of her family, filed a
civil action charging that Mark Putnam "wrongfully caused
the death of Susan Smith." Webster said he would be asking "millions of dollars" in punitive damages. From that
point on, the suit would be a silent factor in much of the
controversy that was about to occur over the plea arrangement and confession.

Runyon had anticipated a certain amount of backlash.
"Mountain people think that certain people can get *anything* done," he would later say. "They're real quick to
say, 'Well, hell, he was bought off'—and I have to admit
with a certain degree of justification." But he was surprised
and somewhat overwhelmed by the resonance of Shelby's
protests, reflected in a strong and negative reaction in the
out-of-town papers. Runyon had expected controversy, but
he hadn't expected anyone to say he'd let the killer off with

a light sentence. He was proud of the bargain he had driven.

Yet it was true that the plea arrangement was drafted and adjudicated in a way that precluded any public examination of the complexities of the case—including the questionable performance of the FBI both in tolerating the exploitation of informants like Susan Smith and in neglecting to investigate aggressively when circumstances indicated that one of its agents was involved in a scandal and perhaps a crime. The killer was in and out of court in a flash, and the record reflected only his formal seven-page written confession. There was no opportunity for dispassionate examination of the events that had led to the crime.

With the victim's aggrieved family denouncing the result, this was a recipe for a kind of media reaction that fed not on information but on well-placed and quite reasonable-sounding innuendo. Runyon was about to learn that he couldn't control it with a few phone calls and an avuncular chat.

After the sentencing, Runyon held his first press conference in eighteen years as Pike County commonwealth attorney.

"Someone here this afternoon asked if justice has been rendered," Runyon said. "Justice is a result of doing the best you can with what you have. Justice, like beauty, is in the eye of the beholder." Without the confession, authorities had "absolutely no evidence," he said. "Not one scintilla or shred of evidence to bring a charge or convict this man."

"Well, what if the body was found?" he was asked.

"Believe me, they couldn't have ever found it." He didn't mention that by the time Mark told them where the body was, the ravine was about to be filled in by the mining company. He tried to explain that he saw only two options when Mark's lawyer phoned to discuss a deal: "To hang up the phone and do nothing, or to start negotiations of some kind."

Why did the suspect confess, then?

"I happen to believe that his conscience played a major role, conscience and a hope to save his soul." The prosecutor happened to believe that it was as simple as that.

The prosecutor had been annoyed by the FBI's official dismissal of the matter as a state case, and Runyon insisted that Terry O'Connor from the Lexington office attend the press conference to answer questions. Runyon had no intention of letting the FBI off the hook, but the questions were perfunctory and reflected no interest in the systemic problem underlying the case. Media apathy enabled the FBI man to say merely, "This incident has damaged the FBI's reputation and its most valuable asset, that being the public trust. We are following up on this, and I would expect some administrative changes to result from it."

It would be the last official statement the FBI would make on the case.

Meanwhile, Shelby had her own reckoning with the law. The state police officers stayed with her through the sentencing proceedings and then took her to headquarters in Pikeville, where she was cited for carrying a concealed weapon and released on her own recognizance in time to get back to the courthouse a few blocks away and talk to reporters out front.

What about the gun charge? "I told them, 'Lord, I wasn't going to do nothing. I wouldn't shoot nobody at all. I always keep my pistol in my purse, but when I get out of the car, I take it out and put it on the seat. This morning I forgot.' "

Runyon didn't think she intended to shoot Mark Putnam either, no matter how it looked. In eastern Kentucky, carrying a gun in your purse was something even the best of people might do. Runyon could recall a tearful phone call he had received a few years ago from a prominent Pikeville woman who had gone to Washington, D.C., on a trip and ended up in federal custody. It seems she had forgotten about the pistol in her purse when she went on a White

House tour. Runyon had to make a number of phone calls to get her out of jail and have the charges dropped.

Shelby's explanation about the gun was at least plausible, although one state police official maintained that she had really brought in the weapon for "publicity purposes." The fact was, for a woman with a gun charge over her head, Shelby was getting a lot of publicity denouncing as a slap on the wrist the sentence for the man who killed her sister. "This is the dirtiest county I've ever seen in my life," she said. "I think they're covering everything up."

In the hubbub over the plea agreement and Mark Putnam himself, it was easy to lose sight of the victim. And Shelby was determined that that not happen. Even though they fought, the sisters had been close—it was to Shelby whom Susan turned when she was most in trouble. Whatever else might be said about Susan, she had been exploited and abandoned by an institution that employed her and by a man she trusted. Shelby was determined that attention be paid to Susan, even if she did tend to trumpet her own role in her sister's life.

"She was more like a daughter to me than a sister," Shelby told the *Williamson Daily News,* published in a small coal city up the Tug Fork on the West Virginia side. She said she had warned Susan to stop seeing Mark "because he was married and had a family. And also, I didn't want her to because I felt she was in danger, that he was using her as an informant, informing on people around where she lived and I lived and she was staying with me. I felt like we were all in danger because of her fooling with him. . . . He had a violent temper, she told me that."

Later in the summer, scheduled to appear in court on the misdemeanor gun charge, Shelby retracted her denunciation of the prosecutor's office: "I do apologize; he, Runyon, was right and I was wrong. I just didn't understand what they were telling me before." She insisted that her about-face had nothing to do with the gun charge: "I was not told to make an apology. I hold my hand to God, I have never been coerced. I talked to my mom and dad and we all think John Paul Runyon and the state police done real good on this.''

Why the change of heart? "Once I got my rest and got to thinking about it, they just did the best they could with what they had. The FBI is the one to blame. I got no cooperation from the FBI and, in fact, was insulted by one of their agents. An FBI agent killed my sister and the FBI tried to cover it up. I believe the role that the FBI played should be thoroughly investigated and a full public disclosure made.''

Still, she expressed sympathy for Mark. "I do feel sorry for the boy," she said, having had her first look at him in the courtroom. "He did look pitiful.'' She explained that her sister was "so in love with him" that she wouldn't heed her warnings about the dangers of working as an informant. Susan "just went crazy" when Mark told her that he and his wife would adopt the child if it was his. "Right to this day, I don't think she would want us to say anything about Mark.'' But Shelby added, "There is no excuse for what he done and he will pay for the rest of his life. I don't think he really meant to kill her. He just panicked.'' Still, she said, "I will never forgive him for what he did to my sister; I just hope that one of these days he can forgive himself.''

The peace Shelby decreed with the prosecutor's office did not hold for long. After the gun charge was dropped, she changed her position and again withdrew her apology, "I didn't mean a word of it,'' she said.

Shelby's instincts for publicity were unfailing. The prosecutor's office, which had been quietly pleased with the sentence extracted from the negotiations with Putnam, was pummeled in the press for letting the killer off lightly. While the state's most respected newspaper, the *Courier Journal* in Louisville, applauded the plea arrangement, the only daily newspaper circulated throughout eastern Kentucky, the *Lexington Herald-Leader*, set a tone that would influence other newspapers and television stations in Lexington. In the absence of detailed information about the investigation, assertions were treated as fact. One editorial stated, "Putnam once threatened Smith when she talked to him about the pregnancy"—an allegation made solely by Shelby.

An editorial in the *Ashland* (Ky.) *Daily Independent*, denounced the "light sentence" given to Mark Putnam and proclaimed that a "murder charge would have been more appropriate." Among the grounds it cited, inaccurately, were that there was "evidence of Putnam's involvement in Smith's death before his confession"; that "an argument between Smith and Putnam could apparently be heard in the motel"; and that "a cracked windshield in the rental car indicated that a scuffle could have taken place," which ignored the fact that the windshield was repaired long before anyone had reason to believe Susan Smith was dead.

Runyon thought such editorials were idiotic and encouraged wild conspiracy theories, but he also believed that they validated one of his favorite axioms: "A lie can go around the world twice before the truth gets its socks on."

In Pikeville, of course, the controversy reached feud proportions immediately. Shelby's lawyer, Larry Webster, had a regular column in the twice-weekly Pikeville paper, the *Appalachian News-Express*, which ran under the pen name Red Dog. He wrote, "It used to be that the crooks had to do their own killing of informants. The government is so efficient now that they do it for the crooks. The agent who strangled that girl sure was lucky he didn't accidentally kill her in a car wreck. He could get life for that."

Meanwhile, the newspaper's publisher, LeJeune Waggoner, offered these tips in a column under the headline "How to Get Away With Murder":

> 1. Be sure and commit the crime in eastern Kentucky, preferably Pike County.
> 2. Make sure your victim is poor and white. Do not kill a minority or a man.

3. Make sure the prosecution, grand jury and judge dance to your jig.

4. Be specific where you want to spend your time. Do not accept any ole Kentucky state pen.

5. Be sure and make enough money to be a yuppie so you can hire a fancy out-of-state lawyer.

6. It helps if the taxpayers furnish the money to buy drinks and other party favors. Most any man can impress girls if Uncle Sam is paying the tab.

7. Remember hillbillies from eastern Kentucky are kind of second-class citizens and sometimes you can kill two for the price of one—it helps if you're the father of one.

The prosecutor's defenders rushed to respond. Ten members of the grand jury released a statement denouncing Waggoner's column as "irrational and without any basis in fact."

"From a prosecutor's perspective, sixteen years was pretty darn good," William E. Johnson, the president of the Kentucky Association of Defense Attorneys told reporters. Frank Haddad, a past president of the same association, said that as a defense lawyer he would never have considered trying to make a deal with a prosecutor who had no evidence. "I would have said, 'Bring your indictment and let's go to trial.' They would never have been able to make the case."

Unaccustomed to public criticism, agitated at having not only his ability but his integrity challenged, Runyon went on a Lexington television program called "Your Government" to defend his actions. "It'll stand out, in my opinion, as one of the few cases, if not the only case, in

Kentucky where a man's conscience has driven him to plead guilty to murder and take sixteen years in the penitentiary,'' he insisted. ''I don't have many people coming into my office and saying, 'Look, I'm a criminal, I violated the law, and I want you to send me to the penitentiary.'

''When we started out on this plea agreement, obviously, when he was willing to confess, he wasn't willing to take the maximum penalty when we had no case. I probably would have been a little easier on John Q. Public—this boy was in a position of trust. He was an FBI agent.''

David Wolf, the forensic anthropologist conducting the autopsy on Susan's remains at his laboratory in Frankfort, made no secret of his contempt for the FBI, which he had long regarded as haughty and not suitably respectful toward state officials such as himself. Though seriously ill with cancer, Wolf also had another reason to insert himself as publicly as possible in the controversy in Pikeville. A Hollywood production company had made inquiries about obtaining the rights to the stories of various principals in the case. Hearing about this, Wolf thought of an old television program, ''Quincy, M.E.'' which had starred Jack Klugman as a crusty medical examiner. Already, Wolf was wondering out loud who would play himself.

This prospect evidently had an impact on the conduct of an autopsy that would normally have taken only a few days. At the end of the week, after Mark had already pled guilty, Wolf was still at work cataloging the remains.

Susan's family wanted to have a funeral on Wednesday, June 20. The Friday before, Wolf was asked to return the remains, but he declined, saying that his work was only one-quarter finished. Shelby, charging that Wolf was engaged in a ''science project,'' not an autopsy, went to Runyon's office for help. Runyon notified Charles Morris, the county coroner, and said that he would comply with the request to have the remains returned for burial. But he warned them both, ''If you want anything additional on an autopsy, you better get it before you bury this girl.''

"The poor little thing's been laying out long enough," Shelby said. "We just think it would be best to have her buried because Mommy and Daddy have been worried enough."

Runyon had his assistant prosecutor, Rick Bartley, call Wolf. Bartley had to threaten an indignant Wolf with a court order to have the remains released.

But even before they arrived from Frankfort, Shelby again changed her position. She now insisted that the autopsy be resumed immediately, placing the state in the position of having to refuse publicly. The criminal case was closed, said David Jones, the administrator of the state medical examiner's office. "We are a state agency. We can't do an investigation to assist someone in civil litigation."

The family lacked the money to pay a private pathologist to do an autopsy for its lawsuit, Shelby responded. Furthermore, she said, the funeral could go ahead only if someone could be found to pay for that.

Runyon phoned Alice Eldridge, who owned the Phelps Funeral Home, where Susan's remains were being sent, and asked, "Alice, what's your absolute bottom-line price on a nonprofit funeral?"

Alice did some quick calculations on the old Burroughs adding machine on her desk. "Five hundred dollars, John Paul."

Runyon made more calls, and a purchase order was drafted for the Pike County Fiscal Court. Under *Description of Goods* on the form it read, *Burial of body found on Harmon's Branch.* A maximum payment of five hundred dollars was specified under *Aid to Needy.*

Alice Mullins Eldridge had founded her funeral home in the late 1950s with her first husband, Haskell, who died in 1983. The pride she took in her position was reflected in her "business cards," actually cardboard hand-fans with balsam handles, imprinted with the name of the funeral home, a stanza of inspirational poetry, and under that the words *Alice Eldridge, Lady Embalmer & Director.*

Alice's second husband, Luther Eldridge, was a coal miner who played gospel hymns on the electric organ in the parlor during funerals. As a member of one of Peter Creek's oldest families, he was a fourth cousin to Susan's mother.

Alice knew that burying Susan Smith would be a thankless task, but she resolved to bring as much dignity and forbearance as she could to the job. Aware of the notoriety of the case, she made careful note of what was inside the box before preparing the remains for burial.

The family told her they wanted to have a public viewing of the closed casket at her funeral parlor. "Shelby wanted to put on a big show," Alice would later say. She was the kind of woman who took in strays of all sorts, and she felt great sadness over the short life and tragic death of Susie Smith. She worked hard to make the funeral as decorous as she could. She placed the pitiful remains in a child-sized Excello fiberglass casket, "a good child's casket." The grave marker was small, about the size of a cereal box, but not cheap—it was bronze and engraved: "Susan Daniels Smith—1961–1989."

Susie Smith went to her grave surrounded by the people she had known all of her life. Family and neighbors, about forty in all, gathered in the viewing room of the Phelps funeral home with the Reverend DeWitt Furrow, pastor of the Peter Creek Presbyterian Church.

As Luther loomed over the organ, the mourners sang hymns, and the service concluded with "The Rose," Susan's favorite.

The next day, a sheriff's car led a small procession of vehicles through Phelps, around the mountain to Freeburn, and up the steep path beside the creek in Barrenshea Hollow, to the Eldridge family plot on the side of the hill next to the frame house where Susan had grown up.

The gravediggers were three muscular local boys, Billie Joe Wolford, Gregory Prater, and Kenneth Wolford. Alice paid them $300 of the $500 allotted for the funeral.

Addressing the mourners, the preacher asked, "How could this ever happen in America, in Pike County? With as

many Christian people as there are among us, how could
this have ever happened? Yet it did happen and it was very
real. We see and read about it every day. We never think it
will happen to us, but it is us. And every one of us is part
of the guilt.'' He took as his text the Lamentations of Jer-
emiah:

> She weeps bitterly in the night,
>   tears on her cheeks;
> among all her lovers
>   she has none to comfort her;
> all her friends have dealt treacherously with
>   her,
> they have become her enemies.

*   *   *

Mark Putnam left the Pikeville courthouse with two state
police officers and no idea where he was going. He felt
himself carried along like a stick on a current, head down
through a sea of yapping faces, cameras scattering like
gulls. Propelled headlong, balance awry with manacled
wrists, he fell into the backseat of the police cruiser, his feet
pushed in like cargo; the vehicle lurched forward as if besieged in a motorcade. He righted himself, pressed his cheek
against the cool glass, not caring about the pictures.

At a brief stop at the state police post he stared mutely at
fingertips stained with fingerprint ink. Firm hands on his
shoulder, averted eyes. Men stumped by uncertain protocol.
''Hang in there,'' said one, and a second one affirmed the
sentiment gruffly. ''Hey, Mark,'' another said, with nothing
to add to the greeting. Said still another, with clumsy kind-
ness, ''Hey, you want a sandwich or something?'' Cops. Not
knowing words to say, they were glad to see him leave.

To where they did not say, except that it was on an
airplane. Two detectives with whom he once worked cases
were assigned to drive him up to Lexington in a new Crown
Victoria. En route, making talk from the backseat, Mark
said, ''You guys are coming up in the world.'' Up front,

Det. Joel Newsome, the big man at the wheel, replied silently with stricken eyes in the rearview mirror. But the cuffs were off for the ride. And in the hills they relaxed a little. Riding shotgun, Det. Claude Tackett, tall and wiry, sat back, draped his arm across the seat, shifting a bit to display more of his face, and told the prisoner as if sharing a secret, "We're going to Otisville, New York. Wherever the hell that is."

Where it was, mostly, was out of sight. The bureau had been worried about major media attention—in fact, there was far less than anybody had anticipated, undoubtedly because places like Pikeville seldom show up on the media radar screens and the publicity of the Putnam case had been a contained explosion, quick and local. Otisville was a medium-security federal prison in the foothills of the Catskill Mountains, coincidentally near the last big stretch of the Appalachian Trail.

Mark said, "Claude, you remember when I first arrived in Pikeville, you were the only detective who traded business cards with me?"

Claude remembered and said that he was sorry about the way it worked out. He coughed and fell silent.

Mark asked about a robbery case he knew they had going. Neither replied. Joel's eyes found his in the mirror. That was the moment Mark realized he was no longer a cop.

The weather was nice, a warm and fragrant afternoon with big clouds in the sky like sails on top of the hills. They fell silent to the hum of the road winding down from the mountains into the open bluegrass flatland of Kentucky radiant in late-springtime sunlight.

On the New Circle Road skirting busy Lexington the driver stiffened, gaped at signs and exit ramps flying by with billboards, slowed to forty.

"Do you know where the airport is?" Joel asked.

"Joel, I am not rightly sure."

From the backseat Mark said softly, "You can take the Versailles Road, two exits ahead." He pronounced the word

the local way: *Ver-SALES*. Joel frowned, watching for the
turn.

On the plane, neutral turf, they were more accommodating
and less troubled with him in the middle seat. The state cops
stared out the window on takeoff and landing, like people
who don't fly much and are still thrilled with the sight.

There was a two-hour layover at O'Hare before the connection to New York. They made him feel comfortable, not
obviously watching while he ducked into the men's room,
clearing their throats and standing back a way while he went
to call Kathy collect. Clinging to the phone, he glanced up
at a television just inside a bar and saw his own image
flicker across the screen, his eyes wide with fear that might
have looked furtive in the instant sweep of the frame, words
he could not make out imposed beneath. His face disappeared and the picture rearranged itself into the generic
visage of a Chicago anchorman changing the subject.
Kathy, numbly composed, told him that the television pictures from Pikeville had been on the Miami news—they
hadn't managed to track her down in Sunrise for the requisite reaction—and on CNN, but not on the network news
programs, which she and Chris had monitored from the
bedroom so the children wouldn't see.

On the second leg of the flight Mark dug out of his pocket
a photograph of himself and the children. He and Danielle
and little Mark all had their arms outstretched, as if beckoning to the photographer. Kathy, as usual, had taken the
picture; she seldom appeared in family photos.

The twin-engine plane touched down in darkness at a
quiet airport in a small city called Middletown. Near the
terminal, three uniformed New York state policemen
waited, arms folded with impatience, flinty eyes shifting
from one to the other as the three men got off the plane and
approached across the asphalt.

"Which one of you men is the prisoner?"

Feeling foolish, Mark raised his hand. Ignoring the Kentucky officers, two of the New York State cops grabbed him, locked his arms in theirs, and duckwalked him over to one of their cars, then pushed him onto the hood and roughly patted him down. Jerking his arms back violently for cuffing, one of the cops used the opportunity to yank Mark's elbows upward, sending a searing jolt through his shoulders that almost knocked him out. As he reeled, his eyes hot with rage, Mark thought of the occasions he had done the same thing to a particularly distasteful prisoner, a cheap cop stunt to release a little aggression and send a painful message about who was in charge.

They drove for a long time on country roads over dark rolling farmland, the Kentucky troopers in the car behind. One of the New York cops told his partner that this prisoner wasn't the only "hotshot fed" who belonged in jail, but he would do for now.

Mark worried about how he would handle himself. Contempt and rude treatment from state cops were one thing; in prison, with the cops on the other side of the bars, it was going to be a different story. As he rode, he devised a new challenge for himself, handling that inevitable first confrontation with another prisoner eager to confront a cop in jail— not backing down, not whining, complaining, or asking for help. Above all, handling it like a man and not behaving in any way that would embarrass the FBI.

Ahead, against a black sky, on the crest of a hill, he saw the prison in white light. Razor wire glinted like ice atop a twenty-foot fence that curled around drab buildings with blazing windows. The gate swung open; he was taken from the car and hustled inside without a chance to say good-bye to the Kentucky boys, who stood back from the glare. The transformation was as abrupt as it was total: the papers and photograph in his pocket were taken away, a bundle of clothing was thrust into his arms. He was stripped naked and stood there appraised and poked by men who, he thought with his own initial flash of contempt, did this every day for a living.

Steeling himself, propelled along a gleaming hallway

through gates that doubled like decompression chambers, he kept his chin up. Mentally, he groped to find a new role for himself. He toyed with the fantasy that he was not in prison as a killer, but as a cop on the ultimate undercover mission—lengthy, arduous, and extremely dangerous. He imagined himself still a special agent of the FBI, no matter what they said. He had a job to do and responsibilities to uphold. And he would prevail, he vowed, even if they kept him there until the very last day of his sixteen years.

EPILOGUE

After Mark pled guilty, the FBI conducted an internal review into the case but did not release its findings and has declined to comment on it, or to allow its agents to comment publicly.

Ron Poole, the agent who had brought Susan Smith to the Pikeville motel to force a confrontation with Mark, was subsequently transferred to the Lexington bureau, where he continued to do undercover work.

In August of 1991, the *Lexington Herald-Leader* excoriated the FBI for Poole's activities after an informant, who had been working with him in another case, was accused of committing two murders while on bail. "If the FBI has a woodshed, it should take Ron Poole there for some serious career counseling," the newspaper's editorial said. "Clearly, the FBI needs to take a long, close look at its policies and practices involving informants. With one FBI informant dead and another charged with two murders, Poole's superiors have a lot to talk over with him."

Three months later, the paper called on the FBI to put tighter reins on Poole:

> The trend is that questions and bodies keep piling up in Poole's wake. The FBI is now investigating Poole and it's easy to see why. But you don't need an investigation to tell that the whole matter smells like a 20-pound carp that's been left out in the sun for a week. And you don't need a degree in criminology to know that, as long as Poole is operating as an agent in the field, the bureau's reputation and credibility are at risk.

Under the circumstances, the FBI has to do more than just investigate. It has to do something to assure the public that it understands how serious this situation is. The FBI has plenty of ways to do that. It could suspend Poole until the investigation is completed. Or it could assign him to a purely routine desk job and keep him under close wraps until the investigation is over. . . . Leaving Poole to go about his business as usual should not be an option. Business as usual with this agent is just too risky.

In March 1992, Kathy Putnam gave a lengthy statement to the FBI concerning Poole's conduct in the Pikeville office and his relationship with Susan. According to sources, Poole has denied any improper conduct. In a sworn statement to his FBI supervisor in May 1990, Poole did concede that he forced a confrontation between Mark and Susan. "I wanted her to accuse him in front of me to see what his reaction was," he said. However, the FBI has forbidden Poole to comment publicly.

Det. Richard Ray was named Trooper of the Year by the Kentucky State Police in 1991. He took his plaque and resigned, disgusted by the department's general penny-pinching on investigations, in particular its foot-dragging in pressing the FBI on the Putnam case.

John Paul Runyon, the Pike County commonwealth attorney, was reelected to a sixth term in 1992, without opposition. In 1992, Runyon said he was convinced that Mark Putnam never meant to kill Susan Smith. "I believe it was accidental," he said. He continued to be distressed by the FBI's casual attitude toward using informants, and by what he saw as its failure to heed the warnings sent up by the Putnam case. "I was very emphatic. They sent agents to my home to talk to me about it, and I told them flat out, if there's one thing you need to learn from this case if nothing else, you need to take a real close look at how you deal with informants—what kind of protection you give them and what concern you have for them. I told them, if you don't have a policy already, you need to develop one, and if you have a policy, by God, you need to start enforcing it.''

In October of 1990, four months after Susan's body was found, Shelby Jean Ward went to court to file harassment and criminal-trespass charges against her brother Billy Joe, a day after he helped their father, Sid, to petition to replace her as administrator of Susan's estate.

Shelby's lawyer later filed an administrative complaint with the Justice Department charging that FBI negligence ''was a proximate cause of the death of Susan Smith.'' The claim alleged that agents Ron Poole and Terry Hulse ''were negligent in failing to see that the relationship between Smith and Putnam was terminated, failing to take steps to protect Smith from the consequences of that relationship, and failing to see that Smith received personal protection from Putnam,'' who, the claim alleged, had been placed ''under an extreme amount of pressure . . . to carry out some untoward act on learning of the pregnancy.'' The claim charged that Mark ''furthered not only his own purposes but also the purposes of the FBI'' in killing Susan, since various criminal cases that Mark helped to prosecute with Susan's assistance could have been jeopardized by disclosure of the relationship between the two.

In May of 1991, eleven months after Susan was buried, Shelby and other family members who had filed the wrongful death lawsuit against Mark obtained a court order to have the body exhumed for a second autopsy conducted by Wolf. The forensic anthropologist spent nearly a year on the task but died before it was completed. The state's chief medical examiner, Dr. George R. Nichols, then stepped in and concluded: ''The identity of the decedent as Susan Daniels Smith is confirmed by odontologic comparison. Further, it is my opinion that the findings are consistent with suffocation.''

*   *   *

As for Susan herself, she left no letters. She barely left behind photographs. Like Kathy, Susan was usually the one who took the pictures.

In May 1992, a year after her remains had been exhumed, Susan was reburied in another spot farther up Barrenshea Hollow, next to her brother Raymond Daniels, who had been killed earlier in the year in a car wreck. Only a handful of people, including her father and her sister Shelby, stood by in a cold drizzle to see her laid once more to rest.

Four months afterward, a visitor walked across the plank bridge over Peter Creek to Johnson Bottom, where Kenneth Smith was living in a trailer with the two children, Miranda and Brady.

A relaxed and amiable if wary host, still barefoot on an early fall day, Kenneth, who denied ever physically abusing Susan, spoke about his relationship with Susan with apparent affection mixed with bewilderment—especially when he was asked what he thought she saw in Mark Putnam. He stroked his chin before replying, "Well, I don't want to be bragging on myself, but Mark Putnam was no better looking than I am." Pondering the question, he said, "I guess it was just that he made her feel like she was important. Susie always wanted to feel good about herself. And for a while, I guess, she did."

Outside, saying good-bye, Kenneth introduced the visitor to young Brady, a fresh-faced, blond-haired boy of seven who had just skidded up to the trailer in a cloud of dust with three young friends on bicycles.

Looking the visitor over in a place where outsiders are nothing but trouble, one of the boys asked, "Brady, is that the man killed your mama?"

Kathy Putnam sold the condo and most of their furniture in Fort Lauderdale and moved with her children to Minnesota to be near Mark, who was transferred from Otisville to a federal prison in Rochester, Minnesota. A year later, she and the children later returned to Connecticut, living with the help of welfare payments.

She remained bitter about what she felt was the FBI's disinclination to thoroughly reevaluate its policies about the use of informants in general, as well as the training and supervision of agents in an office like Pikeville. "Left unchecked, the FBI remains a law unto itself," she said.

Three years after he went to prison, she continued to proclaim her love for her husband. On sleepless nights, she blamed herself for not being able to prevent the tragedy.

"In hindsight, it's always easy to see the mistakes, and I feel that I messed up the worst of all three of us. I knew Mark's position and I knew what Susan was thinking. What I didn't see was that there was too much going on for all of us, Mark, Susan, and me, to be able to evaluate it on our own.

"We each had our own agenda. For Susan, Mark was the only man she ever knew who treated her with respect. She never woke up in the morning, opened her eyes, and felt that she meant something to someone. Was it so wrong for her to want him for herself?

"I was fighting a different battle. I knew how much Mark's job meant to him, but I could see that it was beginning to destroy us. I was determined to get out of Pikeville, desperately trying to hold on to the part of us that existed before. Doing that, I lost Mark. Poole was interfering, and Susan saw her opportunity.

"I know that Mark didn't understand all of what was going on. He only saw me at home, coming apart at the seams. He had never seen me like that before. We were on a collision course, and there are no rules in that kind of game."

Kathy said she is haunted by the thought of Susan. "I never sleep more than three hours at a time. Some nights, I actually wake up with the phone in my hand, thinking I'm talking to her."

Meanwhile, Kathy struggled to provide as normal a life

as she could for the two children and to shore up her husband in prison. In the summer of 1993, she was making plans to move back to Minnesota to be near him.

"He tells me from prison, 'I think about the kids, how I screwed up their lives'—and I say, 'You can't think about that anymore, Mark. It's done. You have a responsibility here, and that's not to give up, and not to become a product of that place. Your responsibility is to come back to us as the man we knew. Think about what we still have. We love each other—we have something many people never find. We have beautiful, healthy children who are getting through this. Time is all that's between us. Time will pass and we'll be okay.' "

In prison, Mark endlessly analyzes the circumstances that led to his downfall, looking for wisdom in hindsight. "I often think about whether Susan was really pregnant. I don't think she was. If she was, I don't think now that it could have been mine. That's one of the places I get totally aggravated with myself—in the hysteria of the moment, I never looked in a cool way at the situation. The baby was most likely someone else's, if there even was one. She certainly believed there was, but then Susan believed a lot of things.

"I broke my standards. That was the compelling reason that I had to do what I did in confessing. Was I stupid? I don't know. Here I am for the next twelve or fourteen years, whatever. Maybe I am just stupid. If I could take back those two minutes in that car . . .

"But I had a responsibility to live up to, and I failed it. For what I did, I sentenced myself. I didn't have to give myself up, I know that better than anybody. And even then, I didn't have to take sixteen years. Confessing was the only way I could see of even being able to start over with a clean slate.

"I know I could be on the beach right now with my family in Florida. I lost all of that. I lost my children's childhood, and they lost their father. But I also know that now I can sleep at night; I can look myself in the mirror. I couldn't do that for a whole year. Slowly, I am becoming at peace with myself.

"Why am I going to lie to anybody at this point about a trivial issue such as where and when I slept with her? I admitted to killing somebody. Anything else pales. It's the most unconscionable thing you can do to somebody. By admitting it and doing the time that I have to do, I did the thing that I thought would square it away as much as I humanly could, by taking my punishment like a man, by accepting full responsibility for my own actions. This will be the worst thing that will ever happen to me, and I can only go one place from here: straight up."

Just as his wife does, Mark worries that he will sound cold about Susan. "I cared for her. She accepted me when I first got there, when a lot of other people didn't. For that reason, I was very grateful to her. She helped me to get on the map. I felt a certain amount of gratitude. She hung in there with me. She was as patient with me as I was with her.

"I felt a great amount of pity for her, for her upbringing and for the environment she had to live in. In that respect, I cared for her. I wanted to help her.

"The most important thing is that Susan lost her life because of me. I didn't mean to kill her, but that changes nothing, because I did kill her.

"I had to explain all of this to Kathy. Can you imagine just coming home and telling your wife, 'I'm going to jail. I killed somebody, Kathy'? At that point, my life was so miserable internally that I thought, 'Just put me in jail and throw away the key. I deserve it.' I had let the situation exacerbate, and it never should have happened.

"But I did the crime. I gave myself up when anyone else might say I didn't really have to. What was gained from that? Well, Susan's parents know where their daughter is, which they didn't know for a year, and Susan's children know. What else? I can't think of anything else.

"I walk around here, I can't *believe* I'm in prison. I ask, 'How did this happen to you?' It's just unfathomable to me that I'm here. But dammit, I did it. I have to live with the consequences.

"And now I can live with myself. There are no secrets between Kathy and me anymore. When I come home, if she is still there for me, I know there're going to be problems, but we're going to beat it. There's just no question in my mind.

"One of the things that hurts me most is the effect on my relationship with my son—we never got to know each other. Danielle and I had five years together, five good years. My son knows me as a voice on the phone."

In prison, he reads and rereads the letters he gets from his daughter, especially the first one, folded and creased until it is nearly in tatters:

Dear Old Pop:

I got this special paper for writing to you. I hope you like it. I have been a very good girl. I have been helping Mommy around the house sometimes without even being asked. I have been eating all my suppers. I stay up later now because I am older than my brother. And I should be able to. He is still being a pain. But I love him anyway. I can't wait until we'll be able to visit you and give you hugs and kisses. I want you to know that we are ok. We miss you but we are taking care of business. You take care of yourself for us. Eat good, sleep good, and brush your teeth. I got your letters and my heart puffed with love. Please write when you can and I will. I love you as big as the universe. Be good, and be careful.

                              Love,
                              Danielle Your #1 Girl